THE CAT STAR CHRONICLES

OUTCAST

CHERYL BROOKS

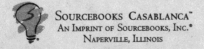

SOURCEBOOKS CASABLANCA™
AN IMPRINT OF SOURCEBOOKS, INC.®
NAPERVILLE, ILLINOIS

Published by Sourcebooks Casablanca, an imprint of Sourcebooks,
Inc.
P.O. Box 4410, Naperville, Illinois 60567–4410
(630) 961–3900
FAX: (630) 961–2168
www.sourcebooks.com

Printed and bound in the United States of America
QW 10 9 8 7 6 5 4 3 2 1

For those who find love
when they least expect it.

Prologue

Every man's dream…
One man's nightmare…

LYNX WAS ONLY SEVENTEEN WHEN HE WAS TAKEN prisoner in the war that destroyed his planet. Slated to be executed, he and the other members of his unit were instead sold into slavery. Thrown into the hold of a ship with no food and very little water, the new slaves were smuggled halfway across the galaxy to a slave auction on a distant world.

Dragged onto the auction block, the terrified boy almost wished he'd been killed. To be bought and sold like an animal was unheard of on his own planet of Zetith, where the world had been green and beautiful and the people were free. On this planet, whose name he never knew, he was sold to a trader who then sold him to someone else.

Stowed in the hold of yet another ship, exhaustion outweighed his fear, and Lynx fell asleep on the journey, only to be rudely awakened by two men. As one held him down, a flexible tube was painfully injected into the soft skin of the inner side of his left upper arm.

"Take that out, and you die," he was told, then was given a drink and left alone again in the darkness.

Lynx lay sobbing with fear and pain and hunger. Even war had not terrified him like this. He had no idea

where he was, or where he was going, and he believed
that death would have been preferable to the life he now
faced. He felt completely and utterly alone. Not knowing if the journey lasted for days or weeks, he lost all
track of time and was fed at odd intervals, which served
to disorient him that much more.

At last, the ship landed, and the bright glare nearly
blinded Lynx as he was pulled into the harsh sunlight by
his captors, who marched him down a dusty street and
into a large palatial building.

"Pretty, isn't he?" the ugly, harsh-voiced man remarked to his cohort as they stripped Lynx of his bonds
and his clothing.

"He'll fit right in!" the other man laughed. Unlocking
a large, ornate door, he pushed Lynx inside. "You're
their slave now," he said with a nod. "You do whatever
they tell you."

The light inside was much brighter than the corri-
dor through which Lynx had been brought, and it took
a moment for his eyes to adjust as the scent of perfume
wafted forward and curled into his sensitive nose. Green
was the first color he saw: lush, tropical plants growing in profusion. Then he saw the women—scores of
them, all beautiful, and all as naked as he was himself.
They smelled of desire, and, despite his fear, that desire
aroused him instantly.

Not knowing what to do, Lynx simply stood by the
door but was beginning to feel somewhat relieved by
what he saw. Being the slave of women wouldn't be so
bad; he was fairly certain they wouldn't beat or torture
him. But Lynx had never understood women. Most of
the time, he felt intimidated by them—never knowing

what to say or do—and had remained alone in the background while his friends found lovers. Granted, he was young, but the concept of enticement was something that Zetithian males generally grasped at an early age; Lynx, however, was mystified.

As he stood there waiting, the women ignored him at first, but his erection eventually elicited a few stares, and soon he was being touched by several soft hands—hands which soon found his hard cock and played in the fluid which had begun to ooze from the scalloped edges of the wide corona on the head. Lynx gasped as they fondled him before pulling him down onto the soft cushions on the floor. He'd never felt such pleasure before in his life. Then one of the women licked him, savoring his fluids until her body contracted in a powerful orgasm. Then another tasted him, and another, and another. He had the same effect on all of them, and they marveled at his attractive feline features and his sexual prowess.

He was the slave of other slaves, and he did whatever they asked, though his own needs were never considered. Not even given food of his own, to survive he had to scavenge what he could from what the women left behind. If they ever felt the need to punish him, they made sure that there was nothing left for him. When they finally gave him permission to eat, they laughed at the way he wolfed down his food.

Still, it was easy at first, for he was young and his sexual desires were at their peak. Day after day he fucked them, fed them, licked them, and massaged them. He catered to their needs and overheard their conversations, but more than anything, they craved his body, for he affected them in a way that no other man had ever done.

He was both lover and slave to each of them, who were, in turn, the slaves of a man who owned far more women than he could possibly service.

At first, Lynx didn't understand their language very well, but as he learned, he discovered that the women's greatest fear seemed to be that of bearing his child. Whenever one of them discovered her pregnancy, he saw the terror in her eyes as the others reassured her that Lynx couldn't possibly be the father. This puzzled him greatly, for he could never understand why having his child was such a horrible thing—or why they never did—but he heard it constantly, and his heart grew bitter. They would take what pleasure he could give them but wanted nothing more; not his children, and certainly not his love.

And so, for many years he lived with them, at first only watching as their children were born, then later assisting with the births and caring for the children. He liked the babies and never held it against them that they weren't his own. He could never understand why none of the children ever resembled him, though he'd had intercourse with each and every one of their mothers. After a while, he came to realize that he must have been unable to father children, and this weakened his self-esteem even further.

His sleep was seldom undisturbed, for there was always a woman seeking his attention—whether it was to bring her food or to make love to her—and before long, it all began to seem the same to him. What he had initially considered to be a blessing now became a curse. The sound of female voices began to grate on his nerves, and the constant bickering among them irritated him almost to the point of screaming. There was no respite, no time to himself; they were always there, always demanding his undivided attention and the sexual gratification he could give them.

His bitterness grew, and his exhaustion was never-ending. As time went on, his erections began to diminish, becoming infrequent before finally ceasing altogether. Then one day, three men marched into the harem, seized Lynx, and dragged him out to be resold. He heard some of the women laughing, and, knowing that they must have complained about his impotence, any feelings he might have had for them turned to dust.

Marched naked to the auction block, Lynx was sold again, but this time, his companions were all male, which was a welcome change. The men might have been rough and crude, but they were undemanding, and Lynx slept well for the first time in many years. His new owner, a just man who didn't believe in slavery, told Lynx that after five years of service, he would be freed. Seeing hope for the first time since he was enslaved, Lynx put in his time, working hard and learning what the men could teach him, after which he was freed. He stayed on for several more years, working in the diamond mines and saving his pay, for he had heard of a new colony on a planet called Terra Minor where he could be his own master and live out the remainder of his days in peaceful solitude.

Peace and quiet were the things he longed for most of all, but to find that peace, Lynx needed money, so he saved his own and watched as other men gambled away their pay or wasted it on the favors of women. As a free man, Lynx saw women and could smell their desire, but he was never aroused by them, and he avoided them whenever he could, for, having been used and betrayed by women, he now despised them all.

But their voices still haunted his dreams, and he would wake up in a cold sweat with the sound of their laughter echoing through his mind as he was dragged away—not one of them even whispering good-bye.

Chapter 1

THE DAY BEFORE LYNX CAME, BONNIE CUT HER HAIR. Not artfully or with any skill whatsoever; just pulled it away from her scalp and kept right on cutting until it was no longer than the width of her fingers. As a result, she could easily have passed for a boy, but her pregnant belly was there to give her away. She'd been told many times that her hair was beautiful—blonde and shining like spun gold, as Drummond always said—but she no longer had any use for it. It only attracted attention—unwanted male attention—and all she wanted was to be invisible. Men were all liars, cheats, and scoundrels, and she had no more use for them than she did for her hair. As a farmer, her style of dress did nothing to attract notice, either—just sturdy boots, rugged trousers, and a pullover shirt. She didn't even own a dress.

The young apple trees blossoming in the orchard were there to remind her that one bad apple didn't spoil the whole bunch, but she was having a very difficult time convincing herself that there was such a thing as a decent, honest, moral man.

Unfortunately, a man was what she needed—moral or otherwise—which was why she'd advertised for a hired hand at the immigration office in the spaceport at Nimbaza. The mines weren't hiring, so anyone coming there in hope of finding work would be sent her way. At least, that was the plan. Drummond, head of the regional immigration office, had been skeptical.

"Don't know how long it will take," Drummond had said, scratching his bearded chin. "Could be months now that word's gotten out about the mines."

"I don't care," Bonnie said grimly. "I need help, and I'll need it even more after the baby comes. Just send me whoever you get."

"Not particular about the species, then?" he asked. "Not many Terrans come here to work in the mines, you know—well, not many good ones, anyway." Drummond was Terran himself, as were many of the planet's inhabitants, but the miners were a hodgepodge of species from throughout the quadrant.

"I don't care *what* they are as long as they're willing to work!" Bonnie declared. "I can't pay much at first, but it'll be a place to live and food to eat for anyone who shows up and would rather stay here than get back on the cruiser."

There were laws about that on Terra Minor, enacted in an effort to keep the riffraff of the galaxy at bay, though it wasn't completely foolproof. Any immigrant either had to have money to buy land or start a business, or had to have a job within a week of their arrival, otherwise they were deported—and the authorities had some highly effective means of enforcing that law. They electronically tagged anyone who landed and could then track them no matter where they tried to hide—and since the tags were deeply embedded in the skull, they were nearly impossible to remove. Some had tried, of course, though they usually wound up dead as a result. Sylor hadn't cared for the idea—the reason for which was perfectly clear to Bonnie now—but she hadn't objected to the implants herself. After all, *she* wasn't the one who'd absconded with money stolen from a pregnant girlfriend.

The trackers would have caught up with him and returned her money quickly enough—if she'd ever bothered to report it. Bonnie thought it was callous of Sylor to leave her in such a way, but he *had* worked hard helping her build the place, so if he wanted to leave and take the ready cash, she couldn't very well say no. The part that stuck in her craw was the way he'd done it. No note, no good-bye, just gone one morning, taking his clothes and all the money they'd saved, along with anything portable that had any value at all—which, unfortunately, included her grandmother's engagement ring. That ring was the only thing Bonnie had left of what she'd inherited, the bulk of the estate having gone to pay for the land and the farming equipment. He took the good speeder, too, leaving her with the relic out in the equipment shed that didn't work half the time, along with a mortgage on the house.

It couldn't be said that Sylor hadn't worked for the money he'd taken; he'd helped her build a house, fences, and the big shed—though it was prefabricated and hadn't taken nearly as much work as the house—and he'd helped her plant the crops. He'd captured their herd of enocks, too, running down each one in the speeder, throwing a net over it, and hauling it back to the corral he'd built. He hadn't seemed to mind the work when it was all new and exciting—and capturing enocks was more exciting than most things—but, as it turned out, the daily grind of rural life just wasn't his cup of tea.

Bonnie's only wish was that he'd realized that before they decided to have a baby.

Sylor had always said he wasn't the marrying kind, which should have been Bonnie's first clue not to trust him—though it was now apparent that was the one thing he'd been completely honest about. He'd had such grand plans for their future on the newly colonized planet, and he'd infected Bonnie with them. Unfortunately, once she'd been bitten by the bug, he had gotten over it.

Terra Minor had been haggled over for centuries, with several worlds laying claim before it was finally bought outright by a consortium that sent in a team of scientists and ecologists to catalog everything from the insects to the weather patterns. Next they sent in timberdroids to harvest most of the trees on the flatlands, after which they planted tough grasses, creating a savanna.

The climate where Bonnie's property was located was temperate year-round, with one season slightly cooler and rainier than the other. The weather and terrain being similar to Central Africa on Earth, some official had decided that the names of places in the region should sound African in origin. This was more a tribute to the Old World than anything, and while it was doubtful that the names had any actual meaning, if they did, those original meanings had been lost with the passage of time.

The only thing to fear from the weather was the storms, with their heavy rains, high winds, and spectacular lightning, which started the occasional wildfire. Though the fires did serve to keep the savanna from growing back into forest, they were dangerous, and each homestead was required to have a wide firebreak around it for protection.

Living there may have been risky, but the land was fertile, and Bonnie had yet to plant anything that wouldn't grow. Sylor hadn't been interested in farming, preferring the excitement of chasing enocks, but she enjoyed raising the plants as well as the more domesticated livestock. At least *they* didn't try to take a piece out of her every time her back was turned.

Enocks were what had caught Sylor's fancy from the beginning, though Bonnie now realized that he had seen it as a get-rich-quick scheme, rather than a lifelong pursuit. Much like the ostriches of Earth, enocks were large, flightless birds, but they were far more vicious than any ostrich, with razor-sharp beaks, daggerlike claws, and a belligerent, carnivorous nature. They were dangerous to work around, but their eggs, which were huge and very tasty, were highly prized and brought an excellent return on any investment. The enocks were omnivorous, so they fed them mostly fruits and grain, but occasionally one of Bonnie's chickens would stray into their pen, which meant certain death for the chicken. She'd put wire mesh around the lower part of the fence to keep them apart, though it wasn't always successful. What she needed was a force field, but such things were expensive luxuries, and since chickens were cheap, she'd yet to earn enough money on their eggs to justify the cost.

Just feeding the enocks was an adventure in itself, but gathering their eggs bordered on suicide—which was something Sylor had always enjoyed. Bonnie would throw out feed to distract them, and then he would make a run for the eggs. She'd been doing it alone since he left and had had a number of close calls—as well as the scars to prove it. Even before Sylor left, Captain Jack had noticed the bites on Bonnie's arms when she'd been in Nimbaza last and had sold Bonnie some excellent ointment, but Bonnie was beginning to believe that what she really needed was a suit of armor—which, of course, Jack hadn't had in the hold of her ship, though as a successful interplanetary trader, she had just about everything else.

Bonnie had begun to despair of ever finding a hired hand, but thankfully, her temperamental comlink was actually working the day that Drummond finally called her.

"Got someone for you, Bon-bon!" Drummond said, his raspy voice booming out over the comlink. "Not Terran, of course, but I think he'll do. Actually, he kinda reminds me of Cat—you know, Captain Jack's husband?—and Leo, too, of course. Anyway, they look like they might be the same species, but so far, this guy hasn't mentioned where he's from. Says he was a slave but earned his freedom, or some such bullshit. He's probably a runaway, but I don't hold with slavery, so it wouldn't matter a hairy rat's ass to me if he was."

"I don't care what he is or where he's from as long as he's honest and able-bodied!" Bonnie declared. Cat and Leo seemed to be both, but whether all Zetithians were, Bonnie had no idea. According to Jack, there were very few of their kind remaining; their home planet had been destroyed, and their species was nearly extinct.

"Looks able enough, but he's not what you'd call talkative," Drummond reported. "'Course honesty isn't something you can spot just by looking at a man."

"I know," Bonnie sighed. Sylor had been a nice looking man and had seemed sincere, but he'd run out on her eventually, just as all the others had done. *No, you couldn't tell by looking.* "Handsome is as handsome does—isn't that how that saying goes?"

"Don't know about handsome," Drummond chuckled. "I only know pretty."

"Yeah, well, pretty doesn't always mean anything, either," Bonnie said dryly. "It's what's inside that counts."

"And you've got both."

"Thanks, Drummond," she said wearily, "but I'm really not in the mood to hear that right now." Men had been admiring Bonnie all her life, but as far as she could tell, it hadn't done her a bit of good.

"It's the truth, though," he protested. "Can't say it's not."

"Maybe," Bonnie conceded without much conviction, because if the type of man she tended to attract was any indication, then being pretty was more of a curse than a blessing. Men had always seemed to think that, along with being easy on the eyes, she was also stupid and gullible—and perhaps she *had* been easily taken in—but she had put that past firmly behind her. She would never let another man—of *any* species—take advantage of her again; her heart, as well as her purse, had been tromped on enough.

"Well, his immigration chip's got everything it should," Drummond went on. "And I was right; he's originally from Zetith. I'm sure Leo and Cat'll be happy to meet up with him. Hmmm… got something else here… looks like an emancipation decree—hold on while I run it through the translator." Bonnie could see him tapping the screen, grumbling to himself, "Damn backwoods planets… don't even put their legal stuff in

Stantongue! How the hell do they expect anyone to read it?" He peered at it intently for a moment. "Yep, that's what it is, all right. Dated about five years ago. All legal and neat—though it could be a forgery."

"Well, gee, thanks," Bonnie said, rolling her eyes. "That makes me feel *so* much better."

He grinned into the viewscreen. "Don't it though?"

Drummond had been around a long time, knew every immigrant to the sector, and considered it part of his duties to look after them. He wasn't a clergyman—though in his capacity as magistrate, he did perform the occasional marriage—but tended to view the entire population of the Nimbaza region as his flock. Bonnie figured he'd probably seen it all. Maybe he was better at spotting a liar than he knew. "Does it *look* like a forgery?" she inquired.

"Well, no," he conceded, "but they get better at it all the time, though maybe they're really lousy at it where he came from."

"Well, let's hope so," she said fervently. "I need help, not more trouble!"

Drummond leaned closer to peer at her, his eyes distorted by their close proximity to the sensor and his mustache seeming to grow to startling proportions. "Looks like you've already had that," he observed. "What the devil happened to your hair?"

"Got tired of messing with it and cut it off," she said shortly.

"Looks more like you got mad at it," he remarked. Cocking his head to one side he asked hopefully, "What'd you do with it?"

"Gave it to the chickens to line their nests," Bonnie replied. "That's about all it's good for."

Drummond shook his head and sighed. "Wouldn't mind having a lock of it myself," he said. "Beautiful stuff, that."

"And just what would your wife say if she knew you had a lock of my hair?" Bonnie asked with a wry smile.

"Dunno," he said, scratching his bald spot. "Probably beat the livin' shit out of me. Still… it might be worth it."

"I doubt that," she said with a reluctant chuckle. "Just tell that man how to get here and stop feeding me a line."

"Sure thing, Bon-bon," he grinned.

She hated the nickname—which, unfortunately, was one she'd heard from various people throughout her life— but she liked Drummond, so the irritation she normally felt was missing from her voice when she retorted, "And would you please stop calling me Bon-bon? My name is Bonnie! How many times do I have to tell you that?"

"A few more, Bon-bon. A few more." Still chuckling, Drummond reached forward and terminated the connection. Bonnie was a feisty little woman, and he liked her more than most. It was too bad she had such lousy taste in men, but then some people just weren't meant to find happiness—no matter how much they might deserve it.

Bonnie was glad that help was finally on the way, but so far all she knew was that he wasn't talkative and, if he looked anything like Cat and Leo, he probably had pointed ears and long, curly hair like they did. They both had fanglike canines that looked as if they could tear a hole in you, too. But Bonnie had always liked Cat; he was friendly and had a very dry sense of humor, and Captain Jack seemed real taken with him—in fact, Bonnie had hardly ever seen them more than a few meters apart. Their three boys were pretty cute, too—looked just like their dad—and Leo and the witch, Tisana, had three babies, as well: two sons and one daughter. The little girl had her mother's black hair and green eyes, but the boys both had their father's tawny curls—which made Bonnie wonder who her own baby would resemble. Sylor was tall and powerfully built, with jet black hair and rakish good looks, while Bonnie was petite for a Terran female and was as fair as he was dark. Telling herself it didn't matter, she went back to work.

Bonnie was out weeding the vegetable garden when it occurred to her that she was completely unprepared for her new helper. There was nowhere for him to sleep in her house; no spare bedroom, and not even another bed. She didn't know where to put him, even in the outbuildings, which consisted of the cavernous equipment shed and the henhouse. Then she remembered that he'd been a slave at one time, and perhaps he wouldn't expect a bed or a room to himself. As things stood, the only way Bonnie could give him a room of his own would be for him to help her build it—and pay for it, too, since Sylor had taken the money earmarked for home improvements. Adding *two* rooms would be better, she decided, because that way everyone could have his own: one for Bonnie, one for her baby, and one for him—whatever his name was.

For now, though, that would just have to wait. They would all be crammed in together, but she knew that the baby wouldn't take up much space for a while, and perhaps a former slave wouldn't object to camping out on the floor.

Having slept badly the night before, Bonnie was exhausted. Dreams had kept biting at her like flies, but snatches of them were all she could remember, and nothing that made any sense at all. Her dreams never did. She had plenty of daydreams, but they weren't romantic and sweet; she'd quit dreaming about love long ago, and now her daydreams were spent going over details. How would she be able to care for enocks in addition to a child? How many eggs would she have to sell to get enough money to add on to the house?

What would she give for a man she could trust?

Her right arm was the first thing that came to mind, but she preferred to keep it, since it was so much more useful to her than any man had ever been. Men had always been trouble, and she had no need for any more of that—or for pretty things, either. She needed stuff she could use, like a new speeder, or a force field for the enocks, or, as always, more money.

Sighing, she bent down to pull a weed that was too close to a bean plant to use her hoe, noting that it was getting harder to bend over, and the baby kicked her sharply to remind her not to squash it. Maybe she should have used a spray on the weeds, but they were expensive, and, because they weren't good for the environment, there was a limit on how much you could use and where you could use it. Not wanting to be the one to poison the water or foul the air, Bonnie had opted not to use any herbicides at all, but it made her work that much harder.

She and Sylor had been required to attend some extensive orientation classes before they were allowed to build a place of their own and begin farming. There were a multitude of regulations, and although Bonnie felt that she'd signed away most of her freedom, she could understand the need for it. With a staggering number of ruined planets across the galaxy to serve as examples, and Earth itself only having been brought back from the brink of death when the inhabitants made some very tough choices, the powers that be had taken their time and had given considerable thought to the details.

By midday there was still no sign of her new hired hand, so Bonnie ate some lunch and wondered if he'd opted to be deported rather than work for her. Then she remembered what a long walk it was from Nimbaza and wished she could have gone to fetch him—which was what she would have done if the speeder hadn't been so worthless. She had been intending to work on it—even though she wasn't the best mechanic in the world—but the simple fact was that she just hadn't had the time.

After lunch she went out to feed the chickens and noticed that one of them was missing. There were always predators about, but she hadn't had any problems with them for a while; her little border collie, Kipper, had seen to that. Bonnie looked around a bit and finally spotted it—as luck would have it—in the enock pen. Gasping in dismay, she didn't know who she was most annoyed with; the chicken for being so stupid, or the enocks for being so murderous.

Her only consolation was that the enocks were still busy picking at the feed she'd put out for them that morning, and the chicken was at the far side of the enclosure. After throwing out more feed to keep them busy, she went around to the gate. Even though the chicken was close by, she knew the best she could hope to do was herd it toward the gate, because if startled, she would never be able to catch it. With that in mind, she went back to the equipment shed and got the net she and Sylor had used to catch the enocks.

The enocks were busy eating, and the chicken was strutting around as if it had no idea it was in mortal peril. *I'm going to eat that chicken myself,* Bonnie thought grimly. *Damn thing is too stupid to live and reproduce.* She needed smarter chickens than that if they were going to stay alive long enough to lay eggs.

Slipping quietly through the gate so as not to startle any of the birds, Bonnie inched her way toward the chicken, noting that there was an enock egg there as well. The egg was worth far more than the chicken—and was less mobile—so she retrieved it first and set it outside the gate.

Returning quickly, she saw that the chicken was now even farther from the gate, but the enocks still hadn't spotted it. Moving along the fence, she managed to trap the chicken, but it squawked loudly, arousing the interest of the big male enock. She had no choice now but to make a dash for it and took off running, but tripped on the net and fell. Cursing, she stumbled to her feet and ran, flinging the chicken over the fence, net and all. She would have climbed it herself, but Sylor had modified the fence to prevent the enocks from getting a toehold in the lower third of it, and, therefore, neither could she.

Bonnie was still a good three meters from the gate when she felt the enock's beak sink into her shoulder. She'd been bitten many times, but had never been caught. They were amazingly strong, and, as if to prove it, the bird flung her to the ground as though she weighed no more than the chicken she'd rescued. Screaming loudly, she fought off his attack, punching him in the head with her fist in desperation, but nothing stopped him for long. Then, to her horror, she saw that the others were now headed toward her, looking as though they'd like a piece of her too.

Scrambling to her feet, regardless of the bites she was taking, Bonnie ran for her life, but the enock was faster, this time catching her by the forearm. She tried in vain to work her way toward the gate, but not only did the bird outweigh her, he had also dug in his heels, making him impossible to budge. With a bloodcurdling chill, she realized that his intention was not to kill her outright, but simply to hold her there until the others caught up—*then* they would kill her. In desperation, Bonnie fought back the only way she could think of, grabbing the giant bird by the throat with her free hand and trying to choke him into letting go. It wasn't enough, because her hand wasn't large enough to encircle his neck, nor was it strong enough to do any damage.

The pain she felt was indescribable, and her vision was growing misty when, seemingly from out of nowhere, two large hands gripped the bird's neck beneath her own and squeezed. The enock gagged and opened his mouth just enough to set her free.

"Run, you fool!" someone shouted.

Barely able to stand, much less run, Bonnie staggered toward the gate. Moments later she was seized by those same hands and was half carried, half dragged to safety. Slamming the gate shut behind them, her rescuer snarled, "You stupid female! They might have killed you!"

Gazing up at him with eyes that could barely focus and taking note of his blazing yellow eyes, pointed ears, and fangs, she said, "Well, hello to you too," and promptly fainted.

Lynx's heart was pounding like a drum; he'd heard her screams and had run to her rescue. The horrifying scene he'd found was enough to make him fear he was too late, but now that he had her safe, his fear gave way to anger, and as Lynx gathered Bonnie up in his arms and headed toward the house, his irritation with his predicament grew. He had come so far and had such plans. Now he found himself not only working on a farm, but for a woman—and a very stupid woman, at that! All the jibes and laughter of the men he'd worked alongside in the diamond mines of Paemay came back to him. "You'll wind up a slave again," they had jeered. "You wait and see." Lynx had sworn to prove them wrong, but so far, his plans had all gone awry. What money he had left after paying his passage had been stolen from him, and he'd landed on Terra Minor without a single credit; at the mercy of a system of government that looked upon the homeless and unemployed as little better than vermin. With nothing but a few meager possessions and the clothes on his back, he'd had no choice but to take the job Drummond had offered or be deported.

His only consolation was that at least it would be quiet here. The chatter of voices—particularly female—disturbed him. The deafening clang of hammers in the mines wasn't much better, but didn't torment him nearly as much as words whispered behind his back or screamed in his face.

But now he had this woman bleeding all over the place, and he focused on the task at hand. Carrying her into the house, he dropped her in a chair and grabbed the first thing he could find to wrap around her arm in an effort to staunch the bleeding. She was a small woman, too, and no match for the huge birds. What an idiotic thing for a woman alone to have been doing! It was a wonder she hadn't been killed.

But Lynx had heard her screams and come running, saving her from certain death. He wondered if she would acknowledge that fact or find some way of putting him in his place. Lynx was so accustomed to having even his best efforts laughed at by women that he expected nothing less. He would leave this place just as soon as he possibly could. He would not remain here to be treated as a worthless slave by another woman—no matter how beautiful she was.

Because she *was* beautiful—and so different from the women he'd known before, who had been all allure and seductive sexuality. This woman was small and delicately made, and even with her roughly cropped hair, there was no hiding the fact that she had the face of an angel. Not that he cared about that sort of thing anymore… not that he ever would again…

Bonnie was not one to faint easily, but when an enock all but bites off your arm, it's hard to do much else. When she came to, she was in her kitchen, and her rescuer was binding up her arm. Blood was splattered everywhere—though she knew that spilled blood always looked like more than it really was, especially when it happened to be your own.

His first words to her were not a comforting, "Hello,

my name is George, and don't worry, you're not going to lose your arm," but instead were a half-shouted, "What were you doing in there?"

"Rescuing a chicken," Bonnie replied weakly. "And an egg," she added as an afterthought.

"A chicken," he repeated. Lynx had never heard the term before. "And what is a chicken?"

"It's a kind of bird," she replied. "You probably saw some of them on your way up from the road."

"The small, feathered creatures?"

"Yeah."

"They are very valuable?" he inquired curiously, hoping that this, at least, was the case.

"Not really," she admitted.

"Then why would you risk your life to save one?"

"Just didn't want the enocks to get it, that's all," Bonnie muttered.

Lynx had seen much loss of life in his time, and the thought of anyone putting themselves in danger for such a pointless reason was enough to feed his anger. "It was not worth the risk," he said fiercely.

"Maybe not to you," she conceded, "but at the time, I thought it was."

His eyebrows rose with an emotional significance Bonnie couldn't identify, but the gesture drew her attention to the small black tufts at the upswept tips of a pair of light brown brows that matched his short cap of curls. The vertical pupils of his large yellow eyes were glowing with anger, and while there could be no doubt that he was of the same species as Cat and Leo, the similarities ended there. Cat and Leo were both good-natured and friendly; this man was not.

Bonnie looked down at her bloody hand and experimentally moved her fingers. It hurt like hell, but she could move all of them, which was a good sign. "It's not too bad," she commented.

This time only one of Lynx's eyebrows went up. He'd seen the deep gash in her arm, and how crushed the surrounding tissue was. She was nothing but a pretty little fool.

"No, really, I've been hurt a lot worse," she lied, not wanting him to see her as weak and defenseless. "All I need is some of Captain Jack's Derivian ointment, and I'll be just fine."

Lynx eyed her skeptically, thinking that she was either intoxicated or a raving lunatic. "Your arm needs to be stitched," he said bluntly. "There is nothing that will heal so deep a cut."

"Well, you just go right ahead and stitch it then," Bonnie said roundly, though she considered this form of treatment to be a bit outmoded. "Don't think I can sew with my left hand." Another treatment option flitted through her mind, but she couldn't quite bring it to the forefront of her brain, and, instead, giggled, "Did you drug me with something?"

"No," he replied. "The pain has affected your senses."

"Is that right?" she muttered. "What pain?" She giggled again, thinking that he *had* to have poured a half a liter of whiskey down her throat. "God, I feel weird."

"It is also from the shock and loss of blood," Lynx said, applying pressure to the bandage.

"I'm bleeding to death then?" Bonnie said as her eyes drifted shut. "That's funny; I'd have thought it would hurt more."

"You need to lie down." Lifting her from the chair, Lynx carried her to the bedroom, placing her gently on the bed. His gaze took in her rounded abdomen and his eyes widened. "You are with child?"

"Give the man a prize," Bonnie mumbled. "Get another prize for guessing when it's due."

"In three months," Lynx replied. He said it so automatically that Bonnie thought he must have chosen a number at random, but, as it happened, he was correct.

"Ooo, that's two for two!" she said admiringly. "Care to go double or nothing and tell me whose it is?"

"I have no way of knowing that," he said stiffly. The only thing Lynx could be certain of was that it wasn't his—after all, they never were.

"Yeah, well, his name is Sylor," Bonnie said informatively. "Sylor Halen. Long gone Sylor... caught the enocks... but took the money and ran." She paused for a moment before giggling again. "There's a song in that somewhere, I think." Her voice trailed off as she nearly slipped into slumber again, but roused up when she remembered that she didn't even know this man's name. "And what should I call you—besides 'my hero,' that is?"

"My name is Lynxsander Dackelov," he replied.

"Lynxsander Dackelov," she echoed. "Hmm, it'll sound pretty strange hollering *that* out when I call you in for dinner. How about just Lynx? You do sort of look like one, you know."

Lynx had no idea what a lynx was beyond the fact that it was the first four letters of his own name, but he didn't bother to comment, focusing, instead, on things that he did understand. "And you are Bonnie Neurath."

"Mmmhmm. That's me." She knew she was mumbling again and tried to remember what else might help someone who'd lost a lot of blood. She had donated blood one time and had felt perfectly awful afterwards, but for the life of her, she couldn't seem to remember what they'd done for her. "Fluids!" she blurted out. "I need something to drink." She thought a moment longer and added, "Something salty… or sweet… or something…"

Taking this as an order, Lynx pulled a sheet up over her and went back out to the kitchen. He felt strange prowling around her house, looking for what she'd requested. Not only did he feel out of place, but her disturbing female scent was everywhere, and the smell of her blood was even more unsettling to him. It brought back too many memories—unpleasant memories—that he never wanted to revisit. His only consolation was that she didn't wear perfume, the scent of which was guaranteed to make him feel ill.

Lynx found some sort of liquid in a container and looked for salt and sugar to add to it. He didn't care how it tasted to her; he was just doing as he was told. It was still so automatic to him that he had to continually remind himself that he did, indeed, have a will of his own.

Returning to the bedroom where she lay, he lifted her up and held the glass to her lips. How many times had he done this for a woman in the past? He couldn't remember, but he knew it was too many times for one man's life.

Bonnie took a sip. He'd mixed apple juice with a little salt and extra sugar, which didn't taste too bad, and she drank every drop.

Despite the fact that Lynx was doing his best to help her, Bonnie didn't think he was being very nice about it, and the tone of his next question proved that. "You risked your child for a chicken?" he snapped contemptuously.

"And an egg," she reminded him. "Don't forget the egg—but I guess you did. It's still out by the gate, and, unlike the chicken, it *is* somewhat valuable. Why don't you go get it, and we'll eat it." That was the other thing they'd done when she'd felt faint; made her drink juice and eat something. "Should be good for me to eat a really big egg, now, don't you think?"

Bonnie didn't understand his reply since it was in another language, but she was fairly certain that it wasn't very nice—at least it didn't sound that way to her. She was getting the distinct impression that Lynx didn't like her—which was fine, because she didn't *want* him to like her. All she wanted him to do was to work hard… and feed her.

"Actually, those eggs are so big, they're a full meal for a family of six," she added informatively, "—and they taste really good, too, which is why people are willing to pay so much for them." She looked up at him curiously. "Are you hungry?"

Lynx didn't answer that at all—in any language. Bonnie recalled Drummond saying that he wasn't very talkative, but it had never occurred to her that he wouldn't even answer a direct question, which she considered to be very rude.

"I don't usually eat them myself," she went on, trying to fill the gap in the conversation, though her speech was still slurred, "but I think this time I should make an exception. Can you cook, or should I get up and do it myself?" Since this seemed to be the obvious answer to her question, she attempted to sit up, but lay back down as her head began swimming again.

"Do not get up," Lynx said curtly. "You need a healer."

"Don't have one—well, not handy, anyway. Vladen's the only one we've got, and he's in Wasaba this month—long way from here. He… travels."

"Will he be here when your child is born?"

"Maybe," Bonnie replied. "I'm not sure. He thought he might be, but you never know."

"What will you do if he is not?" Lynx asked, although he was afraid he already knew the answer to that.

"Don't know," she mumbled. "Sylor thought he could help, and he read up on it, but he's gone." Bonnie gave a fatalistic shrug. "Guess I'll just do it by myself."

Lynx had yet to see a woman—*any* woman—look after anything for herself. Those he had known had always put the responsibility for just about everything on him, and he was used to being a scapegoat. But he also knew—all too well—that giving birth was often fraught with danger. She could not possibly do it alone. "And if there is trouble?" he prompted.

"Guess I'll die, then." Bonnie had already thought about that, which may have been the reason why she did seemingly stupid things like trying to rescue one of her chickens from the enocks. She wasn't sure if it stemmed from the desire to preserve other lives or to simply let the enocks kill her before she had the chance to die in childbirth, but it had seemed like a good idea at the time.

"You should not be living here alone," Lynx said firmly.

"Well, you're here now," she pointed out, "so I'm not alone anymore, am I?"

Lynx didn't comment, but Bonnie could see the emotions roiling within him. She had already decided he didn't like her, and just as surely disliked the idea of having to work on her farm. "You don't want to be here, do you?" she observed.

"No," he said shortly.

"Working on a farm wasn't what you had in mind?" she suggested, but then the most obvious reason occurred to her. "Oh, I get it! You don't like the idea of working for a woman, do you?"

"No," he replied.

Bonnie let out a loud crack of mirthless laughter. "Not even gonna bother to soften that up, are you? Just a flat-out no?"

"Yes."

"Well, I'm sorry to disappoint you," she said with a sigh, "but the mines aren't hiring. Something about quotas or working conditions—I forget which."

"That is what I was told."

Bonnie studied him for a moment. A worker who disliked you spelled trouble, and trouble was something she could very well do without. "Listen, if it makes you feel so much better to work for a man, you can go apply for a job at the mines—or somewhere else, if you like. I don't know how much good it'll do you, but you can try."

"I have done that already," he said bluntly. "They said it might be several years before I could work in the mines, so I had no choice. It was either work for you or be deported."

Bonnie knew this couldn't be true—there had to be another job *somewhere* on Terra Minor—but decided that Drummond must have been concerned enough to ensure that Lynx would take the job she was offering and no other. "Well, I think I'd rather work just about anywhere *but* a mine myself," she said candidly. "But if you prefer it, I guess that's the place to go." She was doing her best to be nice to him, but it was becoming more difficult with each passing moment. After all, *she* was the one with her arm half bitten off, and here she was having to make *him* feel better about working for her instead of slaving away in the mines! She was beginning to wish that Drummond had sent her a woman, instead—especially since a woman would at least have known how to fry an egg; she wasn't so sure about Lynx, who was still glaring at her as though he didn't know whether to slap her or feed her.

"Well," she said at length, "if you aren't going to fix any eggs for me, would you at least give me some cookies?"

This was something else Lynx didn't understand. His working knowledge of Stantongue didn't seem to be helping him very much in this instance, because he had no idea what cookies were, let alone where to find them. Trying not to appear too bewildered, he asked, "Where are the… cookies?"

"In the kitchen, on the table in a green tin marked 'Cookies,'" she said patiently. "You *can* read, can't you?"

"Yes," he replied defensively. "But not in your language."

"My language?" she repeated. "You mean Stantongue? What language *can* you read?"

"Zetithian."

"Ah, so you *are* from Zetith then," she said. "I thought so."

"You know of Zetith?" he asked in surprise. In all the years of his enslavement, he had yet to meet anyone who had ever heard of his homeworld. Sometimes Lynx wondered if he'd imagined that early part of his life, since there was nothing left to remind him of it. Even his memories had begun to fade.

"Yeah, I know of it," Bonnie said grimly. "Did you know it was destroyed?"

Lynx nodded. Yes, he knew—all too well. The sense of loss he felt whenever he thought of it assailed him once again. So many lives, so much waste. His planet had been beautiful once; now it was only space dust. "How do you know of my world?"

"Captain Jack told me about it—her husband is a Zetithian, by the way. I don't know what his real name is, but she calls him Cat."

Lynx felt his eyes widen in disbelief. *"There is another of us still living?"* he gasped.

Bonnie gave him a nod and continued. "Yep, and he's not the only one. There's another one called Leo who travels with them, along with his wife, Tisana. Jack says there are two brothers around somewhere too. One of them's a rock singer and the other one's a pilot." *And any one of them has to be nicer than you are,* Bonnie thought. She had never met the two brothers, but was certain that Cat or Leo would have already gotten that egg and had it cooked.

Ignoring that, he asked, "They are still slaves?"

"I just *told* you that Cat is Captain Jack's husband," Bonnie said patiently. "Weren't you listening? They have three kids, too."

Lynx felt the floor waver slightly beneath him and

his eyes widened even further. "She gave birth to his children?"

"Well, yeah!" Bonnie said, slightly mystified by his question. "They're married." Eyeing him curiously, she added, "Why wouldn't she have his children?"

Lynx was still too stunned to reply, and when he didn't answer, Bonnie decided that this business of not answering direct questions could get old in a hurry. Then she realized that she must have misunderstood his last question; perhaps it wasn't a matter of whether or not Jack had been *willing* to have Cat's children, but whether or not it was *possible.*

"Oh, I see what you mean," she said. "They're different species, of course, but the cross between a Terran and a Zetithian obviously works." As another example, she added, "Leo and Tisana have two boys and a girl."

Bonnie waited a moment or two, wondering if he'd ever snap out of it and get her something to eat. He'd been pretty good about doing whatever she'd asked him to do up until now, but this balking at getting cookies seemed a bit odd. Perhaps she hadn't asked him correctly.

Taking a deep breath, she tried to phrase it as politely as possible. "May I please have some more juice with my cookies?" She started to add, "before I pass out again," but decided that wouldn't be quite as polite.

Lynx jumped as though she'd startled him out of some really deep thoughts, but all he did was nod before going back out to the kitchen.

What a strange bird he is, Bonnie thought. Cat had

been a slave—up until fairly recently, too—but he
didn't act anything like this one did, and neither did
Leo. She wondered what had happened to Lynx to
make him this way, but figured that unless he were to
suddenly become a whole lot more talkative, she would
probably never know.

However reticent he might be, he was very much like
the other men in one respect: Bonnie couldn't help but
notice that he was every bit as physically attractive as
the other Zetithians, and if it hadn't been for his surly
attitude—and her own distrust of men in general—she
probably would have fallen for him at the outset. Unfortunately, given Bonnie's current attitude toward attractive men, this didn't do very much to endear him to her.
She'd have been happier if he'd been not only grouchy,
but ugly, because then she wouldn't have to worry about
being taken in by his charm.

But charm was something Lynx was sadly lacking,
though Bonnie realized that his attitude might have
been partly her fault. If she'd thought about it at all,
she would have planned things better. She would simply have let that chicken get eaten alive by enocks and
then used it as an example to demonstrate just how
dangerous they could be. Then she would have shown
Lynx around the farm, asked him what he liked to eat,
fed him, given him a place to sleep, and they would
have gotten along just fine. But she'd blown it by getting hurt and demonstrating that she was nothing more
than a helpless female—which, ordinarily, she wasn't,
and never had been—and, first impressions being
what they are, she would now have to spend God only
knew how long trying to prove it to him. Not that his

opinion mattered, as long as he was willing to work. Besides, she shouldn't have to prove anything to him; if anything, *he* should be the one proving things to *her*.

If Bonnie was wishing he'd be more friendly, Lynx went back to the kitchen wishing he didn't feel quite so dense. The men he'd worked alongside hadn't made him feel that way—at least, not after he'd learned all they had to teach him—but women? They usually made him feel stupid and then laughed at him.

Casting about for a likely object, Lynx picked up a green container from the table, noting that something rattled inside it. There was a word inscribed on the side, but he didn't recognize the style of writing. For all he knew, it might have said cookies, but even looking inside the tin wouldn't have helped him, because he had no idea what she'd been talking about. What were cookies?

Hoping he wasn't making a mistake, Lynx poured another glass of juice and took it back to the bedroom along with the tin and handed them to Bonnie.

"Would you like some?" she asked as she pulled the lid off the tin. To Bonnie's eyes, he appeared to be *much* too thin—not precisely sickly, but definitely undernourished—and she knew just how far he'd walked to get to her house, because she'd made that walk a few times herself.

It took him a long time to reply, and for a while Bonnie thought he wasn't going to answer her at all. "I do not know what a cookie is."

"Never been to Earth, have you?" she chided him.

"No." His voice was wooden and his eyes wary. She was making him feel stupid again. *Just as women have always done.*

"I didn't think so," she said pleasantly, "otherwise you'd know all about cookies! Here, try one; they're really good, and I know you've got to be hungry." When he still seemed hesitant, she waved it in front of him tantalizingly. "Chocolate chip," she said in a lilting tone. "One thousand-year-old original Toll House recipe…"

Lynx took the one she offered but pulled his hand away quickly, as though she might have been using the cookie to trap him. Then he did something else she thought was strange; he moved away from her and turned around so she couldn't watch him eat it. This was disappointing to her, because when someone eats a chocolate chip cookie for the first time, their expression is worth noting. When he turned toward her again, she couldn't tell if he'd liked it or not.

Lynx, as always, chewed and swallowed his food almost before he could taste it—which was normally the best way to choke down things that were barely fit to eat—but, this time, what lingered on his tongue made him wish he could have started over again. This woman had given him something he'd never tasted before; something rich and delicious, unlike the garbage he'd always had to live on. He stared at her blankly, not quite believing his eyes as she held out her hand again.

"Here," she said, giving him four more of them. "Have some more, and help yourself to some juice, too. It's made from last year's apples. Not as good as fresh, of course, but not bad."

As he took the small treasures from her, Lynx's first thought concerned where he would put them to keep them safe. "Where will I sleep?" he asked.

Bonnie didn't know what that had to do with juice and cookies, but thought perhaps she'd missed something. "Wherever you like," she replied.

"Then I will sleep in the other building." It was large, it was private, and, most importantly, away from her scent, which was already beginning to alter subtly.

She was pretty sure he didn't mean the henhouse. "The equipment shed? Are you sure? It's not very homey."

"It will be quiet," he said, as though that were his only requirement. When he took his cookies and left, Bonnie assumed that he didn't want to eat them in front of her, but he was gone a long time—much longer than it would have taken anyone to eat a few cookies.

Long enough for her to doze off, too, despite the fact that her arm and shoulder were still stinging and throbbing. It was late afternoon when she awoke, and she wondered if he'd asked where he would sleep and then went and took a nap himself, or if he'd just taken the cookies and left altogether. It didn't really matter, except that *someone* needed to feed the enocks. Bonnie tried sitting up and didn't feel too bad—at least she didn't faint—and her arm hadn't bled through the bandage. It was only then that she noticed that he'd wrapped it up with a dish towel.

Moving slowly, Bonnie made her way out to the kitchen and saw that, while the blood was all cleaned up, Lynx was nowhere to be seen. She thought he might have been in the shed, but when she looked out, she saw him over by the enock pen, building a fence.

He was nearly finished with it, and it didn't take her long to figure out his plan. All he'd done was build a small pen that shared one panel with the original, and he was in the process of pulling off the boards between them when she went out. As she watched from a distance, he replaced the boards with poles that could be slid aside to connect the two pens. Then he put food in the new pen and pulled out the poles. As if on cue, the enocks came strutting through the opening. He slid the poles back into place, neatly trapping them in the smaller pen. Then he went around to the main gate and, completely safe and unmolested, went in to gather the eggs. That done, he came out, pulled out the poles, and headed back toward the house without a scratch on him.

And all Bonnie wanted to do was to kick herself for not thinking of it first.

Chapter 2

LYNX HAD BUILT MANY FENCES IN THE PAST AND, AFTER finding some materials in the shed, had set about making enock raising a little safer. He had seen firsthand what the giant birds could do to a person and decided that some modifications were necessary. It was a simple solution, which made him wonder why a pregnant woman wouldn't have done it herself. Perhaps she was lazy, he decided—in keeping with the women he'd served. They never did anything for themselves if they could get someone—such as him—to do it for them.

Bonnie, however, was no stranger to hard work, and knew that Lynx must have been working like a little fiend. He'd set five or six posts and nailed up the panels between them, which was a lot of work for one afternoon, especially after the walk from Nimbaza and only a few cookies to eat. Bonnie didn't even know if he'd drunk any of the apple juice, and though he did have access to water from the pumps to the well, there had been plenty of things he hadn't seemed to understand, so he might not have known what the pumps were for.

Bonnie fed the chickens and went back to the house, noting that Lynx had put the eggs in a crate on the porch, and she put them away in the storage unit until market day. This was another nice thing about enock eggs; they kept well, and their flavor actually improved after a week or so.

Lynx wasn't anywhere in the house, and when Bonnie looked out, she saw him washing up at the pump by the shed. He had taken off his shirt and appeared to be tanned, as though he was accustomed to working outside without one. She stood there, watching him, wondering about his life. She knew where he was from originally, but where had he been since the war? Who had owned him, and who had finally set him free? Watching his impassive, enigmatic face, Bonnie had an idea that she might never know the answers to any of those questions.

She was thinking about checking her arm when he came up to the door and knocked.

"I see you've been busy," she commented as she let him in. "That feeding pen was a truly brilliant idea!" She grinned at him in what she hoped was a friendly, appreciative manner. "You're hired!"

Her smile was wasted, because Lynx didn't bother to smile back. "I came to check on you," he said flatly, "but you were gone."

Since the henhouse was on the opposite side of the house from the shed, it wasn't surprising that he hadn't seen her, but she didn't understand why it would make him snap at her. "I just fed the chickens is all," she said, trying to ignore the little twinge of pain near her heart. "I'm feeling a lot better now, but I do want to work on this arm."

Lynx didn't say anything, but just stared at her with his big yellow cat's eyes. He'd already told her what he thought about her needing to see a doctor and saw no need to repeat it.

Avoiding his angry glare, she went on to explain, "I've got a thing that's supposed to seal up cuts, but I don't know if I can do it left-handed. Don't know why I didn't think of it earlier. Jack sold it to me along with the ointment, but I've never used it."

A black-tipped eyebrow went up.

"Think you could help me with it?"

Lynx nodded in reply, so Bonnie went off and found what she was looking for at the back of a shelf in the bathroom closet. It was called "Seal 'n' Heal" and the directions on it were simple enough: *"Power on. Scan area to be sealed four centimeters from source. Power off. Do not use on eyes."*

Bonnie went back out to the kitchen and handed it to Lynx, who examined the device with a natural curiosity about such things. Slowly unwrapping the towel, Bonnie took a peek at her arm. "Well, that looks downright gross," she commented. Holding up her hand with her thumb and forefinger four centimeters apart to demon-strate, she said, "Scan it this far from the skin."

Lynx was skeptical, but he did what she told him, and the results were nothing short of amazing. Bonnie could feel it stinging just a little, but the gaping skin edges magically closed and were now held snuggly to-gether. "Well, I'll be!" she exclaimed. "I never thought it would work so well! Would you do the place on my shoulder, too?"

Pulling her arm out of her sleeve, she turned around. She couldn't see it, of course, but once Lynx sealed it, the pain diminished immediately, and after applying the ointment, she felt almost good as new. She marveled at the magic of it and wondered why she'd never used it before. She hadn't paid much for it, but decided that Jack must have really thought she needed the little gismo, because, now that she'd used it, it was obvious that Jack hadn't charged her anywhere near what it was worth. "Well, then, guess I'll fix supper now," Bonnie said brightly. "What would you like?"

Lynx didn't reply, being totally confused by her question. What would he *like?* He had no idea what to say to that, since he'd always eaten whatever he could find. Choice had never been a factor; in fact, he didn't even know what sort of food he *did* like.

Still having no idea why he never answered her questions, Bonnie shook her head, saying grimly, "Never mind, I'll come up with something." Gesturing toward a chair, she said, "Just have a seat. This won't take long," and got started. Her arm seemed to be working just fine, but, not wanting to push her luck, she simply grated some onions and peppers in the processor and then fried them up along with some scrambled eggs— chicken eggs, this time—and some cheese. When it was done, she dished it up and set his plate in front of him, along with a couple of pieces of buttered toast and a glass of juice.

Pulling up a chair, Bonnie sat down and dug in. It was good and hot and she was as hungry as an enock. After a few moments, though, she noticed that Lynx hadn't touched his but was staring at the plate of eggs as though it might bite him.

The smell of hot food drifted up to Lynx's sensitive nose, making him feel dizzy. What a heavenly scent! He wanted to devour it but remembered the woman sitting across from him. He couldn't take a bite with her watching; he refused to be laughed at again—or to give anyone the opportunity to do so.

"Oh, don't tell me you're a vegetarian!" Bonnie groaned. "You aren't, are you?"

Lynx shook his head, but Bonnie wasn't sure whether he knew what she'd meant by that or not.

"Well, then, go ahead and eat it," she said irritably. "You *will* eat more than cookies, won't you?"

He nodded, but said, "I cannot eat it here," which seemed a bit bizarre to her, until she remembered the way he'd turned away when he'd eaten a cookie.

"Thanksgiving must have been real interesting at your house," Bonnie remarked dryly.

Lynx didn't understand her remark and looked at her questioningly.

"Never mind," she said with a wave of her hand. Though she did her best to brush it off, she was hurt that he wouldn't even share a meal with her. If nothing else, it seemed very snobbish of him. "You can eat it wherever you like."

Appearing greatly relieved, Lynx picked up his plate and glass and left the house. Bonnie comforted herself with the fact that he was an alien—and while she'd heard of some odd alien customs, this one was right up there with some of the strangest. She wondered if Cat would eat in the same room with Jack and decided that perhaps it was something you could only do if you were married.

In a way, the idea made her jealous of Cat and Jack, who seemed like the happiest couple in the galaxy. Apparently Bonnie wasn't deserving of that kind of happiness, because it sure as hell hadn't happened to her yet. Like most of her boyfriends, Sylor had been handsome and charming, though in retrospect, she couldn't honestly say that she'd loved him very much, and had been more irritated than heartbroken when he left her. Lynx, on the other hand, was very attractive, but he wasn't charming at all, although it might have just been because he was a stranger to her. Lynx hadn't wanted to work for a woman, and it was obvious to Bonnie that he already thought she was a foolish idiot. The trouble was, they were sort of stuck with each other—for a while, at least—because she needed help, and he needed a job.

Still, Bonnie wished they could at least become friends. She missed having someone to talk with, though given his dislike of sharing a meal with anyone, it was fairly obvious that they wouldn't be having much in the way of dinner table conversation. It made her feel even lonelier than she'd been before he came. Maybe it's my short haircut he doesn't like, she mused, though Jack's hair was short, and Cat didn't seem to mind. Cat himself had long, beautiful hair hanging in shiny, black spirals down to his waist, making him appear dashing and sexy. Leo's hair was also very attractive, and she liked him, too, but in a sort of different way. He was more reserved than Cat, but you could tell he loved Tisana with all his heart—maybe it had something to do with Tisana's long, dark hair and bewitching eyes…

However, in contrast to the other two Zetithians, there was nothing the least bit dashing or sexy about Lynx; in fact, he seemed intent on being nondescript and invisible. He was very thin, and his hair color was as neutral as the clothes he wore. Aside from the typical Zetithian features, the only things about him that were remarkable in any way were his eye color—which wasn't something he could change—and his black-tipped eyebrows. He was by no means unattractive, but so far, his personality wasn't what Bonnie would have called endearing.

But perhaps she wasn't being quite fair to Lynx. He'd come here intending to work in the mines, didn't seem to like being around women, and he'd wound up working on a woman's farm. In such a situation, Bonnie thought she might have been a bit surly herself and hoped that he would lighten up after a while.

While she ate her dinner, she kept thinking about him; why he might have acted the way he did, what horrible things he'd been forced to endure, all the while feeling odd little waves of sadness—tiny twinges near her heart that made her want to cry. Lynx had a certain aura that hung about him like a cloud of despair. He shouldn't have been feeling despair, because Bonnie knew she would pay him all she could and wouldn't work him to death, either. Food was plentiful, so he need never go hungry. Aside from that, there wasn't much more she could do for him. He didn't seem to want to talk—not even wanting her companionship—and love wasn't something he would ever want from her, which was no hardship, because she didn't think she could give it to him anyway.

But I can give him something soft to sleep on! She put her dish in the sink and went in search of some spare bedding. Gathering up all the blankets and sheets she could find—what he didn't need in the way of covers, he could use to pad the floor—she carried them out to the shed. Having him sleep out there hadn't been her first choice, but if that was what he wanted, she would do her best to see that he was comfortable. She smiled ironically, as the pillow she chose to give him was the one Sylor had always slept on. Lynx could rip it to shreds with those fangs of his, and it wouldn't matter to her; she had no use for it now.

Chapter 3

As the *Jolly Roger* left orbit of Harabba Five, Captain Jacinth "Jack" Tshevnoe sat alone in the cockpit, tapping the console to adjust their flight to Terra Minor. Unlike the barren rock they'd just left, Terra Minor was a pretty planet when viewed from space, all green and blue with swirling clouds—like many others, perhaps, but even the shape of the continents was interesting. One reminded Jack of the shape of a dog—sort of like Tisana's black hound, Max. She looked forward to seeing that world again and visiting with its inhabitants.

As though he heard her thoughts, Max padded over to place his head on Jack's knee. As Tisana was always in mental communication with her pet, Jack figured Max already knew, but she told him anyway.

"Hey, Max!" she said brightly. "We're going to Terra Minor! You'll get to see Kipper again."

Max gave a muffled bark. He knew to keep his voice down, because Jack didn't like loud, sudden noises. It made her react as if the Nedwuts were firing on them. Max hated Nedwuts and wished he could have done more to help Jack fight them, but the hairy, snarling beasts were more than he could take on alone. Not that he hadn't tried.

In the past, as an honest trader, Jack had never had to fight any battles in space, but harboring a Zetithian was something the Nedwuts apparently considered to be an

open declaration of war. After teaming up with Cat, Jack
had equipped her ship with weapons, which put them
on more even footing, but didn't guarantee their safety.
Jack didn't mind the expense or the danger, though. She
loved Cat enough to fight for him, and she wasn't about
to let a bunch of slimeball Nedwuts interfere with her
life. The way she saw it, anyone who threatened Cat got
blasted. Period.

Jack had never asked any of them how much the
bounty was on a Zetithian—she'd never left a Nedwut
alive long enough to answer any questions—but it must
have been a huge amount to keep them out there hunting.
The information that the Nedwuts had been responsible
for destroying the entire planet of Zetith had spread,
with the result that they were refused landing permission on most worlds, but there were still quite a few of
them lurking around some of the seedier planets. Jack
tended to avoid regions of space where Nedwuts were
known to congregate, but you never knew when a pack
of them might decide to get adventurous, so she stayed
ready with the sensors always on the alert.

Setting the autopilot, Jack leaned back and absently
petted Max. What would her life be like without Cat?
Not worth living, she decided—though she did have her
three sons to think of. She'd have to keep on going for
them, but having loved a man like Cat was guaranteed
to make any other man seem pale in comparison. She'd
lived a long time without a man, and now, she knew she
could want no other—and she wanted him all the time.

Following the trail of his wife's scent, Cat stole softly
up behind Jack just as he had done the first day he spent
on her ship. He'd been naked and chained then, but he'd

been drawn to her like a magnet. He remembered the feeling of utter loss after she'd purchased him at auction, then freed him and left him in the plaza. She'd asked if he would try to escape if she removed his restraints, and he'd been dumb enough to say what any self-respecting slave would have said: "I am a slave and a prisoner. I will attempt to escape"—and she'd believed him! Hadn't she *seen* the effect she had on him?

But Cat knew very well that his Jacinth was impulsive, and though tough and determined, there was a vulnerable streak in her, one that he'd unknowingly hit upon. The way she'd tried to resist him had been pointless, because he could smell her desire for him, and it was strong—strong enough for him to pick up her scent, even on the stinking hellhole that was Orpheseus Prime. Her face had been covered by the respirator she wore to shield her from the stench, but while everyone else had assumed she was male, Cat had known the difference. There had been something about the way she spoke to him that set her apart, and he'd fallen for her completely, without even being able to see her face.

He still recalled the questions she'd asked him—details about himself that no one else had ever even thought to ask. She didn't know him at all—he'd been chained like an animal and put up for sale to the highest bidder—and yet it had been so obvious that she cared about him—where he had been, how he had come to be a slave, and why she'd never heard of his planet.

Looking at her now filled him with the desire to move closer, to inhale her scent—especially knowing what it would do to him. The urge to take her was strong, and she affected him like no other woman on any world had ever done. She was his life: she had rescued him from slavery, and he, in turn, had rescued her from a lifetime of loneliness.

Purring deep in his throat, Cat rested his hands on her shoulders, breathing in her scent, feeling his cock stir in response. They were bound together by an alien ritual; Jack could only tolerate being a short distance from him without becoming agitated and could follow his scent as though it were visible. Staying close to her was no hardship for Cat, however, since it was where he wanted to be anyway.

"Is the course set?" he asked.

Nodding in reply, she added, "It'll be good to see everyone again, but that damn doctor—what's his name?—might not want to see me! I've got a bone to pick with him!"

"You mean Vladen," said Cat.

"Yeah, well, he told me there was nothing stopping me from having more kids, and God knows we've done nothing to prevent it, but I'm getting tired of wondering when it's gonna happen."

"I am not tired of trying, though," Cat purred. Max still sat at Jack's side, thumping his tail, but all it took was a raised eyebrow from Cat to have him on his feet, trotting out the door. It wasn't the first time Max had been asked to leave.

"They never let me watch," Max grumbled to himself. He'd go talk to Tisana instead. It might not be as entertaining as Cat and Jack going at it, but it was better than nothing.

"That's what I like about you, Cat," Jack declared, not even noticing the dog had gone. "You're an incurable optimist."

"No," he said regretfully. "I enjoy mating with you—and will continue to do so, whether we ever have any more children or not."

Reaching over her shoulder to the console, he touched the control for the door and smiled as it sealed behind him.

"Looks like I'm about to get nailed again," Jack muttered, but couldn't quite suppress her smile.

"Yes, my lovely master, you are."

Jack sighed. "You know I can't resist when you call me that, Kittycat."

Purring louder, he pulled her from her chair and into his arms. "You cannot resist me at all," he said knowingly. "And I cannot stay away."

"You know, maybe that's why we haven't had any more kids," Jack said reflectively as Cat licked her ear, sending thrills racing down her spine. "We go at it so often your sperm count is probably too low."

"It is not," he assured her. "Vladen checked that, too, if you will recall."

"Yeah, well, I still think he's a quack," Jack argued. "Never did trust Levitians."

"Shh," Cat whispered. "Let us not speak of him now." The feel of her in his arms sent his mind drifting into a sexual haze. She was his mate for life, and he never tired of demonstrating his claim on her. She kept him laughing, could get a bargain out of the devil himself, and may have called herself by a man's name, but she still melted at his touch. He liked that.

Jack's head fell back, exposing her slender throat for his kiss as her eyes blissfully closed. Cat felt a rush of blood to his groin as the flow of the orgasm-inducing fluid from the glands of his scalloped cockhead began. Knowing that she would scold him for letting it go to waste, he pushed off his loose-fitting pants, leaving them puddled on the floor at his feet. In the past, Jack had always worn a flightsuit and boots while on board the ship, but since she and Cat had been together, she'd taken to wearing only a tank top and shorts. It was easy for him to remove, which was just as well, because they never stayed dressed for long.

Cat heard Jack's soft sigh as he kissed her parted lips, felt their warmth as he inhaled her essence. With a low growl, he deepened the kiss, his tongue diving past her lips to devour her. She ignited a fire in every cell of his body, driving him wild with a passionate desire to join with her.

Pressing her back to the door, he got rid of her clothing as effortlessly as he had his own and pulled her legs up around his waist. His cock unerringly found its way into her soft warmth as with one swift stroke he sheathed himself in her. Her gasp of pleasure sent him further into the abyss where his only thought was to fill her with his seed and his love.

"Ohhh," Jack sighed. "I just love the way you do that."

Cat's voice was deep and rough when he replied. "And I love to make you moan, Jacinth."

"Always do," she murmured. "Can't help it." Shuddering as her first orgasm had her body writhing in ecstasy, she pulled him closer. "Harder, Cat. Make me do more than just moan."

Cat laughed devilishly. "I always do that, as well."

"Cocky Cat!" she gasped. "Can't let me alone for a minute, can you?"

"Do you want me to?"

"No," she replied truthfully. "Don't stop. Ever."

He purred his appreciation for her reply. "Hold on," he said, thinking it was a good thing the *Jolly Roger* was so well built; if it hadn't been, they'd have broken through a bulkhead and spaced themselves long ago. He drilled his cock into her relentlessly, wishing he could get his whole body inside her. She was the one he loved beyond reason; he couldn't help loving her any more than he could help feeling hunger or pain. She had accused him of being addicting, but he knew differently; he was the one who was addicted—to *her*. His body craved her touch; his senses craved her scent and the sound of her voice. And his eyes sought her face... the most beautiful vision his mind could conceive. Jack had never thought of herself as being even passably pretty—her younger sister had been the beauty of the family—but Cat disagreed wholeheartedly.

"My lovely Jacinth," he sighed, gazing into her deep brown eyes—eyes now blurred with passion. "I will never stop loving you."

Jack wrapped her arms around his neck, clutching at his long black curls as he thrust into her, wishing the same thing he had; that she could somehow wrap herself around him completely so that they became one being. It was a feeling she sought each time they were together.

Cat leaned back, balancing her on his groin as his penis swirled deeply inside her. He would leave no place untouched, no chance that she might not feel the greatest possible pleasure. Grasping her hips, he pushed her down hard, driving himself in deeper.

Jack gazed into her husband's dark, exotic eyes, her own widening in awe as he took her to new heights. The moans Cat had hoped for escaped her lips as her pleasure reached its peak again and again, sending him higher still until he felt his own imminent climax begin to swell inside him. Thrusting deeply inside her to plant his seed where it would not only grow, but give her the joy he wished for her to feel, he felt his balls tighten as he came with a growl.

Jack waited breathlessly for the rush of pure delight that would soon follow, and when it came, it sent tendrils of "Ahhh…" throughout her body. Cat smiled, his fingers teasing the hair back from her face.

"Joy, unlike any you have ever known?"

"Oh, yeah," she sighed. "How do you do it? It's always like that—even better than I remember." And she didn't have to think very far back, either.

"That is because of you." Cat kissed her deeply, lovingly, inhaling her scent and tasting her. She was like wine to him—sweet, delicious, and intoxicating.

As Jack slid down to her feet, Max gave a cautious bark from the other side of the door. "Hold on, Max. I'll be out in a minute," Jack said, reluctantly breaking off the kiss. With a furtive glance at Cat, she asked, "Has Tisana been teaching you how to talk to him?"

Cat smiled. "No, but we do understand one another—in some matters more than others."

One man to another, Jack decided. She was just glad that her man was a cat, rather than a dog.

In a barroom well beyond the fringes of the Nimbaza district, Sylor Halen sat with a drink in front of him, listening to the discussion at a nearby table.

"You'll never make it here," a dark-visaged Plaotian man was saying quietly. "The rules are too strict. You'll never get away with it."

Sylor's ears, though peculiarly slanted, were quite sharp, and as usual, the idea of "getting away with" anything piqued his interest.

"If no one is around to report it?" the Plaotian's companion scoffed. "I don't think so. Just don't tell anyone where I've gone." This man was Terran, though of a paler skin than Sylor had ever seen. Pale to the point of sickliness.

"You'll need money, Krall," the Plaotian said. "And lots of it. How're you going to get it?"

"I've got a plan," Krall said earnestly. "All I need is a little seed money."

Sylor's cache of credits was dwindling, and though he prided himself on taking advantage of every opportunity to expand it, since moving on from Bonnie he had been less than successful. The last woman he'd taken the time to romance had not been as well-heeled as he had hoped. He'd taken her for all he could, but even that wasn't enough. Still, he had Bonnie's grandmother's engagement ring: a platinum setting with a flawless, two-carat stone. It had meant a lot to Bonnie for purely sentimental reasons, but the fact that it was very valuable was what had appealed to Sylor. He'd been contemplating how best to turn it into cash: perhaps it would be adequate "seed money."

"Gentlemen," Sylor began, "I couldn't help but overhear that you find yourselves on the horns of a dilemma. Perhaps I can be of assistance."

The two men looked at Sylor warily, but Sylor possessed all the charm that a man of his ilk needed. They would fall in with his plans and feel that it had been their own idea from the start. As Sylor held out his hand in friendship, the process began. "Krall, is it?" he said with a winning smile. "I'm very pleased to meet you."

If it didn't pan out and they became suspicious enough to report him, Sylor still had a few tricks up his sleeve. Anyone who crossed Sylor usually ended up dead… one way or another.

Chapter 4

LYNX HAD LEFT THE HOUSE, BUT HE HAD BARELY rounded the corner of the porch before his stomach got the better of him. Setting down the glass of juice on a nearby tree stump, he tore into his food like a wild dog. After the first few bites, he made himself slow down enough to taste it. It was so good it almost hurt to eat it, and there were actually tears in his eyes when he swallowed the last bite. Kipper sat nearby, looking up at him eagerly.

"You have always been well fed," he told the collie as he tipped up his glass to drink the sweet juice. "I have not been so fortunate."

Lynx left his empty dishes by the door—after which Kipper polished them to a high sheen—and went out to inspect his new quarters.

The shed was spacious, and though it smelled of machinery and dust, to Lynx, it was a palace. The emptiness of it was an attraction for him, and he liked hearing the echo of his footsteps as he walked across the bare concrete floor. There were birds nesting in the rafters, and their chirping didn't annoy him in the slightest, unlike the chirping voices of women. He blinked hard in an attempt to banish the memory. This woman, Bonnie, was a fool to risk her child for a chicken, but at least her voice wasn't a chirp. He'd grown so tired of hearing women's voices! They whined, they pleaded, they screamed, or they *chirped*. Shuddering in revulsion at the memory, Lynx crossed over to the far corner. There, he would be hidden from anyone entering the shed, and it was the farthest place from the door. He would have plenty of warning should Bonnie ever enter there.

What would he do if she ever came there seeking his company? He sincerely hoped she never would, but he also intended to make it quite plain that if she did, she would not be welcome. All he wanted was a place where he could be alone and think of absolutely nothing. When he had been with the women, he'd rarely been allowed a moment to himself, and even after the time spent among men, he still craved solitude. Sitting down in the corner, his hand resting on the pack that contained all he owned, he closed his eyes and drifted into nothingness.

It wasn't long before his worst fears were realized when he heard a tap on the door to his sanctuary and the sound of Bonnie calling his name. *She could not leave me alone even for a moment,* he thought as Bonnie slipped in with Kipper at her heels, carrying a stack of pillows and blankets.

Threading her way between the tractor and various other implements, Bonnie couldn't see clearly, but noticed a movement in the far corner behind the harvester droid. Thinking that she would have slept in the speeder herself, which was comfortable enough and wasn't good for much else, she noted that he appeared to have simply been sitting—or lying—in the corner on the floor. There was a small pack next to him, and from the dent in it, she assumed he had been using it as a pillow.

"I brought you some things," she said. "You can use them to sleep on until I can get you a proper bed. You could probably stand a chair, too."

Glancing around, Bonnie remembered the empty crates she used for the eggs and figured they could stack them up and then put a board across them to make a table. That way he wouldn't have to eat outside, though she wasn't sure if that was what he preferred or not. So far, the only preference she knew about was that he wouldn't eat in her house. Perhaps someday he would explain to her just why that was.

Handing him the bedding, she pulled out two crates and went off to find a board. There was plenty of scrap material left over from building the house, and Bonnie soon found one the right size and put it on top of the crates. It wasn't fancy, but it did have the virtue of being relatively sturdy. Lynx merely stood watching her, unable to understand what she was doing. Doing her best to ignore the blank stare she was receiving in return for her kind efforts, Bonnie then went back to the house and returned with a kitchen chair and a lamp. Her power source would run anything within thirty meters of the house, and the far end of the shed fell just within its range. There were overhead lights in the shed, but Bonnie thought a lamp would make it seem a little homier.

"Got any clothes you need to have washed?" she asked. Lynx's pack was very small and couldn't have held much of a wardrobe, but she thought she should ask anyway.

"No," he replied. "I only have these."

Lynx drew back slightly as he said this, hoping that she wouldn't ask him to take them off so she could wash them. Being left naked and vulnerable in front of a woman was something he never wished to experience again. She would laugh at him, and he couldn't stand that anymore. He'd have thought that after so many years, he'd have gotten used to it, but he never had. Women's laughter still cut through him like a knife.

Laughing at Lynx was the very last thing on Bonnie's mind, however. She was thinking about getting something else for him to wear—after all, everyone needed a change of clothes! She had fabric and a sewing machine—both courtesy of her mother, who didn't think a primitive place like Terra Minor would have ready-made clothes—so she could make him something. The shirt and pants he had on didn't look as though they'd been made for him; they hung loosely on his thin frame, though it was possible that they'd fit him better at one time. The style was simple enough—a tunic that crossed over in front and tucked into trousers with a drawstring waist—and would be easy to duplicate. It was obvious that whoever had dressed him in the past hadn't gone to much expense, and, unfortunately, neither could Bonnie. When she'd asked Drummond to find her a hired hand, it had never occurred to her that he wouldn't have any clothes to speak of. Her only consolation was that he wasn't barefoot, though his sturdy sandals were more serviceable than stylish.

He was such a mystery to her! How did he get there, and where had he been? Why had he come to Terra Minor at all? With anyone else, a long talk over a pot of coffee and a batch of cookies would have filled her in nicely, but Lynx seemed so uncomfortable with her there that after a few awkward moments, she went back to the house, leaving him to make his own bed. She was almost glad to be away from him, for he seemed to exude sadness, uncertainty, and even fear. He had been brusque with her earlier in the day, but now he seemed wary, as though he suspected that she might harm him in some way.

Bonnie couldn't help but wonder if he'd gone outside to eat only because he couldn't stomach what she'd given him and had fed it to the dog instead. The plate had been licked clean, but that might only mean that Kipper had polished it off after Lynx was finished. It was possible that he was allergic to eggs—after all, many people were—and was too polite to refuse what she'd given him—though if his behavior constituted politeness, it was a different brand than she'd ever encountered before. If she hadn't already known Cat and Leo, she might have said it was from having been a slave or was possibly a Zetithian trait, but since they acted nothing like Lynx, she doubted it.

Entering the house, it seemed so empty to her now. There were only three months to go until her baby was born, and then she would have someone besides Kipper for company. She was looking forward to that. She was pretty sure she couldn't count on Lynx.

She told herself that it was probably better that Lynx didn't want to stay in the house—after all, she knew very little about him and might be safer with him out in the shed—but for some reason, it felt wrong. He'd saved her life, and she felt she owed him more than just a corner of the shed to sleep in. He seemed to have a great deal of difficulty accepting things from her—perhaps from anyone. Surely *someone* had shown him kindness in the past; it couldn't be so foreign to him that he didn't even recognize it! Bonnie had a much softer heart than she cared to admit, and that same heart was what had gotten her into a plethora of man trouble in the past. Still, it was her nature to be kind, and she vowed to continue to show him kindness—whether he liked it or not. Reminding herself that she had only advertised for a hired hand, not a roommate—and certainly not a husband—she went to bed.

One of the Nimbaza region's more violent storms passed through that night, and Bonnie was very glad she was safe inside her house when it hit. Knowing how deafening the sound of a heavy downpour could be when it pounded on the metal roof of the shed, she doubted that Lynx was getting much in the way of sleep on his first night. She listened for the sound of him pounding on the door, wondering if he might have been rethinking his decision to sleep out there, but the sound never came—or if it did, she couldn't hear it.

She needn't have worried. With only half of what she'd given him, Lynx had put together the most comfortable bed he had ever slept on in his entire life. He was tired, having walked all the way from Nimbaza and then run to Bonnie's rescue. After binding her wounds, he'd been so angry that he had to do something to work off a little steam. Building the fence had been as much a mental exercise as a physical one; he'd come up with the idea almost immediately and had acted on it. He still didn't quite understand why he'd been so angry with her. Even though he'd rarely been treated with kindness, he did understand the concept. He thought briefly about what else he could do to repay her, but exhaustion finally closed down his mind. He never even heard the thunder.

Bonnie, however, slept fitfully. Perhaps it was from thinking about Cat and Leo—how friendly they were and how happy their wives seemed to be—and, most of all, how different they were from Lynx. She knew that there were wide variations in every species, but for some reason, his behavior just didn't seem to fit.

At last she fell asleep from sheer exhaustion, but Lynx was still on her mind even while she slept. In her dreams, she could see his eyes glowing with passion, could feel his warm hands on her body, could almost taste his soft, sensuous kisses...

Bonnie awoke with a start, her lips tingling as though Lynx had actually kissed her. "Don't be silly," she whispered to herself. "He's not like Cat and Leo at all. I shouldn't expect it of him." But she couldn't quite shake the notion that it wasn't an unrealistic expectation. There was far more to him than met the eye.

When Bonnie let Kipper out the next morning, Lynx was already feeding the enocks. Watching him through the window, she realized that while she had yet to tell him what his duties would be, he had already assumed many of them himself. He certainly wasn't lazy, she decided, even if he *was* a little strange. Not to mention the fact that he had somehow managed to invade her dreams.

Figuring that he probably didn't want eggs again, Bonnie fixed some cold cereal with fruit instead. She wasn't sure whether to call him or just wait for him to knock on the door, but when he didn't show up by the time she'd finished her own, she decided to yell.

Lynx heard the call and came promptly, though it never occurred to him that she would have called her dog the same way. He was used to that and hardly noticed. He did notice that she had at least called him by name, which was better than being referred to as "Boy" or "Slave," as he had so often been called in the past. He put out of his mind the other names he'd been given—they didn't apply to him any more than boy or slave did. When he reached the back door, Bonnie handed him his breakfast, which he took from her without a word.

Thinking that Kipper would at least have wagged his tail, Bonnie watched Lynx through the window, hoping to find out whether he would eat what she'd given him or feed it to the chickens. What she saw made her stare in horror.

Bonnie had never seen anyone eat so fast in her life; he wolfed down the cereal and then drank the juice in what seemed like one big gulp. It was no wonder he was so thin and didn't care what she gave him to eat! He was practically starving! Bonnie stared blindly at him for a long moment and then sprang into action. After stuffing bread in the toaster, she called for him again.

"I forgot to give you some toast," she said, trying not to make it obvious that she'd been watching him. "I didn't know if you liked butter or jelly, so I made it with both." She hesitated a moment before adding, "It's market day, so after I pick whatever's ripe and gather the eggs, I've got to pack up and go into Nimbaza. I won't be back until late, so when you get hungry, just help yourself to whatever you like. There's plenty of cheese and bread and fruit—and eggs, of course!"

He nodded, his expression as neutral as ever. "The speeder does not function," he said flatly.

"Oh, I'll walk," she replied. "I've got a cart to carry everything in, so—"

Lynx took a breath as though he was about to interrupt, but seemed to think better of it. He would not remind her again to think of the child she carried.

"What were you going to say?" she asked.

"I have already gathered the eggs," he said, changing the subject.

"The chicken eggs too? Well, that's great! If you'd give me a hand with the fruits and vegetables, I'll get there quicker and maybe sell it all before it gets too late. Is there anything you need in town?"

His expression was so blank, Bonnie wasn't sure he'd even heard her, let alone understood what she'd asked, and when she began to explain, he just said, "No."

Bonnie could think of about a million things that he might need in town, but took him at his word. "Well," she said doubtfully, "finish your breakfast then, and we'll get started in the garden."

Lynx had never done any farm work before, but he was a quick study, and they had the crates full in no time, after which he loaded them onto the cart. The cart, which not only moved under its own power but also had the virtue of being refrigerated, was what had saved Bonnie when the speeder had finally died on her. Before, she'd always hitched it to the speeder and zoomed on into town, but the cart moved along nicely at a walking pace and, though she was pretty sure Kipper missed riding in the speeder, it served her well.

As she set out, Bonnie's heart felt much lighter than it had in some time. It was a pleasant spring day, and she had plenty to sell; there might even be enough left over to pay Lynx a little bit after she paid her bills—and she had as many bills as anyone. The grain and sunflowers were her main source of income for the year, but the garden produce and the eggs were her cash crops, and now that she could get enock eggs without risking life and limb, she considered trying to trap more of them. Unfortunately, without a working speeder, she was unlikely to have much success.

Bonnie's outlook on the future had improved considerably now that she had Lynx around to help. Before, she'd always dreaded trying to get those eggs every day and had been concerned about what she would do when the baby came. But now, she wasn't worried, and it felt good.

The hike to Nimbaza was about eight kilometers, and though Bonnie and Kipper made it in good time, it was getting hot when she set up her cart in the marketplace. As usual, the enock eggs were the first things to sell out. She saved two of them to trade for cheese and butter from her neighbor, Salan, whose father ran a dairy. Her friend, Zuannis, was a baker, and though she also traded for Bonnie's eggs, she preferred chicken eggs. "They are better for baking," she had told Bonnie. "I would have to make too big a batch to use an enock egg—*and* have to charge too much for my bread!" There were several other people who raised cows, pigs, and chickens, but since Bonnie was the only one in the region who raised enocks, she pretty much had a corner on the market. People just couldn't seem to get enough of those eggs, and she knew she could sell as many as her enocks could produce. She grudgingly admitted to herself that Sylor had been right about them being a good source of income. They had spotted several adult enocks eating the fallen fruit of an indigenous tree, and, knowing how much people delighted in finding the occasional egg, Sylor had gotten the idea to trap them. They tried several different ways before coming up with the speeder and net method, which had been risky, but effective. It took two people and a fast speeder, though—neither of which Bonnie had had since Sylor left.

It was midmorning when the region's only two Norludians, Gerna and Hatul, approached her booth and touched every single thing Bonnie had set out—including the eggs—with their strange sucker-tipped fingers before deciding what they wanted to buy, just as they always did. Jack had once warned her not to ask why they did that, just to let them do their thing and move on, but on this particular day, Bonnie was feeling adventurous.

"Why do you do that, Gerna?" she asked curiously as they finished up their transaction. "I can understand wanting to see if the fruit is ripe, but why the eggs?"

Laughing conspiratorially as she glanced at her mate, her bulbous eyes blinking rapidly, Gerna replied. "We only choose the things that affect us in a... *sexual* manner."

Since they were both quite thin, Bonnie was left to assume that there weren't many fruits and vegetables that met their requirements. "And you feel this through your fingertips?" Shaking her head in bewilderment, she added, "I don't get it."

"Perhaps if I touched you, you would understand," Hatul said in his odd, piping voice. "Just a touch on your hand—"

"Don't let him do that!" a nearby voice called out.

Bonnie looked up to see Zuannis heading toward her, waving her arms in protest, her colorful robes billowing out behind her. Zuannis was a Twilana, and, as such, was tall, bald-headed, and had a nose like the snout of a rhino—horn and all. Twilanas were one of the few species Bonnie had ever encountered whose males were much more attractive, and smaller, than their females. Their style of dress didn't seem to be gender specific, and Bonnie had made the mistake of thinking that Zuannis was a male when they first met. Zuannis had a good sense of humor and didn't make a fuss, but her husband had been less forgiving, pointing out that *he* wasn't the one wearing the earrings. "He'll… well… you don't want to know what he'll do if he sucks onto your skin with one of those things!"

"I've been hearing that from Jack for ages," Bonnie grumbled. "Why won't anyone tell me? Everyone else seems to know, but no one will talk about it! Is it really *that* disgusting?" Then she remembered what Gerna had said about touching the fruit and looked back at Hatul. There was a decidedly mischievous glint in his big, round eyes as he pursed his fishlike lips and smooched at her.

"Hatul," Bonnie said teasingly. "You wouldn't be trying to get off on me while your wife was watching, would you?"

"She likes it," Hatul said, extending his fingers. "Just one little touch…"

Gerna didn't protest, but looked on encouragingly. Zuannis, however, took Bonnie's arm and pulled her out of reach.

"She might not mind it," Zuannis said, "—but it grosses me out."

"Aw, Zuannis, you're no fun at all," Bonnie said, laughing. "Sorry, Hatul!"

Hatul kissed his fingertips and waggled them at her. "Until the next market day, my pretty one!"

Zuannis and Bonnie watched as the pair moved on to another stall. "They are the strangest creatures I've ever seen in my life," Zuannis remarked. "Just plain weird."

"Is it my imagination, or did you just interrupt the closest thing to sex I've had since, well… probably since I got pregnant?" Bonnie inquired dryly.

"I don't think you would have gotten much out of it," Zuannis said, "but he would have come all over himself."

Since Norludians didn't wear clothing, this would have been noticeable. However, never having seen any obvious genitalia on either of the Norludians, Bonnie wouldn't have known where to look for it. "All over his… what?" she prompted her friend.

A pained expression contorted Zuannis' already bizarre features. "His face, Bonnie," she replied. "Their tongues are their, um, sex organ—ever notice him flicking it at you? They use those sucker fingers to hold on while they fuck your—"

"Okay," Bonnie said, holding up a hand. "You're right. I don't want to hear any more."

Zuannis smiled and looked at Bonnie appraisingly. "So, how are you?"

"Fine, Bonnie replied. "Drummond finally sent me some help."

"And?"

"He's… a little… different."

"How so?"

"Well, he's Zetithian—you know, like Cat and Leo? But—"

"And you said you haven't had sex since *when?*" Zuannis asked incredulously.

Bonnie wasn't sure just what this had to do with Lynx. "Sylor left a good while back, Zuannis," she said witheringly. "You know that."

"And this guy has been working for you for *how* long?"

"Just a few days." Bonnie stared at Zuannis curiously, still not sure what she was getting at.

"Older man, is he?" Zuannis suggested, rubbing a finger on her horn, much like a Terran might tap their chin when perplexed.

"No," Bonnie replied. "I'm guessing he's a little younger than Cat and Leo. They aren't that old."

Zuannis nodded. "Zetithians don't age as quickly as humans do," she said informatively. With a curious tilt of her odd head, she went on to ask, "Is he... attractive?"

"Well, he might be if he smiled more and put on a little weight," Bonnie admitted, not even wanting to admit to herself that she considered Lynx to be quite handsome. "He's not nearly as friendly as Cat or Leo— though maybe it's just me he doesn't like."

"I find that hard to believe," Zuannis remarked. "Everyone seems to like *you.*"

"Well, I don't know about that," Bonnie said doubtfully, "but Lynx is... different. He was all set to get a job in the mines, but wound up working for me instead—which he doesn't seem very happy about. And I get the distinct impression that it isn't just me; he doesn't like women in general—didn't want to work for one, anyway."

Zuannis's big, brown eyes widened, and she drew herself up to her full height. "Uh-uh," she said with a decisive shake of her head. *"Couldn't* be a Zetithian! Must be something that just looks like one."

"Well, he said he was—and it was on his immigration chip, too, according to Drummond."

Zuannis shook her head again. "There's something wrong with him then." Zuannis then turned to examine the dried plums as she spoke and picked up a bag to put them in. "I'll take these," she said, handing her purchase to Bonnie. "You can stop by my shop later for your bread."

Bonnie stared up at her tall friend in surprise. "You're just going to leave it at that?"

"It'll be better if you don't know everything," Zuannis said with a firm nod, "especially since he's not… right."

"Great!" Bonnie said with a twinge of amusement. "Something *else* no one will tell me about."

"Believe me, it's for the best," Zuannis assured her.

Bonnie didn't think so, but Zuannis was notoriously stubborn. Bonnie was surprised she'd actually told her about Hatul's sticky fingers—but perhaps it was only to make sure she never let him touch her.

"Well, thanks, Zuannis," she said, bowing to the inevitable. "How's Joachen?"

"Fine," Zuannis replied. "Still feeling a bit touchy about that last fight we had."

Bonnie nodded. Joachen was touchy about a lot of things. "He'll get over it."

"Yes, I suppose so," Zuannis agreed. "He's such a horny little devil. Never can stay standoffish for long." Zuannis laughed, her big earrings jangling. "I can't stay mad at him for long, either. He's such a handsome little thing."

Bonnie didn't exactly share Zuannis's opinion of her husband, and after nodding in a noncommittal fashion, thought it best to change the subject altogether. "Seen Vladen around?" Bonnie asked. "He said he might be here to give me another checkup." As the regional physician, Vladen covered a wide territory, and while he could always be reached by comlink—day or night—he was sometimes a hard man to catch in person.

"Don't think so," Zuannis replied, "but when you do see him, you should have him run a scan on your Zetithian. Might find out why he's behaving so strangely."

Bonnie wasn't sure that Lynx's attitude was the result of a medical condition. "It's probably normal for him," she said with a shrug. "Besides, Vladen has to have run one on him already—immigration requirements, you know."

"I suppose so," Zuannis sighed. "Well, too bad about that." Shaking her head sadly, she lumbered off with a regretful wave, leaving Bonnie to wonder just what in the world she'd been talking about.

Drummond came by later—to buy enock eggs, he said, but Bonnie was pretty sure he only wanted to see how she was doing with her new man.

Feigning disappointment that she had nothing left to sell but chicken eggs, he commented, "That boy I sent you ever show up?"

"He's back at the farm," Bonnie replied. "And thanks for sending him. He's already been a big help."

"Said much yet?"

"No, you were right about him not being talkative—he's not particularly friendly, either."

"Well, if he gives you any trouble, you know who to complain to," Drummond said heartily. "Just say the word, and I'll zap his ass all the way back to that backwater world he came from."

"And what backwater world would that be?" asked Bonnie. "He hasn't told me anything, and the way he acts, I don't think I'll ever ask."

"Place called Paemay," Drummond replied. "One of those worlds where the natives wouldn't have come up with space flight capability on their own, but they did have money—mostly from mining diamonds, I hear. Some technology, of course, but primitive customs—he was a slave, after all. Not many places hold with that sort of crap anymore, but how a Zetithian would wind up there beats the shit out of me. Though Cat did tell me once that a bunch of guys in his unit were sold as slaves after the war, which is how he knew Leo. Wouldn't be surprised if they knew this one, too."

"Well, Cat and Leo must have had it a lot better than he did," Bonnie said roundly, "because Lynx has got some very strange ways! He's very shy and secretive, and he certainly didn't want to work for me. But like I said, he's already made a big difference at the farm. He probably won't stay on once the mines start hiring again, but I'll hang onto him as long as I can."

"Pretty woman like you shouldn't have any trouble doing that," Drummond remarked with a grin.

"Just in case you haven't noticed, Drummond, I have a really rotten track record when it comes to men," Bonnie said ruefully. "I might be able to grow anything that has seeds, but I don't seem to be capable of finding a good man."

"Well, if what I've heard about Zetithians is true," Drummond said, "I'm surprised you don't have him purring all over you by now."

This was more information than she'd gotten from Zuannis, and Bonnie's eyes widened with interest. "They can *purr?*"

"Oh, yeah! Never heard one of them do it myself, but Jack says they can—she also said that if other women ever got wind of what *else* they could do, she'd have to keep Cat locked up on her ship so he wouldn't get stolen."

Judging from Drummond's expression, the "what else" had to be something sexual, which supported what Zuannis had been hinting at.

"Yeah, well, maybe they aren't all alike in that respect," Bonnie said dismissively. She had a feeling that if there was anything sexual about Lynx, she'd certainly never have any firsthand experience with it and hoped that Drummond would stop before he gave her any more clues as to what she might be missing. She decided she wouldn't ever want to compare notes with Jack or Tisana, either—it would be much too depressing! Perhaps Zuannis was right not to tell her. Changing the subject, she said, "So, did you want anything besides eggs?"

Drummond chuckled. "Don't want to talk about it, eh, Bon-bon?" Noting her grimace at his use of her nickname, he added, "I know you don't like the name, but believe it or not, it *did* refer to a type of candy at one time—means you're really sweet, doncha know." Abandoning the effort and giving her crates a cursory glance, he asked, "Got any avocados yet?"

Bonnie shook her head, grateful that Drummond had dropped the issue of her name. "Not yet," she replied cheerfully, despite the fact that she'd already answered that question about fifty times. "The trees are blooming, but they're still pretty small. I don't know if they'll bear fruit this year or not."

He nodded. "Well, I want the first crop when you get any," he said. "Pay you anything you want for them." Grumbling, he added, "Haven't had decent guacamole since I left Texas."

Bonnie couldn't help but smile. "If you liked guacamole that much, what'd you leave for?"

"I needed some space!" he replied. "Not enough room left there to breathe! Now I got plenty of space, but no avocados—except what Jack brings once in a blue moon, and they always taste like crap. How was I to know?"

Due to the planetary regulation against importing live plants, Bonnie had had to grow her plants from seed, and since most of the avocado trees on Earth had been grafted, she knew there was no guarantee that hers would taste decent either. She'd learned that avocado trees didn't like wind or frost, and though frost was unheard of in the region, they did have a fair amount of wind. With that in mind, she'd planted them on the leeward side of the equipment shed and hoped it would be enough of a windbreak for them to tolerate it, but she also knew that Drummond didn't want to hear the details; he just wanted his avocados. "You just keep your britches on," she advised. "When I have any, you'll be the first to know."

"Well, just make sure that Zetithian boy doesn't eat them all," he said. "He looked pretty hungry to me."

"I'll keep him fed," she promised. And she silently vowed that she always would—but what she didn't realize was that he wouldn't feed himself.

By the time she returned home, it was late evening, and if there was any food missing out of her pantry, Bonnie certainly couldn't tell. She was bewildered, and also a little put out with Lynx, because she knew she had made it perfectly clear that he could eat all he wanted while she was gone. Thinking that there might have been some sort of Zetithian taboo about entering someone's home without them being there, whether you had permission or not, she went looking for him.

The lights were on in the shed, and she found him in there working on the speeder.

"I'm home," she announced unnecessarily. "Everything go okay today?"

"Yes," he replied, not even looking up.

"Did you get anything to eat after I left?" she asked.

"No," he replied. "I have not… had time."

This was completely ridiculous, because Bonnie had worked the farm all by herself for the past three months, and she had *always* found time to eat. She started to fuss at him, but decided it was pointless. "Well, I'm hungry as a snarkle myself," she said, "so I'll fix something real quick and bring it out to you."

Lynx didn't say anything or even nod. Bonnie tried not to see this as being impolite, but it was difficult.

"Think you can get that thing running again?" she asked doubtfully. "I've tried, but I couldn't fix it the last time it broke down."

Lynx pointed to a pile of engine parts on the floor beside him. "Those need to be replaced."

"*All* of those?" she exclaimed incredulously. "Why so many?"

"The parts are worn out," he said shortly. "They last much longer if you keep them lubricated."

Something in the way he said it led Bonnie to suspect that he didn't think much of her ability to maintain machinery. This was true, he didn't, but the repairs had given him something to do while she was gone.

"I did," she said defensively. "But I don't think the previous owner bothered with it. We got it real cheap when we first came here."

What he thought of that, Lynx never said, and having stood there for a moment trying in vain to come up with something else to say, Bonnie finally gave up trying to talk to him and went in to fix dinner.

Lynx hadn't been fibbing when he'd said he was busy, but that he had been too busy to eat was a blatant lie. His stomach was growling so loudly, he was surprised she hadn't heard it. The truth was that he'd approached the house more than once with every intention of entering and getting something to eat, but the feeling that Bonnie had been lying when she told him to help himself to her food prevented him. He'd been trapped into doing stupid things before and had been punished. Severely. He had to have permission to eat and only after the women he served were finished. Sometimes they forgot to tell him, but subsequent days of starvation had taught him to know his place, and he hadn't forgotten. He reminded himself that his situation was different now, and that he was not Bonnie's slave, but old habits often die hard, and there are some wounds that never heal.

Chapter 5

IT WAS COMPLETELY DARK BY THE TIME DINNER WAS ready, so instead of yelling for Lynx, Bonnie took a plate out to the shed. He was still working on the speeder, so she just set his food on the table, knowing he wouldn't eat it until she was gone anyway.

"Thank you for doing that," she said with a gesture toward the speeder. "You didn't have to. I gave up on it a long time ago."

Lynx nodded curtly, and Bonnie couldn't decide whether to burst into tears or kick him in the ass. In the end, deciding that she was too tired and hungry to do either one, she went back to the house to her own lonely meal.

Waiting until the door closed behind her, Lynx wiped his hands on a rag and approached the table. He didn't know what it was, but it certainly smelled good. He'd had nothing to eat since breakfast, and he was as hungry as he'd ever been—perhaps even more so, because he knew that what he would be eating would be better than most meals he'd ever had.

He was right. It was delicious. The vegetables had been cooked in a creamy sauce that was so orgasmic in nature that if his testicles still worked, he was sure he would have ejaculated. But, as it was, the experience was purely mental.

Lynx felt a sudden wave of shame pass over him. How Bonnie would mock him if she ever knew of his impotence! His skin crawled at the mere thought of it, and he vowed that she would never get close enough to him to discover his secret. Never. And he would never let himself become indebted to her in any way. He would work as hard as he could and take the pay she owed him and the food she gave him, but he would accept nothing else and would owe her no favors—no matter how beautiful she was. *She will not control me. I am a free man.* With that litany running through his mind, he went back to work on the speeder.

He might have told himself he was free, but that night his sleep was troubled with dreams of his past, and he awoke wondering when, or if, they would ever cease. The huge shed was dark and silent, but his sharp eyes would have been able to see anyone who entered, just as Bonnie had walked in on him that first day. He tried to put it out of his mind, but couldn't shake the idea that if he had beckoned to her—just smiled at her—she would have helped him make his bed—might even have lain down beside him and... And what? Mated with him? There was a time when he would have given anything to be loved by so beautiful and kind a woman. But that time had passed. There was no going back.

A few days later, Bonnie was already heading out to feed the animals before she remembered that she had Lynx to do that for her now. So instead of feeding the enocks, she dragged out her sewing machine and the fabric her mother had sent with her—five years ago, now—and looked at some of the patterns she'd thrown in along with the machine.

Most of the patterns were for women's clothing, but there were some that had been intended for Sylor. Bonnie examined them thoughtfully. Lynx was taller and thinner than Sylor, but she figured she could adapt the pattern easily enough. She worked on it for a couple of hours, and then did some weeding in the herb beds around the house before going out to check on the fruit trees.

Her fruit trees had done well thus far, though she was pretty sure this was due to the fact that the native soil didn't harbor the same microbes as Earth's soil did— either that, or they just hadn't found her trees yet. She had apples, pears, plums, and peaches in addition to Drummond's avocados. The berries were blooming, too, and if all went well, she would have a good crop to make jam. Few people were willing to take the time to make jam anymore, but they certainly enjoyed eating it, so Bonnie had never had any trouble making money from her fruit. She hadn't branched out beyond the standard types that were grown on Earth, but was well aware that there was a whole galaxy full of exotic fruits just waiting for her to plant. Unfortunately, planetary regulations prohibited anything that might take over and become a weed. Bonnie always chuckled whenever she thought of those misinformed officials, because if they'd truly known their fruit, they would *never* have let her plant blackberries!

After checking on the fruit, Bonnie tilled up a new spot in the garden and planted radishes, broccoli, and basil. The best part about the climate on Terra Minor was that the growing season lasted year-round, and you could pretty much plant anything anytime you liked. There were a few plants that didn't grow well in the rainy season, but others thrived, and Bonnie had an irrigation system to tide them over during the dry spells. She and Sylor had dug a pond next to the equipment shed so that the gutters could divert the rain that fell on the roof into the pond to be conserved, and there was also a pump and hose system to water the garden. It was primitive, and though the grain fields had their own irrigation system, the idea of catching the water when it was plentiful seemed more natural and environmentally friendly to her than drilling into the ground for it.

Lynx had been working on the harvester droid that morning and hadn't mentioned anything about engine lubrication, so Bonnie concluded that her maintenance of it must have met with his approval. After lunch, she asked him to help her in the garden and showed him what plants were weeds and what were not, before leaving him to work by himself while she went back to her sewing.

Sometime during the afternoon it occurred to her that, while he might never use her bathroom to take a shower, he might want a towel, so she took him a toothbrush, a towel, some soap, and a cup, and put everything in a spare crate. While she was there, she couldn't help but notice his pack sitting on the table. What would a man like that carry with him? She knew he didn't have any other clothes, but what else would he have? Pictures of friends and family? A knife and a fork? Bonnie had no idea, but knew that his belongings were private and to search through them would have been intrusive. She left his pack untouched, but her thoughts still lingered on him.

What *did* he do out there all alone each night? Was he so exhausted that he fell asleep immediately, or did he lie awake thinking about happier times? She looked down at his pallet in the corner of the floor and was instantly assailed with the mental image of Lynx sprawled on the blankets, his naked body uncovered and his rock-hard cock glistening as he slid his fist up and down the shaft. She could almost see the slick, engorged head, imagine the tightening of his balls as he came, and the spurt of semen splattering across his chest. Bonnie's breath caught in her throat as she felt a tingling ache between her thighs. *It's just because I'm pregnant,* she told herself firmly. *I'm not really attracted to him... I can't be! This is nothing but the effect of raging hormones... isn't it?*

Shaking off the vision, Bonnie left the shed, promising herself that she would never again let herself fall victim to such disturbing thoughts, but they persisted, triggering other memories—what Drummond had said about the Zetithians, Zuannis's strangely evasive manner, how much Jack and Tisana adored their husbands, and why she was so determined to be kind to Lynx, regardless of his surly behavior. There was a reason for that... something about Zetithians. Lynx was different in many ways, but *still...*

Returning to the house, Bonnie noticed Lynx out by the enock pen, standing a little too close to them for safety and actually feeding them by hand. She considered chastising him for taking such a risk when she saw what he was doing. He was feeding them a dead rat.

Bonnie had known there were rats and mice living in the shed, the other side of which housed the grain she kept from the last harvest to feed to the chickens and enocks, but she'd never managed to eradicate them. Apparently Lynx had had better luck.

As Bonnie approached, Lynx looked up warily, as though expecting a reprimand, or at the very least, a heated argument.

"Sure they won't bite you?" she remarked casually.

"No," he replied, "they have not tried to harm me."

Lulling him into a false sense of security, Bonnie decided. *Then* they would strike. "Well, just be careful," she cautioned him, not wanting to imagine what horrible gashes she might have to seal up if one of them were to tear into Lynx the way they were tearing into the rats he'd dropped over the fence. "Where'd you get the rats?"

"They have been eating the grain," he replied. "I am catching them."

"Enocks like them, huh?"

"The birds are carnivores," he said bluntly. "They like meat better than grain."

"Omnivores, actually," she corrected him. "They were researched pretty well before anyone settled here."

"Their beaks are made for tearing meat," Lynx insisted, obviously not believing that the biologists who'd studied them knew what they were talking about.

"But they do like fruit," Bonnie pointed out. "When Sylor and I were trying to catch them, seemed like they were always under a rabasha tree eating the fruit."

"They will eat fruit if there is nothing else," Lynx said, his tone still curt, "but they prefer meat."

Bonnie wondered if Lynx felt the same way. The food she'd given him had been primarily plant-based; perhaps he was trying to tell her something. The enocks certainly seemed happy, and Bonnie had about decided to trade her eggs for beef next time, rather than the usual butter and cheese, when she noticed an odd sound. At first she thought it was coming from the birds. Listening more closely, she realized that it wasn't the birds, but Lynx, and he was *purring*. Apparently, Drummond hadn't been kidding about that.

"Well, feed them all the rats you like," she said, trying not to display her fascination with the way he purred. It was a very soothing sound, and obviously the enocks liked it, too. "How are you catching them?"

"They are easily trapped," he replied, and said no more.

Obviously he wasn't going to let her in on his secret. Bonnie had tried to trap them herself, but for a species that hadn't been around humans for eons like the rats of Earth, they were still pretty cagey. They were supposedly an indigenous variety, but they looked pretty much like any other rat Bonnie had ever seen, and they acted like them too. Maybe Lynx was catching them in self-defense—yet another reason she'd have preferred that he not live in the shed—and ought to have been enough to make him want to sleep somewhere else as well. In case he was regretting his original decision, Bonnie suggested carelessly, "Well, if you decide you can't sleep with them running around in there, you can always sleep in the house."

"No," he said. Which was just what she expected him to say. She thought that perhaps he was like Drummond and needed the space. There was certainly plenty of that in the shed; the harvester droid was huge, dwarfing the rest of her equipment, and it took a large building to house it.

"Suit yourself," she said with a shrug. "I wouldn't want to sleep out there, but that's up to you."

Shaking her head, Bonnie turned and went back to the house to finish making his pants. The length was a guess, because if the way he avoided any kind of contact with her—physical or otherwise—was any indication, she knew he would *never* let her measure his inseam! In fact, since that first day when he had carried her into the house and bound up her arm, they hadn't even been close enough to shake hands.

While she worked, the purring sound he'd made stole into Bonnie's thoughts. What would it feel like to kiss him while he was purring? Her mind made the leap, and she could feel his soft, wet lips as he delved inside her mouth with his hot tongue, the sensuous vibrations driving her wild. It was only one tiny step further to imagine him caressing her nipples with his lips and tongue while he purred—or his tongue on her tingling clitoris, teasing and driving her to new heights of rapturous delight.

Bonnie realized she'd stopped sewing, and her body was aching for him, almost crying out with hunger. I can't *do* this, she told herself again, but the sensations seemed so real, the memory of them etched into her mind.

By this time, Bonnie had given up on letting Lynx get his own food from the kitchen; he simply would not set foot in there, whether she was home or not. If she wasn't there to feed him, he wouldn't eat unless he was picking it fresh out of the garden. She made a point of giving him something extra before she left because, while the thought of him going hungry made her a little sick, the idea that he might be eating rats made her feel even worse.

By that evening, Bonnie was barely able to cloak her embarrassment as she gave Lynx his new clothes along

with his dinner. Not wanting to meet his eyes for fear
that he might guess the erotic nature of her thoughts,
she simply said, "I thought you could use a change
of clothes," and laid them on the table, leaving him
abruptly, not giving him the opportunity to refuse.

While outright refusal had been his first impulse,
knowing that his own clothing would wear out eventually had made Lynx reluctantly nod his acceptance. He
didn't like the idea of being in Bonnie's debt but decided
that he would repay her somehow, vowing not to wear
them until he did.

He'd had no money whatsoever when he arrived on
Terra Minor; it had taken nearly every credit he had just
to get there, and what little he had left was stolen. He
had never intended to land on Terra Minor with nothing but the clothes on his back and, while he continued
to chastise himself for not being more careful with his
money, he still had no idea how it had been stolen. The
unfortunate truth was that, naïve in the ways of space-
ports and the predators who lurked there, he'd simply
fallen prey to a pickpocket. He could have exchanged
his ticket to Terra Minor for passage to a planet more
tolerant of the poor, but the lure of a new planet had
been a strong one for Lynx. He knew there were places
on this world that had never been seen by an intelligent
being, and he longed to find them, to pass days on end
without ever seeing another living soul.

Unfortunately, on Terra Minor you weren't allowed
to simply exist. This had been the only drawback to im-
migrating there, but he had worked in mines before and
was certain that if he worked hard, he would be able to
buy a place of his own eventually. Then he could work

in the mines and retreat each night to his own home—built somewhere well away from other people—and find the solitude he craved. He might have to hike a long way as a result, but it would have been worth it.

Worth it, because then he would never again have to inhale the scent of a woman's desire—an aroma that still lingered even after Bonnie had left him.

As Bonnie expected, she never saw those clothes again. Lynx seemed to stay clean enough, but then she realized that he must have been washing his own clothes late at night and hanging them up in the shed to dry while he slept. She hoped she never had to go out there at night for any reason, because she had a feeling it would absolutely mortify him to be caught without his pants, and she had no intention of ever letting him know that Lynx with his pants off was a sight that she'd very much like to see.

Bonnie felt her nipples tingle as the fantasy struck her again. She'd vowed not to become interested in another man, and the realization that she was beginning to feel a strong attraction to Lynx was disturbing. She fought against it, biting her lip and telling herself that it was only a side effect of their close proximity, or because she was already becoming accustomed to his ways, or, what was more likely, her pregnancy made her more susceptible. But whatever the reason, Lynx was looking better to her all the time. The odd thing was she couldn't even say she liked him—and he clearly didn't like *her*.

Bonnie assured herself that she wasn't falling in love with Lynx, but she caught herself watching him more and more, her thoughtful gaze lingering on him long after it should have moved on to something less… disturbing.

Because he *was* disturbing, and her woman's eye couldn't help but be attracted to him. Looking at him evoked erotic fantasies that sent her mind delving into areas best left unexplored. Drummond had said that Jack might have to lock Cat up to keep him from being stolen if his abilities became known. What made Zetithians so different from the males of any other species? Was it just the purring? Bonnie had no idea, but the need to discover for herself just what that difference was grew stronger by the hour.

She tried to convince herself that it was *what* he was rather than *who* he was that intrigued her. Even excluding the comments from Zuannis and Drummond, the other Zetithians were still attractive in the extreme, and if they hadn't been married, Bonnie was honest enough with herself to admit that she would have been interested. She told herself that she might have felt the same way about Lynx initially—especially if he'd smiled at her or at least been civil—because he *was* a handsome man and moved with the same feline grace that Cat and Leo possessed.

But while his alien features intrigued her, if Lynx had ever smiled at her, she hadn't seen it, nor was he in any way flirtatious; in fact, Bonnie had never received less encouragement from a man in her life. But there was still something about him that tugged at her psyche, causing her to ponder what she might be missing.

She had more dreams—and since all of them involved Lynx and tended to wake her up in midorgasm, they made quite an impression on her. In those dreams, he held her close while he purred, loving her like no other had ever done; making her feel alive and strong, but also cherished and desired. She had no firsthand experience with a Zetithian lover, but in her dreams they were among the best in the galaxy. When she awoke, she could still imagine him purring while he made love to her; his eyes glowing with desire, his hot, hard body penetrating her, filling her with his heat...

But perhaps the purring *wasn't* sexual—after all, the only time Bonnie had ever heard Lynx purr had been for the enocks, so it might have had nothing to do with sex, but the more she thought about it, the more the idea of making love with such a man nearly drove her insane with desire.

Unfortunately, with this newly discovered interest, the object of that interest became more elusive and secretive than ever. Lynx now knew what Bonnie expected of him and could therefore go about his chores with very little need for discussion. The chores always got done—he never shirked them—but they rarely did anything together. To Bonnie, it was like living with a ghost.

One evening, Lynx didn't answer her call to dinner, and, not seeing him around anywhere, Bonnie went out to the shed, struck with a sudden, irrational fear that he was gone—gone for good, and without a word, just like Sylor. He wasn't there, but his pack still lay on the makeshift table, along with the clothes she'd given him. No, she thought, taking a steadying breath, he wouldn't have left without his things; if he'd carried them this far, he wouldn't leave them behind now.

Standing there staring at his meager belongings, Bonnie suddenly forgot all about her decision to avoid invading his privacy; the need to know what was precious to him was so overwhelming, she couldn't fight it any longer. With trembling hands, she carefully checked inside his pack. There she found a medallion with an unfamiliar emblem embossed upon it, some strips of leather (presumably to repair his sandals), a slingshot (which was undoubtedly how he was catching the rats) and two very stale chocolate chip cookies.

Emotions flooded through her, and she felt the blood drain from her head as tears began to flow even before her mind could register what it meant.

He'd been hoarding food—but why? Was he afraid she wouldn't feed him, or were the cookies just so tasty that he wanted to save them for later? Had he seen the cookies as payment for saving her life? Bonnie tried to come up with all sorts of reasons why he might have kept them so long, even thinking that they might have made good rat bait, but nothing could stop her from crying like a baby.

No, he wouldn't leave these things behind, she decided, and there were no credits in his pack. Unless he carried them in his pocket, he had nothing but what Bonnie owed him—and she hadn't paid him yet. Surely he wouldn't leave before he had money! Her mind went wild, trying desperately to make sense of it all, until the baby kicked her into motion. Fighting back tears, she put everything back just the way she'd found it and ran out into the yard, screaming his name.

Bonnie was understandably upset, but when she finally saw Lynx coming out from behind the shed, presumably having been answering the call of nature, she was unnecessarily dramatic.

"Where were you?" she shouted at him. "I couldn't find you anywhere!" She was still crying, still wrestling with emotions she had thought were completely dead. "I thought you were gone!"

Lynx looked at her as though she'd lost her mind completely, but all he said was, "I am still here. I would not leave without telling you."

His frank tone brought her up short, because she believed him. No, he wouldn't leave without a word; he was far too honest for that. But Bonnie was speaking her mind at last, and she wasn't about to stop yet.

"But I never see you, Lynx!" she wailed. "The work gets done, the food disappears, but you aren't there!" She took a deep breath in an effort to steady herself before adding. "You avoid me like the plague. Would you mind telling me why?"

She could see his feline eyes glowing in the twilight and had a feeling this was another of those questions he wouldn't answer, but, to her surprise, he did.

"It is because you smell of desire," he replied.

Bonnie could scarcely believe her ears. "Excuse me?" she said. "You don't like the way I smell?" This was completely ridiculous; she used the same soap he did—and probably more often!

"It is your desire," he said. "I can smell it."

Bonnie was bewildered on two points. "You don't like being desired, or you don't like the smell of it?"

"I do not like being desired by a woman," he replied.

"Would you rather be desired by a man?" she asked, groping desperately for an explanation.

He shook his head. "I would not."

"But you don't like women at all, do you?"

"No."

The irony of her predicament struck her then, and Bonnie began laughing through her tears. She had finally found her decent, honest, moral man: one who wouldn't take anything she hadn't given him and who wouldn't leave without telling her—and she'd almost given her right arm to get him, too—but he would never love her, and not because of her, specifically, but on principle! She'd never met a true misogynist before and had certainly never been attracted to one. Obviously she should have been more careful about what she wished for.

Bonnie's laughter soon gave way to anger and then shame. She hadn't said anything to him or treated him any differently, but even trying to hide her feelings wouldn't work if he could actually smell them. She could try to mask it with another scent, perhaps, but if his nose was that good, what hope did she have?

"Well," she said bitterly, "your dinner is getting cold. Better hurry up and eat it." Avoiding his eyes, she turned on her heel and went back to her empty house.

Lynx stared after her, her aroma wafting back toward him on the wind. There had been a time when a scent like that would have had him running after her, his cock as hard as diamonds and dripping with eagerness to mate. He would have let her run, then gone after her, pouncing on her playfully out of the darkness and ripping her clothes in his haste to bury himself in her body. But there was nothing; no matter what his senses told him, his body ignored the signals and would not respond. Lynx returned to his refuge to eat the food she'd left for him, but for once, it seemed to have no flavor.

That night, sleep eluded him long after he would normally have slept, but when he finally drifted off, he slept fitfully. It was nearly dawn when he awoke, drenched in sweat and trembling with fear and anger. In his dream, Bonnie had seen him—naked and exposed—and, realizing his failing, had laughed.

Chapter 6

STARING AT HER DINNER SITTING THERE ON THE TABLE, Bonnie felt an overwhelming urge to throw it against the wall. What was wrong with her? Why was he affecting her this way, and why had she let it happen? Worse still, how could she hide her desire for a man when he could actually *smell* it?

The answer to that was to do the same thing he was doing: avoid him—and since he was already avoiding *her,* it wouldn't take much effort. If she never saw him, she couldn't feel desire and couldn't ever actually love him, could she?

The answer to that was probably that, yes, she could still love him—if that was, indeed, what she was feeling. It might only have been lust, but she couldn't recall unrequited lust ever making her feel like her heart had been ripped out—despite numerous failed romances. She'd felt bad enough before, but now, she felt even worse, and it seemed impossible to stop crying; as soon as she would dry her tears, believing she was over it, she would remember the things he'd said to her and start all over again.

Bonnie had never felt so helpless. Lynx wouldn't love her no matter what she did. She could pay him, feed him, clothe him, love him, even hand over the deed to her land, and it wouldn't make any difference. She couldn't make him love her, and if she even got close enough to him to speak, he'd just catch a whiff of her desire and be repulsed all over again. Bonnie was normally pretty tough, but just then, all she wanted to do was crawl under a rock and die. His rejection of her was so complete, so all-encompassing; he not only despised her, but her entire gender!

Unfortunately, they still needed one another. Bonnie knew that one call to Drummond might get Lynx a different job, or even deported, but that was one of those things that only a woman scorned would do. Bonnie wasn't about to have him kicked off the planet just because he didn't like women. She would get over him. She knew she could. She always did.

Sleep was a long time coming that night, but when it finally crept over her, Bonnie had another dream about Lynx. In it, he was walking away from her, and she was calling to him, but he never looked back and never even slowed down.

Awakening with cold tears on her cheeks and feeling a despair that went far beyond what she should have been feeling, the rational part of her mind knew that the whole thing was just plain silly. He couldn't possibly mean so much to her after such a short time. He might have saved her life and helped her out a great deal, but he'd never been nice to her. She'd never even seen him smile. It was illogical; she should have grown to hate him, not love him! Still, it was impossible for Bonnie to imagine ever truly hating Lynx. The man had been a slave; at the very least, he deserved her compassion.

She was doing her best to understand him, but it was hard to understand a man who wouldn't talk. He must have had some bad experiences with women, but what kind? Bonnie hadn't had much luck with men, either, but she had always managed to come through the hard times reasonably unscathed.

Or had she? It was possible that the chip on her shoulder was every bit as big as the one Lynx carried. Running her fingers through her cropped locks, Bonnie remembered feeling just as much enmity toward men as he seemed to have toward women. Lynx had changed that by possessing all of the attributes Bonnie was searching for in a man—with the possible exception of the most important one.

In an attempt to divert her mind, Bonnie took the worn speeder parts, went through the catalog, and ordered new ones. Lynx might never love her, but if he could get that speeder running, he would be worth his weight in gold.

As her pregnancy progressed, Bonnie was so exhausted each evening that even if Lynx *had* come seeking her company, it wouldn't have been very enjoyable—for either of them. Each market day she went walking into Nimbaza with her wares. She made a lot of money, chiefly due to Lynx's help. With more time to devote to tilling and planting, she was now able to grow more vegetables and herbs, and with Lynx providing a steady supply of rats, the enock egg production had doubled. With the money she earned, she paid her bills, and whatever was left over, she split evenly with Lynx, sometimes even giving him all of it. Bonnie lived in fear that the mines would start hiring again and that he would hear of it and leave her, so she knew she had to pay him as well as she could.

The weekly trek into Nimbaza was hard but enjoyable for Bonnie, and though Zuannis knew there was something troubling her friend, she kept those thoughts to herself, focusing instead on preparing for the new arrival.

"I still have the clothes my children wore when they were young," Zuannis announced. "Would you like to have them?"

Bonnie smiled as she looked at Zuannis, trying to imagine the size of any infant she might have given birth to and decided that the clothes might fit her own child in about three years. Still, it was better than nothing. "Sure," Bonnie replied. "I've made a few things, but I probably don't have nearly enough. You know how it is."

"Never enough time, is there?" Zuannis said airily. "Which is why I have offered. I'll have Joachen bring them by before you leave today. How is Lynx faring?"

Zuannis always asked, and Bonnie always replied, "Fine. Working hard, just like always."

Zuannis shook her head sadly. "He needs to come with you to market sometime," she said. "He is too isolated. It would do him good. Or perhaps I should bring Joachen with me the next time I visit."

"He might like that," Bonnie said. "But he sure doesn't like it when Salan happens by! I mean, he actually disappears! Must be able to smell her coming or something."

"Zetithians have very good noses," Zuannis said knowledgeably. She had met Lynx a few times at the farm, and the fact that he could sniff out the aroma of her freshly baked bread was a testament to the fact that there was nothing wrong with his nose—though she still remained convinced that there was something else wrong with him—something hormonal, perhaps.

Bonnie knew just how good Lynx's nose was and merely nodded her agreement, preferring not to get into another discussion of Lynx's apparently nonexistent libido.

Market days were both a blessing and a curse for Lynx. He could work without Bonnie's disturbing scent in the air, but while she was gone, he envisioned all manner of dire consequences. He wished the speeder parts would come soon, and though he told himself that it was only because he wanted to work on it, the truth was that he knew just how far it was to Nimbaza.

"Pregnant females should not travel alone," he muttered to the chickens, but at the same time, he balked at offering to accompany her. She'd never asked him to, and he reasoned that this was a good enough excuse, but couldn't escape the feeling that it wasn't. "What if the child comes early?" He knew there was usually some traffic on the road—especially on market days—and doubted that anyone would pass her by and not come to her aid, but it still worried him, and he wished Bonnie's farm hadn't been quite so remote. Her friend Zuannis had come by a few times, and that girl from the dairy, Salan. So far, Lynx had managed to avoid Salan, but had to admit that he liked Zuannis. Of course, the main reason for that was that Salan smelled like a female in heat from a kilometer away, while Zuannis smelled of fresh bread.

Smiling ruefully, he shook his head. "Not that it matters," he said, realizing that he was now talking to the animals more than he did to Bonnie, or any other person, for that matter, and he wondered how much longer it would be before the mines would hire him. It wasn't as though he didn't enjoy the work he was doing—if he hadn't been working for a female, it would have been just fine, especially since it involved maintaining her farm implements. It might not have been as glamorous as some other occupations, but he loved working on machinery. It was straightforward and unemotional; machines only required certain, specific things, unlike women whose minds he had yet to understand, though he'd lived among them for years.

Bonnie was a little different, however. He had to admit that she wasn't like other females, and if he'd met her years before, he might be feeling differently now. She was nice to him, she was lovely, and she smelled like heaven. If only…

Then one day Bonnie got a call from Drummond. Jack was coming.

"Said she'd be here for the next market day," Drummond reported. "You need to bring that boy with you."

"Boy?" Bonnie echoed. "I'm not sure, Drummond, but I think he's older than I am."

"Maybe," said Drummond, "but he seems like a boy. You know: tall and thin with big eyes and curly hair?"

Bonnie knew this was true, and it made her wish that

Lynx *had* been a boy—still young and innocent. He might have liked her better.

"He still working out all right for you?"

"Sure. He's a—" she paused there, letting out a long breath. What was he, anyway? A blessing? A big help? A godsend? A curse? "—good worker."

"Well, you be sure and bring him then," Drummond urged. "Cat and Leo will want to see him, I'm sure."

"And I'm dying to see Jack again too," Bonnie said. "She's… well… you know Jack."

"Yeah, I know Jack," he said, chuckling. "She's one of a kind."

Bonnie might have been a farmer, and Tisana might have claimed to be a witch, but how did one describe Jack? A shrewd trader, she was tough as shoe leather with a mouth like a drunken pirate and a heart the size of a red giant star. Maybe she would have some suggestions for dealing with Lynx other than letting him go on living like a hermit. Or perhaps Tisana could put a hex on him—after all, she *was* a witch—though Bonnie didn't think that she counted hexes among her powers. She could talk to animals and start fires with a glance, but to the best of Bonnie's knowledge, magical spells weren't part of Tisana's repertoire. She did know a lot about herbs, though. Maybe she could brew up a potion that would improve Lynx's disposition.

Bonnie decided not to tell Lynx about Jack's visit, because even though he knew the other Zetithians existed, she wanted his meeting with Cat and Leo to be a surprise—just to see if it would squeeze some sort of spontaneous emotion out of him—something other than the ones she'd already seen.

The evening before market day, the cart was loaded except for the fresh eggs, but by day's end, Bonnie still hadn't asked Lynx to go with her. Recognizing that she was putting it off intentionally didn't make it any easier; she was still afraid to ask him. As a result, it was after dark when she went out to the shed.

"Lynx?" she called from the doorway. "I need to talk to you."

Lynx turned on his lamp, and in the dim light, Bonnie could see him, backed into his corner and pulling a sheet up over himself as though trying to disappear into the wall. It took Bonnie only a moment to realize that he had to have been naked, because his wet clothes were hanging from the harvester droid; she could hear the water dripping onto the hard floor. Her mouth went dry in an instant, and her first impulse was to rip that sheet right out of his hands. She stared at him as he lay there, but he was nothing like she'd imagined him. His hard body wasn't beckoning to her, nor were his eyes, which clearly warned her not to take another step closer. No, she thought regretfully, he would never let her catch him naked, no matter how much she might want him to.

Anger, mingled with irritation at being caught in just the sort of situation he most wished to avoid, colored Lynx's voice. "What do you want?"

Bonnie knew it was a bad time to ask, but hadn't really expected him to snap at her. Still, her reaction to seeing him in bed was more disturbing than she would have cared to admit, and the thought that she might have interrupted a "private" activity didn't help matters. "It's nothing serious," she said quickly. "You don't need to get up. It's just that I need you to go with me to Nimbaza tomorrow."

"You have never needed me before," Lynx pointed out.

Bonnie bit her lip, hoping that Lynx couldn't smell what the thought of ripping that sheet off of him evoked. "I know that," she said evenly. "But I need you to go with me this time."

Lynx wasn't a bit happy at the prospect of the trek into town. Walking beside Bonnie while being constantly bombarded with the suggestion that his body refused to consider would be pure torture. Unfortunately, she was his employer and paid him to work. If she needed him to accompany her, he could hardly refuse. "What would I do?"

He would probably thank her in the end, since he would be meeting Cat and Leo, but his obvious reluctance had Bonnie's eyes stinging with tears. "I just need help," she said miserably. "You might not have noticed, since you haven't even been in the same *field* with me in weeks, but I'm getting bigger every day, and my feet are swollen up like a couple of melons. I feel awful, and I *still* have to walk into town!" She hated to beg and really saw no need to, but she did it anyway. "Please come with me, Lynx. I need you."

The trace of desperation in her voice triggered a response so automatic that Lynx had to take a moment to control it before he could reply. It was a tone that women had often used to manipulate him in the past— knowing that he was a sucker for it—but he refused to let it affect him now. Even so, Lynx knew he had no choice but to comply. "I will come with you," he said, but the note of resignation in his voice only served as fuel to feed Bonnie's despair.

"I wish I could understand you, Lynx," she said sadly. "But I haven't got the first clue." She turned to go, but paused as another thought struck her. "By the way, have you been eating the food I've been giving you, or are you just using it to trap the rats?"

Lynx stared blankly at her, unable to imagine why Bonnie would think he hadn't been eating—and also why she would be asking him that now. He'd eaten every scrap of food she'd ever given him, and he was *still* hungry. If his stomach had ever been completely full, it must have been before the war. "I have been eating it."

"Well, you sure could've fooled me," she muttered. "The plate comes back clean, but I never get so much as a thank you, and you're still as skinny as a rail. Would it kill you to even acknowledge the fact that I'm—oh, never mind! It doesn't matter; I don't know why I bother." Waving a dismissive hand, she said, "Just be ready to go in the morning, okay? And you might wear the clothes I gave you—clothes that I made for you myself, I might add—instead of those rags you seem to be so fond of."

Lynx was beginning to wish he'd just said "yes" to begin with, because then she would have already left, and they wouldn't be having this discussion. Perhaps he shouldn't have said anything more, but the fact that she was irritated with him for no good reason egged him on. "Is my work not to your liking?"

"What?" she asked, momentarily diverted. "No—I mean, yes. Your work is just fine. I haven't seen a weed in the garden in ages. The alteration to the enock pen was an absolutely brilliant idea, and feeding them rats has got them laying eggs like crazy. Things have been running smoother than they ever did. Why do you ask?"

"You are angry with me," he replied.

She sighed. "I think it's more frustration than anger," she replied. "And it isn't because you don't do a good job!" Pausing a moment to take a deep breath, she went on, "It's *lonely* here, Lynx! I get the occasional visitor, but it isn't the same as... well, *you* might enjoy the solitude, but I certainly don't, and this was *never* how I intended to live when I came here with Sylor. I know that working for me wasn't what you had in mind, and I'm really sorry you don't like women, but, Lynx, *it's not my fault!* I've done the best I can to make you feel comfortable here, but you still act like I'm no better than the dirt under your feet. I just wish it could be different, that's all."

"I cannot be your lover," he said abruptly.

Bonnie stared at him in bewilderment. She must have missed something. "What? Who said anything about being my lover? I mean, look at me, Lynx! I can hardly move! The very last thing I need right now is a lover, and if you're smelling any 'desire,' it certainly isn't coming from me!" This wasn't true—she knew it, and he probably did, as well—but Bonnie saw no point in admitting it when it was so abhorrent to him. Letting out a deep breath, she looked at him beseechingly. "I sure could use a friend, though. Would it kill you to try?"

If the look on his face was any indication, it probably would have.

"Oh, just forget it," she mumbled. "I give up."

Chapter 7

THE HIKE INTO NIMBAZA WAS A SILENT ONE. BONNIE WAS still wishing that Lynx would at least talk to her, but the fact that he hadn't worn the clothes she'd given him didn't offer much in the way of encouragement. Bonnie couldn't understand him at all. To her, it seemed that having gotten a job working for her was one of the best things that could have happened to him—the miners didn't have that great a life; the pay was good, but the work was hard and being stuck in a mine all day didn't appeal to Bonnie in the slightest. She'd given him a good job that had kept him from being deported, and he was acting like he'd been sent to prison. The whole thing made her want to pull out her hair, not just cut it.

Bonnie mulled it over for the entire eight kilometers to Nimbaza and came to the conclusion that perhaps she'd been going about this all wrong. She'd obviously been too nice to Lynx and should be demanding a little more respect, if nothing else. She should be starving him into submission, not trying to fatten him up for market. No, she couldn't starve him—Bonnie didn't have the heart to starve the male enock who'd tried to kill her—but she *could* cut down his portions. That way, if he got hungry enough, he might appreciate her more, though she doubted it.

Then she remembered the cookies and figured she ought to feed him more, not less, because just the

thought of Lynx hoarding cookies made her want to cry
all over again. That was the problem, she told herself;
she was just too emotional right now. If she hadn't been
pregnant, none of this would have gotten to her. She
wouldn't have cared whether he ate anything or not as
long as he did what she expected of him.

Lynx knew Bonnie wasn't very happy with him, but
considered this to be a good thing. If she disliked him
enough, she wouldn't feel desire, he wouldn't have to
smell it and be reminded of the effect that the scent of
a woman *should* have had on him. He hadn't explained
just why it was that he couldn't be her lover. He'd left
that to her imagination.

Still, Bonnie had been good to him, and he'd repulsed
her. He was well-fed and had money in his pocket for
the first time in what seemed like his entire life, and
she was the one responsible for that. He was sorry for
upsetting her, but there was nothing he could do about it.
If he'd apologized, she might have begun to desire him
again, and he didn't want to take that risk.

Trying not to think about her, he focused on the
money instead. When he'd worked in the mines of
Paemay, he hadn't considered the money he earned to
be his own; it was being saved for his passage to Terra
Minor, and he rarely spent any of it unless it was absolutely necessary, even to the point of going hungry
most of the time. He'd had a goal back then, and he'd
been single-minded enough to see himself through
some difficult times.

But it was different now. He had money, but no real

reason to spend it—or even save it—and the dream of buying his own land seemed so remote. He told himself that it wasn't true, that he could do it eventually, but he was having a hard time convincing himself.

Lynx wondered how it was that Bonnie had ever had the wherewithal to buy her land. Had she inherited it? Had she earned it? He didn't know. There were so many things he didn't know about her. She was having a child, but she rarely spoke of it. Lynx only knew the father's name was Sylor Halen, and that he'd left her. Took the money and ran, she'd said. He wondered why. Once Zetithians chose a mate, it was for life, unless circumstances made it impossible to stay together. If he could have mated with Bonnie, they would not be walking together in stony silence. The journey would have been a pleasant one, if only…

Lynx had been doing his best to look anywhere *but* at Bonnie, but since he had fallen a few steps behind he could hardly avoid seeing her—and catching whiffs of her. She might have thought she didn't smell of desire, but she did; pregnant women had always smelled like pure, sweet love to him. Her description of her own body might have been accurate, but he'd always considered pregnant women to be beautiful, and she was no less so than any other. The curves of her body called out to him—her hips, her breasts, her round belly. Yes, she was beautiful—even with her jaw set and her brow furrowed in a scowl.

Arriving in Nimbaza in reasonably good time, Bonnie and Lynx set up the cart in the marketplace. Her problems with Lynx had overshadowed the excitement of knowing that Jack would be there—and Cat and Leo and Tisana, too—but once they reached the outskirts of town, Bonnie found it difficult to appear nonchalant. It wasn't every day that something as momentous as meeting up with two other survivors of the holocaust of Zetith took place. She busied herself with arranging her produce but couldn't help looking up from her work to scan the crowd for Jack. Knowing that she would have a stall set up somewhere nearby, Bonnie held back a crate of enock eggs for Jack, who always had something interesting to trade for them.

She didn't have to wait long. Jack came over very casually, as though only intending to talk, but when she winked at her, Bonnie knew that wasn't her only motive. Jack could wheel and deal with the best of them.

"How the hell you been?" she called out as she approached. Jack (Bonnie didn't think her real name, Jacinth, suited her at all) was tall with short, dark hair and, unlike the typical woman, walked with a bit of a swagger. She'd ventured farther out into space than anyone Bonnie had ever run across and, wearing a short-sleeved flightsuit and boots with a big pulse pistol strapped to her thigh, looked as though she could take on anything and everything and still come out on top. To Bonnie's mind, Jack was just too damn cool for words. "Baby about to pop out of there?"

"Not soon enough," Bonnie replied. "I've had just about enough of being pregnant. Makes it way too hard to pick cucumbers."

"I can believe that," Jack agreed. "I had triplets, you know, but then, I'm not a farmer." Giving her a sweeping glance that might have seen more than Bonnie would have liked, Jack added, "Been doing okay otherwise?"

Bonnie did her best to put up a good front, but knew that while Jack might have been astute enough to see right through the ruse, she'd also had time to catch up on the local gossip. "Just fine, unless you want to count Sylor running off and one of the enocks trying to amputate my arm. That Seal 'n' Heal came in real handy, by the way." Holding up her arm, she added, "See? Thanks to that and your Derivian ointment, there's hardly even a scar."

"No shit?" Jack exclaimed, examining Bonnie's arm. "Hmm. I never had a chance to test one of those things on a really bad wound. Never would've thought it would work so well! Should've bought a whole case of the damn things instead of just a dozen. Might have to go back—if I could just remember what planet I got 'em on," she added with a laugh. Abandoning that line of conversation for the ploy it was, she eyed Bonnie speculatively. "So, Sylor ran out on you, huh? You know, I never cared much for that smooth-talking bastard—had shifty eyes. You're probably better off without him. Getting along okay?"

"Not too bad," Bonnie replied. "I hired someone to help me. He's around here somewhere."

Bonnie didn't have to turn around to see just where he was, either, because Jack's curious gaze soon found Lynx, and her eyes widened in disbelief. "Holy shit!" she exclaimed. "He's Zetithian!" She turned and shouted across the plaza. "Hey, Cat! Get over here and bring Leo with you!"

Following her gaze, Bonnie watched as Cat left their booth, thinking that he had to be the sexiest thing she'd ever seen in her life. Tall and lean with black curls down to his waist, just the way he moved was enough to make most women fall at his feet, but his smile would have melted a stone. Even the way he dressed was sexy—a loose white tunic, black breeches, and tall black boots— and reminded Bonnie of a pirate. Bonnie turned to look at Lynx, standing there behind her, and noted that while the two men had the same kind of eyes, ears, and fangs, the resemblance ended there. Cat was outgoing and confident and positively exuded sexuality, whereas Lynx was so sullen and withdrawn, it was hard to believe they were even from the same planet.

Bonnie was glad she was looking at Lynx when he saw Cat, because there was plenty of emotion there, all right: his mouth dropped open and, for a second or two, she thought his knees were going to give way beneath him.

"Cark?" he said in an unsteady voice.

"Lynxsander?" Cat said more after that, but it was in a language that Bonnie could only assume was Zetithian. Lynx ran to him then, and they hugged each other tightly; Cat laughing joyously, and Lynx sobbing as though his heart would break. *So, he does have emotions after all...*

A moment later, Leccarian "Leo" Banadänsk crossed the plaza, and Bonnie hoped Salan wasn't around to see him, or she probably would have swooned where she stood. As tall as Cat, but golden rather than dark, he reminded Bonnie of the lions that his wife, Tisana, had nicknamed him for. Exuding leonine grace and power, he also had a smile that would warm a much colder heart than Salan's—a smile that right now was positively beaming with delight.

Lynx's eyes were glowing with a fire Bonnie had never seen there before as Leo raced forward to hug him even harder than Cat had done.

"Where have you been, Lynxsander?" Leo said laughing. "We feared you were dead!"

Lynx couldn't even utter a reply, but it didn't seem to matter, because Leo obviously didn't expect one. The explanations could come later.

"Honest to God, they turn up everywhere we go!" Jack declared, still completely astonished. "It must be fate or something. First we picked up Leo on Utopia and then we ran into two brothers on Darconia! Cat always said there were others in his unit who were sold as slaves, but I never dreamed we'd ever find any of them! Where the hell did he come from?"

"He just showed up one day," Bonnie replied with a shrug. "He was looking for work, and since the mines weren't hiring, Drummond sent him to me."

"Oh, wow!" Jack said with a heartfelt sigh. Then, seeming to come to her senses, she looked at Bonnie and grinned. "So, are you happy with him?"

"Happy?" she said blankly.

"Oh, of course you are!" Jack exclaimed. "How could you possibly have been with one of *them* and not be happy?"

"Been with one of them?" Bonnie echoed. "As in…?"

Jack stared at Bonnie as though she'd gone barking mad. "You mean you aren't lovers?"

"No," Bonnie said hastily. "He just works for me… and he doesn't like women."

"You've *got* to be kidding!" Jack scoffed. "Why the hell doesn't he like women?"

"I wouldn't know," Bonnie replied. "He barely even talks to me."

Jack shrugged. "Well, Cat was a bit standoffish when I first found him, but he warmed up real quick." Her eyes narrowed. "How long's he been working for you?"

"Several weeks," Bonnie replied. "He does a great job, but he doesn't like me at all."

"Been too tough on him?" suggested Jack.

"Nope, not really—haven't needed to be," Bonnie admitted. "I hardly ever have to tell him what to do. That part is pretty nice, but *he's* not! Not nice, not friendly, and not interested in me at all—or any other woman, for that matter."

"Well, that's pretty fuckin' strange!" declared Jack. "Huh! Guess they aren't all alike, then. Shoots the shit out of *my* theory."

"Your *theory?*"

"About why their planet got blown to bits," Jack replied. "You see, I think it was because the guys were so irresistible that someone decided to get rid of them."

"Irresistible?" Bonnie glanced at Lynx, thinking that while the word *did* fit Cat, Lynx had nowhere near as engaging a personality. Still, she'd been strongly attracted to him—even without trying, he'd gotten to her in ways she wouldn't have thought possible. Maybe it *was* true.

"Oh, yeah! *Completely* irresistible!" Jack went on. Moving closer to Bonnie, she whispered, "They secrete a fluid that triggers orgasms—effortless, continuous, *multiple* orgasms." She gazed at Lynx in amazement.

"A Zetithian man who doesn't like women," she mused, shaking her head. "Unbelievable."

It wasn't really—at least not to Bonnie. It was simply the story of her life. It was ironic—but only fitting— that of the few remaining members of a species who were apparently the best lovers in the galaxy, Bonnie had somehow managed to wind up with the dud.

Chapter 8

THEY HADN'T ALL BEEN DUDS, OF COURSE, OR EVEN dishonest—sometimes it was simply a matter of bad timing—but when it came to men, Bonnie hadn't had much luck.

When Bonnie was sixteen, her best friend's boyfriend tried to get her to spend the night with him. When she told him she wouldn't, he told her friend that she had. It's easy to imagine what happened after that.

At seventeen, she became good friends with a boy in her geometry class, but before love had the opportunity to blossom, his family moved to Cleveland.

At eighteen, Bonnie fell in love for the first time. It was no secret that Ray was in trouble most of the time, but Bonnie was sure that her love could reform him. When she finally got him talked into going to a graduation party with her, the night of the party he was arrested for shoplifting. She never saw him again.

At twenty-one, Marv came into her life. He was handsome, courteous, and thoughtful, and treated Bonnie more like a lady than anyone else ever had. She was certain that they would be together forever—until he got sent back to prison.

Bonnie swore off men after that, but then she had one love affair that began with a great deal of promise, but it didn't quite pan out. Though they parted amicably, Bonnie had always felt it could have been so much more.

At twenty-four, another charmer stole her heart, but before it could even begin, the affair ended when he wound up falling in love with Bonnie's sister. They'd always gotten along well and became good friends, but Bonnie wasn't the one he married in the end.

Not long after that, Bonnie found love at long last with someone who wouldn't marry her, but who swore he'd never leave—and he didn't, until Bonnie was pregnant with his child.

Now she had a Zetithian who might have been as honest and dependable as the day is long, but who, aside from being a confirmed misogynist, couldn't even stand to be downwind of her.

Deep down, Bonnie knew there were plenty of decent men in the universe, but unfortunately, they didn't seem to be meant for her. Even knowing that it was probably her own fault for always choosing the wrong sort didn't help because, as often as not, the wrong sort seemed to choose *her*.

Bonnie was recalled to her surroundings when she heard Cat asking Lynx what had ever possessed him to cut his hair. Lynx muttered something that Bonnie didn't catch, but she could see that he was embarrassed by the question. Cat seemed almost as appalled as he would have been if Lynx had cut off his balls. It seemed sort of silly to Bonnie—after all, it was just hair—but then, perhaps it was symbolic, much like the way she'd cut her own. She chuckled to herself, thinking that if Lynx ever let his hair grow out, she might have had hope—though there would be no guarantee that he'd been letting it grow because of her.

Jack wandered back to her own booth muttering something about having Tisana brew up a potion of some kind, and Cat, Leo, and Lynx went off to catch up on the past twenty years. Bonnie was still amazed that they all knew each other.

She went back to selling her produce, and Drummond dropped by for some eggs. He scrutinized the crates closely, still searching in vain for his avocados. Bonnie sold him some Janlian pears, which looked like avocados but would have made really lousy guacamole.

Vladen, the regional physician, came by later in the morning and bought a lot of vegetables—said he was headed back to Wasaba, and the produce there wasn't nearly as good as Bonnie's. While she considered this to be a nice sentiment and a testament to her ability as a farmer, a woman late in her third trimester does *not* want to hear that her doctor is leaving the vicinity!

"Guess you could get Mobray to help out," Vladen suggested when Bonnie reminded him that Sylor was no longer an option. Mobray was Salan's father, a Terran neighbor of Bonnie's who ran the dairy. He'd delivered plenty of cows, and though the basic principles were undoubtedly the same, it didn't leave Bonnie feeling very encouraged.

"We need to get a midwife in the area!" Vladen declared, running a hand through his bristly blond hair. "I can't deliver every baby in the sector—it just isn't feasible!"

This was one aspect of colonial life that hadn't occurred to Bonnie when she'd listened to Sylor's plans for their future. It had probably occurred to Bonnie's mother, though. She had delivered all of her children in an ultramodern birthing facility, and they had drugs there that could make you positively *enjoy* being in labor! Where Bonnie lived it was hard to find an aspirin, let alone an obstetrician.

Lynx had returned from his reunion with Cat and Leo and was busy stacking the empty crates into the cart. Bonnie watched him carefully, searching for some sign of his earlier excitement, but he seemed once again to be his quiet, stoic self.

"What about him?" Vladen asked with a gesture toward Lynx.

Bonnie's reply to that was something of a snort. "Lynx? I doubt if he'd care much for that."

Actually, she had an idea that when she went into labor, Lynx would probably hide out somewhere until it was all over. If he didn't like the scent of her desire, catching a whiff of newly-delivered placenta would probably make him throw up.

"What about it, Lynx?" Vladen asked him. "Think you could deliver a baby?"

Despite having just found two long-lost friends, Lynx was apparently unchanged—at least, on the outside. "Yes," he replied tonelessly.

"Ever done it before?"

"Yes."

"Well, there you go then!" Vladen said brightly. "He'll be all the help you'll need—and I really don't think there'll be any trouble." Reaching into one of the many pockets on his jacket, he retrieved his scanner and leaned down from his two and a half meter height to peer at Bonnie's rounded belly. As a result of being constantly on the move and having no real office of any kind, Vladen carried most of his medical equipment on his rather large person and tended to rattle when he walked. She wasn't sure how he managed to keep it all straight, but Bonnie had yet to need anything he hadn't been carrying in his pockets. "Yes, in perfect position and should be dropping any time now," he said heartily. "Then it'll be a walk in the park."

"A walk in the park?" Bonnie echoed. She'd heard plenty of descriptions of labor and delivery, but never had anyone referred to it in that manner. Bonnie felt a strong urge to slap him but knew that it would have hurt her hand like the devil. Being a Levitian, Vladen had bony ridges along the edge of his jaw that looked sharp enough to cut your hand if you were to hit him. Bonnie had often suspected that this trait had developed out of self-defense, because Levitians had a tendency to say things that made you want to slug them, and the bony spikes on the top of their feet would have deterred anyone from stomping on them.

"Yes, yes," Vladen said soothingly. "No trouble at all. A novice could do it, and if he's had some experience, why, that's even better!"

Even though Lynx claimed to have delivered a baby before, Bonnie wasn't sure she wanted his help. However, if Lynx wasn't lying—and knowing how blatantly honest he could be, she had no reason not to believe him—she knew that he could probably do it again, though it was possible that this might have been what had turned him against women.

"Sure you don't want to know what it is?" Vladen prompted, still eyeing his scanner. "I can see quite clearly."

"No," Bonnie said firmly. "I want it to be a surprise."

Vladen shook his head. "Too many surprises in this life," he said. "I'd want to know myself."

"It doesn't matter to me," said Bonnie. "I'll dress it

the same way whether it's male or female—at first, that is—which is all that matters. Zuannis gave me some baby clothes," she added, "and they look like they could go either way. Who knows, they might even fit."

Vladen nodded, but couldn't help feeling thankful that Bonnie wasn't having a boy. "Got any names picked out?" he asked, stowing his scanner in a different pocket, which made Bonnie wonder how he kept track of it all.

"No," she replied. "I want to get to know the baby first. Then I'll decide."

Vladen smiled knowingly, his pale blue eyes crinkling at the corners. "Every new mother has her own pet notions," he said with an airy wave of his hand. "I've heard them all." He glanced down at Bonnie's feet. "Now, *my* pet notion is that women in your condition shouldn't be on their feet all day. It's bad for the veins." Taking her hand, he examined it carefully. "Hmm, no swelling there. Been taking your vitamins?"

"Yes, I have," Bonnie assured him. She wasn't completely sure they'd been developed for Terran women, but she'd been taking them anyway.

"Well, you be sure to rest with your feet up several times a day," he told her. Turning to Lynx, he added, "And call me if you need any instructions during the delivery. My comlink is always on."

With that parting shot, Vladen shuffled off, and Bonnie was left staring at Lynx, who appeared to be acutely uncomfortable—especially since the look she was giving him should have at least made him break out in hives.

"So," she began. "You've delivered babies before?"

"Yes." Having made his reply, Lynx closed his lips firmly, refusing to elaborate.

"How many?" she asked.

"I do not know."

"That many, huh? Well, if you ever decide you don't want to work on a farm or in the mines, I'm sure you could get a job as a midwife." Noting his expression of revulsion, she added, "And yes, I know just how much you would dislike it—but it would probably pay very well."

"I have enough pay," he said. Which wasn't entirely true, because if Lynx were ever to be able to buy his own land, he would have to earn a great deal more than Bonnie was paying him. But taking a job as a midwife? He simply couldn't do it. It would have brought back too many painful memories.

"Then I must be paying you too much," Bonnie declared. "Of course, if you never actually *spend* any of it, I suppose it doesn't matter."

"I will spend it," Lynx said defensively. Unfortunately, since Bonnie was currently providing for all of his needs and he'd never had enough extra money to buy anything beyond the bare necessities, he had no idea just what he would spend it *on*.

Bonnie didn't either. "On what?" she demanded, giving free rein to her skepticism. "Couldn't be loose women, and I *know* you don't like new clothes, so that leaves booze, drugs, gambling—or a speeder of your own, perhaps? No, wait! I've got it! You want your own private dining room where you can eat all alone." Then she remembered that she hadn't asked Jack about Cat's eating habits. "By the way, is that a Zetithian custom or just one of your own little peculiarities?"

Bonnie knew she was skating on thin ice; another crack like that and he'd probably deck her, but she didn't care, because if he decided to quit his job, he'd have to find another one pretty quick, or Drummond would deport him. Then Mobray could deliver the baby, and Bonnie would feed rats to the enocks and live long and well without Lynx. She didn't need to spend the rest of her life trying to love someone who despised her entire gender. Life was too darn short for that.

"You do not understand," Lynx said bitterly.

"You're absolutely right, Lynx," Bonnie said equably. "I *don't* understand. And do you know why that is?"

"Because I have not told you," he said, knowing full well that he never had and never would.

"No kidding! You haven't told me a thing; you just sit out there in the shed and sulk because you had to work for me instead of going off to dig in the mines. Being kind to you obviously hasn't helped matters any, so from now on, no more Mr. Nice Guy."

"But you are a woman," he reminded her.

"So what?" she said, making a vague attempt at a snarl. "I can be as mean as anyone. You just watch me."

Bonnie almost missed it, but could have sworn she caught a faint glimmer of a smile. Not quite what it should have been, but a smile, nonetheless.

"Ah, so, you *can* smile," she said. "I was beginning to think it wasn't possible."

Lynx was spared from having to reply to that, because just then Cat came over, followed by his three sons—who actually looked more like his clones than his children. Carrying a large box and flashing a grin that made Lynx's pitiful smile look like a grimace, he said, "We will trade?"

"I dunno," Bonnie said doubtfully. "What've you got there?"

Cat's grin became a full smirk. "I believe you will trade anything for this."

Bonnie peered into the box and nearly fainted. It was full of bags of dark chocolate chips. "You drive a hard bargain, Cat," she sighed. "How many eggs do you want for that?"

"How many do you have?" he asked with a suggestive smile.

"Well, I saved a full crate for you," she said, "but I might have to throw in something else for a treasure like that."

Cat shook his head, and his dark eyes flashed. Bonnie noticed for the first time that Cat's pupils seemed to have a faint blue glow to them. Lynx didn't even have that much color, she thought ruefully. His pupils seemed to be the same color as his yellow eyes. "It is an even trade," Cat said. "We have many children to feed."

"And they can't live on chocolate, can they?" Bonnie certainly wished that she could. She also wished she could grow it, but hadn't bothered to try because cacao required a more tropical climate.

"No," he admitted. "But I believe they would like to."

All three nodded vigorously in agreement.

"Well, they seem to be thriving," Bonnie observed. "I don't think I've ever seen cuter kids in my life."

Cat seemed very pleased to hear that. "They resemble their mother, do they not?" he said proudly.

"Well, no, Cat," Bonnie said truthfully. "They look just like you."

"But they have their mother's eyes," he protested.

Bonnie shook her head. She had noticed before that Jack's eyes had a slight reddish glow to the pupil, but the kids didn't have even that. "I honestly can't see any resemblance to Jack at all," she said. "You're *sure* she's their mother?"

Smiling devilishly, Cat assured Bonnie that she was. Then he cocked his head slightly. "Your child will resemble her father, too, I believe."

"Aw, don't tell me that!" Bonnie groaned as the full meaning of his words sunk in. "I wanted it to be a surprise!"

"I may be wrong," Cat said, hedging just a bit. Bonnie had learned from Jack that Zetithians were prone to occasional insights that usually turned out to be true. Cat himself had seen who was responsible for the destruction of their planet in just such a vision, and no one had ever doubted him. Of course, since the culprits had been Nedwuts, no one was too surprised, since they were generally regarded as the premier badasses of the galaxy. There were plenty of other species around who caused just about as much trouble, but the Nedwuts had managed to acquire the reputation for being the worst.

"I doubt it," Bonnie grumbled, knowing that Cat's assessment was probably correct. "Vladen was dying to tell me himself. You're sure it's a girl?"

"I believe it is," Cat said meekly.

"Not that I *mind* having a girl, you understand, but if she looks like Sylor… well, I'm sure she'll turn out okay."

Cat grinned. "She will be beautiful."

"Thanks, Cat," Bonnie said graciously. "But as long as she's healthy, it doesn't matter what she looks like. I'll love her anyway."

Cocking his head to one side, he peered at Bonnie curiously. "Lynxsander's children would be more to your liking?"

Bonnie stared back at him blankly. She had no clue as to where he'd gotten that idea, but it was hitting a little too close to the mark for comfort. "I—I don't think he has any intention of *ever* having any children," she stammered, hoping that Lynx wasn't overhearing their conversation. "At least, not with me." Glancing over at Lynx, Bonnie noted that he had gone to get the crate of eggs out of the cart where she had hidden them. When he returned, he gave no hint of having heard anything, but with ears like that, she couldn't be sure.

With a skeptical lift of his exotic brow, Cat seemed to disagree but said nothing more on the subject.

Salan came by later on with some cheese to trade— Bonnie had saved some eggs for her too—and she noticed Lynx right away. The dairyman's daughter was a pretty girl with long auburn hair and a knowing smile, and, being half Terran and half Davordian, had the most luminous blue eyes Bonnie had ever seen. If the way she was looking at Lynx with those fabulous eyes was any indication, it was apparent that she'd gotten the scoop on Zetithians from someone.

"So, he's your new hand?" Salan asked, not taking her eyes off Lynx.

"Yes," Bonnie replied. "He's pretty good help, too. Not very chatty, though."

Salan nodded absently, still gazing at him. "I like the quiet type."

"He's quieter than most, Salan, but—who knows?—he might actually talk to *you.*" Since Lynx had always managed to disappear whenever Salan came to the house, this was doubtful, but he couldn't run away this time—and for all Bonnie knew, the two of them might have been destined to be together forever. "Hey, Lynx," Bonnie called out, "Salan gets those last two eggs."

Lynx got the eggs without a word, then took the box of cheese and stowed it in the cart. He didn't say one word.

"So, Lynx, I hear you're from the same planet as Cat and Leo?" Salan prompted him. Bonnie smiled to herself as she noted the change in the milkmaid's posture—a change that drew attention to her two largest attributes.

Lynx nodded warily.

"I've always thought they were just about the handsomest men I've ever seen," she gushed. "But that was before I met *you!* I must say, I like the shorter hair—*and* your black-tipped eyebrows! They're so… *exotic.*"

Salan was openly flirting with him, and Bonnie held her breath waiting for his response.

"You are Davordian," Lynx said. "I have seen your kind before."

"Oh, really?" Salan purred, taking a step closer to him. "And where was that?"

"There were many in the brothels of Paemay," Lynx replied, taking a step backward. "Their blue eyes were greatly admired."

Bonnie bit back a laugh while Salan, completely missing the insult, went on to ask, "And did *you* admire them?"

"No," he said. "I did not frequent the brothels."

"Well, then," she said with a sly smile, "how did you know they were there?"

"Other men told me of them," Lynx replied, "and I have seen them lying drunk in the street." In a bitter voice, he went on to add, "Some were slaves as I was and were used as concubines."

That got through to her, leaving her momentarily speechless. Blushing scarlet, Salan turned away from him, muttering, *"Nothing* like Cat or Leo!" To Bonnie, she merely said, "Thanks for the eggs," and stalked off.

Well, thought Bonnie, Salan couldn't say no one had warned her.

After they closed up shop, Bonnie went round to the receiving office and picked up the engine parts for the speeder from Wilisan.

Wilisan was a Terran of Middle Eastern descent, and if there was any man, aside from Lynx, living on Terra Minor that might have inspired Bonnie to fall in love, it would have been him. He had a long, lean body, flashing black eyes with dramatically up-swept brows, dark skin, and lots of wavy black hair. He was a feast for female eyes, almost as much as the Zetithians were, and, better yet, he was single. Salan had tried catching his eye more than once, but he'd never seemed interested.

"Finally going to fix that old clunker, eh?" Wilisan asked Bonnie with a smirk.

"No," she replied firmly. "Lynx is going to do that."

Wilisan looked at Lynx with interest. "Ah! You can fix it?"

Lynx nodded. "It only needs replacement parts and"—with a glance in Bonnie's direction, he added—"better maintenance."

"Not my fault," Bonnie muttered under her breath.

Wilisan exchanged a look with Lynx that plainly stated what he thought of female mechanics—which wasn't a whole lot, apparently.

"You two should get along just fine," Bonnie said dryly. "I can see you have a lot in common."

Completely missing the barb, Wilisan nodded at Lynx, saying smoothly, "I have an old speeder I would like to rebuild. Perhaps you could look at it?"

Lynx glanced at Bonnie as though seeking her permission, which surprised her a bit. "Uh, sounds like a great idea to me," she said, hoping it was the right thing to say. "He's been working on all of my equipment, and it's running much better than it ever did before."

"I will pay you well," Wilisan said.

Lynx nodded, and Bonnie thought he looked… better… for some reason. Then she realized that it was the prospect of doing work for someone other than herself that had brightened his countenance. He was almost smiling.

Not wanting to be one to deny him what he clearly saw as a treat, she said, "Sure, take a day off whenever you like, Lynx. I can manage without you."

Wilisan seemed very eager to discuss this with Lynx, so Bonnie left them to make arrangements while she carried the box of parts out to the cart. "Wish he could get that excited about working for me," she said to Kipper as he trotted alongside her. "But I guess that's too much to hope for."

Kipper could sense that Bonnie was unhappy, but why that was escaped him, so he just wagged his tail, wishing for perhaps the millionth time that Tisana was around to translate for him.

The return trip wasn't quite as silent as it had been that morning, but Bonnie was the one doing most of the talking. As she saw it, Lynx was a captive audience, and she should have taken advantage of that fact on their previous hike—though he could have always turned around and gone home then. This time, he pretty much had to go in the same direction as Bonnie did, whether he liked it or not. She pumped him for information about Zetith, figuring that was a more neutral topic than what had happened to him since the war. As it turned out, he had been in the same unit as Cat and Leo, but the similarities ended there.

"Cark was good with all weapons," he said, giving Bonnie the distinct impression that Lynx didn't consider himself to be as adept. "But Leccarian, whom you call Leo, was the best with a blade."

"Well, you seemed awfully glad to see them," Bonnie observed. "Were you good friends?"

"We were in the same unit," he said, his expression becoming wary.

Which had to count for something, but his attitude now was quite different from the way he'd acted when he'd first seen Cat. At the time, he'd seemed overjoyed, but now he was reticent again—almost as if meeting up with his former comrades reminded him of things he would have preferred to forget.

"All soldiers, huh?" Bonnie said with a nod. "I guess facing life and death together makes you closer."

"I was not a soldier," Lynx muttered, suddenly appearing fascinated with the ground in front of his feet.

"Oh, then what did you do?"

"I did not… fight," he said uncomfortably.

"I didn't ask what you *didn't* do," she said pointedly. "I asked you what you *did.*"

"I… helped."

"Helped with what?" The way he was acting, Bonnie thought he might have been the one responsible for making sure everyone had shoelaces—which was certainly important, though not particularly heroic.

Head down and still not looking Bonnie in the eyes, he replied, "I maintained the weapons and the other machines."

While this might have explained why he'd been able to tear apart a speeder engine, it didn't explain why he'd feel ashamed about it. "And I'm sure you were very good at it, too," she said promptly.

Lynx's response to that was a noncommittal shrug.

"You couldn't *all* be warriors," Bonnie said reasonably. "I mean, *somebody* has to work in the support positions! I've always felt that the cooks were the most important people in anyone's army, because if the soldiers don't eat, it's pretty hard for them to keep on fighting! And with a weapon that doesn't work, you can't do much of anything either."

Lynx still didn't seem convinced, so Bonnie kept talking. "I think I'd much prefer to have a good mechanic helping me on the farm; a soldier wouldn't be much use when it came to keeping my equipment up and running. Wilisan seemed to think it was pretty neat that you could fix a speeder too."

He made no comment about that, either, though to Bonnie's eyes it was perfectly obvious that he didn't give a damn what she thought.

"And a guy who can deliver a baby is a wonderful thing for a pregnant woman to have around—not that someone else couldn't help me out, but experience in such situations is always comforting." Bonnie was rapidly running out of appreciative things to say. "Guess you'd rather I just shut up, huh?"

Another shrug was all she received in reply. Bonnie was trying to be admiring, but he obviously wasn't buying it. "Lynx," she said, trying her best to smile, "all I'm asking for is a little conversation! It's fairly obvious you don't like me, and I know you'd rather be anywhere else but here, but couldn't you at least *pretend* once in a while? I'm *not* the enemy!"

The look he shot in her direction said otherwise.

Bonnie tried to see it from his side but was having trouble relating. "What *happened* to you, Lynx? Cat doesn't act anything like you, and when Jack found him, he was in chains! You're driving me nuts! Just when I think I might actually be getting somewhere, you clam up again! You're not a slave anymore, Lynx! That part of your life is over and done with, but you've got a chip on your shoulder the size of Arcturus, and it's *got* to be getting heavy!"

Realizing that her little speech had been liberally laced with Terran expressions, Bonnie knew that Lynx probably didn't get the exact meaning of a lot of it, but she didn't care. It was happening again; she'd been trying so hard to be nice to him and was finding it extremely frustrating when it didn't work. Lynx had nothing further to say, so Bonnie just gave up after that. Indulging in an erotic fantasy might have kept her mind off her swollen, aching feet, but she figured that Lynx would have smelled her desire and gotten all weirded out again, so she focused on her baby instead.

Her little *girl,* actually. It might have been better to know it was a girl or a boy ahead of time so she could think of it as something other than an "it." A name was needed, too. A girl name… something that sounded good with Neurath, because Bonnie wasn't about to give her baby girl Sylor's last name! They hadn't been married anyway, so she didn't need to—wouldn't have needed to even if they were—though she thought that Halen might have been easier to match up a first name with than Neurath.

With a grandmother named Lucretia and a mother named Eudora, Bonnie didn't have any intention of naming her daughter after either of them, so she knew she would have to come up with something else. On a whim, she asked Lynx what his mother's name was.

As deep in thought as Bonnie had been, she'd almost forgotten how reticent Lynx could be, but, surprisingly, he answered her quite normally—not even asking Bonnie why she wanted to know. Perhaps he saw it as a welcome change of subject.

"Shaulla," he replied.

Shaulla Neurath… it sounded exotic and mysterious, and shortening it to Ulla wasn't bad either. It was a thought, but then another occurred to her, completely erasing the original.

"So tell me, Lynx," she began. "Did you dislike your mother?"

He wasn't sure why she needed to know, but answered her anyway. "No," he replied.

"Did you love her?"

It may have been Bonnie's imagination, but his expression seemed to soften slightly.

"Yes." Lynx recalled his mother's gentle touch and her warm smile. She had loved him as a mother should, and he had loved her in return—but that was very long ago.

"So you don't hate all women," Bonnie asked, interrupting his reminiscent thoughts. "Just all of us except your mother?"

When he didn't reply immediately, it became evident that he was giving this some thought, so Bonnie pushed a little further. "There are some of us who are probably a lot like your mother, you know," she said neutrally. "Would you hate them too?"

"Perhaps not," he admitted.

"But you haven't met any of them yet, have you?"

"No."

Apparently Bonnie wasn't anything like his mother—which was probably just as well. "Would you be inclined to think more kindly of a girl who had your mother's name?"

"Perhaps," Lynx said cautiously, still unclear as to her purpose.

"Well, then," Bonnie said roundly, "if Cat's right about my baby being a girl, I'll name her Shaulla."

Bonnie couldn't tell if he approved or not—his expression was once again as enigmatic as ever—but if her baby girl was going to be growing up around Lynx,

Bonnie did *not* want him acting as though he despised her! It was bad enough that he felt that way about her, and besides, she *did* like the name.

"And her last name?" Lynx prompted—though Bonnie couldn't begin to guess why it would have mattered to him.

"Neurath," she replied firmly. "Unless I marry someone in the next few weeks."

"You will not give the child her father's name?"

"I wasn't married to Sylor," Bonnie said evenly, "and he left us. I see no point in giving her his name. Any man who would leave a woman while she carries his child deserves no recognition." She tried to keep the anger and bitterness out of her voice, but it was difficult.

Whether Lynx agreed with her sentiments on that subject didn't matter to Bonnie. Sylor was gone, having left shortly after her pregnancy was confirmed. It was possible that the reality of becoming a father may have frightened him—though they'd talked it over and he'd agreed to it—but so far he hadn't found the courage to return, and with Bonnie's delivery date rapidly approaching, it would be very difficult, if not impossible, for him to convince her to trust him again.

"You no longer like men?" Lynx inquired.

Bonnie wasn't sure why he thought she wouldn't like *any* of them—she'd already admitted to liking Cat, and Lynx had been sniffing out her desire—but she didn't bother to quibble, because for all she knew it was true. "Yeah, and you don't like women—though you could have at least tried to be a little nicer to Salan. A few more exchanges like that and she might start charging me more than two eggs for her cheese!"

Trudging onward, her mind nearly as weary as her feet, all Bonnie could think of was how sick she was of it all. She was tired of playing this stupid game; there ought to be at least one person in everyone's life that could be counted on, and she hadn't had someone like that in a very long time—probably not since her mother. So far Lynx had proved to be trustworthy, but not friendly, and Bonnie figured that it would have been too much to ask for a man to be likable *and* trustworthy. She was reminded of an old joke she'd heard once about how men were like parking spaces; the good ones were always taken and the rest were handicapped. Unfortunately, she knew from experience that it was too true to be very funny.

"It isn't that I don't like men, Lynx," she said after a bit. "I just want one I can trust. You wouldn't think that was too much to ask, but apparently it is—for me, anyway." Looking ahead, Bonnie could see her home just coming into view, and it had never looked so good. "Thank God we're almost there," she sighed. "I can't remember ever being so tired."

The thought of having to make that walk to Nimbaza again was almost enough to make Bonnie want to lay down and die—though it was either that or let Lynx go to market by himself the next week. It would be in keeping with her usual luck if he simply sold everything, including her cart, and then took off the way Sylor had. But as bad as she was feeling, she concluded that it might be worth the risk.

Lynx might have said he wouldn't leave without telling her, but that didn't necessarily mean he would stay forever. If he would just stay on another month or two,

Bonnie thought she could make it on her own after that. The mines might not be hiring, but there were bound to be other people looking for help—some place that Lynx would be happier. Drummond must have known that Lynx wouldn't like working for Bonnie—and while she might have been at the top of his list, the job at her farm surely hadn't been the only one available when Lynx arrived—but perhaps he'd felt sorry for Bonnie, or thought that having additional help would make the avocados grow faster.

After unloading what she'd bought at the market, Bonnie sent Lynx off to put the cart in the shed. Tossing him a bag of chocolate chips as an afterthought, she said offhandedly, "You never know when you might get a craving. Thanks for going with me today."

Lynx put the bag of candy in his pocket but didn't say anything.

"The correct response to that is to say 'you're welcome,'" Bonnie pointed out. "Try to remember that."

"You're welcome," Lynx said over his shoulder as he walked away with the cart.

It wasn't bad for a start, she thought. Now if he could only say it like he meant it.

Lynx walked quickly back to the shed. What a nightmare of a day he'd had! The only good thing he had to show for it was the bag of candy in his pocket—and the prospect of working on Wilisan's speeder, of course. Of all the Zetithians who could have survived the war, the two he'd met up with had to have been some he actually knew! Men who'd known him the way he was before he was sold as a slave. They didn't seem to have been changed a bit by being enslaved, even though they'd both been beaten within an inch of their lives—and more than once, too. No, they hadn't been changed, at least, not the way he had been, and they both had wives and children to prove it. They were successful, too—had traveled the galaxy and had found a type of freedom that Lynx knew he would never possess.

When he had first seen Cark—or Cat, as he was now called—he'd felt a surge of happiness beyond anything he'd ever felt in his life, which was increased exponentially by the added joy of seeing Leccarian again. But all too soon the reality began to sink in. Those two were everything he was not, as were brothers Trag and Tychar, who had also been members of his unit. Cat and Leo told him the brothers had been owned by a reptilian queen who had pampered them, and while they might not have been with a woman in twenty years, they'd subsequently found a Terran woman who loved one and took pity on the other.

Lynx had listened to their stories, but when prompted to tell his own, he was reluctant to relate the story of his life as a slave to so many women. His talents as a lover would have been worth telling—but only if he still possessed those abilities. He was able to tell his old friends of his life since then—he even got them laughing when he told a few stories about the exploits of his fellow miners on Paemay—but didn't want to see their reactions when he told them he no longer cared for women. It was an attitude in such direct opposition to that of other Zetithian males as to be unheard of. He wished with all his heart that it wasn't so; that he could tell them of his new life with Bonnie—as her friend, if not her lover—but he wasn't even her friend, and he would have had a great deal of difficulty finding the words to explain why.

Cark—Lynx had trouble thinking of him as "Cat"— had seemed to sense his distress and had not pressed him. Even so, he'd been about to tell them everything when Cark's sons had come running up to meet the "uncle" they didn't know they had. Such things were not to be discussed in front of children, and so Lynx had remained silent.

"These are Larsanken, Moriconthan, and Curlanikund," Cat said, introducing his sons one by one. "They are named after some of my ancestors, but Jacinth has a problem with the length of our Zetithian names and calls them Larry, Moe, and Curly." Then he added with a droll expression: "I will explain the origin of *those* names later."

"And I have two sons and a daughter," Leo reported proudly. "But they are babies still and are back at our ship with their mother."

Lynx stared at the boys in wonder. Cark had not only fathered children, but they all appeared to be pure Zetithian! He took each of their hands in his own and gazed wistfully into their softly glowing eyes—eyes that he had longed to see in a child for so long…

If only Lynx had met Bonnie long ago, and if only he had been capable of fathering children, things might have turned out as well for him. Bonnie was different from the other women he had known; he knew that, and there were times when he wished he could allow himself to have normal feelings toward her. Without the demons of his past to haunt him, he would have been her lover long before this—perhaps even from the very beginning. He knew deep down that she wouldn't have abused him or taunted him the way the others had; she would have loved him—just as surely as Cat and Leo's wives loved their husbands—not like those other women who had quite literally used him up.

Lover, they'd called him. Lover Boy, Slave Boy, or just Boy—or Slave, when they were angry with him. Anything but his own name. In fact, not one of them had ever even asked him what his name really was. Not that it mattered. He told himself it would have been different if he'd actually loved any of them, but he hadn't. He didn't even know how.

A quiet but persistent voice inside his head reminded him that Bonnie had asked him his name—even though she'd been bleeding and in pain at the time—and he felt a pang of regret for the way he'd treated her. She'd been very kind to him; he knew that, and he also knew that she was right; it wasn't her fault. None of it was.

It was difficult to even look at her, because he couldn't deny the fact that she was beautiful. Her angelic face, the soft curves of her body, added to her kind nature, should have made him want her. There was a time—albeit a brief one—when he would have admired such a woman and knowing the level of pleasure he could give her would have emboldened him to act; to entice her into his arms and delight in her reaction to him. He would have loved her and given her such joy.

But the fact that he couldn't do any of those things angered him. If only he had never scented her desire! He could have been nicer to her if only she hadn't smelled

like that. Her scent was tantalizing but tormenting at
the same time. One whiff of her should have sent him
into full arousal, but it only reminded him of things he'd
rather forget. He didn't intend to seem ungrateful, but
he knew that in thanking her, he might lead her to think
he felt differently toward her, and he didn't want that to
happen. All he could do to thank her for her kindness
was to do the best job for her that he possibly could.

He couldn't even risk smiling at her. She had caught
the one smile he'd ever sent her way. *"No more Mr. Nice
Guy,"* she'd said. Hearing that, Lynx couldn't help but
smile; Bonnie didn't have a mean bone in her body. He
would do his best not to give her any other reason to
complain about him and vowed to work harder. As he
saw it, it was all he could do.

She said she only wanted conversation with him. He
didn't believe it, though he almost wished he could. If
he'd been one of those men who could rattle on for hours
about nothing of importance, he could have at least kept
her satisfied in that respect, but he wasn't. He couldn't
lie, either—couldn't even begin to come up with a less
sensitive excuse for his behavior—and since he had no
intention of telling her the real story, he had decided
that the less he said to her the better. He almost wished
he *could* have lied, because it might have made things
easier for him—and for her.

Chapter 9

OVER THE NEXT TWO WEEKS, BONNIE SPENT MORE TIME with her feet up than a Davordian girl in a Paemayan brothel, but she certainly wasn't having any fun. She couldn't breathe, couldn't eat, couldn't sleep worth a darn, and picking vegetables was completely out of the question. Kipper moped around, looking up at her with big, sad eyes, wondering what was wrong with her. She wished she could have had Tisana around to talk to her pet and explain that she would get back to normal eventually, but Jack had gone off on another trading run, taking Tisana with her. Then one day, Shaulla dropped and life was good, except Bonnie now had to pee constantly, and her feet swelled up even more.

Lynx might not have liked it, but except for the cooking, he was now doing everything—and Bonnie cheated a bit on that, too. Breakfast was usually eggs and toast, but for the other meals she fixed a pot of vegetable soup. Each time they ate some of it, she would add more water and vegetables to it and just let it keep on cooking. Lynx never complained, and though Bonnie knew he had to be getting sick of it, quite honestly, she didn't care.

Lynx had the speeder up and running within two days of getting the parts, and he'd taken the next day to work on Wilisan's speeder, with equal success. Bonnie was impressed, and said so, but for all the good it did, she might have been complimenting one of Mobray's cows on her excellent cheese. What it would take to get through to him was beyond her.

Then one day, Bonnie decided to play dirty and introduced him to cookie dough.

Even after having traveled across the galaxy to a new world, Bonnie still considered chocolate chip cookie dough to be one of the ultimate taste sensations in the universe—right up there with turkey gravy on Thanksgiving—especially when she made it with dark brown sugar. Bonnie wasn't sure which one evoked a more orgasmic response, but since there were no turkeys on Terra Minor—something that she considered to be a serious oversight—she was left with cookie dough.

It might have been that burst of energy one gets at some point just prior to delivery, but though her back was killing her, Bonnie was feeling downright industrious one day. She'd been mopping floors and was in the process of cleaning the kitchen sink when she noticed Lynx out working in the garden. Since the inconsiderate wretch was doing it without a shirt, she felt that a bit of retaliation was in order. Gathering up her own milled flour and fresh eggs, Mobray's excellent butter, and Jack's out-of-this-world chocolate chips, she whipped up the fluffiest, creamiest dough her culinary skills could produce. Then she went out on the porch and yelled for Lynx.

Apparently not wishing to entice her into an odoriferous state of desire, she noted that the little snit put his shirt back on before coming over.

"Hey, would do me a favor and taste this?" she asked, holding out a spoonful. "I want to know what you think."

Warily, he reached out for the spoon, but Bonnie

pulled it back. "Uh-uh," she said with an evil shake of her head. "Just take a bite."

Backing off, he said, "I will not."

"Oh, yes you will," she said roundly, "because if you don't, I'll never fix another meal for you again! You'll have to pick your own vegetables out of the garden and cook them yourself!"

This wasn't much of a threat—and she never would have followed through with it anyway—but crossing his arms belligerently, Lynx did his best to top it with one of his own.

"I will not help you give birth to your child if you do not feed me."

Bonnie couldn't help but laugh. "Women have been having babies for millions of years, Lynx. I wouldn't be the first to go it alone. Besides, I can always call one of the neighbors. Zuannis or Salan would come for moral support, if nothing else." Bonnie knew this wasn't entirely true, for while Zuannis had given birth to several children, the mere thought of being present while someone else was in labor made her feel faint. She'd offered her husband's help instead, but Joachen hadn't seemed any more excited at the prospect than Lynx was. Hatul, however, had overheard the conversation while he was fingering the vegetables and had been quick to offer his assistance. Bonnie had hastily declined, though upon further reflection decided that his sucker-tipped fingers might be useful when it came to pulling a reluctant infant out into the world.

Not backing down one bit, Lynx just stood there, glaring at her.

"Oh, come on, Lynx!" she cajoled. "It won't kill you,

and I don't care what religion you belong to, tasting this won't send you to hell."

Still wary, he asked, "What is it?" Ordinarily, Lynx wouldn't have asked that question, but something in her manner warned him that she was trying to trick him in some way.

"Not gonna tell ya," Bonnie taunted him. "You have to guess. Come on, open your mouth—close your eyes if you have to—but just taste it."

Lynx was standing a step down from her on the side of the porch, and as Bonnie had set the bowl down on the railing before she poked a spoonful in his mouth, she had a hand free when he tried to bolt. Catching him by the front of his shirt, she said, "Oh, no you don't! You aren't running off this time! Now, you just chew that up and swallow it—slowly!—and look at me while you do it; I want to see your reaction."

Bonnie watched as Lynx's expression changed from one of stubborn denial to an unabashed display of pleasure. Having been caught completely unawares by her ploy—his first thought had been that it was going to taste horrible—it struck him with as much impact as she'd hoped it would. Knowing how the creamy butter was melting on his tongue as the sugar, vanilla, and salt sent his taste buds into overdrive, Bonnie's mind reeled for a moment; if only she could elicit such a response from him with a kiss or the touch of her hand! As he bit down on the chips and the chocolate added its own magic, she fought the urge to glance down at his groin and see if the effect was as profound as it appeared.

"Good?" she inquired curiously, though the look on his face was proof enough.

Lynx nodded, blinking slowly. "It is what the cookies are made from."

"Good guess," she said. "Now, tell me, Lynx, isn't that the best thing you've ever tasted in your life?"

Lynx couldn't lie. "I believe it is," he replied.

"And it didn't kill you to eat it in front of me, did it?"

"No," he admitted. "It did not."

"You know, Lynx, food is one of those things that should be shared," Bonnie said gently. "Please, tell me why you can't sit down at the table with me." When he hesitated she almost poked another spoonful in his mouth but instead added, "I promise, I won't laugh."

Lynx didn't know why he spoke, perhaps it was her assurance that she wouldn't laugh, but whatever the reason, to her surprise, he answered her question. "I was the slave of other slaves," he said, "and was starved when I did not please them." Bonnie could see the pain and humiliation he must have felt sweep across his features. This was more difficult for him than she would ever have imagined. "And when they finally let me eat, I had to eat as quickly as I could." He paused as a tremor shook him. "I can still hear their laughter."

So that was why he had to carry his food off to eat it, she thought, the way a stray dog would do when it knows it's about to be kicked for stealing scraps. Bonnie wondered if Lynx had been abused in that way, but also knew that abuse wasn't always physical. The humiliation had undoubtedly hurt him far more than the starvation ever had.

"I won't laugh," she promised. "And Lynx, I know you don't like being around me, but could you please try—at least have dinner with me once in a while?"

She'd lost him, though. Having partially spilled his guts, he clammed up again. She could almost see the walls going back up around him.

"I'll always keep you well-fed!" she said desperately. "Don't ever believe me when I say I won't! It's nothing more than an idle threat—to be honest, I really have no hold over you at all! You could leave here right now, and Drummond would find you another job—I'm sure there's a long list of others who could use your help— and it's good help, Lynx!" she said earnestly. "I'm paying you all I can, and it's still not enough." She felt tears filling her eyes. "You've helped me in so many ways. I'd like to return the favor, but all I can do is pay you and feed you—you won't live in the house, and that's okay, not many hired hands do, but I want to talk to you, or something—anything! Like I said before, it's *lonely* out here! I see my friends now and then, but it isn't the same as talking to someone you actually see every day. Don't you ever get lonely? Don't you sometimes wish all you had to do was reach out and know that someone would be there for you?"

Bonnie knew what his reply would be even before she asked that, but it still hurt.

It hurt him, as well. Lynx could see the pain he was inflicting, but if he relented, he knew he would have to spend more time close to her, knowing she wanted something from him that he was unable to give. "I prefer to be alone," he said, and it wasn't a lie, either. Being alone was much easier for him.

"Is that something else you never had, like a decent meal?"

Nodding, he replied, "Yes. I find that solitude is even more important than getting enough to eat."

"Well," she said, doing her best to bow to the inevitable, "if you ever change your mind, you know where to find me." With a heavy sigh, she picked up the bowl of cookie dough and turned to go back inside, half intending to eat every last bit of it, when her water chose that moment to break, completely ruining her exit.

"Well, of all the rotten timing!" she exclaimed. "Though I probably ought to be glad it happened on the porch and not in the middle of the kitchen floor!" She looked at Lynx questioningly. "So, what do we do now, Lynx? Boil water?"

"Boil water?" he echoed.

"Never mind," she replied. "Old Earth joke. Guess I'll just bake these cookies and then go lie down or something—or is it better to walk around?"

"You may do whatever you wish," he replied. He stood there hesitantly. Lynx had never asked her for anything before and wasn't quite sure how to do it.

Bonnie could see the assortment of emotions roiling inside him. She didn't know what his problem was, but she had an idea he was about to back out on her. "What now?"

"Before you bake the cookies," he began.

"Do what? Take a shower?"

He shook his head and sighed. "I would like more," he said, gesturing toward the bowl.

"Ah-ha!" she said gleefully. "I *knew* I could get to you with that! C'mon, Lynx. Let's get sick on cookie dough, and then we'll have a baby."

❖ ❖ ❖

That's not exactly how it went, but they did start off that way—and it at least got Lynx inside the house. Unfortunately, Bonnie hadn't eaten much more than the equivalent of two cookies before she began having some serious pains and decided that her bed was probably the best place to be.

It was hot as hell. Bonnie was totally miserable. Lynx, on the other hand, was wonderful.

It was obvious he'd delivered babies before, and if there was anything else he could possibly have done to help her, Bonnie couldn't imagine what it might have been. He rubbed her back, encouraged her, and coached her on how to breathe correctly to ease the pains. He sponged her overheated body with cool water, and as her labor stretched on into the night, he even held her in his arms and purred. His warm body against her back felt more soothing than anything ever had before, but, unfortunately, it made her feel that much worse, knowing what she was missing the rest of the time. She knew she would never get that kind of attention from him again unless she had another baby, which was doubtful, given the circumstances, nor would she ever sleep with him again. There were a few times when her tears had nothing to do with labor pains.

Dozing at intervals, Bonnie drifted into a marvelous fantasy, imagining what it would be like to be loved by this man. He was so patient, so gentle, his nature so completely different from the way he'd acted around her before, and her eyes filled with tears whenever she thought about it. She knew quite well that she would never be loved by him, not like this, and it was breaking her heart.

Lynx relaxed into the old ways with practiced ease. He'd always loved caring for women in labor, because that was when they seemed to appreciate his efforts the most. No one had ever yelled at him to do anything else; they let him be, let him focus his attention on the one woman for as long as it took. In a way, it was one of the few times he was able to rest. He would lie down with the woman and hold her, caress her and, yes, pretend that he loved her—that she was giving birth to their child—a child whom she wanted more than anything. He could pretend that he was loved, as well. After the birth, things would go back to the way they were, but for that short space of time, Lynx was content.

Bonnie's labor lasted well into the night, and Lynx stayed with her. He knew it was only what she needed that mattered, but he forgot that for a brief interval when he allowed himself to pretend as he had done so many times in the past. Drowning in her scent and intoxicated by the feel of her body in his arms, he forgot where he was, even *who* he was, and kissed her lovingly while she slept.

The day was dawning when Bonnie's daughter was born, and when Lynx took the baby in his arms and held her with such tenderness, all Bonnie wanted to do was cry. He held her for what seemed like an eternity before taking a deep breath and, in a very matter-of-fact tone, said, "Your child is not normal."

Bonnie's heart slid to her feet. "What do you mean, 'not normal'?"

He brought the baby closer, showing Bonnie the ridged forehead and backwardly slanted ears.

Quickly regaining her composure, Bonnie said: "She's normal enough for a half-Vessonian. I should have warned you. Sylor wasn't Terran."

"Forgive me," Lynx said stiffly. "I did not intend to cause you distress. I did not know about her father."

If Bonnie felt any distress at that point, it had nothing to do with whether or not her daughter was normal, but with whether or not Lynx would hate the child as much as he hated all other women. He can mess with my mind all he likes, Bonnie thought, but she didn't want her daughter brought into it.

"You didn't know about Sylor because I didn't tell you," Bonnie said wearily. "He's gone, and I'm trying very hard to forget about him—which won't be easy with Shaulla looking just like him." Jack's three boys looked just like their father, too, she remembered. Lynx's kids would probably be every bit as cute, but that was something Bonnie would never know—no matter what Cat might suggest.

Reaching out, Bonnie took her baby from Lynx, wondering if the child could feel how much he despised her. Bonnie wanted to tell him to go away and never come back, but couldn't bring herself to do it.

"Thank you, Lynx," she said instead. "I couldn't have done it without you."

His face was an unreadable mask. Now that Shaulla was born, he'd retreated again; Bonnie didn't even have to be looking at him to know that. Unfortunately, Bonnie now knew what she'd been missing—had seen a side of Lynx that she hadn't even known existed—and having learned that, she knew she couldn't stand the fact that she loved him while he despised her. She made up her mind to send him back to Drummond as soon as she was sure she could manage everything without him. She knew very well he wouldn't be deported; he could get a job as a mechanic anywhere.

Nodding in reply, he said, "Call me if you need me."

Bonnie made up her mind not to call him unless one of them was dying. Then he left her alone with her new daughter, and they both cried.

Lynx left the house in more torment than ever before. How could he have said such a thing to a new mother? He knew very well that having an abnormal child was a woman's worst fear, though the other women of his experience had always been more afraid that the child would look like him—even more so than if they'd given birth to a monster.

Shaulla might have been half-Vessonian, but to Lynx, she was still beautiful—so innocent and new. Not like the ones who were grown. If only she could stay that way, he thought wistfully, and not grow up to become the stuff of his nightmares.

But perhaps this one would be different. After all, she had the same name as his mother, and it was possible that she would grow up liking him and not learn to treat him with contempt.

Reminding himself that he only worked for Bonnie, and that Shaulla would always know him as the "hired hand," he still longed for a closer relationship with her. They could at least be friends. He would teach her all he knew about machinery and construction and anything else she wanted to learn from him. Of course, he knew that he couldn't expect Bonnie to encourage this sort of thing.

Lynx found himself wishing that he could have had a chance with a woman who had grown up knowing him and at least liking him. But all of those young girls he had known before the war were gone now, and he couldn't have given them joy the way he once had anyway. That part of him was lost forever.

Lynx went to the pump and turned it on full force, letting the cold water run through his hair and down his back, washing away the tension and the fragments of his dreams—dreams that were pointless to indulge in, because they never came true and never would. He had felt it every time he brought a child out into the light, that quick surge of hope, only to have it be cast down again when he realized that once again it hadn't happened. And even though he knew it to be completely impossible, Shaulla's birth affected him no differently than any of the others. As always, the child he delivered hadn't resembled him in the slightest. She belonged to someone else.

When Bonnie contacted Drummond the next day to report Shaulla's birth, he listened carefully but still wasn't sure what he was hearing. "You're *sure* you want it to read like that?"

"Yes, I'm sure," she said firmly. "If Sylor ever comes back, I don't want him meddling or trying to share custody or anything like that. I don't want his name anywhere on it."

"Suit yourself," he said, shaking his head. "Not sure this is the answer, but—"

"Do I have to remind you of what happened between us?"

"No, but it could be disproved easily enough if he

ever decided to put up a fight," Drummond pointed out. "But if you're sure that's what you want to do, while you're at it, you might want to get his name off the deed to your land, too."

"Is there any way to do that?"

"Hmmm, been gone long enough that you could claim abandonment," suggested Drummond. "Or since he took money, you could claim that as the purchase price for his share." Scratching his chin, he added, "Might even be able to make it look legal."

"That'd be great," Bonnie said. "Now that you mention it, I don't want him coming back claiming to own the place, either. I'm done with him."

"Sounds like it," Drummond commented, thinking that getting on Bonnie's bad side hadn't been in Sylor's best interests. "Still don't want to report him? Just say the word, and I'll sic Zerk and the boys on him to track him down—really should, you know."

"No," she said. "He's probably hooked up with some other gullible woman by now and has his name on her property too."

"I haven't seen anything to that effect," Drummond said. "But then, he might have gone out of my territory."

Bonnie could only hope that was true. Trying to sound nonchalant, she said: "Hey, do you have anyone else looking for a job?"

Not answering her question, he asked, "You need more help? What's the matter? That Zetithian boy not working out?"

"It's not that," Bonnie said truthfully. "I just don't think he's very happy working here."

"Well, he's a fool not to!" Drummond said roundly.

"Working for you is a damn sight better than working in the mines!"

"Yes, but it's not what he had planned," she said, not wanting to explain any further. "Don't you have any other jobs for him?"

"Sure," he said. "But nothing any different than what he's doing now."

Perhaps not, Bonnie thought, but at least it would be a job working for someone else. Her chest constricted, and she swallowed hard, fighting back sudden tears. That sort of thing was happening to her more frequently than ever, and she was getting tired of it.

"I could give him a list, and he could check it out," Drummond went on. "But if I were you, I'd hang onto him until someone else shows up. It's still not a good time for you to be working that place all by yourself, especially now that you've had the baby."

"I'm not helpless!" Bonnie protested. "You know I'm not!"

"Never said you were," he returned promptly. "But plenty of other people need help, and I thought you needed it the most, so I sent him to you. You should keep him."

"Lynx isn't a slave anymore," Bonnie reminded him. "I can't very well keep him if he doesn't want to stay."

"Then why are you the one telling me this?" Drummond demanded. "Seems to me if he wants a different job so damn bad, he should be talking to me himself."

"He hasn't actually *said* anything," Bonnie admitted. "I just... thought I'd ask."

"And now you have, and I've told you there's no

one to replace him." Drummond leveled a stern look at Bonnie through the viewscreen. "If he's unhappy enough to want to quit, then he can see me about another job, but in the meantime, *you keep him.*"

"That's what I thought you'd say," Bonnie said with a sigh. "But please, tell me if anything changes."

Something in his expression made Bonnie think he wasn't going to, but he said, "Sure thing, Bon-bon. But don't you go worrying yourself about it. Just take good care of that baby."

"I will," she replied and terminated the link. She shook her head sadly, thinking that Drummond was probably just as untrustworthy as all the rest. It just wasn't as obvious.

Bonnie stayed inside for the next day or two, simply setting Lynx's plate out on the porch for him. She felt very clumsy with Ulla at first and figured that, as good as he was at delivering babies, Lynx probably knew a whole lot more about caring for one than she did. At one point she was wishing she could ask him for some advice on breast-feeding, but she and Ulla finally got the hang of it. While she lay beside her happily suckling infant, Bonnie laughed out loud as she imagined the look on Lynx's face if she actually *had* asked him.

On the third day, having rigged up a sling to carry Ulla in, Bonnie ventured out with her after lunch and wound up doing some work in the garden. Not surprisingly, she tired pretty quickly, and Ulla went to sleep. Bonnie was so exhausted she didn't think she could even make it back to the house without lying down for a while, but was able to make it to the shade of a peach tree before she sank down gratefully in the cool grass.

Putting Ulla down gently so as not to wake her, Bonnie lay down beside her with Kipper curled up against her back. She quickly fell asleep and dreamed of making love with Lynx in the shade while her baby slept. In her dream, Lynx looked at her with the eyes of a lover; aglow with the kind of tenderness she'd yet to see there while she was awake. She could almost feel him purring, feel his body sinking into her own, feel the heat, and most of all, feel the love.

Waking from her dream, Bonnie was startled to discover Lynx sitting nearby holding Ulla. The tenderness Bonnie was longing for was all there, but it was for her daughter, not for herself. Lynx held Ulla as though she were his own child, his eyes closed as he purred softly. Seeming to sense Bonnie's gaze, he opened his eyes to find her watching him.

"You did not call me," he said quietly.

"Should I have?" she asked.

Lynx seemed puzzled for a moment, as though unable to form a reply. Finally, he said, "I thought you would." He'd actually *hoped* she would, but he wasn't ready to admit it—not yet.

"Didn't need anything," she said with what she hoped was a nonchalant shrug. "I'm not helpless, you know." Which was what she had told Drummond—and it was true; she *wasn't* helpless. Bonnie didn't ask for much from anybody. The only thing above and beyond the call of duty that she'd ever asked Lynx for was a little companionship, and she hadn't gotten it. "And she's a good baby," Bonnie added.

Lynx nodded, still holding Bonnie's daughter as though reluctant to give her up. It seemed that Lynx's dislike of women didn't include infants, but how long would it be before he began to treat Ulla with the same contempt he had for her mother? Bonnie knew that it would be very hurtful for a young girl to be treated with kindness until she reached a certain age and then suddenly be rejected by him for no apparent reason. She hated to put Ulla through that, but the next words that Lynx uttered proved that rejecting her was the farthest thing from his mind.

"I… like children," he said finally. "If you ever need help with her…" His voice trailed off as he gazed down at Ulla's tiny face where she lay sleeping in his arms.

Bonnie stared at him in frank disbelief. She'd assumed that he was experienced in their care, but that he actually *liked* children hadn't occurred to her. It seemed impossible, but his rapt expression was enough to assure her that he was telling the truth. Bonnie reminded herself that he had always been honest with her—she might not have always liked what he had to say, but if he'd ever lied, Bonnie certainly couldn't prove it. It seemed odd to her that a man with such a fondness for children could have such a negative attitude toward women—which made it extremely doubtful that he'd ever have any children of his own—but perhaps he only liked other people's kids.

She shook her head and said with an odd laugh, "I can't figure you out, Lynx. Maybe I should just quit trying."

Looking up at him, Bonnie realized that it was only a matter of time before her "desire" for him returned—in fact, she was surprised he couldn't pick up the scent of what she'd been dreaming. She'd had her baby, and though she knew that a new baby often disrupted the intimacy between a husband and wife, Bonnie had only to look at Lynx sitting there holding her child to know that watching him with Ulla would only make her want him that much more.

Seeing this gentler side of him was stimulus enough, but Lynx had also grown more attractive during the three months he'd spent on Bonnie's farm. He'd lost the hunted, starved look he'd had when she first met him, and his hair was growing longer. Why he hadn't cut it, Bonnie didn't know and didn't ask, but it was possible that Cat's words on the subject had made a difference to him. He'd had plenty of muscle to begin with, but the work he'd been doing had built him up, and he was filling out his clothes much better than he had before. He might not have had Cat's personality—or his long black hair—but he was developing the same stunning physique.

As Ulla began to cry, Bonnie reached out to take her from Lynx, but the child's crying ceased immediately as Lynx began to rock back and forth, his purring becoming even louder as he patted her.

"Well, you obviously know what you're doing," Bonnie admitted with some reluctance. Taking a deep breath to steady her emotions, she went on to say, "I—I'll let you know if I ever need any help." As she lay there watching him, though, her curiosity got the better of her. "Where'd you learn that, anyway? Have a lot of brothers and sisters?"

He nodded. "Yes," he replied. "On Zetith, it was customary for older children to take care of the young ones, and when I was a slave, the other slaves had many children."

Bonnie remembered that he said he'd been the slave of other slaves, and apparently at least some of them had been female. If it was during that time that he'd developed his dislike of women, Bonnie thought it odd that he liked children any more than he liked their mothers. She reminded herself that it was hard not to like babies—they have the knack of bringing out the nurturing instincts in just about everyone.

"That was where you learned to deliver babies then?"

He nodded, his purring never ceasing.

"Well," Bonnie said briskly, "you're *very* good at it! You should think more about what Vladen said. We could use someone like you around here to help with other births."

As soon as she'd said it, Bonnie wished she hadn't, because Lynx looked positively stricken at the mere mention of the idea.

"Okay, then, maybe not," she went on smoothly. "Look, you can rock Ulla anytime you like. I'm sure she'll enjoy it." Which she seemed to be doing right then; utterly content and completely relaxed in his arms.

In his arms. Bonnie knew what that felt like, too, and began to envy her daughter.

Putting those painful thoughts firmly aside, she got to her feet, noting that the sun was beginning to set. "I'll just go get dinner started," she said hastily. "You can play with Ulla while I'm cooking."

Lynx nodded and closed his eyes again, his face taking on an expression of serenity the likes of which Bonnie had never seen. *No, he doesn't want me to stay here with him. I am the farthest thing from his mind. He only wants to hold my child.*

When Lynx had seen Bonnie lying there, fast asleep, his first impulse was to lie down beside her and take her in his arms and kiss her until she couldn't think anymore—until *he* couldn't think anymore—and show her how sorry he was that they couldn't be together. He wanted to look down into her deep blue eyes and see his own desire reflected there; watch her expression as he gave her everything he had to give. He thought back to the time when mating with a woman could truly take him away to a better place, one where nothing bad had ever happened to him or to his world. But he couldn't do that, so he did the next best thing.

And with his eyes closed and Shaulla in his arms, Lynx *could* pretend again. Pretend that all the horrors of his past had never taken place, and that he was sitting in the shade while the sun set and his child slept. It was another of his dreams. His mind flowed outward, touching the sky, the clouds, the grass, and the trees. He was at peace with a baby in his arms. Even in his former life, it was one of the few times he'd ever been left alone, because no mother wanted to disturb him while he purred and rocked her crying child to sleep, and neither had Bonnie. He was safe for now.

Chapter 10

THE MORE TIME BONNIE SPENT WITH ULLA, THE MORE she began to understand why Sylor had left when he did. If he'd had second thoughts about starting a family, then leaving before Bonnie even *looked* pregnant had probably been his best move. It would be so much harder to leave after your child was born and you had gazed into her eyes.

The bond between mother and child was strong, and Bonnie could now understand why her own mother hadn't wanted her to leave Earth to begin a new life on Terra Minor. Bonnie didn't want Ulla out of her sight, let alone living on another planet.

The bond between father and child must have counted for something, too, because even though Lynx wasn't her father, he went to a lot of trouble to see that Ulla was comfortable.

The first thing he did was build a cradle for her to nap in while they worked in the garden. The cradle was about waist-high with a roof over it to keep the sun out of her eyes—she wouldn't have gotten wet if it rained, either. Then he began carving toys for her; highly polished wooden toys, with not a splinter or a rough spot on them anywhere. He was quick on his feet, too. She had only to whimper before he was right there to see what the trouble was, and he could change a diaper three times faster than Bonnie could. Plus, he could wrap her up in a neat little bundle, while Bonnie's efforts always seemed to leave a foot sticking out.

He began taking care of Bonnie, too. He would bring her water, telling her that she needed to drink more fluids, or tell her to rest when even Bonnie knew she had worked too long and was getting tired. Bonnie suspected it was just to help her produce more milk to nurture his little darling, but fortunately, he never put it that way.

Vladen came by when Ulla was about two weeks old and proclaimed that all was well with both mother and child. "Thought you might have some trouble with those forehead ridges during the delivery," he remarked. "But it looks as though you did just fine."

"Do you mean to tell me you were concerned about that?" Bonnie said ominously.

"Just a thought, my dear," he said soothingly. "Nothing to worry about—as you can readily see! Won't have any trouble at all with the next one!"

"There won't *be* a next one," she said.

"Oh?" he said, nonplussed. "I would have thought…" His voice trailed off suggestively, obviously referring to Lynx.

"No," Bonnie said firmly. "There will be no more."

"But, Cat and Leo can cross with—"

"What they can do has nothing to do with me and Lynx," she said, cutting him off before he could finish. Things were bad enough as it was; hearing all the details of what she'd been missing would only make it worse.

"But Zetithians are—"

"I don't know what you've heard about them—from Jack or Tisana or anyone else," Bonnie said evenly, "but this one is different. He likes the baby just fine, but he doesn't like women at all."

Vladen obviously didn't believe her. "Perhaps his nose is congested," he muttered, idly rubbing his jaw ridges. "I have treatments for that."

"Trust me, his nose works just fine!" Bonnie said, rapidly becoming exasperated. "And don't you dare say a word to him about it!"

"A bit sore on that subject, are we?" Vladen observed, his raised brow pushing his bristly blond hair even farther back on his high forehead.

Bonnie blew out a pent-up breath and glared at him. "For once, *Doctor*," she said firmly, "it's none of your business."

He chuckled knowingly. "Of course it isn't. Don't know what I'm talking about, either, do I?" Then his expression changed abruptly. "But perhaps it isn't his nose that's the problem. Perhaps it's you."

"Me?" she repeated in disbelief. "What's wrong with me?"

"Well, Sylor did you a very nasty turn by leaving you like that," he said, casually picking up Ulla to set her on his knee. "Perhaps you've been taking it out on that Zetithian boy."

"He isn't a boy, Vladen!" Bonnie reminded him.

"Don't change the subject, Bonnie!" Vladen scolded. "All men are not like Sylor! Remember that!"

"No, some of them are like you," she said with a wry smile. "Irritating, overbearing—"

"And wonderfully wise," he finished for her, switching on his scanner to check Ulla. "Perfect child," he said. "Sometimes that Vessonian-Terran mix makes for a weak heart, but she's ticking along just fine."

"Weak heart?" Bonnie exclaimed, feeling her own skip a few beats. *"Weak heart?* You're telling me that *now?"*

"Well, I've checked her right along," he reminded Bonnie, "and her heart was always normal, but until a child is born, you never really know, do you?"

She stood there gaping at him for a long moment before she was even able to speak. "No, I suppose you don't," she said. "But couldn't you have at least warned me about all of this?"

"And had you worried sick the whole time?" he said with a smile. "Not worth the stress, my dear. I do my best to avoid putting unnecessary fears into the heads of pregnant women. Believe me, they find enough things to worry about on their own!" Vladen stood up, handing Ulla back to Bonnie. "Well, then," he said briskly. "Must be off! Take good care of them."

"Them?" she echoed.

"The baby and the Zetithian," he replied. "Though I believe he requires even more care than the child."

"No, he doesn't," she said wistfully. "Lynx doesn't seem to need much of anything. All I do is feed him."

Vladen looked so smug, Bonnie considered it a wonder his jaw ridges didn't pop right through his skin. "I doubt that," he said. "He's one of the neediest men I've ever seen."

"Well, he might be needy," Bonnie grumbled, "but he sure doesn't act like it! He never asks for anything, and most of what I've given him, he doesn't seem to want."

"Yes, well, some women are more needy than they're willing to admit, too," Vladen said mysteriously.

"Oh, I'm sure they are," Bonnie agreed in an effort to shut him up. "And I'm sure you think I'm one of them.

But I'm also sure you have other patients waiting for you, so I won't keep you."

"Any eggs available?" he asked on the way out. "And some of that white squash with the scalloped edges?"

"Sure," she said wearily. "Got plenty of both. Help yourself to anything you like—on the house."

"That would make it seem as though you were paying me for my services!" he said indignantly, clearly affronted by the suggestion. "Which you know very well I cannot do! I will pay for what I get from you!"

Bonnie chuckled in spite of herself. "I suppose the advice was free too?"

"Well, yes—yes, of course it was!" he sputtered.

Bonnie sighed, pulling some eggs out of the fridge. "I guess you get what you pay for."

And in Bonnie's opinion, it *was* lousy advice, because it was obvious to her that Lynx didn't need her or anything she could do for him. He didn't need anything but his precious solitude and the chance to rock Shaulla—and something to eat once in a while.

She was beginning to not only need him again, but want him and crave him. When she looked at Lynx, all she could think about was kissing those lips, running her fingers through his curls, and holding his purring body close to her own. She was jealous of Shaulla, because she got to do those things. Not the way Bonnie would have, perhaps, but Bonnie had seen Ulla grasp his hair in her tiny fists, and he held her so closely. Bonnie would never get the chance unless she charged Lynx a hug or a kiss before she let him hold Ulla, and she wasn't even sure she could get it then.

Lynx knew what she was feeling, too. Bonnie was feeding the enocks one morning while he gathered the eggs, and something in the way he moved triggered her emotions. Within moments, his head went up and his nostrils flared. There it was again, he thought; her desire. Lynx breathed in the scent and waited for a response from his body, but none came. His lips hardened into a thin line as he turned away from her.

Bonnie saw his reaction and wanted to run away and hide—which is essentially what she did. Throwing the remainder of the feed at the birds, she turned and left so quickly, she nearly tripped over Kipper on the way back to the house.

Bonnie knew there was nothing she could do to make herself more attractive to him, either; the usual feminine wiles were useless on a man who disliked women. And besides, she didn't just want him to *make* love to her— she wanted him to *love* her.

Late one night, Bonnie was up feeding Ulla. Before she went back to bed, she went out to the kitchen for a drink, not bothering to turn on a light, for the moonlight lit her way quite well. If the moon hadn't been shining so brightly, Bonnie doubted that she'd have looked out, but when she did, she saw him.

Lynx was standing by the well pump, completely nude, though Bonnie only saw him from the rear. If she'd been jealous of her daughter before, Bonnie was now jealous of the moon, for its light caressed the contours of his perfect body in the same way she would have liked to touch him with her fingertips. Her only consolation as she watched the droplets of water fall from his skin was that she could stand there and watch, secure in her home, and know that he couldn't catch the scent of her desire wafting toward him with the evening breeze.

As Lynx leaned over to wash his hair, Bonnie was sure she would climax just from the sight of him. All of it was appealing to her on the most basic, elemental level and beyond. The line of his spine as it disappeared into his sculpted buttocks. The way his neck seemed to flow so perfectly into his broad shoulders. And his legs; tapered, muscular, and strong. Bonnie took that vision back to bed, dreaming of him; of the way he would feel, the way he would taste, the way he would touch her. She tried to remember how his body felt pressed tightly against her own while she had been in labor with Shaulla. It was the only memory she had, and she clung to it in desperation. Bonnie tried to imagine more, but kept coming back to what Jack had said about Cat. Did all Zetithians possess the same attributes? Could the fluids he secreted *really* induce orgasms? She'd never heard of a species that could do such things—and she'd heard quite a few tall tales! Sylor certainly had no remarkable abilities in that respect; making love with him had been no different than having sex with a human male. But Bonnie wasn't asking Lynx for that. She only wanted him to hold her and purr the way he had before. She didn't need orgasms to make her love him or want him. *He* was what made her want him, not some chemical reaction.

Then again, perhaps it *was* all chemical—or hormonal—and, given a couple of long, miserable years, it would all go away. Then she could look at his naked body in the moonlight and not care. In the meantime, charging him a hug or a kiss for holding Shaulla was sounding better all the time.

"Lynx," Bonnie whispered to the darkness. "You're a torment to me. Go away and leave me just like all the others have—and, please, do it soon, before I do something stupid."

Lynx stood up tall and shook the excess water from his hair. Glancing down at his penis where it hung from its nest of curling hair, he remembered a time when even cold water couldn't douse his need to mate. He hadn't understood why Bonnie had shut him out after Ulla was born. Holding a woman again had felt so good to him, and even watching the child emerge hadn't been quite as painful as it had been with the others, because he already knew there was no chance that this child could be his own. Still, he always held his breath at that moment when it might still be possible…

Beautiful mother and beautiful child. Lynx knew a moment of jealousy and hatred toward Bonnie's old boyfriend. Sylor should never have left her; a man who would abandon his own child was no better than a common criminal.

But if he had not left, I would not be here. Lynx pondered that for a while, thinking that it might have been easier. He might have gotten a job somewhere else—or been sent offworld—perhaps even back to Paemay. He didn't want to go there—too many bad memories were associated with that planet—but he'd worked and saved to pay his passage before; he could do it again.

Still, this was a nice world to live on; the climate was favorable, the shed he lived in was spacious and quiet, and the work was hard, but simple. If only there had been no females nearby, it would have been perfect.

But was that really true? There had been a time when Lynx loved women—all women, no matter their age or form or personality. He might not have understood their minds, but he loved their smiles, their laughter, and their songs. But that had been on Zetith. Women there were so indifferent to males—until you enticed one enough to become your mate, he reminded himself. Then it was lifelong and everlasting. It saddened him to think that they were all gone and had been gone for many years now. His mother, his sisters—all of them dead; all of those beautiful females, and their wonderful planet nothing but dust.

Nothing could bring them back again. He couldn't even mate with a human female the way his old friends had done in an effort to save the Zetithian race from total extinction. He was one of the last of his kind—and there was nothing he could do to perpetuate his line. Looking over his shoulder, he saw the moonlight reflected in the windows of Bonnie's home. No, there was nothing to be done; not even with a woman who desired him.

Chapter 11

DESPITE BONNIE'S WISH, LYNX NOT ONLY DIDN'T LEAVE, he didn't even mention the possibility. Bonnie didn't suggest it, either, just in case he might want to take Ulla with him when he left. He loved Ulla. It was evident every time he looked at her or touched her.

Bonnie resumed the rhythm of her life, taking back some of the chores that Lynx had assumed over the past few weeks in a futile attempt to get him out of her mind. Salan came by a few times and tried flirting with Lynx again—though after what he'd said to her when they first met, Bonnie was surprised she would even want speak to him—and received no more encouragement than she had before, though he was a bit more tactful. There weren't very many eligible bachelors in that locale, and though Lynx was an attractive creature, Bonnie wondered how anyone could be masochistic enough for another try once they'd been so flatly rejected, though it hadn't stopped Bonnie from wanting him, either. In an effort to cheer Salan up after a particularly disappointing visit, Bonnie confided to her that Lynx didn't like women in general, but doubted that it helped very much. Even though Bonnie knew how she felt, it was amusing and somehow comforting to sit back and watch Salan's thwarted attempts at seduction.

Another bright spot was a visit from Zuannis. She didn't get out that way very often, and when she called ahead, Bonnie knew she was in for some much needed entertainment.

After properly praising Shaulla to the skies, Zuannis had plenty of news to relay.

"And now," she began, with the air of one about to tell a tale of epic proportions, "the story of last week's market day—which you missed."

"Salan hinted at something when she was here last," Bonnie said, eager to hear more. "Something about Hatul?"

"Ah, yes," Zuannis said, laughing. "He went too far."

"Gerna left him?" Bonnie gasped.

"In a manner of speaking," Zuannis replied, her smile brimming with mischief. "She won't speak to him."

This didn't sound like much of a punishment to Bonnie, but then, she'd been getting the cold shoulder from Lynx for so long, perhaps she was becoming immune.

"So?"

"Oh, I was forgetting you didn't know. When a Norludian female won't open her mouth to speak, it's a sign that she is refusing sexual relations."

Bonnie sat for a moment, and Zuannis watched her anxiously, waiting for the implications to sink in. "They don't… *really*… do they?"

Zuannis smiled. "I should have told you before—but if you'll recall, you didn't want to hear any more."

"True," Bonnie admitted. "So, tell me all of it."

"Ever hear how a Norludian gives birth?"

"No," Bonnie replied. "But I would assume it's the same as for other species."

Zuannis shook her large bald head, making her earrings jingle merrily. "It's more like they regurgitate their young."

It didn't take long for Bonnie to figure out the rest. "So when they have sex, it's always… oral?"

Zuannis smiled. "That's right."

"So if the female won't talk… it's like saying 'You're not getting any'?"

"Exactly," Zuannis replied.

Having heard this, Bonnie thought she should stop talking to Hatul altogether, just so he wouldn't get the wrong idea—but it was fascinating that conversation of any kind constituted flirtation. She just wished it could have been as easy with Lynx. "So, who did he, um, do it with?"

"Do you mean to say you can't guess?"

Bonnie's laugh began with a small chuckle and then progressed to a full-blown bout of hysterical laughter. Eyes streaming with tears, she said, "Oh, my God! Not Salan!"

"The very same," Zuannis assured her. "You must understand; Norludians are not opposed to sex with other partners, provided the other mate approves."

"But Gerna has never liked Salan, has she?" Bonnie observed.

"Not one bit."

This made Bonnie laugh even harder. "That poor girl! She must really be getting desperate to say yes to Hatul! She still comes around and flirts with Lynx, even though he was openly insulting the first time they met."

"Poor girl," Zuannis echoed. "We should try to find someone for her."

"Who?" Bonnie said. "Wilisan's always been the best-looking man around here, but he's never seemed interested in her either, otherwise she wouldn't be so desperate. Know any miners?"

"None that are enough like her to be compatible," Zuannis said frankly. "You've seen them, haven't you? They're perfectly hideous!"

Bonnie *had* seen them, and the fact that most of them were Udeelans was a point she considered mentioning to Lynx, if for no other reason than to let him see what he was missing. Udeelans were slimy, smelly, albino hulks, nearly blind from living in darkness, and had hands the size of platters. Even the Norludians thought they were ugly, and they weren't terribly friendly, either. Bonnie couldn't imagine anyone—Salan included—who would want an Udeelan boyfriend, but then, Bonnie would never have encouraged Hatul, either.

"Not much hope, is there? Unless Gerna really does kick Hatul out."

"I don't think Salan truly enjoyed the event," Zuannis said dryly, "and I think that was part of Gerna's problem with the whole thing: she seemed to think that Salan should have appreciated it more and blamed Hatul for not choosing his lovers more wisely."

This insight had Bonnie laughing merrily once more, which did wonders for her morale. "That sounds so… *Norludian,* don't you think?"

Zuannis nodded, wondering just what it was about a particular Zetithian that made *him* so choosy about his lovers—Bonnie, specifically. Zuannis didn't think Lynx could have seen anything objectionable in her friend, but since she had an idea it might be a sore spot with Bonnie, she broached the subject very carefully.

"So, what does Lynx think of Shaulla?" Zuannis said casually—knowing that Lynx must have helped deliver the child. "Or does he think of her at all?"

"He likes her," Bonnie replied woodenly. "Even made her some toys and a crib."

Zuannis didn't miss Bonnie's abrupt change of mood. "Cat seems to be a very devoted father," she remarked, "and so is Leo."

Shaulla began to get fretful, and Zuannis handed her back to her mother. Kissing her daughter on the top of her head, Bonnie said, "Yes, I'm sure they all are, and Lynx is better at taking care of a baby than most women. Better than me, anyway. You should see him change a diaper."

Bonnie sighed—and the regret it contained wasn't lost on Zuannis. Apparently, it *was* a sore spot, and Salan wasn't the only one taken with Lynx.

Zuannis gazed at her friend, realizing that nothing had changed between Bonnie and Lynx—which was most unfortunate. With Cat and Leo as examples, Zuannis knew that Lynx could make Bonnie one of the happiest of women—unfortunately, it wasn't in her power to encourage that.

At this point, Bonnie wasn't looking for Lynx to be her lover; she'd have settled for a whole lot less than that. She was sitting in the shade of the peach tree one afternoon while Lynx held Ulla, clearly smitten with her, ignoring Bonnie completely. "Tell me something, Lynx. Is there a reason why we can't be friends?" she asked thoughtfully. "I know you work for me, but—"

"Women do not want men as friends," he said, not even bothering to look up from Ulla's face. "They want only lovers."

"That's not true!" Bonnie exclaimed. "I'm friends with lots of guys! Drummond, Mobray, Cat, Leo—I even like Hatul up to a point, and Wilisan is, well, *gorgeous,* even if he is a little too macho for my taste— what makes you so different?"

"I have no mate," he replied.

"Well, neither does Vladen," Bonnie said reasonably, "and I like him just fine—when he's not telling me things like forehead ridges might have caused trouble with Ulla's birth, that is—but I don't want *him* for my lover!"

Lynx turned his yellow eyes on Bonnie at last and inhaled deeply; the scent was still there. "But you want me," he said. "You say you want only a friend, but you lie. Your body tells the truth."

Bonnie knew he was right; she might not have been asking for it with words, but he knew differently. Pausing for a moment in an effort to regroup, Bonnie decided that if he knew the truth, there was no point in denying it. "Well, then, what's so wrong with wanting a man as a lover? Most guys like the idea."

"I do not," he said firmly. For a moment, she thought that might be all he had to say, but, surprisingly, he went on to add: "Women have only used me. I cannot love them."

Bonnie had been used plenty of times herself, but she could still feel something for Lynx, which led her to believe that he must have come through much worse times than she ever had. Still, his choice of words had her puzzled. "Can't or won't?"

The look he shot her almost drew blood, but he did answer her question. "Both."

With two couples as her example—as well as their re-
spective children to show as proof—Bonnie knew there
was no reason that your typical Zetithian couldn't mate
with a Terran, therefore, there had to be some other sort
of… problem. "I've got a pretty good idea as to why you
won't, but is the reason you *can't* physical or mental?"

"Both," he said again.

His tone of voice was sharp enough to make Bonnie
wish she hadn't asked, but it explained quite a bit. It
was her rotten luck with men coming back to haunt her.
She'd found a Zetithian dud, all right; one who not only
didn't like women but was impotent to boot! Then she
remembered that he'd been the slave of other slaves—
many of them female—and Bonnie had an idea that if
a man were to own a bunch of slave women, he would
prefer that they have his own offspring rather than that
of another slave. There were plenty of old tales about
eunuchs who guarded the harems of sultans. Bonnie had
only seen Lynx naked from the rear—was it possible
that he'd been castrated? Worse things had been done to
slaves throughout Earth's history alone. Who knew what
might happen on other alien worlds? It made her blood
run cold to think of it, but the possibility was there.

Bonnie tried to put it as delicately as possible.
"They didn't… *do* anything to you to make you that
way, did they?"

"They used me," he repeated.

"Used you?" she echoed. "How?"

"As a slave is used," he replied, biting off his words.

Bonnie knew she'd gotten him pretty well riled,
and was surprised he was still talking to her. Then she
realized that the fact that he was sitting on the ground

holding Ulla would have made stalking away rather
difficult, so she decided to press her advantage. "For
sex?" she asked, probing further. "How could they do
that if you weren't capable?"

"I was at one time!" he spat at her. "As capable as any
man, but they would not leave me alone—ever!"

"They?" she echoed. "You mean there was more
than one?"

At his nod, Bonnie exclaimed, "Good God, Lynx!
Most guys would *kill* to have a problem like that!" However, having said that, it occurred to her that every man
has his limits. "Just how many *were* there?"

"I do not know," he said. "Perhaps fifty or more at
any given time. They came and went. I stayed."

Bonnie stared at him, scarcely believing her ears.
"Fifty women? For how long?"

"I am not certain," he replied, "but I believe I was
with them for ten years—as the years were reckoned on
that planet," he added.

"Let me get this straight, Lynx," Bonnie said. "You
were a love slave to fifty women? For ten years?" She
tried to comprehend what it would have been like to
have been stuck servicing fifty men for that long, and
while she knew it wouldn't have taken quite as much
out of her as it would have for the reverse to be expected
of a man, she could understand him a little better now.
"Why the devil didn't you say so before?"

As soon as Bonnie said it, she knew it was a stupid
question. He didn't want to talk to her at all, let alone
tell her his life story.

Then she remembered what Jack had said about Cat's
sexual abilities. One *Zetithian* man in a harem? It was no

wonder they hadn't left him alone! They must have been after him night and day! No, he hadn't been castrated. They'd simply worn him out.

"How long ago was that, Lynx?"

"Another ten years have passed since I was sold to someone else," he replied, seemingly grateful to have moved on to a less sensitive topic.

"And why were you sold?"

He looked at Bonnie as though she'd lost her mind. "The women I served must have… complained," he replied, "for I was taken away and sold to a man who freed me after five years of service."

"And you still can't… do it," Bonnie said hesitantly. "Even after all this time?"

"No."

Bonnie's body might have been screaming at her, but her heart was even louder in its protests. She loved him anyway. This wasn't terribly surprising considering that, as things stood, she couldn't have him at all and still loved him. Sighing deeply, her voice wistful, she said, "Would it make any difference to you if I said it didn't matter?"

If he'd been holding anything other than Ulla, Bonnie believed he would have slammed it into the ground in frustration. "What do you *want* from me?" he demanded angrily. "I have done the work. I have helped with Shaulla's birth and her care—I have even helped you to name her. I can do no more than that."

"Probably not," Bonnie agreed sadly. "But the thing is… I love you, Lynx. God knows you've given me no encouragement, but there it is, whether we like it or not. You can't help who you fall in love with—no one can—and, believe me, I've fallen for the wrong men my whole life! It's something no one can predict, and quite honestly, I wish I *didn't* love you. It would make things so much easier."

His silence stretched out longer than it should have, and Ulla began to fret even more than she had when Lynx was so angry. Reaching out, Bonnie took Ulla from him.

"She's probably hungry," Bonnie said as she began to pull up her shirt, preparing to feed her.

Lynx didn't move.

Bonnie looked into his fiery feline eyes and saw no warmth there, no love returned, and no hope that there ever would be. "Go away," she whispered. "Leave me alone, now, please… That's something you *can* understand, isn't it? The wanting to be alone?"

And it was true: Bonnie *did* want to be alone—alone to hide her shame. She'd never told anyone she'd loved them before and then been so completely rejected and ignored. Not like that. Not without some sort of response.

Then Bonnie realized that she had never actually spoken those words before—at least, not to a man. Perhaps that was why she was so alone. She thought she might have said, "I love you, too" at one time or another, but had never been the one to say it first. She had always waited to hear the man say it before she risked saying it herself—and sometimes, those words were never uttered. This time was different, though, because she had volunteered the information, and it had gotten her nothing—nothing but a blank look from the man she claimed to love. She was mortified and desolate, knowing that Lynx would never even say, "I love you, too." In fact, he didn't say anything at all, but left her there in the shade while she nursed her daughter.

All Lynx could think as he walked away was that it served him right for being such a fool. He hadn't intended to tell Bonnie that he was incapable of being a lover to her, it had just popped out. How could he have let himself be goaded into revealing such a secret? She didn't need to know, and he didn't want her to know. It was better to let her think he didn't like her, not that he was only half a man.

And what had she said? That it didn't matter? Lynx believed it mattered more than anything. No woman wanted a man who couldn't function. He'd even been sold because of it.

But at least she hadn't laughed. He reminded himself that Bonnie had always been kind to him, even when he was being an ass—which made Lynx feel even worse, because telling her hadn't changed anything. He was still being nasty and rude to the one person who had ever shown him kindness.

And not only that, but she had claimed to love him—not just desire him, but love him! Lynx had no idea what to make of that. No one had ever told him such a thing before, and while he had to admit that he wasn't entirely opposed to the idea, he wasn't completely sure he believed her. As to why they couldn't be friends, the main reason was that most of the contact he'd had with women had been sexual in nature; just being friends with a woman wasn't something Lynx knew anything about.

Bonnie wondered just how much it had cost Lynx to admit his failings as a man—if you could call it a failing. Bonnie knew that Lynx had never asked to be anyone's love slave—let alone slave to more than fifty women!—and though it might have seemed like fun to a young man at first, he was to be commended, rather than condemned, for having lasted as long as he had. No one could have tolerated that forever; in his case, what was surely every man's dream had become a nightmare when translated into reality. Unfortunately, what Bonnie thought didn't seem to matter to him; she'd told him she loved him, in spite of everything he'd told her about himself, and he hadn't said a word.

Bonnie tried to convince herself that she didn't care, but she knew it was a lie because she *did* care, though not for the reason that he, or anyone else, might have expected. She cared because she *did* want something from him—and it wasn't just his love—she wanted what everyone else seemed to think she should want; she wanted his children.

And not even for herself. She wanted them because deep down, Bonnie believed that Lynx wanted them far more than she did. His love for Ulla was obvious, and she knew he would love his own children even more. Bonnie laughed bitterly, knowing that the one thing Lynx might have wanted from her was the one thing she couldn't give him. It was so ironic, so sad, and so unfair…

Vladen had said that Lynx was needy, but Bonnie wondered just how much he had actually known. As the regional physician, Vladen was required to do physical examinations on all immigrants to the sector, so if there had been a physical problem, he would have picked it up on the scanner and would, therefore, never have suggested that Lynx might be the one to father Bonnie's next child. If Vladen had known about it at all, he would therefore have had to assume that the cause was psychological, and that, given the right environment, Lynx's problem would correct itself. Unfortunately, Bonnie didn't think the right environment was to be found anywhere within a thousand kilometers of her house.

It occurred to her to consult Vladen in the matter, but Bonnie knew that as things stood, it was truly none of her business. It wasn't as though she'd been Lynx's wife or girlfriend who was facing an infertility problem. Bonnie was nothing more than his employer—an employer who ought to have known better than to fall in love with her own employee, much less told him about it. She hadn't intended to, but like so many things in life, it had simply happened.

The season progressed, and the rains became more infrequent. Bonnie went to the market in Nimbaza every week, taking Kipper and Ulla with her in the speeder and leaving Lynx behind to tend the farm. To Bonnie's surprise, Lynx seemed happier for some reason, and while she suspected it was from having finally told her something about himself, if Lynx had been asked, it was doubtful that he would have said the same thing. It might have helped to unburden himself—or even to know that he was loved—but he was also becoming more used to his life on Bonnie's farm, and, as he had always done, he took pride in his work—however mundane it might have seemed to anyone else.

Lynx loved coming up with new and better ways to do things around the farm. The enock pen was only the beginning, and he was streamlining work in ways Bonnie had never dreamed of, and also began looking ahead to anticipate any problems that might arise.

Bonnie saw Drummond and Zuannis at the market every week, but knew that Jack wouldn't be back for months. Bonnie and Salan kept right on trading eggs for cheese and butter, and everyone remarked on how beautiful Ulla was and how fast she was growing. That was one nice thing about having a baby along, Bonnie reflected—it gave you something neutral to discuss.

Vladen always followed up his quick assessment of Ulla by asking about Lynx, which made Bonnie wonder if he knew more than he let on. Perhaps he *had* seen something on the scanner.

"How's that Zetithian boy?" he would say—still referring to him as a boy. Bonnie thought he might have been right about that; perhaps Lynx had never truly grown up. She tried to imagine what she would be feeling, what kind of psychological scars she would carry with her always, had she been in a similar situation, and came to the conclusion that no one could overcome them unless they had their memory erased. Vladen had already suggested that the problem was either Bonnie or Lynx's nose, but it went much deeper than that. One thing was certain; the cookie dough ploy would never work again.

Lynx kept the equipment running smoothly and together they brought in Bonnie's best grain harvest ever.

The storage side of the shed was full, and there were buyers lined up for all that she didn't need for her own livestock. Zuannis had put in a large order for grain to make her bread, and Bonnie was looking forward to visiting her. It might have been a Twilianan bakery, but to Bonnie, it smelled every bit as heavenly as her favorite bakery on Earth. In anticipation of that sale, though it was a bit risky of her when she expected Lynx to resign each and every day, she bought some fencing materials and decided to have a go at capturing more enocks.

For this, she needed Lynx's assistance, and when Bonnie told him how she and Sylor had done it, while he might have *thought* it was suicidal—which was Bonnie's own opinion—no one could have guessed it from his neutral expression.

To catch an enock required a speeder that would fly about two meters off the ground carrying the weight of two people, as well as that of an adult enock—who tended to weigh in at about seventy-five kilos—suspended in a net beneath it. The speeder Sylor had taken could do it, but Bonnie wasn't so sure about the other one.

Lynx wasn't either. "It will not fly that high with the added weight," he said flatly. "The enock will be dragged and possibly injured—but I may be able to modify the speeder."

"That'd be great!" Bonnie said. "That fruit the enocks like so well is nearly ripe now, and pretty soon they'll be thick under the rabasha trees."

"Where are the trees?" he asked.

"You know that little grove in the northwest corner of the wheat field? Those are the rabashas." Bonnie had never gathered the fruit herself, mainly because the

enocks would have attacked her, but also because the
fruit smelled like it was rotting even when it wasn't.
Why the enocks liked it so well was beyond her compre-
hension, but then, they liked dead rats, too.

Lynx nodded, saying that he would see to it, leaving Bonnie to assume that he intended to work on the
speeder, and a few days later, he started work on the
new enock pen.

Not long after that, he knocked on the door one morning and asked Bonnie to come and pick out which enocks
she wanted to keep.

"What do you mean, which ones I want to keep?"

"There are a great many of them," he replied. "You
can be… selective."

Gazing back at him with a doubtful eye, she said,
"Show me."

A walk out to the new pen was all it took to demon-
strate his brilliantly simple plan. There were about thirty
enocks of all sizes in there, munching away on a big pile
of rabasha fruit. The stench was incredible, but from the
look of it, the fruit wouldn't last long.

"So, how did you manage to gather up the fruit without getting yourself killed?" she asked.

"I built a fence around the grove to keep them out,"
he replied.

Bonnie shook her head, saying ruefully, "And then
you just gathered it all up and lured the enocks in here
with it."

He nodded. "It seemed simpler than catching them
one at a time."

Bonnie started laughing then and didn't stop until
tears were streaming down her cheeks. "Sylor was *such*

an ass!" she exclaimed when she could speak again. "Always looking for the most exciting way of doing anything! When I think of all the times we nearly got ourselves killed catching those damn things with the speeder…" She paused, staring at the flock of enocks in awe. "What an absolutely brilliant idea!"

Then another problem occurred to her. "You said I could be selective," she reminded him. "We only need one male in each pen. How do we get the other males out of there?"

Lynx had a plan for that too. "The females are attracted to my purring," he said. "I will lure them into the feeding area and then open the main pen with this," he said, holding up a remote control he had rigged to open the gate, "and when all but one of the males is out, I will close it again."

"But if you're outside the pen, how will you keep from being attacked?"

"The males will not attack me if I give them more of the fruit."

"Or dead rats," she suggested. Gazing up at Lynx with frank admiration, Bonnie felt a strong desire to hug him—stronger than usual, that is—but somehow managed to suppress the urge. "I knew the enocks were more docile when you purr, but I didn't realize that the females were actually *attracted* by it. Seems women of all species take to you, Lynx," she remarked. She started to add, "Too bad you don't return the favor," and nearly had to bite her tongue off in an effort to leave those words unsaid.

A moment later, she was glad she'd managed to keep her mouth shut because, to her complete surprise, Lynx responded with the most naturally male gesture she'd yet to see him use. Shrugging his shoulders in a rather self-deprecating fashion, a hint of a smile touched his lips, making him appear to be almost pleased. Bonnie thought she might pass out from the shock, and it made her wish she'd been looking at Lynx instead of the enocks when she'd referred to his idea as being brilliant.

Unfortunately, it wasn't long before Bonnie was sure she'd imagined all of it. He'd leaned toward her for the briefest instant before his face quickly became the same unreadable mask as always. If any woman had ever really seen him smile, Bonnie was certain that it must have been Ulla—and it also had to have been when no one else was looking. Her feeling of disappointment was like a swift slice right to the bone, and this time, she couldn't keep the words to herself.

"Oh, please, don't spoil it," she whispered softly as she turned away from him. Taking a deep breath to ease the pain in her heart, Bonnie leaned against the fence and stared blankly at the ground. "You've done a great job here, Lynx," she said, unable to keep the bitterness out of her voice. "I'll have to pay you a big, fat bonus— maybe triple your usual salary."

Bonnie looked up in time to note that his wooden expression had been replaced with one of utter mystification. She didn't even want to attempt to explain. It was too damned hard.

Lynx had just gone through such a range of emotions that he didn't know *what* he was feeling. Her praise had washed over him like a balm, and his initial impulse was to gather her up in his arms and kiss her. He'd been about to do just that when the knowledge that he couldn't—or shouldn't—do anything of the kind had slammed into him like a hammer. However, Bonnie hadn't taken more than two steps toward the house when Lynx did something he hadn't done in months. He actually touched her. Grabbing hold of her arm, he spun her around to face him, fully intending to kiss her like she'd never been kissed before.

Glaring up at him, she said, "What's the matter? Won't money be enough?—or do you only want my firstborn child?"

He gaped at her as though she'd slapped him. "I—yes, the money will be more than enough—you do not need to—"

"Then let go of me!" Bonnie growled, gripping his arm to push him away with her free hand. She felt something there—something familiar, yet also something that shouldn't have been necessary for someone like him. It took a moment for Bonnie's brain to register the implications and then she froze, staring at him in disbelief. "You lied to me!" she whispered fiercely.

Lynx looked completely bewildered. "I have not."

"Yes, you have!" she insisted. "'I cannot be your lover,' you said! That's bullshit! Here I've been feeling sorry for you and thinking that the way you dote on Ulla, you must want children of your own more than anything in the world, and you've got one of *those* things in your arm!" Bonnie wished she'd paid more attention to some of Jack's more colorful expressions, because they would have come in handy, but just then, she couldn't think of anything bad enough to call him. "Impotent, my foot! An impotent man wouldn't need something like that!"

"Do you mean *this?*" he asked, touching the inside of his upper arm. "It was placed there when I was enslaved. I—I was told never to remove it. I have never known its purpose."

Bonnie stared at him in disbelief. "What kind of backworld moron do you think I am?" she demanded. "Granted, they're a bit antiquated, but lots of guys still use them."

His baffled expression was downright ludicrous, which led Bonnie to conclude that Lynx was either a darn good actor or he was telling her the truth.

"Do you mean to say that you really don't know?"

He nodded apprehensively.

"It's a form of birth control, Lynx," she explained. "Sylor had one when I first met him—and let me tell you, it took some doing to talk him into having it removed! It makes men sterile—you can still function normally, but you sure as hell won't father any children!"

Lynx blinked a couple of times and started to speak, but no words came out. Bonnie had never seen a man look so completely shattered—like he was about to rupture something vital, or already had. Still gripping her arm, he held her away from him for a long moment, and then bent over at the waist, gasping for air before dropping to his knees with a groan.

Bonnie's first thought was that he was dying. It was rare, but humans had been known to die from shock—maybe Zetithians did it more often. How could she have known it would kill him?

"Lynx!" Bonnie cried. "Lynx, I'm sorry—I shouldn't have said it like that! Are you okay?"

"No," he replied, his lips forming the word without his throat uttering a sound. Releasing the death grip he had on her arm, he fell forward, his arms stretched out in front of him as if in supplication. When he spoke again, his words were audible, but they were unintelligible—horrible, strangled sounds that disturbed even the enocks. Bonnie didn't have any idea what to do, but Kipper stepped closer to him and tried to lick him in the face. Lynx didn't even seem to notice.

Knowing that he always wanted to be left alone, Bonnie thought it best to leave him, but her feet seemed to be rooted to the ground. Taking Lynx by the shoulders and shouting his name in a desperate attempt to get his attention, Bonnie rolled him over onto his side.

Lynx was still muttering in an unknown language, his eyes staring straight ahead without focus, and though she had no idea what made her do it—actually, she was thinking of slapping him across the face to bring him to his senses—but perhaps knowing that she might not ever get another chance, Bonnie took his face in her hands and planted a firm kiss right on his warm, succulent lips.

Whoa, bad move, Bon-bon! was Bonnie's last thought as his arm flailed wildly and slammed against her jaw. Everything went black.

Lynx felt like the mass of the entire galaxy was pressing down on him. He couldn't think, couldn't breathe, couldn't even see what was right in front of his face. Anger, horror, and regret were all flooding through his mind at once, filling him with raw emotion. Something took hold of him, and he struck back at it blindly, not even knowing what it was. His mind was splitting apart;

all that he had believed to be true before was now being cast aside by this new truth.

When the flood subsided at last, he heard a voice telling him to forget his past and to go on with his life. There was something else he had to do… he didn't know what, but there was something… He was floating above his body, looking down on himself, lying in the grass next to another inert body.

Bonnie! he thought wildly. *What have I done?*

His essence fanned out and then condensed and dove back into his mind. Within moments, he could feel again, could see and hear, and could move his limbs. Pulling Bonnie into his arms he felt something settle in his chest; a feeling so completely alien to him that he couldn't identify or even begin to describe it.

Remorse and regret filled him, soon to be replaced by anger—at himself and at everyone else. He could now see what his suppressed rage had been doing to him—causing him to lash out against everyone around him. Everyone but small children too innocent to understand contempt. He had always been kind to Ulla; there was nothing for her to forgive, but Bonnie was a different story…

Lynx had vowed not to become indebted to her, had captured a whole herd of enocks to make certain of it, but, in truth, there was nothing he could do for her, nothing he could give her that could outweigh the debt he already owed her, which was nothing less than his life.

Chapter 12

LYNX HAD KNOCKED HER OUT COLD, BUT WHEN BONNIE came to her senses, Lynx had obviously come to his, and, better yet, he was holding her in his arms. Not purring, perhaps, but definitely holding her. Bonnie lay with her eyes closed, doing her best not to reach up and rub her jaw. She had no intention of jumping up and yelling at Lynx for hitting her, since it had been accidental, anyway; all she wanted to do was to lie there and enjoy it, pain and all. Bonnie could feel his warmth, feel him breathing, and hear his heart beating. She wondered how long she could feign unconsciousness before he became suspicious. Not long, she decided, since her "desire" must have been almost to the smellable phase by then. She tried to think about something else.

Vladen! Vladen must have seen the implant on his scan and, therefore, it would never have occurred to him that Lynx would have had any performance difficulties when it came to sex. He must also have assumed that Lynx understood its purpose and would ask to have it removed if he and Bonnie ever intended to have a child together. Bonnie knew that anything physical would have shown up; she had never heard of one of those scans missing much of anything; they would even light up for an ingrown toenail.

Bonnie tried to visualize vicious enocks and rotten peaches and anything else she could think of to kill her desire, but it was probably already too late. Her only hope was that he might assume it was some sort of residual scent and not drop her like a hot potato. Even knowing the risks, Bonnie couldn't seem to stop herself and shifted closer to him, her ear pressed against his chest. She listened to his heart—still beating rapidly, but slowing down as he relaxed. Bonnie fought the urge to sigh and forced her hands to remain where they were, though this wasn't too much of a hardship, since one of them lay across his outstretched thigh.

Lynx began to whisper, but she couldn't understand him. It could have been Zetithian or Paemayan, for all she knew. Bonnie didn't know which one would come more naturally to him, but it didn't matter. The fact that she couldn't understand him left her free to imagine what he might be saying. He could have been whispering words of love—his voice certainly sounded soft and tender—or he could have been beseeching whatever god he worshiped to deliver him from the evil that was womankind.

Bonnie was finding it difficult to pretend to be out cold while trying very hard not to cry, but her tears gave her away as they ran down his chest. She knew the moment he realized it, for his heart rate quickened abruptly, and she let out a sob, knowing that her moment of peace and joy had come to an end.

"Are you okay now?" she asked, surprised that she was able to move her jaw enough to speak—and also that her voice sounded reasonably normal.

"I should be the one asking you that," he said. "You are the one who was hurt—not I."

"Not really," Bonnie disagreed. "You've already been hurt more in your lifetime than I could possibly imagine."

"I have rarely been injured," he said stiffly.

No, Bonnie thought grimly, *just practically fucked to death.* "Yeah, well, pain isn't always physical."

Lynx shifted his weight behind her, and Bonnie knew her little respite was over. Bowing to the inevitable, she sat up. She felt slightly light-headed, and her jaw ached like an enock had kicked her, but she stood up anyway. Turning around, she looked down at him, sitting there in the grass.

"I am sorry you were hurt," he said, his voice slightly softer. "It was not… intentional."

"I know that," Bonnie sighed. Looking over at the pen she noticed that the enocks had eaten nearly all the rabasha fruit. "Thanks again for the enocks," she said lightly. "I'll pay you that bonus as soon as I can."

He nodded but didn't look up. "Whatever you wish," he said in a wooden voice. "It does not matter to me."

Bonnie didn't think much of anything mattered to him, and she wondered why he'd gone to all that trouble and built all those fences. Was it only because she'd asked? Or because he wanted to prove something? *God only knows,* she thought wearily. *I certainly never will.*

When Bonnie returned to the house, Ulla was awake and screaming her hungry little head off. Bonnie picked her up, gave her a big hug and a smooch, got a charming chuckle out of her when she tickled Ulla's tummy, changed her diaper, and then sat down to feed her. That was one nice thing about breast-feeding: it gave her plenty of time to ponder just about anything.

Poor Lynx! She'd already told him she loved him, and now she'd kissed him! She rubbed her jaw, wondering if it was truly worth the pain, and came to the conclusion that it probably was. First her right arm, and now a few loose teeth—not to mention the nearly continuous heartache. The old sages hadn't been kidding when they said love hurts. They knew *exactly* what they were talking about.

Sylor had hurt her, too, but at least he'd left her Ulla. Gazing down at her daughter's adorable little face, Bonnie felt all the motherly love a woman was capable of and knew that Lynx looked at Ulla in almost the same way. *Lucky little Ulla,* she thought. *You've got two of us to love you. Too bad it can't all be hearts and flowers.*

Romance. When was the last time Bonnie had had a little romance? Upon reflection she decided that she probably never had. She'd had boyfriends and lovers, but had never been showered with gifts or wined and dined—possibly because she was too practical. She only wanted things she could use, like—

Her thoughts broke off there as realization slammed her upside the head with as much force as Lynx's arm. Things she could use—like a whole pen full of enocks! Lynx *had* given her a gift, and a terribly useful one at that.

Bonnie tried to remember what she'd said to him. Had she been properly appreciative? Or had *she* been the one to say the wrong thing and spoil it? No, she decided, that wasn't how it happened; it was Lynx's change of expression that ruined everything. *Then* she'd offered to pay him a bonus. And what had he done but make some sort of incoherent protest? Had he seen the birds as a gift? And if so, why?

Any answers Bonnie could come up with were unsatisfactory at best. Lynx might have been trying to get a raise, or might have been trying to butter her up for something, but she had no idea what. Bonnie knew that he could have asked her for anything, and she'd have given it to him; she already owed him more than she could ever repay. She already loved him, too—had even told him it didn't matter that they could never be lovers in the usual sense.

It hurt her to think that the only thing Lynx might have wanted from her would be for her to *stop* loving him. But if that was what he'd truly wanted, he'd certainly picked a strange way to go about doing it. When Bonnie looked out a bit later, she noticed that the male enocks had already been thinned out of the flock and were now outside the pen, eating the rabasha fruit. Was there anything that man couldn't do? He was inventive, resourceful, and wasn't above doing a little hard work. In Bonnie's opinion, he was darn near perfect.

This was also Lynx's opinion of Bonnie. How many women would have asked *him* how he felt after they'd been knocked senseless? Very few, he was certain, and now he owed her again—for so many things. She'd enabled him to see himself as a normal man at last. Not now, perhaps, but he had been at one time. He cursed himself for never realizing the implant's purpose. How could he have been so stupid?

Throwing himself into his work, he tried to silence his mind, but the torment was unrelenting. He had to repay her again… somehow.

With the enocks safe in the feeding area, he cleaned the pen and then spread the manure on the garden and under the fruit trees. The sun was hot, and it was hard work, but he didn't care. The pain in his muscles might help to drive out the pain in his heart but it couldn't stop the words that kept running through his mind. *I could have fathered children. I could have, once—but no more.*

By day's end, Lynx was exhausted but no closer to a solution, nor could he feel any peace returning to his mind. He dreaded the coming night, knowing that even if he did sleep—which was unlikely—it wouldn't ease his pain; his nightmares would haunt him.

That was when he smelled the smoke.

For Bonnie, the day had dragged on, oppressive in its heat. She did all the normal, ordinary things she would have done on any given day, yet all the time knowing that nothing would ever be the same again.

The wind had begun to pick up, blowing in gusts out of the northwest, and Bonnie could see the dust whipping around in the original enock pen. It hadn't rained in over a month, and the rainy season was about to start—with a big bang, apparently. She could rest easy knowing that they'd gotten the crops in before it rained—though she would have been happier with the grain delivered and the money in the bank at Nimbaza. She'd be able to pay Lynx that bonus too.

It was getting near dark when her comlink began beeping. The regional weather control in Nimbaza was issuing a warning about a fire headed their way. Looking out, Bonnie could see that the entire northwestern horizon was ablaze—and the wind was whipping it right toward her.

Bonnie's first thought was that at least her crop was in storage behind the firebreak and not still out in the field. Lynx had tilled the firebreak right after the harvest and there was now only stubble in the fields so, with any luck, the fire should go around them.

But Bonnie couldn't afford to count on luck. Tucking Ulla into her crib, she ran out, shouting for Lynx. The wind was blowing so hard, she could barely move forward against it—and it was blowing straight at the house. The air was already scented with smoke, and she screamed again for Lynx, who was nowhere in sight.

It was possible that the rain might catch up with the fire and put it out, but Bonnie knew she couldn't count on that, either. The firebreak was the regulation width plus a little more, but did those guys really know what they were talking about when they'd made that regulation? Had they tested it in a real fire, with a fierce wind blowing it on?

She doubted it. They'd done a great job getting things started on Terra Minor, but there were always mistakes and oversights, and theory didn't always work well in practice.

She spotted Lynx over by the water tower, which she knew was nearly empty. The dry season had been even drier than usual, and they'd had to irrigate the fields more often than she would have liked. The pond by the shed was still reasonably full, and Lynx had been mulching the trees with enock dung, which had some remarkable water-holding properties, so they'd had to water them less. *Maybe we should make a study of it,* Bonnie thought, as her mind took a strange turn. *Publish a treatise on the virtues of enock dung and then make a mint selling it.* She let out a cynical laugh, thinking about the odd things that come to mind when you know you're about to lose everything.

"Lynx!" she yelled. "What are you doing?"

"I pumped more water into the tower after the last crops came in," he said, shouting to make himself heard above the wind. "There should be enough to flood the field. I thought about this when I worked on the firebreak. With this much wind, it will not be enough to stop the fire from reaching the house."

"That's what I thought too," Bonnie yelled back. "How are you planning to do it?"

"I disconnected the irrigation lines to the field," he shouted. "The water will pool about twenty meters out."

Bonnie looked across the field as the fire raced toward them. "You think of everything, don't you?" she remarked almost absently.

Lynx didn't reply but switched on the pumps. "We can pump more water into the tank, but that might take too long. Get the line that goes to the garden and get ready to soak anything that catches fire on this side of the firebreak."

The buildings were made of materials treated with a flame retardant—another regulation for living on the savanna—but it was only a retardant and wasn't completely foolproof—or fireproof. Given time and enough heat, it would burn just like anything else.

"So this is what you do out there in the shed all alone at night? Think up things like how to catch enocks and put out fires?"

"Yes," he said shortly. "Now, move!"

Running to the garden, she uncoupled the heavy hose from the lines to the plants and put on a smaller line that

she used for other parts of the yard. It would blow up in
her hands if the pressure was too high, but she switched
the pump full on and dragged the hose out toward the
enock pen.

The enocks were agitated, flapping their wings and
running back and forth in the pen. If the fire got too close,
she would have to let them go. Fortunately, aside from the
fence that surrounded them, there wasn't much in the pen
that would burn, except the birds, and Bonnie didn't care
to watch them get roasted alive, not even the big male that
had nearly taken her arm off. *Well, maybe I* would *sacrifice him,* she thought grimly, *but not the females.*

Kipper was racing around like a madman, barking
his head off. The chickens were in the henhouse, which
was small comfort, since it would go up like a pile of
kindling if the fire ever reached it—as would the grain,
and as much as there was in the shed, it would probably smolder for months. Bonnie fought the urge to hose
down the shed, knowing that water wasted now would
mean there might be none to put out the sparks that
would surely fly on the wind ahead of the fire.

The flames drew nearer, sending smoke billowing
into the sky. Lynx stood still for a moment, staring out at
the fire, before suddenly jumping down from his perch
on the tower to run through the field of stubble.

"What are you doing?" Bonnie screamed. The fire
was almost on him. Something must have been jammed,
because she could see him swinging an ax to chop
through the line. Then the water burst out like a foun-
tain, and she couldn't see him anymore.

Sparks were flying everywhere, carried toward her
on the wind. The smoke burned her lungs and enveloped

the entire compound in a hot, dense cloud. She couldn't see Lynx at all and could barely see the house. Then she saw flames and aimed her hose. The fire went out immediately, only to be replaced by another, and another. *My God, they're everywhere!* Bonnie kept on spraying; trying to see, trying to breathe. She had no clue as to where she was, let alone the direction she was facing.

The enocks were going wild; Bonnie could hear them, squawking like a bunch of dying chickens. Turning toward the sound, she could see that some of their feathers must have caught fire, and she was heading toward them when she caught sight of Lynx inside the pen, hitting them with his shirt to smother the flames. She let out a scream, terrified that the enocks would turn on him. Bonnie ran to the gate, dragging her hose.

"Get out of there!" she screamed at him. "They'll kill you!"

In that moment, the air seemed to clear as the fire began to pass around them. Lynx ran toward the gate with the big male at his heels. Bonnie shot the bird with a stream of water, diverting his attention long enough for Lynx to escape.

Slamming the gate closed, Bonnie screamed again as lightning struck and the sky opened up, deluging them with rain. In the glare of the lightning and the roll of thunder that followed, she could see Lynx standing there with rivulets of water coursing down his bare, heaving chest. As she stood gulping the cool, moist air into her burning lungs, her only thought was that Lynx was hers. *I damn near gave my right arm for him, I've fought fire and enocks for him, and he is mine!* Running to him, she flung her arms around his neck, and, pulling him down, kissed him fiercely.

While the storm raged all around them, she clung to his hot, wet body, tasting his lips at last. He smelled of smoke and rain and sweat, and Bonnie twisted her fingers into his hair, refusing to let go. Someday, she would pay for this. Someday, she would be watching him walk away as he had done in her dream, but that would not happen on *this* day. No, on this day, she vowed, he is *mine!*

Somewhere in the back of her mind, Bonnie knew that her logic was faulty, but she didn't care. Kissing him for all she was worth, she pushed her tongue past his sharp fangs, not caring if he bit her; it was worth the risk.

Feeling his hands at her waist, she paused for a moment, knowing that this was the end, and he would push her away now. All of her love for him came crashing down. Crying out in anguished protest against his lips, she cursed the day she'd met him, but with her next breath swore her undying love.

"Don't you dare push me away!" she screamed at him. "I love you so much, Lynx! No one could ever love you more, but it doesn't matter to you, does it? *Nothing* matters to you, and I hate you for that! Go on! Leave here now and take your precious solitude with you!" Giving him a shove, she turned to go back to the house—back to her home, her child, and her life of loneliness.

For the second time that day, Lynx caught her by the arm. She tried to wrestle away from him, but he held her fast, just as the enock had done on the day they'd first met. Bonnie swore at him, pounding on his chest with her free hand, trying desperately to escape. Despite his superior strength, she twisted away from him somehow—and ran.

But Lynx wasn't about to let her go. He hadn't been trying to push her away, he'd been about to take her in his arms and kiss her the way he'd ached to kiss her for so long... Running after her, he caught her arm just as she tripped and fell, pulling him down on top of her.

Bonnie began to fear for her life; she'd pushed him too far, and now she was sure he would have his revenge on all women by killing her. Kicking and screaming, Bonnie swung at him with all her might, wishing she had something—anything—to fight back with. Her strength was beginning to desert her when, suddenly, in a flash of lightning, she could see his face clearly, his yellow eyes blazing down at her out of the storm. His fangs gleamed like pearl daggers, and she could almost feel them ripping out her throat. Then, as the thunder rolled, his head descended. With a growl that she felt more than heard, his tongue swiped across her parted lips and then thrust past them.

It took several moments before Bonnie's astonished brain caught up with her lips and realized that she was being kissed rather than killed. As she kissed him back, sucking hard on his tongue and teasing his lips, she felt desire building as her fears drifted into nothingness. Lynx released his hold on her arms, and she wrapped them around his neck. Their love-hungry souls met, and they kissed like thwarted lovers who had never kissed before: with fierce, demanding, terrifying passion.

"I'm sorry!" she gasped. "I didn't mean it... please... don't ever leave me. I love you." Bonnie's voice trailed off as his lips found hers once more as the darkness of night fell.

Caring nothing for his reply, she only wanted him to keep kissing her until she died. Lynx might not be capable of sex, but he could kiss, and Bonnie couldn't fault him on the way he did it, either—except that he stopped much too soon.

"You need to get inside," he said roughly. "Ulla may need you."

This was where she'd been headed when he'd stopped her so unceremoniously, but she ignored that, saying only, "If I do go inside, you're coming with me."

"Bonnie, I can't—"

"Don't say it," she pleaded. "I already know why you *think* you can't, but, please believe me when I say it doesn't matter! I want you, Lynx, and I don't care what you can or can't do. I only know that I want you in my arms, in my house, in my bed… and most of all, in my life."

"But I *am* in your life," Lynx protested, his body sagging with weariness. He'd tried so hard to resist… and had failed miserably. "I have tried not to be, but I am."

Getting to her feet, Bonnie held out her hand. "Come on, then. Let's get inside where it's warm and dry and we can talk about it."

Lynx stared out her outstretched hand as though he dared not touch it. Not meeting her eye, he said, "You will not be… disappointed… that we cannot be lovers?"

"Maybe a little," Bonnie admitted. "I'd like to be able to touch you and hold you as much as I want, but right now, I'll take anything I can get, even if it's just being in the same room with you. Honestly, Lynx. That's all I need."

But it certainly wasn't all she got.

Chapter 13

LYNX KNEW THE MOMENT HE LOST CONTROL. Somewhere in the blazing inferno filled with suffocating smoke and horror, he heard her voice calling out to him, and his body reacted without thought or direction; he went to her—came when she called—just as he always did. And now he knew why. It wasn't from having been a slave, conditioned to responding quickly to a summons. It was because he loved her. There in the midst of chaos, it became so clear to him; the entire pretense, all the denial had been pointless. He was sure he'd fallen in love with her the first moment he saw her about to be torn apart by those vicious birds.

He'd gone to her rescue then, just as he had every time she needed anything. Anything she mentioned— and anything he thought she might want or need—he gave to her, telling himself that it was to keep her in his debt. He knew now that he'd been lying to himself from the very beginning. He hadn't been angry with her for being foolish enough to risk her life for a chicken; he'd only been terrified of what might have happened had he chanced upon her a few moments too late.

She still had hold of his hand, or this revelation might have caused him to fall into another fit. He felt the tug of her grasp, warm and strong, as though she was the anchor that kept him secure and centered in this world, not letting him go careening off into insanity.

"You're sure you're all right?" she whispered. "Not burned or anything?"

Lynx shook his head, not trusting himself to speak yet.

Had she meant those words she'd said before? That she only wanted to be in the same room with him? It was difficult for Lynx to comprehend that anyone could feel that way about him, because if anyone else ever had, he certainly couldn't remember it. People, especially women, always wanted something from him, something more than just himself. They wanted him for what he was capable of, the tasks he could complete, the machinery he could repair, the sexual gratification he could provide. Had he ever been wanted just for himself? He didn't think so. Bonnie was unique in that respect—and in so many other ways as well…

Perhaps the most amazing thing about that night was that Ulla had slept right through the fire and the storm. Bonnie listened for her cries as she carefully opened the door and, hearing no sound other than her occasional contented sigh, slipped inside, pulling Lynx in behind her. Dripping wet and smelling of smoke and rain, the first thing she wanted was a shower, and she wanted to have it with Lynx.

Bonnie might have kissed him and held him, but she still hadn't caught him with his pants off. His shirt must have been out by the enock pen—or even inside it— and since he'd used it to douse the flames, it was doubtful that he would ever wear it again. His pants weren't in much better shape, and Bonnie's own clothes were dotted with holes from sparks she hadn't known had touched them. Tiptoeing through the kitchen so as not to wake Ulla, Bonnie led Lynx into the bathroom and, closing the door, flipped on the light.

He looked wild. His hair was a mass of wet, spiral curls, and his face and torso were streaked with soot and rain. Bonnie had seldom seen him up close without his shirt, but even wet and dirty, he looked seductive. She caught a glimpse of passion simmering in his eyes.

Bonnie didn't fully understand what had happened to suddenly change the way Lynx acted toward her. That kiss had been completely unexpected. She tried to think back, to come up with a reason or a time when she thought he might have changed toward her, but couldn't put her finger on it. Perhaps he hadn't changed; perhaps something was wrong with him.

"Are you *sure* you're okay?" she asked, peering up at him tentatively. "I mean, you didn't get kicked in the head by an enock or struck by lightning—did you?"

"I am uninjured," he replied. This was a bit of an understatement, since not only did he appear to be uninjured, but looked like every woman's wildest erotic fantasy.

"Then would you mind explaining this sudden change of attitude? This morning I wound up getting hurt when I kissed you, which, given your previous attitude toward me, I could have expected—"

"I did not intend—"

"To hit me? I know you didn't, but tonight was so completely different. I'm not sorry it turned out this way, but I *am* a little confused."

Lynx looked uncomfortable and tried to say something to explain but seemed to have trouble finding the words.

"Can't explain it, huh?"

Shaking his head, he said softly, "No, I cannot. I only know that I feel… differently… toward you than

I have for any other woman." To tell her he loved her now would have been too sudden, too pat an answer. He would wait.

"Yeah, well, I can't explain why I feel the way I do either," Bonnie said candidly. "It isn't as though you've ever been friendly or anything."

"It is... difficult," he said. "I thought you would be like the others, but you—" Lynx broke off there, throwing up his hands in a gesture of utter futility. "—are not."

"Well, it's nice to know I'm not anything like your typical harem girl," Bonnie said agreeably, but noticed that the fire had gone out of his eyes. It wasn't his usual stoic expression, but still... The words were difficult to utter, but she knew she had to say them. "Lynx, would you rather go back out to the shed for the night? I may have been a bit... premature in bringing you in here."

His expression grew wary, and his voice sounded hollow when he replied. "I will do as you wish."

"What I wish is immaterial right now," Bonnie said evenly, hoping she was saying the right thing—for once. "The question is, what do *you* wish?"

His gaze dropped to the floor. "I wish to stay and give you joy," he said. Looking up, he added, "But I know that I cannot."

"Yes, you can," she whispered. "In fact, you may have done it already."

He seemed puzzled by this. "But I have not mated with you," he protested, "and I—"

"Lynx," she said earnestly, cutting off his protests, "I'd trade all the enocks on this whole damn planet just for the chance to see you smile—and to hear you laugh would bring me the greatest joy I can possibly imagine."

Lynx stood there gaping at her in disbelief. This was not at all what he'd expected her to say. "But my laughter is worth nothing," he said.

"Not to me."

He shook his head, seeming to find it difficult to believe that such a plain and simple thing would matter to her—or to anyone; he was used to being asked for a great deal more than a smile.

"Lynx," she said gently, trying to explain, "what I'm trying to say is that I want you to be happy. Nothing more, nothing less. You've said before that you only want peace and solitude, but, tell me truthfully: is that *really* all you want? Isn't there something else you dream about and wish for?"

It took him a long time to form his reply. Lynx knew what he wanted, but he also knew that it was no longer possible. "What I want most of all, I cannot have," he said at last. "It is useless to wish for it."

He went no further with his answer, which left Bonnie to assume that whatever he wanted was something she couldn't give him. His face gave nothing away, and Bonnie wanted to kick herself because, while this conversation hadn't been without merit, it had certainly killed the mood. *I should have kept my mouth shut,* she thought. *Just stripped him down, pushed him in the shower, and asked questions later.*

"And I suppose peace and solitude come right after that—whatever it is." Sighing regretfully, she said, "Well, go on, then. Take a nice, hot shower, and I'll try to find you something dry to wear." Actually, she had already made more clothes for him, but so far hadn't felt masochistic enough to give them to him. Lynx made no gesture of protest, nor did he say a word as she left the room.

It took Lynx a few moments to realize she'd given up again. She was so beautiful, so kind, and he wanted to give her everything, including his love, but he didn't know how.

Shaking his head as though doing so might help him think more clearly, he was recalled to his surroundings. Lynx had never been in such a room before. He had noted her gesture and moved closer to the bathtub, turning knobs at random. The water grew warm and then hot. With the instinct of a born mechanic, he had it figured out in seconds. Removing what was left of his clothing, he stepped beneath the spray and let out an ecstatic groan. The cookies had nearly robbed him of speech, but to someone who had always had to bathe in cold water, this went far beyond that. Lynx thought he would have to build her another enock pen as payment for this treat. *No, you don't have to do that anymore,* he told himself. *She wants you, not a fence.*

Still not believing it fully, he picked up the soap. It was the same as what she had given him to use; proving that, even then, she had considered him her equal. The concept of equality was the one he'd had difficulty grasping since earning his freedom. The conditioning of his mind had been very thorough in that respect. Would he ever feel that anything was his due, rather than a treat tossed to him the way you would reward a dog? He certainly hoped so.

Stripping off her own sodden garments, Bonnie put on
a robe and then took down the clothes she had made for
Lynx from the shelf where she had laid them, not knowing when she would ever give them to him—if indeed
she ever would. They weren't fancy but were made from
heavy, unbleached cotton, comfortable and sturdy. Lynx
had never explained why he wouldn't wear the others—
though it was possible that they simply didn't fit him. If
that was the case, she thought miserably, he wouldn't be
able to wear these, either. She wished he would tell her,
because she was tired of trying to figure everything out
for herself. Those quiet, uncommunicative types were
hard to deal with; they left you guessing their motives
at every turn.

With any other man, Bonnie would have slipped out
of her robe and climbed into the shower with him, knowing that he would understand the gesture and respond in
kind. She wasn't sure she could count on that with Lynx,
who had undoubtedly seen plenty of unclothed females
in his lifetime—what was one more? But if he truly felt
differently toward her, perhaps it was worth the risk.

A quick listen at the door was enough to assure her that
he was already in the shower; she could hear the water
running, sluicing down his body before splashing against
the tub. Opening the door a crack, she was relieved to discover that he hadn't locked it, and slipping inside, set his
clothes on the cabinet. Selecting a soft, fluffy towel from
the closet, she laid it on the stool near the shower. Even
behind the frosted glass of the door, his body called out to
her, telling her that she'd given up much too easily.

"Um… need your back washed?" she asked. Not very
subtle, perhaps, but it was one way of breaking the ice.

Lynx's answer surprised her. "I have already washed my back," he said. "But, if you wish, I will wash yours."

Bonnie knew she might regret it if that turned out to be all he had in mind, but it was still an offer she couldn't refuse. Getting out another towel, she dropped her robe on the floor, and stepped into the tub.

And let out a gasp of sheer astonishment. She tried desperately to remember some of Jack's more colorful expressions, but couldn't come up with one that quite fit. His cock might not have been erect, but it was still impressive—as was the rest of him.

Lynx had put on some weight since his arrival at Bonnie's farm, and it looked damn good on him. No longer painfully thin, he was all strong bones, tanned skin, and sleek muscle, rippling with feline power.

"No wonder those women wouldn't leave you alone!" she exclaimed, staring at him in wonder. "Did they ever even let you get dressed?"

His curling hair had grown to the point that it almost reached his shoulders, and droplets of water scattered when Lynx shook his head. "No," he replied. "I wore nothing during the years I spent with them."

Bonnie began to quiver with excitement. "I just might rip all of your clothes to shreds myself," she whispered. She stared at him a moment longer before adding, "That's a joke, son. Come on now, at least give me one tiny little grin!"

It was genuine, but pretty tiny.

"Oh, you can do better than that," she scolded, advancing closer. "Are you ticklish?"

"Ticklish?"

"Yeah, ticklish," she said, running a finger down his chest. "Doesn't that make you want to laugh?"

"No," he replied.

"How about this?" she asked coyly, teasing his navel with a fingertip. "Sylor would double over and scream when I did that to him."

"It does not affect me," Lynx said, but Bonnie could see the effort it was taking to maintain his composure. Delving deeper into his navel, she brushed her other hand over his chest, skimming his nipples.

His shout of laughter nearly sent her into orgasm. She'd gotten her wish—though it might be all she would ever get. Then she decided that whatever she *did* get, she was probably going to have to take. Taking advantage of his laughter, she hooked an arm behind his head and pulled him down for a kiss. The heat where their skin made contact would have rivaled a fire, and the soft touch of his lips, strong hands, and warm body melted her. Bonnie slid her hands around him, delighting in the feel of his hot, wet skin beneath her fingers, and her body responded with a tight knot of desire deep inside her and a growing ache between her thighs.

"Mmmm," she moaned as he began to purr softly. "You feel so good. Like hot, wet silk."

"And you smell of desire," he murmured. Purring louder, he rubbed his cheek against hers, breathing in her scent, but felt a pang of disappointment at his body's lack of response. She felt *so* good…

"I thought that was a *bad* thing."

"No," he said. "It is something that I cannot respond to as I once did, but I never said it was bad."

"Oh," she murmured as his hands cupped her bottom and pulled her tightly against him. "I guess I didn't understand…"

"That is my fault," Lynx said, nuzzling her ear. "I am sorry to have hurt you, Bonnie. You are not to blame for anything that has happened to me. It has taken me a long time to realize that."

"And I can't judge you by what other men have done to me, either," she whispered. "But, please, Lynx, promise me just one thing. Don't shut me out. Tell me what you're feeling, what you like, and what you don't. Don't leave me in the dark."

"I will try," he said hesitantly, "but such things are very difficult for me."

Lynx wasn't even sure what he *did* like. His own preferences had always been deemed insignificant in the past. He had emerged from slavery craving only peaceful solitude, but this was clearly not the time for that.

It was second nature for a Zetithian man to entice women, to be seductive and teasing, but Lynx had been sure he'd forgotten how until he watched Bonnie move toward him in an intoxicating blend of soft curves and sleek muscle. He'd never beheld anything he considered more beautiful, but knew that what he could see with his eyes went much deeper.

Bonnie had longed to let her hands roam all over him, but wanted to understand his own desires. "Any good spots?" she inquired. "Any places that are off limits?"

Barely able to breathe, his arms encircled her, seeking contact without conscious effort and when he opened his mouth to speak, though he had no idea what he was going to say, long-buried patterns of behavior resurfaced. "You may touch any part of me you like," he said, his voice dropping to a deep, seductive purr. "Unless you tickle."

"Didn't like that, huh?"

Lynx shook his head slowly. "There are better ways to make me laugh," he said with a suggestive lift of a black-tipped eyebrow.

Bonnie stared at him as though seeing him for the first time. "Well, you'll have to clue me in, Lynx," she said hoarsely, "because I'm at a complete loss."

Leaning down, he murmured, "Lick the tip of my ear."

Bonnie took a cautious swipe at it with her tongue, and Lynx laughed even harder than he had when she'd poked him in the belly button. Then she tried sucking on it, and he practically screamed. She relished the sound, only stopping when she remembered that they should at least *try* not to wake Ulla.

"Well, that's certainly effective," Bonnie remarked. "What else do you like?"

"I like many things," Lynx said mysteriously. "But I will let you discover them."

Bonnie could scarcely believe this was the same man; he'd suddenly gone from someone she should have disliked to someone capable of melting her down to a puddle.

"Who *are* you, and what the hell have you done with Lynx?" she whispered.

A smile tugged at the corner of his mouth, but all he said was, "I will wash your back now."

With soap-slick hands, Lynx not only washed her back, he caressed her entire body, driving her desire to a fever pitch. Gazing hungrily at his cock, Bonnie waited for some reaction, but though it was thick and long, the head never even peeked past its foreskin. She toyed with the idea of doing a bit of exploring to see what was hidden underneath there, but cautioned herself that this might be one of those places he would rather she not touch.

However, after he'd massaged her nipples to the point that her milk was about to let down, Bonnie decided that if Lynx didn't want her playing with his dick, he was going to have to slap her hands away. Wet and aching with need, she took his balls in her hands, washing them thoroughly before slipping her fingers along his shaft, teasing back his foreskin.

"Wow," she whispered, gingerly touching the scalloped edge of the head. "I'd sure like to see this thing in full bloom."

"I do not believe you will," Lynx said with marked regret. "It has not functioned in many years."

Eyeing it hungrily, she asked, "Is it okay if I suck it anyway?"

"You may do anything with me you like," he said, putting that soft, deep tone in his voice again—something that Bonnie didn't think she would ever tire of hearing, nor would it ever lose its effect. "Unlike the way it has been with others, I long for your touch."

"Then I'll touch you as much as I can," Bonnie promised. "I'll massage you, tickle you, fondle you, and caress you. I've wanted to do all of those things for so long—you've no idea."

Lynx couldn't help but laugh at this. "I have been inhaling your scent since I first came here," he said. "I know what you want, and I know just how long you have wanted it."

No secrets there. "Nasty of you to deny me, wasn't it?"

"I will repay you," he said seriously. "You will never want for anything, ever again."

Which was quite a promise for a man who couldn't get it up.

Chapter 14

BONNIE'S MOUTH WENT DRY AS SHE REMEMBERED where Lynx had received his "training." He'd probably already forgotten more about pleasuring a woman than most men ever learn to begin with—and undoubtedly still knew more than any man alive. Oddly enough, Bonnie wasn't interested in anything fancy; all she wanted was Lynx.

After toweling each other dry—which was an intensely erotic experience in itself—Bonnie combed out Lynx's tangled curls and dried them. Stepping back to view her handiwork, she shuddered with excitement, thinking that with a hard cock he'd have been absolutely perfect. She thought if she sucked it long enough it might get hard—if she was lucky.

Sighing regretfully, Bonnie decided that if it didn't feel good to him, it was pointless to try. It would be hard leaving it alone, though, because while she knew very well that he could use his hands and mouth to have her writhing in ecstasy in no time, what could she possibly do for him? With other men, she'd always gone straight for the dick and, generally speaking, they didn't complain. But with Lynx, Bonnie knew she'd have to be more inventive.

Bonnie had never met anyone who didn't like having their back rubbed, and though it wasn't much, he seemed to like it—at least he wasn't complaining. Just lying in bed with Lynx was a treat in itself—one Bonnie had gotten a taste of when Ulla was born. His warm, purring body had felt wonderful then, but this time he was there because he chose to be, not because it was required of him, and the difference was shocking.

Bonnie still couldn't understand what had changed him. Lynx had been smitten with Ulla from the start but had barely tolerated Bonnie. Was this merely his way of ensuring that he would get to see Ulla more often? The idea was painful, and Bonnie hastened to assure herself that Ulla was *not* the only reason he'd kissed her. She tried to play it all back through her mind, trying to remember what he'd said, something—*anything*—that would prove that he was there because of her and not just her child.

Lynx felt Bonnie's hands falter and heard her wistful sigh. Being well versed in feminine moods, while he might not have known the exact nature of the problem, he was well aware that one existed. Looking up at her, he asked: "What is troubling you?"

Storm clouds and lightning had been replaced by a pale moon, but Bonnie didn't need it to see his eyes, for they had a glow all their own. *Oh, he's* very *good,* she thought ruefully, wishing she could be as insightful. Always a total failure when it came to guessing the thoughts of men, Bonnie knew that Vladen had been quite correct in suggesting that her own attitude was the greatest impediment to a closer relationship with Lynx. Men mystified her, and she didn't like being kept in the dark.

"Too much on my mind," she sighed, wishing she could stop thinking and just be, just feel, and not care…

Cocking his head to one side, he speculated, "Is it that you do not understand why I would want you when we cannot mate?"

There was no point in denying the truth. Bonnie blew out a pent-up breath and nodded.

"Bonnie," he said gently, "if I wanted you, but you could not feel any physical pleasure yourself, would you deny me?"

"What?" she blurted out, not understanding him at first. After a moment, she ventured, "You mean like if I was paralyzed or something?"

"Yes."

Bonnie considered this for a moment. Having sex without feeling anything? It would be strange, she decided, but if it was important to him… no, she wouldn't refuse. In fact, the mere thought of being able to look up at his face while he thrust into her bordered on orgasmic, whether she could feel anything or not. "No," she replied. "I wouldn't. Just having you close and knowing that you wanted me would be enough. You could do anything you wanted."

"And have I not said that you could do anything you wanted with me?"

"Yes, you did say that, but—"

"You do not believe me?"

"Yes, but how will I be able to tell whether you like what I'm doing or not?" she asked, the words seeming to burst from her. "A hard, dripping cock is a pretty hard signal to miss, you know."

To her surprise, he laughed. "There are others, as you will soon discover."

"Well, you'd better make them really obvious," she said roundly, "because subtleties are pretty much lost on me. I have to know for sure or this just won't work! In fact, you'd better tell me what to look for right now."

"How will I know if you enjoy what I do to you?" he countered.

This wasn't something Bonnie had ever given much thought to. "Sighs, maybe?" she ventured. "And—and I probably moan a lot, too."

"I do that as well, and I also purr." Cocking his head to one side, he added, "Is that enough?"

"Yes, but you purr for the damned enocks, Lynx!" she grumbled. "It couldn't mean very much if you can do that!"

"But when I purr for *you*," he said in a voice filled with sincerity, "it will mean something else."

His tone should have been enough to reassure her, but Bonnie still had doubts. "Well, okay," she said uncertainly. "If you say so."

Chuckling softly, he asked, "Do you require a demonstration?"

"Yes," she said with a firm nod. "Yes, I believe I do."

"Then lick me."

"Where?"

He didn't reply, but the look he gave her said quite clearly: *"Where do you think?"*

He'd said she could suck his cock, but Bonnie thought perhaps he'd like something else even better. Pushing him onto his back, she leaned down and took a swipe at his balls with her tongue.

In response to her tongue, Lynx let out a gasp, followed by a rather explosive purr.

"Okay," she conceded. "You're right. That *is* different."

Unable to control his reaction, Lynx could scarcely breathe. "No one ever did that to me before!" he said in a hoarse whisper.

"No one?" she echoed. "Not ever?" Obviously the harem girls hadn't been as much fun as she would have thought.

Shaking his head in reply, all Lynx could think of to say was, "Do it again."

Bonnie grinned devilishly. "With pleasure."

Nudging his legs apart, she lay down in the space between them. Lynx had nice, big balls that hung tantalizingly low, and Bonnie knew she could have endless fun with them. His purring became more erratic as she licked him and then sucked his scrotal skin into her mouth and pulled, lifting his testicles. Then she let them drop.

Bonnie heard Lynx suck a breath in between his teeth and felt herself getting wet—to the point that she was now dripping on the sheets and the hot, slick feeling between her legs was driving her absolutely wild.

"I'm not hurting you, am I?" she asked anxiously as she realized that his reaction might have indicated pain as well as pleasure.

"No!" he said fiercely. Spreading his legs farther apart, he settled down into the bed, making his balls sway back and forth. "Suck them."

"Ooo, getting pushy, are we?" Since Lynx had likely never been given the opportunity to tell any of his lovers what he wanted, Bonnie figured it was probably a real turn-on for him… "What did you say?"

"Put them in your mouth," he growled.

With a wayward grin, she taunted, "Make me."

Lynx hesitated only a moment before seizing Bonnie's head with both hands and pulling her up against him. "Suck," was all she heard him say—all that she could understand, that is.

As she took one in her mouth and teased it with her tongue, Lynx traded his purrs for groans. *Oh, yeah!* No doubt about it; she could tell what he liked whether his cock got stiff or not. After a bit, she picked up on the flavor, and, no pun intended, thought he tasted sort of nutty. Jack hadn't mentioned anything about how a Zetithian would taste, and Bonnie wondered if they came in different flavors. It was all so strange! Here she was, having a great time, and he hadn't even done anything to her yet! Experimentally, she tried sucking his cock, and though she preferred them hard, found that a soft one fit in her mouth better.

Lynx seemed to appreciate the gesture—if clutching the sheets, holding his breath, and thrusting his hips up against her face meant anything. Lying there, devouring him, Bonnie lost all track of time. She went hunting for a sweet spot that might make him come, licking every place between his navel and his buns, but didn't find one. She knew that on human males, the best way to do that was to go after his prostate, but she wasn't sure Lynx would like it—some guys didn't. She would save that for another time, seeing no point in doing everything she could think of the first time around.

Ulla sighed, and Bonnie waited breathlessly until the baby settled back down to sleep. Lynx then took advantage of the momentary pause in the assault on his groin to roll Bonnie over and bury his face between her legs in a move quick enough to have been practiced.

However, she didn't complain, since he had the courtesy to leave his penis within range of her tongue. His own tongue was quite talented, but then he got his hands into the act, making her revise her opinion of which might be better.

If Bonnie had thought it would seem mechanical before they started, she'd have been wrong because Lynx touched her like a lover, not like a slave who was simply doing as he was told. Even if she *had* been giving directions, she couldn't have told him to do what he was currently doing, because she'd never even thought of it before. With any other man, if they'd ever used anything but their penis on her, it had been their fingers, but Lynx used his thumb, a technique that quickly took her to the combustion point. Then, with a thumb in her pussy and his tongue on her clitoris, he got another finger wet and went after her ass.

Lynx knew a little something about female anatomy, and he soon found her sweet spot, circling it tantalizingly before homing in with a deep, mind-numbing massage. Unable to concentrate on anything else, Bonnie let go and lay with his cock resting against her cheek. Even flaccid, his equipment was a handful—or a mouthful, depending on what she happened to be doing with it—and having it on her face was quite an erotic treat. Bonnie was trying hard not to scream or moan too loud—this was most definitely *not* the time to wake the baby!—and just about had to bite her tongue in order to keep quiet.

It was incredible, but as if that weren't enough, that finger he'd been using to tease her ass soon found her best spot from the other side. Bonnie's mouth fell open, and her eyes widened in disbelief; she'd never known anything could feel so exquisite. She had a few brief, thrilling moments to realize what was about to happen before she careened into orgasm. She thought that was it, but soon discovered that she couldn't breathe, couldn't move—couldn't do *anything*—without setting off another wave of ecstasy. Her body was tied in knots as her mind reeled in amazement.

Granted, she hadn't had actual intercourse with him, but she knew that if those slave women had ratted on Lynx when he could still do what he'd just done to her, then what she *hadn't* gotten from him had to have been mind-blowing in the extreme. She now felt some slight empathy for those women—knowing that the disappointment they had faced when he could no longer function must have been severe. But she would never have complained herself.

Her body wasn't able to move just yet, but her mind was running wild. Jack said she suspected that Zetith had been destroyed because of what their males could do. She'd thought that Lynx disproved her theory, but Bonnie had a strong feeling that Jack had been right all along. Lynx must have been every bit as sensuous as Cat or any of the others at one time—in fact, it seemed to be coming back to him fairly quickly—so Bonnie could only assume that most Zetithian males were like that. She tried to imagine what it would be like with one who was fully functional and decided that if what Lynx had done to her were increased only by half, it was a wonder that Jack and Tisana were still able to walk.

Jack had also said that they could secrete a fluid which triggered orgasms—undoubtedly a chemical effect—and the obvious source of such a fluid had to be the penis. Bonnie made a mental note to suck harder on Lynx's the next time to see if she could suck some of it out of him—or perhaps stimulate its production.

It was a crying shame Lynx's dick didn't work, because if it had, Bonnie would have pulled that sterility implant out of him in a heartbeat, even if she had to tie him down to do it. Upon further reflection, she decided she might do it anyway, because she didn't need two obstacles standing in the way of having his children, which was something she was now determined to do.

Lynx let go of Bonnie, but very reluctantly. What she'd been doing to him had nearly cost him his sanity. Her tongue on his sensitive skin had nearly been his undoing. Her hot breath was a stimulant, her touch intoxicating. Even the memory of it sent his mind into a spin. She'd been so anxious to please him, too, even asking what he liked. If anyone had ever done that before, he couldn't remember, and if a woman had ever licked him, it was to achieve her own orgasm by tasting him, not to give him pleasure. His only thought was to repay her in kind, and he'd pounced on her, using as many techniques as he could remember. Lynx was certain that more would come back to him in time, and he had every intention of using every last one of them.

Chapter 15

BONNIE AWOKE THE NEXT MORNING TO THE SOUND OF Lynx purring, Ulla crying, and her comlink beeping like crazy. Reluctantly, she left Lynx in bed, pulled on a robe, picked up Ulla, and answered the hail from Drummond.

"What's up?" she asked, slipping Ulla up to her breast to quiet her cries.

"Just checking to see if you all were still there," he said. "Nasty fire we had last night, wasn't it?"

"Almost lost the farm," Bonnie said, nodding in agreement. "But we made it through. Lynx flooded the field, and the fire went around us, but it was a little scary there for a while!"

Drummond grinned. "And did you thank him properly?"

Bonnie knew exactly what Drummond meant, but decided to tease him a little. Cocking her head at him curiously, she said, "Mind explaining that?"

Drummond smiled knowingly. "Not in front of the baby," he replied. "But I think you know what I mean, Bon-bon!"

He waited for her to take the bait and was slightly disappointed, because for once, she failed to rag on him about his use of her nickname. Something was *definitely* up!

"Vladen still around?" Bonnie asked casually.

"No, but he's headed back this way," Drummond reported. "Some injuries from the fire needing his expert touch, I guess. Not too many, though. What do you need him for?" Peering at his viewscreen, he added, "Thought you said you were okay."

"Oh, I am," Bonnie replied. "I've just got a few questions for him. I'll give him a call after awhile."

"Well, I guess I'll see you around then," he said, still not sure quite what to make of her odd attitude. "Take care."

"I will," she promised. "You do the same." Terminating the link, she leaned back in her chair. Ulla sighed deeply as she drank her breakfast. "Yeah, me, too, kid," Bonnie murmured. "What a night!"

Bonnie could hear Lynx stirring in the bedroom, and for a moment, was almost afraid to hear what he would have to say the morning after. He wouldn't have been the first man to wake up with a totally different attitude than the one he'd gone to bed with, and Bonnie could just imagine him fully dressed, with eyes averted as he hightailed it back to the shed.

It was possible that he might be having similar fears, so when she heard his footstep in the doorway, she looked up with what she hoped was a welcoming smile—a smile that widened when she caught that first glimpse of him.

Yawning as he ran a hand through his tousled locks, Lynx hadn't even bothered to put on his clothes—*any* of them. As he entered, his sheepish smile melted the tightness around Bonnie's heart. No, he hadn't changed his mind, and when he came closer, he leaned down to kiss her and then Ulla.

"She slept through it all, did she not?" he inquired as he stroked her soft cheek with his knuckle.

"Yeah, must be nice," Bonnie said, realizing that while her heart might be feeling more relaxed, the rest

of her certainly wasn't. "Lynx… I didn't… *imagine*…
any of that, did I?"

Lynx shook his head. "No, you did not."

"No regrets?"

"No."

Bonnie felt like laughing and crying at the same time.
"Me either," she said, switching Ulla to the other side.
"I was afraid you might decide you didn't want…" Her
voice trailed off. Not trusting herself to look at him, she
stared down at her baby.

"To be loved anymore?" he ventured. "Yesterday, I
realized that I do want your love, Bonnie, and I want it
more than I have ever wanted anything—more than solitude, more than money, more, even, than my freedom.
Those things mean nothing to me now."

Lynx came closer, and she leaned into him, her
head resting on his thigh. She couldn't say anything—
couldn't even think of anything to say—all she could
do was nod. Blinking back her tears, it occurred to her
that she could be happy now. She didn't have to cry
over every little thing. He hadn't said he loved her, but
his acceptance of her love was quite enough to satisfy
her. When it came to technique, she knew he was un-
surpassed, but perhaps he didn't know how to love in
the emotional sense. He would learn. She would teach
him—by example, if nothing else. She would make him
feel more loved than any man ever had; wide open, no-
holds-barred, unconditional love.

Turning her head and slipping an arm around his legs,
she kissed him in the hollow of his flank and was rewarded with a soft purr. Lynx sank to his knees beside
her chair and took Bonnie's face in his hands, kissing

her gently, sweetly, before nipping at her earlobe with his fangs.

"My beautiful Bonnie," he murmured. "What would you like to do today?"

Bonnie's practical nature surfaced briefly. "You mean after we feed all the animals and clean up the mess from the fire?"

"Mmmm, do you know that at one time, such activities would have been enjoyment for me? I would prefer to work hard, rather than have to spend my time pleasing a woman."

"And now?"

"Now I want nothing more than to spend all my time tantalizing you and filling you with joy."

A soft laugh escaped Bonnie's lips before he captured them again with his own, melting her with his heat, fusing them together. She'd never known a man could say such things and have her believe him. It was amazing.

Lynx took Ulla from her and then grasped Bonnie's hand, pulling her to her feet. "Come back to bed," he said. "As of today, I am your slave, and I will see to your every need."

Bonnie gaped at him in frank disbelief. "Aw, not every day, surely?" she scoffed when she finally found her tongue. "I mean, I have to do *something!*"

"Not today," he said, shaking his head. "You have given me much, and today is the day I thank you."

So, I'll only get one day? It might not have seemed like much, but it was still more than most people got—and certainly more than Bonnie had ever had. "And tomorrow everything goes back to normal?"

He smiled seductively, his lips curling to reveal his gleaming fangs. "I do not believe so, but you may judge that for yourself."

If he did nothing more than smile at her in that particular fashion, Bonnie knew it would be a welcome change.

Lynx took her to bed and after changing Ulla's diaper and putting her down in her crib, placed pillows around Bonnie in a most strategic manner. She didn't think she'd ever felt quite so comfortable before. He was an artist. Then, kissing her soundly, he disappeared for a while, returning with a breakfast of hot, cooked grain mixed with fruit and crisp toast dripping with butter and honey. "So, you *can* cook," she murmured when he handed her a plate.

"Not as well as you, perhaps," he said. "But I will learn."

He fed her, letting Bonnie taste him along with the food. It was hot and good and made her sleepy. Lynx was still naked, a state which stirred her desire for him. He'd combed his hair—even his pubic hair looked fluffy—and she wanted to feel it tickling her face. His kisses were hot, wet, and delicious and promised other delights yet to come.

"I will feed the animals now," he said. "But before I go, is there anything else you require?"

Staring at his beautiful cock, she said impulsively, "I'd like some of… you… with honey."

His breath went out with a loud purr. "As you wish." Kneeling beside her on the bed, he took the honey dipper, letting the golden syrup run down his penis.

"All of you," she said, eyeing his balls hungrily.

His dick truly must have been beyond repair, because Bonnie couldn't imagine any man alive who wouldn't get an erection at the thought of having honey licked and sucked from his genitals. However, his penis never moved, but his exotic brow flicked up as he gathered up his nuts to douse them with the sweetness.

"Now, feed them to me," she said hoarsely.

Lynx filled her mouth with his hot, sweet meat, and while he might have been playing naked slave boy for her, he obviously hadn't forgotten what he'd enjoyed so much the night before. "Suck me," he groaned, taking her head in his hands. His breath went in through his teeth with a hiss. "That feels *so* good…" Their eyes met, and Bonnie knew she had never been faced with such an expression of raw, naked lust before. Something told her the enocks were going to have to wait just a bit…

Bonnie let go of his dick and sucked in a testicle. In response, Lynx drew in a ragged, purring breath and arched his back, offering himself to her completely. His words were rapid and unintelligible, leaving Bonnie to imagine what sort of wild, erotic things he might be saying. Dipping a finger in the honey on his scrotum, she prodded him from behind, and Lynx went wild trying to let her in and still keep his balls shoved up against her face. Finally, Bonnie gave up any pretense of letting him give her pleasure and pushed him onto his back, devouring him while her finger delved deeply into his body. Quickly locating his most sensitive spot, she went after it; softly at first and then, upon hearing his gasps of pleasure, with a vengeance. Bonnie was hot and dripping with moisture as she massaged him, sucked him, and fondled him, but didn't stop until she got what she wanted. She waited to see the hot semen burst from his body, but none came as Lynx climaxed with a roar.

Bonnie had never seen a man come so hard, nor had she ever seen an orgasm that lasted so long. Dripping with sweat and panting hard by the time it was done, his expression of wonderment was quickly replaced with one of fierce determination. Pulling her up over his body, he gasped, "Sit."

He didn't have to ask her twice. As she lowered her scorching pussy onto his waiting mouth, he thrust his tongue inside her. Gripping her hips, he pumped her up and down on him, driving Bonnie absolutely wild before pulling out his tongue and sucking in her clitoris. Screaming as he pulled on her, she let him tease her to the breaking point with the hot suction of his lips and the rough surface of his tongue.

"Lynx!" she gasped. "I can't—" And then it happened; a great, crashing orgasm that shook her like an earthquake and sent her keeling over onto the bed. Lynx let out a satisfied purr and continued on; licking her lazily as though there was nothing in the world he would rather do, seeming to enjoy making her body pulse and hearing her moan.

And he *did* enjoy it. Lynx's mind drifted back, remembering what it had been like so many years ago when he'd thrust his hard, young cock into every woman he could reach. He'd liked watching them spread their legs for him, begging him to fuck them, their nipples taut with anticipation. The smell of hot woman had surrounded him all the time back then, and his erections were nearly constant. He'd finish with one and move on to the next. Some of the women couldn't wait and would caress themselves, or each other. He liked watching that while he was slamming his cock into their beautiful, eager bodies. They drove him wild, and he could hardly stop long enough to sleep. But he'd been young then, and didn't care... The women he'd known on Zetith were never like that. They hardly ever wanted anyone at all, and when they did, it had never been him. He reminded himself that he'd been very young, but he knew of others his own age who were already sexually active. Until he'd been thrust among the slave women, he'd never inhaled the scent of a woman who actually desired *him*. They might not have loved him, but they certainly wanted him, and he'd been more than willing to comply.

But Bonnie was different. True, she was human, which accounted for part of the contrast, but her scent had undergone a subtle change during the time he'd known her. He'd been told as a boy that there was a difference, that the scent of lust was sharper, less pleasing than the aroma of love, but he hadn't understood then. The scent of the slave women had gone straight to his cock, filling him with a lust he'd never dreamed he was capable of feeling. But Bonnie smelled of love—a softer, gentler fragrance—and he thought perhaps that was what had changed him. He didn't know for certain; he only wished he hadn't wasted all of his ability on women who felt nothing for him. Now he had a woman who loved him, and he couldn't do the things he longed to do with her. She'd seemed pleased by what he *had* done, but he knew that the difference between what he wanted to do and what he was capable of doing was vast, indeed.

And then, there was what she'd done to him. He'd never known that a man could climax without his cock being touched. It was just as good, just as cleansing a feeling as it had ever been. She'd done things he'd never imagined, and he'd never known a woman could be so giving. She was different, he reminded himself, so very, very different…

Lynx knew he should get up to do the chores, but lying beside Bonnie, relaxed and at peace, left him feeling better than he'd felt for a very long time. Being able to lie there, his arm thrown over Bonnie's warm, languid body, was a luxury he'd always been denied, and he relished every moment of it.

Approval. Perhaps that was what had changed him. She approved of him and the work he'd done. That had been it. Surely that was what had begun the process of change. He must have known it somehow, and had done as much as he could for her, just to win that very thing.

An hour or two later, Bonnie and Ulla both awakened, the baby being very hungry, and the mother feeling more sated than ever before. Lynx was right there to change Ulla's diaper before placing her gently in the bed beside Bonnie. As he slipped in behind her and held her against his purring chest, Bonnie realized that this was how it could have been—and possibly would have been—right after Ulla was born if only she hadn't been too stubborn to ask for his help. She couldn't have been sure that the tenderness he'd shown toward her during her labor would have persisted after the birth, and it might not have turned out to be as good as it was now, but she still should have given him the chance. It might have spared them all some pain.

But Bonnie was determined not to think that way anymore. She would think positively and do her utmost to make Lynx and Ulla's lives the best they could be. Her mind drifted, and she smiled to herself, because just knowing that she could bring Lynx to climax made her very happy indeed.

Bonnie noted that Lynx either hadn't bothered to dress when he went out, or if he had, he'd stripped down as soon as he returned. It was funny in a way, because after all the time she had spent wondering if she would ever catch him with his pants off, she was beginning to wonder if he'd ever wear them again. Not that she minded in the slightest, because snuggling in with his warm, naked body against hers was a treasure beyond price.

"I hope you never get dressed again," she sighed. "I love looking at you, feeling you, touching you."

Lynx breathed in her scent. Yes, she loved him, and that knowledge sent rivers of warmth coursing through his body. "I will do as you wish," he murmured. "I enjoy pleasing you."

"Stay naked then, at least for today," she pleaded. "I saw you once, late at night. I—I thought you were beautiful."

"But I am a man, and men are not beautiful," he whispered. "It must have been the moonlight tricking your eyes."

"I disagree," she said. "I look at you and I feel… something… something I've never felt before. It's… hard to explain."

"Do not try," he said, kissing her neck. Her hair was growing longer, too, and it tickled his cheek. He liked that sensation.

As Ulla sighed and fell into blissful slumber, Lynx pulled Bonnie onto her back and lay between her outstretched legs with his head pillowed on her chest. "*You* are beautiful," he told her, raising his head to look into her eyes. "Your golden hair, your sparkling blue eyes…" His gaze drifted over her breasts, full and heavy, the nipples pink and firm. He blew gently on the damp nipple Ulla had just left behind and watched it harden before his eyes. He moved up to kiss the hard bud, flicking it with his tongue, hearing Bonnie's soft moan of pleasure. If his cock had been hard, he would have moved higher, forcing his way inside her waiting body, loving her as she deserved to be loved.

"Kiss me," she whispered, pulling him toward her.

Following her command, Lynx slid across her soft skin, seeking her wet lips to delve into her mouth; taking her, tasting her.

Bonnie's mind went swirling into a maelstrom of delight; Lynx was in her arms, kissing her, his strong body covering her own. Oh, yes… this was joy… He knew he couldn't do it without an erection, but Lynx tried anyway. Bonnie felt his cock and balls sliding over her wet flesh and smiled with warm delight as he broke the kiss and pushed himself up with a hand on either side of her shoulders.

This was how he should always look, she thought; gazing down at her, his eyes filled with tenderness and love, though clouded with desire. And his smile knowing and teasing. His *smile*…

His balls felt heavy and full as Lynx pushed against her, feeling her heat, her wet softness. She felt so good.

His cock pressed against her, his balls getting wet with her creamy moisture.

Moving side to side, Bonnie took up the challenge and, wiggling her hips to get him where she wanted him, with a sharp abdominal contraction, sucked him inside.

Lynx gasped as he felt the pull. His cock was finally inside her, where it belonged. He was afraid to move, to break the connection, the spell…

"Mmm, you feel nice," Bonnie purred. "Thick and soft and warm." She felt him slipping away and sucked him in again. "Stay there for a while. I like it." She liked looking up at him, too; his handsome face poised above her wearing an expression of pure delight.

His balls tingled with an excitement Lynx hadn't felt in a very long time. He was actually inside her! He couldn't help it; he ground in tighter, forcing his cock in deeper, feeling her sweet sheath caressing him. Softness surrounded him, and the scent of her filled his senses. "I wish I could—"

Bonnie shook her head. "Don't think about that. I love you, Lynx, just the way you are. There is more to you than any other man I've ever known. Much more." She smiled. "You feel absolutely fabulous."

Lynx arched his back, reveling in the feel of her as she held him; it felt so good, he forgot to purr. There had been a time when his cock could thrust deeply inside a woman and literally dance, but this was good, this was *very* good. He'd hardly ever gotten to just hold still and feel—not once the other slaves learned what he could do; and they'd pushed him to the point that he could not only move his cock inside them, but could practically vibrate it. He tried not to think about it; what Bonnie was missing. She was happy with him as he was. She loved him. He knew it; he could smell it and feel it. It should have been enough for him. But he wanted so much to give her everything.

Bonnie thought she had it all then. It felt good to move with him; gentle, undemanding yet fulfilling just the same. Experimentally, Lynx contracted a long un-used muscle, only to have Bonnie lose her tentative hold on him.

Since Ulla chose that moment to awaken from her nap, Bonnie considered it to be nothing to be concerned about, but Lynx nearly cursed out loud.

Ulla began to fret, but seeing Lynx there changed her cry into a smiling coo.

"I think she likes having you here," Bonnie remarked, giving her baby a tickle. "I don't blame her for that. I like it too." A fleeting pain passed through her heart. Yes, she liked having him here, but would she have to endure his loss when he left? Would Ulla? She was pretty sure Lynx could be trusted at his word, but she'd been lied to before. Looking up at Lynx, she said quietly, "She would miss you as much as I would if you left us now."

Lynx recognized that statement for what it was; a subtle request for reassurance. "Then she has no reason to fear—until she grows up and leaves us someday."

Bonnie felt relief wash over her like a wave and sighed deeply. "You know, for a guy who used to make me mad every time you opened your mouth, you sure do know the right things to say."

"Telling the truth is usually best," he said. "I have no knowledge of what our future holds in store, but I will not leave you—not willingly."

Bonnie began to speak, but the tightness in her throat stopped her. Instead, she simply nodded and pulled him down for a kiss.

Sweetness and love; he felt it in her lips and smelled it in the air surrounding her. She loved him, and he would stay.

Chapter 16

LYNX MIGHT HAVE HAD EVERY INTENTION OF STAYING, but there was another factor which neither of them had considered. Sylor had spent all the money he'd taken, and his other schemes had failed to live up to their potential. It had proven to be very difficult to survive in his usual manner on such a law-abiding planet, which had been a bitter pill for Sylor to swallow. He had little choice but to admit his mistake and return to Bonnie, and while he had no doubt that he could talk his way back into her good graces, upon his return he found that someone else had taken his place; in his home, in his bed, and in his daughter's life. Sylor knew what Bonnie was like; if this cat-creature was loved by her, he wouldn't leave of his own accord. Sylor still wasn't quite sure why he'd left himself. Perhaps it was because he knew she'd expected him to—though he knew there was more to it than that. There was something within him that rebelled against the idea of settling down to raise a family, or following the rules—*any* rules.

Sylor's own father had been a rather fleeting presence in his life. In fact, Sylor couldn't remember seeing him above five times in the time before he left home, and not at all since then. It wasn't as though he'd had a terrific role model for a parent. But Sylor probably wouldn't have been a model citizen even with a loving family around him. He simply didn't care what happened to anyone but himself, and he was quite willing to let others sacrifice to meet his needs.

Sylor knew the law; he had abandoned his homestead and his child, and legally, they could be declared lost to him. He would have to win her back. He would not risk being caught and deported. Not that the authorities hadn't tried, it was just that he was very hard to find when he was of a mind to disappear, even with the tracking implant. Bonnie must not have told them all they needed to know—if, indeed, she knew anything at all. A man had to have some secrets, after all. There was also the possibility that she hadn't been the one to file the complaint in the first place. Bonnie had had no illusions about him and couldn't have been very surprised when he left.

If only he hadn't agreed to the child! He'd known it was a mistake, but Bonnie had wanted a child so badly, he found it difficult to refuse her. Now it was either come back and pick up where he left off, or be deported. But unless he could get rid of his "replacement," there wasn't much hope for him. Bonnie had had plenty of time to decide he wasn't coming back and put the land in her name exclusively. If that was the case, she probably didn't see the need to file a complaint. But, perhaps someone else had. Someone who would have known she changed the title on the land.

Drummond. He was the only possibility. If Bonnie hadn't filed the complaint, he must have. Otherwise, Sylor knew he would have been pursued long before this.

Sylor had felt the call of the wild; the desire to be free of obligations and duties, and he had listened to it, just as he always had—doing whatever happened to suit him

at the time. And now, it was in his best interest to return.
But how to do it? How to make her want him back?

He hated resorting to murder, which would have been
the easiest way to get rid of such an impediment. Perhaps there was another way…

Sylor might have been invisible to anyone else, but not
to Lynx. Lynx had picked up his scent; the scent embedded in the pillow he'd slept on for months. When
he first became aware of it, it took him a moment to
realize that his pillow wasn't following him, but that
the former owner of it was nearby. His first instinct
was to fight, but the longer Lynx considered the matter, the more he felt that it might be pointless. Bonnie
had never said she didn't love Ulla's father; just that he
was gone. Would she take him back? The realization
that she probably would hit Lynx so hard he nearly fell.
She must have loved him once, Lynx realized, and he
had fathered her child. She'd told Lynx that she loved
him, but why would she keep him when she could have
a man who could be a real lover to her and could give
her more children?

Lynx rubbed the implant in his arm absently. It was
still there; a reminder of his former status as a slave.
As bad as those memories were, it was a wonder he'd
never cut it out before. The moment he was freed, it
should have been removed—whatever its purpose.
Lynx had imagined all manner of reasons for the device,
chief among them that it was a poison that would be
released if he should ever attempt to escape. Now that
he understood the reason for it, it seemed so simple; the

master had not wanted his slave women to give birth to anyone's children but his own.

Lynx had only been there to serve them, not impregnate them. He'd been told he would die if he ever removed the implant, but not the how or the why. He could see it now; if he had removed it, he would have fathered children, and he would have been put to death as a result. Thinking back, Lynx realized that the women must not have known of it either. He'd smelled their fear and heard their whispers. It might have meant their own death to give birth to his child. Some of them might have at least discerned that he was sterile—after all, he'd mated with each one of them, and none of the many children he'd seen born had ever been his own. He understood the reason now, but the pain of it still lingered. It had been cruel, but when did anyone take into account the feelings of a slave?

But he wasn't a slave anymore. He was a free man, and, scenting his rival, he would fight, perhaps even kill, to keep his mate. On Zetith, such confrontations were rare, for when a woman chose a man for her mate, it was for life. Rivalry was nearly unheard of. But as his blood heated and his hackles rose, he knew that this was something deep; an instinct long buried in his species. He would not give her up without a fight.

But first, there was something else that needed to be done.

He found Bonnie in the bathroom on her knees by the tub, engaged in giving a very lively Ulla her bath. Without preamble, he said: "I want to get rid of this."

"What?" she said, glancing over her shoulder. "What are you talking about?"

"This," he said, pointing to the implant in his arm. "I wish to be freed."

Bonnie pushed a stray lock of hair from her eyes and stared up at him curiously. "But you're *already* free, Lynx. How will that change anything?"

"It is a reminder to me of what I once was. I want it gone."

"Lynx," Bonnie said gently, thinking she understood the reason for his urgency. "It only makes you sterile, not impotent."

"Still, I want it removed."

"Right now?" She gathered a squeaky-clean Ulla up in a soft towel and held her close. "Vladen's been gone for a while, so he should be back through here soon. We can probably catch him on the next market day."

"No," he said with a swift shake of his head. "Now."

"Sylor had Vladen take his out," Bonnie said doubtfully. "I'm not sure of the procedure…"

"It should not be difficult," Lynx said impatiently. "If you will not do it, then I will cut it out myself."

"Well, now wait a minute, maybe I could—" But she was talking to empty space.

Now that he'd decided on it, Lynx couldn't wait another moment; not for Vladen to return, nor for Bonnie to reluctantly agree. The knife was sharp, and it stung where he cut himself. Forcing the end of the tube through the opening in his skin, he pulled it out, discovering that it hurt far less to remove than it had to put it there. He held it up to the light. It looked so simple, so innocuous. How could such a small device change his life so profoundly?

Bonnie dressed Ulla quickly and set her down to play on the floor. She found Lynx in the kitchen, bleeding, and the implant gone, smashed into a thousand pieces.

"Boy, when you decide to do something, you don't waste any time, do you?" Bonnie commented. Searching his face, she tried to get some idea of why he'd felt it was so urgent. Her voice sincere and her expression quite serious, she added, "I would have done it for you, Lynx. I was just... busy."

Lynx was already feeling a bit chagrined for his impatience. "I could not wait," he said with a shrug. "I do not know why." He did know, but the fact that Sylor was in the vicinity was one that he was reluctant to impart to Bonnie. How would she react when he told her? He had no idea whether she would be angry or elated, but he was hoping for anger. Sylor had left her, stolen from her, and while she'd told Lynx she loved him, he'd never heard her say she loved Sylor, but Lynx was sure she must have at one time. He knew her well enough by this time to know that she would not treat such a matter lightly.

"Well, no harm done," Bonnie said briskly. "I might have swabbed it with an antiseptic first if *I'd* done it, but I don't think there's anything to worry about." Bonnie was glad Lynx had been the one to insist on removing the implant, because she didn't want him to think that her only interest in the matter was to restore his sexual capability—which wasn't the real reason at all, but it would have been a welcome side effect.

"I am not worried," Lynx said. "I have suffered worse injuries with no ill effect." He hesitated for a moment, debating on what to say to her. Taking a deep breath, he said, "But I was told I would die if it was ever removed."

Bonnie felt the floor give way beneath her feet. "And you pulled it out anyway?" It terrified her to think that she might have been wrong. "Oh, my God," she said faintly. "Maybe it wasn't what I thought it was after all! Maybe we should—"

"No," Lynx said quickly, cutting her off. "You were correct; if I had fathered a child while I was a slave, it probably would have resulted in my being killed." He winced as the other thought came to him, "—along with the child—and possibly the child's mother."

"I didn't think about the possibility of *you* being killed," Bonnie admitted. "But I did think about the children. That's why the women didn't want their babies to be yours, Lynx. It had nothing to do with you personally." Noting his stricken expression, she added, "It was pretty heartless not to explain it to you, but you *were* a slave."

Lynx nodded. She was right. It was nothing more than what he'd told himself already, but hearing it from her made it seem... better somehow. He stared down at the shattered remains of the implant. "And now it is gone, but it still makes no difference."

He was feeling sorry for himself, and he knew it, but he said it anyway. There were demons he needed to exorcise—demons that haunted him constantly.

"You might be surprised," Bonnie murmured.

He looked at her curiously. "Are you really so unlike the others I have known? I feel it; and I want to believe it, but sometimes the past is too strong, and I—"

Bonnie sighed deeply. "Guess I have to come right out and say it, don't I?"

His face went blank, and he stopped breathing, waiting for what she would say.

"I'm glad you took that thing out if it was so important to you. I love you so much, Lynx. You're a good father to Ulla, and you'd be a good father to your own children too."

"Perhaps," he said. Judging from his expression, he didn't believe it.

Bonnie shook her head. "I'll try every way that I can, Lynx. Vladen can help. You'll see."

"What are you saying?" he whispered.

Bonnie smiled at him lovingly. "I want to have your children, Lynx. We'll do whatever it takes to make it happen."

Lynx felt the blood drain out of his face. "But, how is that possible?"

"There are lots of ways," she assured him. "Medical treatment is probably a lot more advanced here than it was on Paemay, or even Zetith. Vladen can do some pretty remarkable things—you haven't gotten to see it yet, but you will." Bonnie had been speaking urgently, encouragingly, but was struck with a sudden shyness as she lost some of her confidence. Maybe she was wrong; maybe that wasn't what he wanted after all. "If—if that's what you want."

Lynx closed his eyes, remembering all the children he'd brought into the world; all the times he'd held his breath until he could see, until he knew. His head began to spin, and Bonnie caught him in her arms to steady him. "No one ever—" he whispered.

"Lynx, you understand why that was, don't you?" she said. "It wasn't you! It was the situation you were in! There's nothing wrong with you—and there never has been! There is absolutely no reason why any woman in her right mind wouldn't love you and want to be with you forever and have your children! It's what I want more than anything in the world—and I'm not what you'd call an easy mark! I was ready to swear off men entirely because I didn't think the kind of man I wanted even existed!" Her eyes filled with tears as she cupped his cheek and gazed into his exotic eyes, at the strong planes of his face. "But you *do* exist, and you *are* real. You're honest, loving, intelligent, and I'm so lucky to have found you." Bonnie paused as she attempted a watery smile. "Of course, the fact that you're downright gorgeous doesn't hurt, either."

Lynx couldn't help but smile back. "It is I who am lucky to have found you," he said. "You are such a stubborn woman! When I think of how I have acted, I am surprised you did not have me sent back to Paemay."

"Don't think I didn't try," Bonnie said dryly. "But Drummond wouldn't let me." She paused a moment before adding reflectively, "Jack probably would have had my hide for getting you deported, too, and I'm sure Cat and Leo wouldn't want to lose track of you now that they've found you." She looked up at him shyly. "And Jack told me a little bit about what it was like to have a Zetithian lover."

Once again, Lynx's face became an unreadable mask. "I am sorry that I cannot—" He dropped his head. "I was once a very skilled lover. I could do such things—"

"Shhh," she said, putting a finger to his lips. "Please, don't apologize for that anymore. It's not your fault, Lynx. None of it is. Besides, if you could still function, you would never have been sold, and you would never have come to this world. You would still be a slave, and we would never have met—and *that* really would have been a tragedy."

She followed those words up with a poignant kiss but felt a fierce determination grow within her. *I will not lose him. He will know what it is to be loved. I promise.*

Lynx couldn't help but feel regret when he kissed her. There had been a time when he could make a woman feel nothing but pleasure, casting an erotic spell that left them sated and sleeping, but always eager for more when they awoke. As much as he'd done to please them, those women should have worshiped the ground he walked on, but they never had. He had given so much but had received nothing in return. Bonnie had been happy with so much less and had shown him so much more kindness. He didn't understand the difference, but he liked it. He only wished he could give her everything, but that was impossible.

Chapter 17

BONNIE COULDN'T HAVE SAID JUST WHEN SHE NOTICED it, but over the next few days Lynx's lovemaking became as mechanical as she had suspected it might be at the outset. He was doing all the same things, and they were having a similar effect, but something had changed. Knowing just how far he had come, she might have expected him to backslide a little, but she also knew that he could progress even further if given the right amount of support and encouragement. Still, she couldn't forget that first night when she'd seen the fire in his eyes. She tried to analyze it; what had been the trigger that set him off? Lynx was still there with her, but the heat was gone, and she wanted it back.

Lynx might have been happy doing what he could for Bonnie if only he hadn't known what he had been capable of before, but he did, and his dissatisfaction grew. The woman who should have been the recipient of the best he had to offer was getting far less than she deserved and far less than he wanted to give. Insecurities redeveloped, sending him back behind the walls he had shielded himself behind for so long. Not completely, of course—he didn't retreat to the shed, but his attitude changed.

To make matters worse, Ulla was teething and grew increasingly irritable and fussy and wanted to chew on anything and everything she could find to relieve the pressure in her gums. Bonnie was having a hard time recognizing her normally happy baby in the miserable wretch Ulla had become. It seemed to Bonnie that the only time Ulla *wasn't* crying was when Lynx held her and let her gnaw on his finger while he purred.

Lynx was outside doing something, she didn't know what, but Bonnie hoped he would come back soon. "Sorry I can't purr like your father," Bonnie told a bawling Ulla as she sat rocking her. "Wish I could, but I've never been able to get the hang of it."

Bonnie jumped about a foot as Lynx put a hand on her shoulder. "I will take her now," he said.

"Please do!" Bonnie exclaimed. "I can't do a thing with her! Vladen gave me some stuff to put on her gums, but I think it makes it even worse!"

Lynx took Ulla without comment, holding her close and patting her back while he purred, still not quite able to comprehend what he'd just heard, but he knew it was wrong.

"Even though we are lovers, I am not her father," Lynx said quietly. "You should not confuse her by referring to me in that manner."

"You're the only father she has ever known, Lynx. I don't see how it's confusing—especially now."

"But how will it be when she grows older and realizes that I could not possibly be her father?"

"She'll think she's adopted, I guess," Bonnie said with a shrug. "I mean, she doesn't look like me, either. She's too much like Sylor for that."

"But she *does* look like you," Lynx said gently. "She has your hair and eyes."

"Maybe," Bonnie conceded, "but that's about all."

Lynx's expression grew wary. "There is nothing in her of me."

"She's got your name."

"My mother's name," Lynx corrected her.

Bonnie hesitated, wondering if this was the time to tell him everything… but perhaps not. "Yes, but I gave her *your* mother's name, not Sylor's. You are more a father to her than Sylor will ever be—not that I'd give him the chance now; not after what he did."

"But he is her father," Lynx insisted.

"Biologically, yes," Bonnie grumbled. "But that's about all the credit I'll give him."

Lynx stared at her, the light beginning to dawn. "You do not still love him?"

Bonnie gaped at him for a long moment in total disbelief. "Well, if I ever did, I certainly don't love him now! For heaven's sake, Lynx! Don't you get it? I've chosen you. You, just you, and only you. I love you, you big dummy! Can't you get that through your thick skull?"

Lynx just stared at her, and then at the now sleeping Ulla in his arms. "I don't understand."

"And here I've been thinking you were so smart all this time! I want you to stay here, Lynx; I want you to be a father to Ulla and a husband to me. I said I wanted to have your children too. Weren't you listening?"

"Yes, but I still don't believe it would be possible."

"Oh, it's possible, all right," Bonnie said roundly. "I brought you to climax once, and I'm sure I can do it again. Not meaning to sound too unromantic and technical about it, but now that you've pulled out that implant, you'll start to produce sperm again, and we can collect your semen and then inseminate me with it. I *will* have your children, Lynx. It's just a matter of time."

"But Shaulla—"

"So what if she doesn't look like you!" Bonnie protested. "You brought her into this world; you've cared for her and loved her. No father could do more than that!" Bonnie was rapidly losing patience with him. "I thought you understood all of this. Where were you when I said it? Another planet?"

"Perhaps I was," Lynx said uncertainly.

"Well, are you back now? How many times do I have to tell you before you'll believe me?"

"I—"

"Put that baby to bed," Bonnie said darkly. "I don't know what else it'll take, but I'm going to prove it to you, once and for all. What's gotten into you anyway? I thought you were doing so much better. Having a relapse?"

Lynx was so confused the only thing he heard was that he should put the baby down, so that's what he did. He looked down at her lying in her bed. She really was his—sort of. How *fascinating*...

Bonnie took his hand. "Come on, 'Dad.' You and 'Mom' need to spend a little time alone."

Pulling him along behind her, Bonnie took him to her bed. Turning, she looked fiercely into his eyes and said, "Okay, Lynx. This time, I want it all."

He gaped at her in surprise. "I've done all I can, there's nothing more I can do," he protested.

"I'm not talking about sex," she said. "And even if I was, it wouldn't matter. Besides, there's nothing wrong with you. You can do anything you want, Lynx. Vladen as good as told me that nothing physical showed up on

that scan he did of you when you first got here—and
those scans are damn near foolproof!"

Lynx just stood there, not having the slightest idea
what to say to her.

"I've done all I can," she went on. "Now it's time for
you to do something."

"But I have!" he said, his anger rising at last. "I have
worked for you, I have helped with the child, and I have
lain with you and given you what pleasure I can!"

"Yes, but the one thing I really want, you've never
given me. You've never given me yourself."

"No?"

"No, you haven't. There's a part of you that you've
never given to anyone—not to me, not to anyone you've
ever been with—and I want it." She raised a hand to
caress his cheek. "I love you more than you will ever
know," she whispered. "Please believe that. I want to
give you everything—myself, my daughter, and children
of our own. But I can't do that if you won't let me."

Bonnie was gazing straight into those big yellow
eyes when she saw the fire ignite behind them. The dam
broke at last, and Lynx lunged at her, pulling her into
his arms, crushing her in his embrace. His mouth found
hers, and as he devoured her soft, full lips, Bonnie became aware of a growing thunder in her ears, and the fire
between her thighs erupted. She didn't care what he did
to her—not even if she died as a result.

Lynx felt a tightness in his balls and something happened, something long forgotten, as a rush of blood
and fire raced through his groin. He didn't remove her
clothes gently, but ripped them to shreds while the crashing sound of his own pulse raged in his head. He felt a

throb and pain, tearing through long-dormant places, and his cock began to ache with lust and need and love and desire. Freeing himself of his clothing, he threw her down on the bed and then pounced on her like a wildcat on its prey.

There was no time to waste; the need to mate was so strong, he had to succumb to it or die. Bonnie's eyes were clouded with desire, and he could smell her scent; surrounding him, enveloping him, and driving him to new pinnacles of passion. Her nipples were hard, her legs spread wide, the golden hair between them wet and waiting for him. Pinning her with his own body, he licked her, savoring the flavor and aroma of hot, passionate woman. The scent of her was stronger than ever and drove him mad. She smelled different, too; the pleasing aroma of love was still there, but was now spiced with the sharp scent of lust. He wanted nothing more than to bury himself in her soft body and get lost inside her forever.

Muscles that hadn't been used in years still remembered the drill, aiming him without conscious thought or effort. He plunged into her in one hot, hard stroke and let loose a cry of triumph. There had been a time when he could fuck a woman in his sleep, but he wanted to be awake for this one; wanted to look into her eyes to see what he was doing to her. Her lips were parted in awe, and her soft moans escaped them with every move he made. Rising up, he looked down at his thick, hard cock, watching as it rammed into her again and again and again. Her heavy breasts rocked back and forth on her chest as he moved against her. He stopped thrusting and then smiled as she cried out in protest.

"Does it feel good to you, Bonnie?"

Nodding, she whispered helplessly, "Please don't stop."

His reply was a loud, satisfied purr, and as his cock began its swirling dance inside her, her eyes seem to lose their focus. Lynx found her sweet spot and raked it with the serrated edge of his cockhead; pulsing it so fast, it was more of a vibration than a stroke. He heard her gasp, and then heard her scream as he drove her to a frenzy. His cock must not have been producing the orgasmic fluids that women had always craved because she wasn't having the continuous, effortless orgasms he remembered; he had to work for every single crescendo she reached. But that didn't matter to him, in fact, he was glad of it. He wanted her to feel what his body alone could do to her; things she never even dreamed of…

Backing out and rolling her over, he dove into her from behind. He liked looking at her round, firm ass while he fucked her. It was beautiful. He'd have to be sure and tell her that—but not now; he would save that for later. Reveling in the sound of their bodies slapping against each other, he picked up the pace, fucking hard and fast and deep. He brought her to one climax, then another, and another before slowing down to undulate his spine, feeling her, teasing her, bringing her up to the peak and sending her crashing down again. And it felt good—fabulously so—to be inside a woman again. Especially this woman. This woman he loved.

She wants my children! He savored the memory of those words. What wouldn't he give her now; now that she said the one thing he'd never heard from a woman— any woman. She really meant it, too; he was certain of it. She wanted babies—*his* babies, and he vowed to plant lots of them in her belly and then watch them grow and would love them, too. He slowed and rolled her over again; he wanted to see her face when he finished. Bonnie moaned in ecstasy, and as Lynx felt his testicles tighten, he reached down to pull her in tighter. At long last, he was going to fill her with his seed, and she would know joy.

Bonnie had seen the inferno blazing in Lynx's eyes and knew she'd unleashed a fury. When his hard cock penetrated her, she felt sure she could match him stroke for stroke and stay with him—but it was impossible. She soon lost all control and had to simply lie back and let him take her. She'd never known anyone who could do what Lynx was doing; had never felt anything like it and had never even dreamed that such a thing was possible. What he had been capable of with his hands and mouth was nothing compared with this! It was like riding a rogue comet through space, one with moves she couldn't even begin to anticipate.

Lynx had rolled her this way and that, giving it to her from every direction to the point where she half expected him to stand her on her head. Where did he learn all this? She was so blown away, she couldn't even remember that she already knew the answer to that question. What she did know was that he could aim the damn thing in any direction and stay inside her at angles no other man would have even dreamed of trying. She looked down once, seeing him on his hands and knees with his ass aimed toward her, his balls bouncing up and down as he fucked, his cock aimed backward to catch her pussy and drive into it with perfect precision. She stared at him in disbelief, thinking that while he might not have been able to use it for several years, he certainly hadn't forgotten how. In response, Bonnie raised her legs high, and then grasping her feet, rotated her pelvis up to meet him.

Lynx let out another explosive purr and pulled out suddenly; his gleaming cock poised above her for a moment, then dove in as deeply as possible, swirling his thick rod inside her. Then he did it again, and again, and again. Bonnie had never felt quite so thoroughly nailed before in her life, and watching him from behind was the most erotic thing she'd ever witnessed—and, best of all, he was doing it to *her*.

When Lynx turned around and took her in his arms, his dick penetrated her once again, and she marveled at his lack of fumbling; his aim was perfect, and he slid right up inside her. "Hold onto me, my lovely Bonnie," he whispered. "And I will give you joy unlike any you have ever known."

Not knowing what to do—and not capable of much else—Bonnie grasped his shoulders, and Lynx then sat back on his heels, lifting her upright and taking her hips in his hands as he bounced her against him. Setting her down hard, he stopped all movement—even his breathing ceased for a moment. Bonnie watched his bright pupils dilate and, with a deep-throated growl, he filled her with his essence.

Within moments, every muscle in her body contracted and a thousand points of orgasmic thunder exploded in a climax which seemed to involve every cell. Her entire being then seemed to expand, as though each molecule suddenly needed more space before condensing into a euphoric sensation that raced through her bloodstream, spreading warmth and contentment throughout her body. It really *is* joy, she marveled… unlike any she had ever known…

Lynx watched as his lover's eyes grew round with astonishment and then wonder and then joy. He knew that peaceful laetralence would soon follow as his snard worked its magic. It had been many years since he'd witnessed the effects; but to his triumph, Bonnie's reactions seemed to be pronounced and prolonged. He didn't know the reason for the difference, but perhaps it took love to reach the highest level—a love for which he was profoundly grateful.

Lynx could feel the wavelike undulations of his coronal ruffle begin and heard Bonnie's gasp of renewed pleasure. He'd seldom had the opportunity to let it all unfold as it was meant to; before, there had always been someone else clamoring for his attention. But this was even more wonderful than he imagined it would be; he was with her, inside her, giving everything to her. He'd felt his own satisfying release before, but had never reveled in the woman's pleasure. As his gaze roamed over her face, taking in her heavy-lidded eyes with lashes that sparkled with tears of joy, her full lips parted with unspoken awe, and the softly glowing blush of her cheek with its light sheen of moisture, Lynx knew he had never looked upon anything more intoxicatingly beautiful in his entire life.

Lynx felt his penis beginning to lose its stiffness, but it didn't matter now. Even if he could never do it again, he'd done it at least once, and he'd done it with the only woman he'd ever truly loved—this one who loved him in return—this woman he adored.

Bonnie didn't want to wake up and forget this lovely dream she was having. Lynx was in her arms; her fretful baby was sleeping—what the chickens and the enocks were up to, she didn't know and didn't much care. Had she ever felt this way before? She didn't think so. It was so peaceful... even her brain was quiet for once; not thinking about anything... just drifting endlessly on a blissful cloud of serenity. At some point she would have to get up—but not yet. Work could wait for just a little longer...

Bonnie had never been one to put off until tomorrow what needed to be done today—all work and no play had been a way of life to her. But Lynx had changed that— just as she had changed him. And everyone thought there was something wrong with him! There was nothing wrong with her darling Lynx. He was perfect. Jack didn't know *everything* about Zetithians...

Just as Cat probably didn't know everything about women. Bonnie smiled to herself, thinking that Lynx had used some techniques she'd be willing to bet even Cat didn't know. But the effortless orgasms? Bonnie had climaxed several times, but there was nothing effortless about what Lynx had been doing to her.

She felt blood begin to surge toward the apex of her thighs at the mere thought of Lynx in action. What was it he had said? *"I was once a skilled lover"?* What a gross understatement! Running a finger delicately along the curve of his shoulder, she sighed with contentment. She loved that spot: the place where Lynx's neck flowed gracefully into his back and shoulders. It seemed odd to consider a man graceful, but the whole of his being seemed to define the word. True, he was strong and masculine, but that touch of the feline in him raised him far above ordinary males.

Remembering how much she would have given to hold him like this—all those months of longing, all those sleepless nights—and now, this; it was nothing short of heaven.

Lynx began purring as soon as he awakened to find himself in Bonnie's embrace with the sweet, glorious scent of love filling his head and spiraling down to his groin, bringing his cock to life once again.

She'd been so right—it had all been in his head—if only she'd told him before, things might have been different, though it might have been more the way she said it than the actual knowledge. He had no idea just how she'd done it, but his cock was now hard as steel, and he wanted nothing more than to use it on her again.

The feel of her sated body told him he'd done well, but he knew he could do better—*would* do better—in the future. There was no reason not to now, and no reason he couldn't meet with his former comrades and feel like one of them again—perhaps more so than he ever had. He'd been younger than the others and had always felt slightly inadequate in comparison—they'd been such proud warriors, whereas he had been more effective behind the scenes.

Bonnie had been right about that, too. They had worked as a unit; each with his own talents and duties, and each one every bit as important as the other. The only difference was that the others had found lovers—lovers who bore their children. The children of the last remaining Zetithians would be scattered like seeds across the galaxy, and Lynx vowed that he would add his own to the mix. Those who would have destroyed them had not succeeded. The spirit of Zetith would prevail.

Lynx nuzzled Bonnie's breast, breathing on her soft nipples and watching with fascination as they hardened. She was his to entice and enjoy, and he would delight in exploring her body; learning its secrets and finding new ways to enthrall her. He would bind her to him. His semen, or snard, as it was referred to in his native tongue, was very effective, but his coronal fluid was best, though it seemed to be absent. Perhaps it would return in time. It was one thing of his that women had never wasted, seeing it as a precious commodity to be savored and enjoyed.

He remembered that first day in the harem when he had naïvely thought that his life as a slave would be one of pure pleasure. They had taken him by the hand and led him to a bed of pillows, laying him down and teasing him to make the fluid flow freely. Had that first taste been accidental, or had he encouraged them, knowing what it would do to them? He couldn't remember, but he could vividly recall the scene in which scores of beautiful, nude females had clustered around his cock like bees to honey; feeding on his fluids, and then gasping and writhing as the orgasms shook their shapely forms. Exotic beauties each one of them, with perfect breasts, slender waists, and lush, rounded hips; if only they'd been less greedy, less demanding, he would be there still. They would have adored him as much as he now adored Bonnie—Bonnie, who didn't want more than he could give, but who only wanted *him*.

And she would get him, too, because just as soon as she woke up, he was fully intending to mate with her again. Suddenly, it seemed that waiting was no longer an option.

"Are you awake?" he whispered.

"I am now," Bonnie murmured. "What's up?"

"It's odd that you would put it that way," he said as he brought her hand to his lips for a kiss. "But if you will just put your hand here," he said, moving it lower, "you will see what is 'up.'"

Bonnie giggled. "I think I've created a monster."

Lynx chuckled softly. "I believe you have… *released* the monster."

"No kidding," Bonnie said. "—and it's *quite* a monster! Persistent little devil, too. You sure you don't need more… recovery time?"

"I have slept," Lynx replied. "—and as you can see, I have already recovered."

"Well, *you* may have," Bonnie said roundly, "—but I'm not so sure about me. You fuck like a world champion, you know that?"

"I *was* very good," Lynx said modestly, "at one time."

"You still *are* very good," she corrected him. "I don't believe I've ever been with anyone else who could literally do it upside down and backwards."

Lynx grinned. "That backwards move was very popular."

"I'm sure it was," she agreed. "Watching your balls

bounce was incredibly erotic! I'll bet even Cat doesn't know that one."

"Possibly not," Lynx admitted. "I did that for a woman who liked watching me mate with other women." Favoring Bonnie with a sly smile, he added, "She liked watching my balls bounce, too."

"Well, you've got some really nice balls there," Bonnie said. "And this cock is freakin' awesome, too."

"Awesome?" he repeated. "I do not understand that word."

"Sorry, my Stantongue isn't as good as my English," she said. "It means inspiring awe, wonder, something that's really cool, absolutely fantastic, wonderful, marvelous, fabulous—" Bonnie paused as she gave his penis a yank. "Are you getting this?"

"You like my cock," he said with a knowing smile.

"That's an understatement if I've ever heard one!" declared Bonnie. "It's absolutely beautiful."

"It does not seem to produce the fluid from the corona anymore," he said regretfully. "That is what would give you the most joy."

"Well, maybe I just need to suck it harder," Bonnie suggested.

Lynx felt his nuts tighten, and his cock pulsed without conscious effort. The mental image of Bonnie with his dick in her mouth was almost enough to send him into orgasm.

"Or maybe I just need to jack you off a few times," she went on conversationally. "You know, to flush out the pipes?"

"Jack me off?"

"You know, with my hands?"

"You would do that for me?"

"Sure, why not? I've done it lots of times before—and you surely have done it to yourself!"

"No, I have not."

"Lynx," she said darkly. "Most guys do it all the time! Do you mean to say you never have? Where the devil have you been?"

"Paemay," he replied with a chuckle. "And Zetith before that. I did not know it was possible."

"Guess you aren't as good as you thought you were—or maybe the slave girls didn't like watching a guy come, whereas I, on the other hand, absolutely *adore* the sight of a spewing cock."

Lynx gave an involuntary gulp. "You do?" He didn't think he could take much more of this kind of talk without having to do something… physical.

"I *do*," she said with a heartfelt sigh. "Especially yours! I love watching it drool and fuck and—"

Lynx had heard enough and suddenly, couldn't wait another moment and pushed her head down to his groin. "Suck me, then, and watch me come."

Bonnie hadn't had the opportunity to suck him when he was hard, and it was something she'd been looking forward to for a long time. And it was beautiful, too: thick, hard, red-hot, and—

"Lynx!" she exclaimed excitedly. "What's that?" Pointing to the clear fluid oozing from the serrated points of his corona, she asked, "Is that it?"

He nodded. "I believe so."

"Hmm, guess a little, um, *discussion* was all it took then." On closer inspection, she noted that, while it seemed to be coming from a slightly different source, it didn't appear to be different from the normal lubricating emissions of human males. "So, does it work if I just taste it?"

"It used to," he said as his face took on an expression of roguish delight. "Lick me and discover for yourself."

Bonnie laughed out loud. "You really like telling me what to do, don't you?"

"Women have never let me do that before," he said. "But you do, and I *like* being able to tell you what I want you to do."

"Yeah, well, anything you like is bound to be good for me, too," Bonnie admitted. "I want you so bad right now, I can hardly stand it. Cocksucking is a favorite pastime of mine, by the way—drives me absolutely wild."

"And Sylor *left* you?" Lynx remarked with an amused smile. "I still do not understand why."

"I guess he just wasn't the type to settle down," Bonnie said with a shrug. "That's the way he was—I can't really hold anything against him, because he always said he didn't want to get married—which was probably for the best."

Lynx drew in a deep, ragged breath. Things were not progressing anywhere near quickly enough to suit him, and his cock pulsed again in anticipation, causing more fluid to exude from the corona. He'd taken just about all he could stand. "Are you going to talk or suck me?" Lynx said, stroking Bonnie's cheek with his slick cock-head. His voice deepened as he added, "I think you will like it."

"I already know that, Lynx!" she said waspishly. "The damn thing even *tastes* good."

"Lick me then," Lynx purred, "and you will know joy."

"Just dying to know if it works, aren't you?"

Lynx nodded. "I am understandably... anxious—and curious."

Bonnie smiled. "There's an old saying about curiosity and cats—perhaps you've heard it? 'Curiosity killed the cat.'"

"Meaning?"

"Cats sometimes get into some very dangerous places by being so curious."

"I am only curious about getting into one place," he said suggestively. "I want you to taste my snard."

"Snard?" she echoed. "That's what you call that fluid?"

"No, snard is what we Zetithians call our semen," he replied. "The other fluid has no name."

"No name?" she said thoughtfully. "I'll have to come up with one."

"Do that," he said. "But taste it first."

"Okay, here goes..." Bonnie teased the coronal edge with the tip of her tongue. His fluid was clear and slightly salty and definitely had the desired effect; within moments, Bonnie felt like a bomb had gone off inside her. She rolled away from him as her body went into spasms. "Yeah," she gasped. "It works—*very* well! So tell me, Lynx, am I still all in one piece?"

"You are," Lynx replied, purring contentedly.

"I think you should call that stuff Orgasmic Explosion, or Cock Thunder, or Joy Juice. No, wait! I've got it! The Zetithian love potion."

"I like that one," he said appreciatively. "The love potion of Zetith."

"Says it all," Bonnie agreed. "Sounds a lot better than 'pre-cum,' too. Of course, now that I think about it, semen isn't that great a word either. It's no wonder people keep coming up with new things to call it." Dipping her finger in his magic potion, she began painting his cock with it. "You know, come to think of it, I'm not sure the fluid humans produce has an official name, either. I've heard lots of euphemisms, but nothing that sounds very… scientific." She continued spreading the slippery stuff all up and down his now-quivering shaft. "I'm surprised Jack hasn't bottled this stuff and made a fortune off of it by now."

"That has been tried," Lynx said, doing his best to keep talking when all he really wanted to do was mount her, "but it does not last. Some of the slave women were curious and collected it, but found that it lost its effect after a few hours."

"Mmm. Just as well." Bonnie started giggling uncontrollably as another use occurred to her. "It'd be a lot of fun at a party, though," she gasped. "You could spike the punch with it."

Lynx grinned. "Now, that *does* work," he said. "But the effect is not as strong."

"Did the slave girls actually *do* that, or was it a popular party drink on Zetith?"

"It was not so highly prized on Zetith," Lynx said dryly. "We had plenty of it there."

"But the slave girls must've thought it was incredible." Noting his nod, she continued. "I'm sure it *had* to get boring living in a harem all the time. I'll bet they were tickled to death to have you—you must have kept them well entertained."

"For a time," he agreed. "And in that place, with women always wanting to mate, my cock was erect almost all the time."

"Didn't that hurt?"

"Sometimes," he admitted. "But I could always find release."

The thought of Lynx randomly plunging his stiff dick into any available woman bothered Bonnie just a bit. She hoped he would be more... selective... in the future. "So, what's your favorite position?" she asked, fully intending to make a list of his preferences and then give him whatever he wanted—if for no other reason than to assure that he didn't go looking for love anywhere else.

It didn't take Lynx long to reply, for the image of a shapely ass bouncing on his groin sprang into his mind, making his cock throb in anticipation. "I liked to lie on my back with a woman sitting on me, so I could see her from behind. They enjoyed it because I could move inside them like—"

But Bonnie had already sprung up to position herself between his legs and was wiggling her bottom at him. "Like this?"

Lynx swallowed hard; if she kept that up, he'd lose a load of snard into the air before he ever got inside her. His reply came out somewhere between a purr and a choke.

"I believe I'll take that as a yes," Bonnie chuckled. Looking over her shoulder, she said wonderingly, "I never dreamed you could be this much fun."

He blinked in surprise. Could mating actually be fun? Perhaps it *had* been in the beginning—before it became such an endless chore to him. Fun. What an interesting concept! "You are having fun?"

"Barrels of it," Bonnie replied. "Aren't you?"

"Yes," he replied hesitantly. Then he realized that he hadn't done anything that could be considered fun in a *very* long time.

"I didn't think I'd ever have fun with a man again as long as I lived," Bonnie went on, "but you changed that. I haven't felt like shaking my ass at a guy in ages."

Actually, she never had, but that was beside the point. What mattered was that she was doing it now—and enjoying herself enormously. Experimentally, she tried it again and was rewarded with a groan from Lynx. Giggling with delight, she twisted around and jiggled her tits at him.

Lynx's long, tortured moan gave Bonnie another idea. Pinching her nipples, she pulled her breasts up as high as they would go and then let them drop.

As her luscious breasts bounced, Lynx lost all control and grabbed her hips, pulling her down on him so hard that if he'd missed, he'd have hurt himself. He didn't know how or why, but being with Bonnie was different. No woman had ever made him lose control the way she did. Her beautiful body stretched out above him nearly drove him insane, and he drank in her image, reveled in her scent, and delighted in the feel of her. She affected him so much more strongly than any of the others had, seeming to merge with him; her pleasure was his pleasure, and he would give her all he could. He had a feeling of oneness with her that was completely alien to him.

He thrust his hips upward, impaling her deeply as he held her down tightly. Bonnie let out a gasp of surprise and then settled down on him, grinding him inside her, deriving intense enjoyment from his soft groans of pure delight. She kept up the movement, reaching down to massage his balls as she rocked him, loving the hard, thick presence inside her—loving *him*. Just being able to do that was a joy to her.

Stopping her own movement, she could still feel him sweeping her inner walls with his talented cock. He didn't need to produce the love potion to drive her wild; his body itself was quite enough.

But not all, because she let out a cry as the first climax burst from the depths of her body. "Oh, *Lynx!*" she sighed. "You don't just give me joy; you're joy itself." Her voice trailed off as she lost her balance and nearly fell off of him. "I don't think I can do it this way…" Falling forward onto her hands, she rocked back against him, driving him in deeper and reveling in the heavenly sensation of his hard cock stretching her to the limit. She could feel her body contracting around him, squeezing him hard and forcing more of his love potion from his engorged cockhead.

It was good, but still not exactly what Lynx wanted. He pulled out from under her and heard her gasp in protest. "Get up," he said, slapping her butt and pulling her up onto her knees.

Bonnie's arms were sprawled out on the bed as Lynx pushed down on her lower back and impaled her slick heat with his gleaming wet cock. If he'd ever felt such an overwhelming urge to drive himself into a woman before, he couldn't remember it. All he wanted was to be up to his nuts in her, ramming in as hard as he possibly could. It was as if all the desire he'd ever felt in his lifetime was now bottled up inside him, trying desperately to get out. He thrust into her with all the strength in his body. The sound of her legs slapping against his thighs and the sight of her bottom bouncing against his groin drove him to new heights of passion.

Bonnie was one gigantic, continuous orgasm. Her body couldn't even respond anymore, the orgasm was all in her mind—shutting out all conscious thought and all sensations, except one—ecstasy—in its purest, most perfect form. Somewhere within that perfect place she heard a hiss and a groan as Lynx erupted inside her, his cock spewing forth his seed.

His climax came from so far inside him, Lynx felt as if he'd given her more of himself than his semen; his life force itself seemed to separate, ripping away part of his soul to send it hurtling forth into her welcoming body. He knew then what had happened; he hadn't just used her to slake his lust, as he had with the slave women. He loved her, and he had *mated* with her. For life.

Chapter 18

SYLOR WAS ALREADY WELL AWARE THAT HE WOULD have a difficult time convincing Bonnie to take him back and call off the hunt, but what he'd just seen through the window convinced him that to eliminate *this* rival, he would have to be more ruthless than ever before. Sylor prided himself on his own sexual abilities, but he was smart enough to realize that between himself and Bonnie's new lover, there could be no comparison.

To say he was disheartened would have been incorrect, for Sylor had never been one to let minor obstacles stand in the way of his desires. He'd wanted his freedom, and he needed money, so he took it. He saw it as rightfully his, anyway—even the ring Bonnie had inherited from her grandmother, though most people would have had difficulty reconciling that as anything other than blatant thievery. He'd even stolen Bonnie from her previous boyfriend—which had been no trouble, really. All he'd had to do was arrange for a meeting between the boyfriend and Bonnie's sister, tell each of them a few lies, and the situation took care of itself. People were so easy to manipulate when you knew how.

He'd misjudged Bonnie, however, having assumed that she would be waiting for him when he decided to return. What was odd was that she'd taken so long to set the dogs on him. They were having trouble finding him, though, and it was downright hilarious to see the looks on their faces when their tracking devices told them that Sylor was right there in front of them, but they still couldn't see him. It was all he could do to keep from laughing out loud.

Sylor knew he could blend in with his surroundings to the point that he was all but invisible, but the Zetithian seemed wary, almost as though he'd known someone was there. Sylor was unfamiliar with the species—he'd met Cat and Leo, of course, but knew very little about their innate abilities—so he backed off for a while, watching from afar while deciding on the best approach to the problem.

Kipper remembered him and had seemed happy to see him—at least not giving him away by barking like a fool. The dog knew him well enough; what about the cat?

Sylor knew he'd been gone too long and that this rival was now firmly entrenched in his old life—but how to get him out of it? Getting him deported would be difficult, since Sylor himself was on the run, and there was nothing incriminating he could plant on him—he'd already sold the only thing traceable when he'd unloaded the ring to fund the deal with Krall, which had proved to be a disastrous mistake. There was nothing to accuse Lynx of; he couldn't even claim adultery—though it wasn't a crime on Terra Minor—because he and Bonnie had never married. That had been a mistake, Sylor now realized, because he'd always intended to come back—when it suited him.

So, Sylor waited and watched, alert for any opportunity. He preferred toying with people over resorting to anything drastic. Could he convince her new lover that Bonnie didn't want him anymore? It was doubtful, but perhaps the man was insecure enough to believe what a stranger might tell him. Could he tell him that Bonnie had a history of using and discarding men? Sylor knew that the reverse was true, but could he make him believe it?

It would be hard for Sylor to insinuate himself into Lynx's confidence in his current predicament. With any other man, a casual meeting, an exchange of news, a few laughs, and then he could have him believing anything he told him—of course, it would be a casual comment; one that anyone might have made, but one that would discredit Bonnie and make it seem as though she was indiscriminate when it came to bestowing her affections. He could pass along some very personal information which would make it apparent that he himself had known Bonnie intimately. Lynx would have no way of knowing just who Sylor was, and would therefore believe that he couldn't trust his new lover to remain faithful.

Which Bonnie would do, though it pained Sylor to admit it. He'd fucked more women on this planet than he could count, but if Bonnie had been promiscuous, she'd managed to keep it a secret from everyone, including Sylor, who prided himself on his ability to know things that others didn't. Perhaps it had been her steadfast heart that had attracted Sylor to her in the first place, but those guileless blue eyes of hers would lead anyone to believe that she was just lonely enough, just gullible enough, to believe a few white lies.

Sylor was desperate enough to consider murder, but wasn't the type to want his hands dirtied with another man's blood—whatever the reason. He considered himself to be a cut above the common criminal and certainly above anyone as low as a murderer. But if he could make it happen in some other way... perhaps set up a fatal accident... yes, that would do very nicely, indeed—and farms were notorious settings for accidents; really nasty, really *horrible* accidents...

Sabotaging the equipment would have been the best method, but it was just as likely that he would wind up killing Bonnie, rather than his intended victim. Too much left to chance, too much margin for error. He would have to think on this a while longer...

The start of the rainy season was a slow time for farmers on Terra Minor. Once the major crops had been harvested, no large-scale planting was done until nearer the time for the rains to taper off again. Then there was a flurry of activity, because timing was everything; if planted too soon in the cool, wet weather, the seeds would rot in the ground, and if planted too late, they would fail to germinate. Bonnie and Lynx kept busy tending the vegetable garden, for there were many plants that enjoyed such conditions, but for the most part, there was time to relax and enjoy their new-found love.

Shaulla kept them both busy and entertained. She was a happy, laughing child—much like her father, Bonnie thought ruefully. Sylor had always been so charming, but how much of what he'd told her had been lies? Bonnie had always tended to believe in the men she loved—so much so that they could tell her just about anything and she would swallow it.

But Lynx had been different; he'd said he didn't like her from the start and had made no bones about it. It was so odd the way men behaved. The one she should have hated turned out to be the one she loved the most.

Not that loving him was difficult, especially now that he was unleashing the full force of his sensuous, loving nature in her direction. Bonnie was glad she'd fallen in love with him before discovering his capabilities, otherwise she could never have been certain that she loved him for himself and not the wide variety of pleasures he could provide.

She was discovering more of his fantasies every day, though it seemed odd to her that he would have any. He'd been vehemently opposed to romance for so long, she wondered just how new some of them were. Along with being able to tell her what he wanted, he seemed to enjoy having sex in odd places—including one remarkable encounter in the henhouse, much to the discomfiture of the hens.

Lynx was experiencing sex from the (for him) novel perspective of the predatory male. On Zetith, men had to entice women and then be ready to go at a moment's notice. Taking a woman by force was impossible, for if a female felt no desire, the male would be unable to function. But for Lynx, Bonnie smelled like love even when she was feeding the chickens, and the fact that he could now be the initiator was heady stuff indeed.

The strange thing was that Bonnie had seemed to enjoy giving him pleasure even when she experienced none for herself—at least, not in the way that other women had. Lynx hadn't believed her when she'd said she would only use her hands on him, but she had done it and had obviously enjoyed it when he ejaculated right in her face. Lynx didn't understand it; he'd never met a woman who didn't want far more from him than that.

Now that his impotence was no longer a factor, Lynx was back to his old ways of being hot and hard almost continuously. How could he have ever believed he could remain indifferent to Bonnie? It had taken fifty slave women to equal what this one, lone woman was doing to him now, and for this reason alone, Lynx was grateful for the lull in the workload. There were still chores to be done, of course, but the pace was slower, less urgent, and he had plenty of time to enjoy his mate.

As he leaned against the rail of the enock pen, feeling the soft rain fall on his face, Lynx thought back to when Bonnie had come out to the shed with his lunch while he'd been working on the harvester droid. With plenty of time until it would be needed again, Lynx had torn it apart and worked on it daily. He was one of those men who had a feel for machinery and could diagnose a problem almost instinctively, but though he had been focusing solely on the work, he had known Bonnie was there even before she spoke.

Her heavenly scent had quickly filled his head and then gone racing to his groin. Did she have any idea what she had done? That she had taken a man as worn-out as that old speeder and made him feel new again? Lynx doubted it, for Bonnie had never seen him as broken to begin with.

She'd smiled at the sight of his grimy hands and had insisted on feeding him, something that Lynx had done for the slave women countless times in the past, and he marveled that someone would do it for him. Bonnie's love for him was still a mystery to Lynx. He'd been unkind to her from the start, but she had seen through the ruse, perhaps understanding him far better than he did himself.

Bringing him fruit, she fed him one succulent bite after another. His cock was so hard he could scarcely think of eating, but she made him swallow every bit of it. Then she had released his clothing and sucked him. He could still feel it; her lips warm and soft on his hot meat, her orgasms seeming to almost interrupt her enjoyment of him. That was the first time she'd used her hands on him, too. She'd teased him, telling him that his hands were too dirty to touch her, but that hadn't stopped *her* from touching *him!* He'd been so wet and slick, and she'd laced her fingers together and made a tunnel of her hands to stroke him while she licked his balls. Lynx would have been starved for a month if he'd ever even suggested that a slave woman do what Bonnie was doing voluntarily, letting him spew his snard all over her—on her face, on her breasts, in her mouth…

As he watched her sucking him, he knew it wouldn't be enough, even after he'd come for her. Rubbing his cock on her face that was now slick with his snard, he felt the need to mate boiling up inside him again. Her desire had not abated, nor had his. Ignoring her feeble protests about his dirty hands, he pushed her down and stripped the clothing from her succulent body and buried his shaft in her soft, wet heat, thrusting hard and deep until he came once more. With a satisfied purr, he withdrew and licked her until she was helpless with ecstasy. Then, just to prove he still could, he did it all over again.

Even with his sexual prowess back to its former level, it was odd that a man who had spent so much time in the company of women could have been so sexually naïve; he knew everything a man could do to a woman, but what a woman could do to a man? He was on uncharted territory there, and he knew it, and though he'd heard other men boast of their exploits and what their women had done for them, Bonnie was doing something amazing every day.

At that moment, he almost wished he was capable of pleasuring himself—something he'd never considered before. Just the thought of what she'd done should have sent blood flooding his groin, stiffening his shaft and making it drip with anticipation. Lynx loved the feel of Bonnie's hands on his cock, her tongue swirling on the head, devouring him... Promising himself to find Bonnie and mate with her just as soon as the chores were done, he tossed more feed to the enocks.

Lynx was startled out of his reverie by Bonnie's approach, but this time, she didn't smell of desire, she smelled of fear.

"Oh, God! You haven't got her either!" Bonnie exclaimed. "I can't find Ulla! She can barely crawl! How could she possibly have gotten out of the house?"

Lynx felt fear slice through him like a knife. Though he hadn't picked up the scent lately, he'd known Sylor had been nearby. Would he have taken his child? Was that his intent?

"She was playing on the floor when I left the house," Lynx said, trying to keep his voice even. "If she had gone outdoors, she would have fallen down the steps.

You would have seen her, or heard her cries. She must still be in the house, hiding perhaps."

Bonnie shook her head. "Kids her age don't do that, do they? I've never had a baby before, so I don't really know for sure, but—"

"We will find her," Lynx said firmly. "She cannot hide from me."

"Well, that sounds pretty darn cocky," Bonnie declared, momentarily diverted. "I know your eyes are pretty good, but—"

"I will find her," Lynx said again.

"If you say that enough times, I might actually believe it," Bonnie muttered. "Come on!"

Dashing across the yard and up the steps, Lynx burst through the door, his keen cat's eyes searching the kitchen. She was there somewhere, she *had* to be! Calling out her name he stopped and waited, listening intently. There was nowhere to hide except under the table, and she wasn't there. Moving to the next room where she'd been playing before, he saw her toys lying by the sofa, but no sign of the child.

"I don't see her, do you?" Bonnie said nervously. "I can't imagine how she could have gotten past me! She was right there just a few minutes ago!" She paused as the idea that Sylor might be involved occurred to her. "If Sylor's come back and taken her—I'll… I don't know what I'll do. Well, yes, I *do* know; I'll sic Drummond on him and he'll track him down. How could I have been so stupid? I should have done it months ago! That's what I get for being so forgiving."

"You forgave him for leaving you?" If she'd forgiven him, she just might take him back…

"Well, not really, but I could have gotten his butt deported if I'd only known..." Bonnie stomped her foot in frustration.

Lynx sniffed the air and put up a hand to silence her. "Sylor has not been here," he said. "Listen."

Bonnie's heart was pounding too loudly for her to hear anything beyond the rush of blood in her ears, but she listened anyway. "I don't hear anything," she said after a few moments.

"I can hear her breathing," Lynx said. "She's here somewhere. Normally, I could locate her by scent alone, but she lives here, and her scent is already strong."

"You can hear her *breathing?*" Bonnie exclaimed. "Are all of your senses that good?"

"Better than yours, perhaps," he said. "Otherwise you would have found her before this."

"Well, then, where *is* she?"

"There," Lynx replied, pointing to the floor by the sofa. "Can you see that the fabric looks odd?"

Bonnie stared at the couch, and as she did, part of the pattern seemed to move and she heard Shaulla giggle. "I don't believe it!" she exclaimed.

"She is able to blend in with her surroundings," Lynx said quietly. "Do you see her now?"

Bonnie could see two points of light that seemed to move. "I see her eyes—at least, I think that's what I see," Bonnie replied. "What is she? Some kind of chameleon?"

Though he'd never heard the word chameleon before, Lynx took her meaning immediately. "There were animals on my planet that could almost disappear," he said. "We had to hunt them by scent alone."

"Like a chameleon," Bonnie whispered, still amazed at what her daughter seemed to be doing. Shaulla giggled again and slowly began to reappear. "Why, you little stinker!" Bonnie exclaimed, scooping Ulla up from the floor. "You had me scared to death!" Shaulla couldn't talk yet, but she seemed to understand a good joke anyway and laughed merrily. "I never knew Vessonians could do that!" Bonnie exclaimed and shuddered as the implications of this ability struck her. "Do you think she can do this at will?"

Lynx shrugged. "Perhaps Vladen would be able to tell us."

"No, he won't," Bonnie said grimly, "because the next time I see him, he's dead meat! He never told me anything of the sort, and neither did Sylor—although Sylor might not be able to do it himself. Vladen told me the Terran-Vessonian cross sometimes produces a child with a weak heart—maybe this is another variation. When you start mixing species together, anything can happen—Tisana came by her powers that way, you know—it might be something like that."

Lynx shook his head. "No. I believe Sylor has this ability as well," he said. "I have been aware of his scent recently, but have seen no one."

"Is *that* how you knew he hadn't been in here? No, wait—you couldn't possibly know what he smells like!"

"Have I not been sleeping on his pillow?"

"I never thought of that," Bonnie said slowly. "And yes, you have." She searched her memories of Sylor, trying to recall anything... "You know, when we first started hunting enocks, Sylor got hurt pretty bad trying to catch one by himself. I'll bet he made himself invisible, and the enock fought back, whether he could see him or not. It was later on that he came up with the net and speeder method." Thinking further, she added, "I'll bet he could have slipped into the pen and gotten eggs without my help, too."

"Possibly," Lynx conceded, "But we could see Shaulla when she moved."

"Sylor may be better at it than she is—or at least, better at holding still when he needs to." Bonnie felt her skin begin to crawl. "He could be anywhere, Lynx, and we'd never even know it!"

"I would be able to hear him and pick up his scent," Lynx assured her. "But only if he was close by."

Bonnie shivered. "I've got to tell Drummond about this! They need to catch Sylor—if they're not already looking for him. Drummond always said I should have filed a formal complaint; this is what comes of not using my head."

"Would Drummond have done it himself?"

"Maybe," Bonnie admitted. "He's always been one to look out for me, but he never said anything about that—he wanted *me* to file the complaint, which I didn't do—not even when I changed the deed."

"You can have this changed?" Lynx asked. "I would not have thought…"

"It's a relic from the old mining laws on Earth," Bonnie explained. "Though God knows why they chose that one! After six months, you can consider a claim on a homestead abandoned, and someone else can take it over. Of course, if you abandon your claim, you usually wind up getting deported."

"I am aware of the deportation policy," Lynx said dryly. "It is why I came to work for you."

Bonnie grinned. "Yeah, I figured as much. Did you realize that Drummond got you here under false pretenses?"

"No," Lynx said cautiously.

"He told you this was the only job, didn't he?"

Lynx nodded.

"I'm sure there were other possibilities—just not any in the mines. It was another of his ways of looking out for me."

"I was very angry," Lynx admitted.

"Yes, you were!" Bonnie declared. "And you didn't bother to hide it. If I hadn't needed you so badly—and if you hadn't saved my life and then built that enock pen—I might have had you deported myself! Or at least have you sent off to work for someone else."

"I am very glad you did not," Lynx said.

Bonnie laughed softly. "So am I. But I did ask Drummond if there were any other jobs available for you. I was so… well, it's hard to describe just how I felt, but I didn't think I could take it anymore."

Lynx looked at her curiously. "But you needed me," he said. "Would you have done that?"

"I'm not sure," Bonnie admitted, "but you seemed so unhappy here, I thought you would rather work for anyone but me, and I—" Her voice faltered, and she looked away from him, tears filling her eyes.

Lynx took her in his arms and lightly kissed her. "I would not have gone," he said quietly. "It was a torment for me to be here with you, but I couldn't leave."

"Torment?" Bonnie echoed. "Yes, that's pretty much how I felt; loving you when you would hardly talk to me and not being able to escape."

Lynx's arms tightened around her. "I am very sorry," he murmured. "But you understand now, don't you?"

Bonnie shook her head. "No," she said. "I understand why *you* thought it was necessary, but it wasn't that way for me at all! I love you, Lynx. I knew you were once a very skilled lover—and you've proven that—but that isn't everything. When Ulla was born, I got a taste of what it could be like with you… it was very hard to go back to the way things were before."

"But," he said gently, "I could not stay away."

"I thought Ulla was the one you couldn't keep away from," Bonnie said ruefully, though it pained her to admit it. "You seemed so much more interested in being with her than with me."

"She was *not* my only reason for staying," Lynx assured her; though he had always felt an attachment to the children he delivered. He had searched in vain for his own image in each child's face, still wanting to believe they were his own, even after realizing they were not.

Looking down at her daughter there in her arms, Bonnie said quietly, "But I still envied her. She had all the love from you that I wanted so badly."

"You no longer need to envy her," Lynx said. "Perhaps you never did."

It wasn't a declaration of his love, but it was close. Bonnie smiled. "Now I can just envy her ability to disappear! We've got to figure out a way to find her when she does that—you know, tie a bell on her or something—though we probably should be more concerned about Sylor if you've smelled him around here."

Lynx nodded and then looked at Bonnie uncertainly. "Do you know why he would return?" Lynx thought he knew the reason, but was reluctant to say it aloud.

"Probably looking for something else to steal," Bonnie said with a snort of disgust.

"You wouldn't—" Lynx broke off there, uncertain of how to phrase the question.

"Wouldn't what?"

"Take him back."

"Take him back?" Bonnie exclaimed. "Are you out of your mind? Why would I give *you* up for him? Come on now, Lynx. There's no comparison—never was, and there certainly isn't now! Please, don't keep throwing that in my face!"

His expression became neutral to the point of sullenness. "I did not intend to anger you." Lynx appeared uncomfortable, but added, as though it explained everything, "but you *did* have his child."

Bonnie gaped at him. "Any Joe Schmo can father a child, Lynx! There are plenty of times when it doesn't mean a damn thing."

Lynx blinked hard. Not mean anything? How could that be when it meant everything to Lynx? "I cannot understand that."

"Well, neither can I sometimes," Bonnie said with a shrug, "but some men just fuck their way through life and leave children behind wherever they go."

It was true of other men, perhaps—Lynx knew this from experience—but the thought of having a child of his growing up somewhere without him horrified Lynx. And not only his own child, but now Ulla. He would kill rather than let anyone take her from him. He loved her—and her mother—to distraction. No, Sylor would not get them back. Not without a fight.

Chapter 19

JACK HAD BEEN WORRYING OVER WHAT TO DO ABOUT the situation between Bonnie and Lynx ever since her last visit, but as she sat in the cockpit adjusting the course for the approach to Terra Minor, it was gnawing at her like a starving dog on a bone. Jack liked Bonnie, and it bugged the hell out of her that Lynx had turned out to be such a stick in the mud. What the devil were they going to do with him?

She glanced at Tisana, who sat nearby feeding her daughter while her two fair-haired boys, Alrik and Aidan, lay at her feet playing with the dog. Jack didn't think she would have liked having babies pull on her ears if she'd been a dog, but Max seemed to view this activity with a fatherly tolerance, though perhaps this was due to Tisana's intervention. Aside from her ability to communicate with animals, Jack knew that Tisana was capable of many remarkable things, and she had been trying to convince Tisana to make a potion for Lynx ever since learning of Bonnie's plight. Tisana had always staunchly refused, but since they were about to land, Jack thought she'd give it one more try.

"We're almost there," Jack said heartily. "Got Lynx's love potion brewed up, yet?"

"Jack," Tisana said wearily. "How many times do I have to tell you I don't make love potions?" Smiling as she fed Althea another spoonful, she added, "And even if I did, I certainly wouldn't allow anyone to use it on an unsuspecting person. It's unethical."

"Ethics be damned!" Jack declared. "Bonnie's got one of the last remaining Zetithians, and he's not living up to his potential! If Lynx's line dies out, there will be too few bloodlines to reestablish the species. Think about our children, Tisana! They need mates!"

"And I've told you a million times, their genes appear to be dominant," Tisana said patiently. "It doesn't seem to matter who they mate with, you still wind up with what are essentially pure Zetithian offspring, and our children are living proof!"

Jack ignored that. She'd heard all of this before. "Haven't you been listening to the guys talk? Zetithian women only go for Zetithian males, and even that takes some doing! It's all very well for my sons, but you've got a daughter! Who will Althea marry if she doesn't like my boys? They need more options!"

Tisana shook her head, smiling. Jack had such a one-track mind. She seemed determined to scatter Zetithians all across the galaxy and stamp out their enemies as she went. That last trio of Nedwuts they'd run into hadn't made it out of Rocky's Cantina alive, though they *had* made the mistake of firing the first shot. *Nobody* took potshots at Cat and lived if Jack was anywhere around, and Cat was no slouch when it came to looking after himself, either. Tisana had considered posting warning signs wherever they went, just to avoid any bloodshed. She'd had to shoot a fireball to deflect the shot herself, but that was mainly due to the fact that Leo had also been in the line of fire. The fact that they'd been cruising all around the galaxy and hadn't lost either of their men was a testament to just what lengths a woman would go to hang onto a Zetithian once she'd found one. It required constant vigilance, and Tisana sometimes wondered if going off with Jack and Cat hadn't been a mistake. Leo had been much safer on Utopia—though she hadn't exactly had to twist his arm to get him to leave; they were both much happier having escaped from life on that world.

"I know what you mean, Jack," Tisana sighed. "But it isn't up to us to decide who they'll marry! My daughter's choice of mates is with the gods."

"Oh, fiddle-faddle," Jack said dismissively. "Sometimes even the gods need a little help."

"Yes, I know," Tisana said, rolling her eyes. "The gods thrive on the sweat of human endeavor or some such thing. You don't have to tell me again."

Cat sauntered into the cockpit and, with one look at his wife, got the gist of the conversation immediately. "She is worried about Lynx, is she not?"

"Yes, but you know how she feels about Zetithians," Tisana said with a smile. "I still can't believe she let Trag go off with those gun runners."

Cat grinned knowingly. "She is our greatest champion. If she had been leading the fight, Zetith never would have been destroyed."

"Aw, now, Cat, don't start with that!" Jack warned. "It's not my fault I'd never heard of Zetith before I met you. But you're right," she added reflectively. "I'd have blasted that asteroid to smithereens, even if I had to sacrifice my ship to do it!"

"My lovely master," Cat purred, planting a kiss on Jack's cheek. "You are truly a mate beyond price."

"Go on, now," Jack said, making a feeble attempt to brush him off. She never was able to resist him. "Not in front of Tisana."

"We have made love in public before," Cat reminded her. "With strangers watching."

"Yes, and we decided we didn't really like it," Jack pointed out. "Besides, Tisana isn't a stranger."

Cat leaned closer and inhaled deeply. "But I can smell your desire, my master. You cannot hide it from me."

"I'm not trying to hide it," Jack insisted. "It's just that I'm in the middle of trying to land the bloody ship! Why do you always want nooky when I'm busy?"

"But I *like* it when you're busy," Cat purred. "That way I can surprise you."

Jack dearly loved being surprised, but she somehow managed to ignore that remark. She would deal with Cat later. "But what *are* we going to do about Lynx?" Jack reiterated, doing her best to recapture the original subject. "I like Bonnie a lot, and I just think she should have the same chance with Lynx that I had with you. It's only fair, you know."

"I do not believe you need to do anything," Cat said wisely. "I believe the problem will resolve itself without any interference."

"Meaning I should mind my own damn business?" Jack grumbled.

"I think you should listen to Cat on this one," Tisana advised. "He knows more about Lynx than you do."

"True," Jack admitted. "I don't know much at all." She threw Cat a speculative glance over her shoulder. "And what you *do* know, you aren't telling, are you?"

"Lynxsander was only a boy when he was taken and sold," Cat said quietly. "Perhaps slavery had a more profound effect on him than it did on the rest of us."

"But Bonnie said he didn't like women," Jack argued. "I could understand him being affected in tons of other ways, but what the hell could have done *that* to him?"

"I do not know," Cat said. "He did not share that story with us."

"You wouldn't be trying to pull the wool over my eyes, would you?" Jack said suspiciously. "I heard you fussing at him about why his hair was so short. I wondered about that myself; I didn't think you guys *ever* cut your hair."

Cat was reluctant to say more, and it showed, but he also felt that Jack deserved an answer. "It is a symbol of a man's virility," he said at last. "For a Zetithian to cut his hair is to proclaim that he is no longer a man."

Jack's eyes grew round with horror. "You never told me that!" she exclaimed. "I never want you to cut yours—but that's just because I like it, not because it means anything!"

Tisana put forth the obvious conclusion. "Lynx was castrated, wasn't he?"

Cat shook his head. "It is possible," he conceded, "but I do not believe so," he replied. "Something else happened to change him."

"Well, we've got to *do* something about it!" declared Jack.

"Jack," Tisana warned. "You shouldn't meddle."

"Yeah, well, what else do I have for entertainment?" she grumbled. "Nothing exciting has happened since—" The ship lurched slightly as it breached the atmosphere of Terra Minor, triggering a sudden wave of nausea that nearly had Jack losing her lunch all over the control panel. There was only one thing that would cause Jack's iron stomach to rebel. "Whoa, shit! I think I've already got something new to keep me busy!"

"You are with child, are you not?" Cat purred.

"Dammit, Cat!" Jack exclaimed. "How the hell could you know that?"

Tisana exchanged a meaningful look with Cat behind Jack's back. "It is what I *do*," Cat said simply.

"What?" Jack demanded, still adjusting the controls as she fought the urge to throw up. "Which part? The knowing or the making it happen?"

Cat shook his head and smiled, but didn't bother to reply. Both were true, and Jack already knew it.

"Leo knew before you did," Tisana whispered to Cat. "He said her scent was different."

"And just *why* did none of you bother to tell me?" Jack demanded.

"It is more fun when you discover it for yourself," Cat purred. "You may thank me later."

"Yeah, well, you know what being pregnant means, don't you?" Jack said grimly. "No cocksucking for about three months. Think you can stand it?"

Having Jacinth sprawled on their bed, sucking him for hours was wonderful, but Cat was well aware that she enjoyed it even more than he did. "I am not the one who will suffer," he chided her.

"Oh... yeah... right." Jack muttered. "Silly *me*..." It would be a very long three months.

❖ ❖ ❖

Landing without further incident, Cat went off to make the mandatory visit to the trade authority while Jack and Leo loaded up the pack droid and headed for the marketplace, leaving Tisana behind with the children.

"I'm dying to see if those sponges we picked up on Ulada will sell," Jack said eagerly. "I mean, a sponge that makes its own soap? Who *wouldn't* want one?"

"Someone who does not want soap?" Leo suggested.

"You always were a killjoy," Jack retorted. "Ooo, look! There's Bonnie! She'd better have Lynx with her, or I'll go looking for him! Never been to Bonnie's farm," she added reflectively. "Maybe we should pay him a visit."

"There is no need," Leo pointed out. "He is there, unloading the cart."

Following Leo's line of sight, Jack watched Lynx as he worked. Something was different. "Holy shit!" she exclaimed softly. "His hair is longer."

Leo smiled. "Did you think it would not be? Human females have a very strong, intoxicating effect on us," he said.

"Yes, but you've never seemed to be too taken with me, Leo," Jack observed. "I've yet to make your dick hard."

"It is different once we have chosen a mate," Leo said equably.

"You guys have so many rules!" Jack grumbled. "Though I guess there had to be a few, or there would have been total mayhem on your planet. Must've created plenty of it on other worlds, though."

"Some," Leo conceded. "But not all."

"Well, better keep your sword handy," Jack advised. "Here comes Salan."

Jack smiled at the dairyman's daughter, and Leo couldn't help but grin back at the girl's seductive smile. She never gave up, even after Tisana had once promised to tell Mobray's cows to kick her whenever she milked them if Salan didn't leave Leo alone. As far as anyone knew, Tisana had never bothered to follow through on the threat because Leo was completely faithful, and Salan's blatant attempts at seduction were always good for a laugh.

"Hel-*lo*, Leo," she said coyly. "Where's Tisana?"

"Back at the ship with the kids," Jack said, pulling Leo back out of Salan's reach. For a milkmaid, Salan had the longest, sharpest-looking talons Jack had ever seen, and she had no intention of letting her sink them into Leo—or Cat, for that matter. Not liking Salan particularly, Jack was of the opinion that she and Sylor would have made a good pair.

"I'm sorry to hear that," Salan said sweetly, gazing adoringly into Leo's golden eyes. Salan thought he was the handsomest man she'd ever seen, with Cat running a close second. Just the thought of running her fingers through his tawny curls and having his strong arms wrapped around her made her head spin. She ought to have known better than to covet the husbands of two women who were so capable of blasting her to bits— the one with her pulse pistol and the other with the fire in her eyes—but Salan simply couldn't help it—nor was she particularly intelligent. "We've been having trouble with one of our cows. I thought she might be able to help."

"She'll probably drop by later on," said Jack. "But I guess you don't have the cow with you."

Salan laughed merrily. "As I said, we are having trouble with her. She will not stand to be milked, no matter who approaches her."

Jack fought hard to suppress a chuckle. Maybe Tisana had made good on her threat after all. "We might be sticking around for a few days this time," Jack said. "Maybe she'll make a house call."

"My father would be pleased," said Salan, still eyeing Leo hungrily. She would have given her father's whole herd to get him alone for just one night. Perhaps while Tisana was busy talking with the cows… Then she remembered the threat Tisana had made. Could it be…?

Just then, Kipper came bounding across the plaza toward Jack and Leo, barking excitedly. "What the devil's gotten into him?" Jack wondered aloud as Kipper continued to bark for a moment and then began sniffing at Leo and whining.

"He wants Tisana," Leo said knowledgeably. "I have seen this type of behavior before."

"He may just want to see Max," Jack suggested, but then remembered that animals knew a whole lot more about what went on in the lives of people than anyone gave them credit for. "Or he may want to tell us that Lynx and Bonnie are—"

"Hey, Jack!" Bonnie called out as she spotted them. "Come see the baby!"

Leo and Jack made their way over to Bonnie's stand and were suitably impressed when introduced to Shaulla. Jack commented that Ulla looked more like her mother than her father—which wasn't true, of course, but she thought it was something Bonnie would like to hear.

"Shaulla?" Leo echoed, looking at Lynx curiously. "That was your mother's name, was it not?"

"Ooo, good sign!" Jack said under her breath as Lynx nodded. She might have been busy tickling Ulla under the chin, but she was watching Lynx out of the corner of her eye. Yes, he *did l*ook different. He was even smiling—sort of—and so was Bonnie. Jack's own expression brightened immediately. "So, how's life on the farm been treating you, Lynx?"

"I am well," Lynx replied warily. He knew Cark trusted this woman with his life, but she was… strange. He was even more wary of Leo, who had been very quick to realize how Shaulla had gotten her name. He knew he shouldn't have been so reluctant to admit that he and Bonnie had mated, but for some reason, he didn't wish to discuss it, even with his old friends.

"Well, huh?" said Jack. "Just *well?* I'd say you look a damn sight better than *well.* Longer hair, picked up a little weight—hell, I even saw you smile!" Her eyes narrowed sharply. "You've been getting some, haven't you?"

"Jack," Bonnie chided. "Couldn't you at least *try* to be a little more discreet? You'll embarrass him."

"Never met a Zetithian yet who was embarrassed about much of anything!" Jack declared. "Hell, they'll walk around naked if you don't make them put clothes on! Of course, they usually start a riot when they do that—but that's beside the point."

"The point is," Leo said, cutting Jack off abruptly, "that Lynx has been thriving on Bonnie's farm. I believe we should not discuss it any further."

Jack laughed out loud. "You think so? Well, you guys just go do your thing, and we girls will talk!" Kipper was still nudging Leo in the leg trying to get his attention. Jack tapped the comstone mounted on the breast pocket of her flightsuit. "Hey, Tisana," she said. "You need to come talk to this mutt of Bonnie's; he's got some sort of bee in his bonnet."

Tisana rolled her eyes, even though Jack was nowhere near. "Would you *please* speak in plain Stantongue," she said wearily. "I know very well that what you meant is not what you said."

"Bonnie's dog needs to talk with you," Jack said, speaking slowly and enunciating each word with care. "Got it?"

"Yes," Tisana replied. "I'll be down later."

"Oh, and Tisana?" Jack added in a quiet voice. "You know that problem we talked about? It's not a problem anymore."

Tisana silently thanked every deity she'd ever heard mention of. Jack on a matchmaking mission was a fiasco waiting to happen. "I'm so glad," she said. "See you later." After tapping her stone pendant to break the link, she added, "And I hope you haven't stuck your nose in where it doesn't belong."

"She always does," Larry piped up. He might have been off in the corner playing with his brothers, but Larry didn't miss much.

"You know, for a three-year-old, you're pretty smart," Tisana remarked.

"About my mother, I am," Larry replied. "We shouldn't have let her go to the market without us."

"Leo's with her," Tisana reminded him. "And your father won't leave her alone for long. They'll keep her out of trouble." She did her best to sound reassuring, but Tisana had often wondered how Jack had managed to stay out of prison for the entirety of her life, because she was forever setting people off. Even now that she didn't have to twist any arms to get information about her sister, she still got into the occasional fight—and not just with the Nedwuts.

"Want me to go check on her?" Max asked, eagerly wagging his tail.

Tisana considered this for a moment. *"No, she'll be all right. She doesn't usually get into trouble on this planet... well, hardly ever."*

Max hoped she was right, but when it came to Jack, he tended to agree with Larry.

"So, what's up?" Jack asked Bonnie when they were finally alone. "Aside from his dick, that is."

Bonnie couldn't help but laugh. She'd never met anyone quite like Jack. "Don't ask me," she said, throwing up her hands. "He just finally... well... I don't know *what* happened, but one day he just decided he didn't hate me anymore. I think Ulla had a lot to do with it."

"Likes kids, huh?" Jack eyed her speculatively. "That's nice. Learn anymore about what happened to him?"

Bonnie wasn't sure she should tell Jack, but on the other hand, she didn't want Jack to embarrass Lynx by asking him. "He was a harem slave, Jack. The women there just... wore him out."

Jack blinked in surprise. "Wore him out? Shit, I didn't think it was possible to wear one of *them* out! What'd it take? Ten, twenty women?"

"Fifty," Bonnie replied grimly. "For ten years."

Jack's low whistle signified her admiration. "Damn! He's got to be either the best or the... well, shit, I don't know!" Shaking her head in disbelief, she added, "Fifty women!" She looked questioningly at Bonnie. "And he was the *only* man they—?" Jack stopped short, realizing her error immediately. No woman in her right mind would have taken another man over Cat, and Lynx had to be just as good—if not better. Lynx would have been the only man the women craved.

Bonnie nodded. "They never left him alone for a minute," she said. "They didn't feed him much, or let him sleep, either."

"No wonder he didn't like women!" Cocking her head, Jack went on to ask, "Sure you didn't do anything to change his mind?"

"Don't know for sure," Bonnie shrugged. "But I think it might have been the food."

Jack grinned. "Then you must be needing more chocolate by now."

Bonnie couldn't argue with that.

Then Jack remembered something else. "Haven't seen anything of Sylor, have you?"

"No, but I think he's around somewhere," Bonnie replied. "Lynx said he could smell him."

"Not surprising," Jack commented. "Think he might cause trouble?"

"I don't know, but it wouldn't surprise me if he did. Did you know Vessonians can disappear? Like chameleons?"

"I've never heard that," Jack admitted, "but I wouldn't put it past them. I never *did* like that bastard!"

"Must be something they like to keep secret then—I could see where they might not want the word to get out. I didn't know it myself until Ulla vanished one day. Scared me half to death!"

"That would make Vessonians about as much trouble as Treslanties, then," Jack remarked. "They're the only ones I've ever heard of that could do stuff like that, which makes it a real pain in the ass if you're ever looking for one. 'Course, Nedwuts are even worse if you're trying to keep a Zetithian safe." Jack had killed a number of Nedwuts since she met Cat—though killing them didn't get you in trouble anywhere anymore. It was a wonder they didn't figure it out and stay home, but they couldn't seem to get the idea into their thick, ugly skulls. "This is one planet you're safe from them on," Jack commented. "Tougher landing regulations than Earth! Good place to raise Zetithians." Eyeing Bonnie speculatively, she went on, "Any possibility of that?"

Bonnie smiled. "Doing everything in my power."

"Good girl," Jack said approvingly. "I *knew* you could do it! I'm doing my part again too."

"You're expecting?" Bonnie exclaimed.

"Yes, I am," Jack said proudly. "Not sure what we'll name this bunch, but if they're all boys again, I'm leaning toward Groucho, Chico, and Harpo—though Cat's more in favor of Kirk, Spock, and Bones. I don't really like the idea of naming a kid 'Bones,' though," she confided. "Sounds a bit macabre to me."

"That's wonderful!" Bonnie said. She was excited about Jack's pregnancy, but, as before when Jack had nicknamed her older sons Larry, Moe, and Curly, the significance was lost on Bonnie. Jack had made a study of ancient Earth culture, so Bonnie could assume that the names referred to someone—she just didn't know who.

"I had enough trouble naming one child," Bonnie said. "So far, I haven't given any thought to what I'd name triplets."

"Well, I'm here to tell you that if Lynx is the father, there will be three of them," Jack declared. "You know, I still haven't figured out how that works. I need to talk to Vladen. I could understand a Zetithian female always having a litter of three, but how it works with a human mother, I haven't got a clue. Tisana said the women in her family only have one daughter, but she had a couple of boys, too, so if you're smart, you'd best be making a list of names you like—and lots of them, because you're gonna need 'em!"

Jack took a deep breath before continuing—though Bonnie felt in need of one as well. Talking with Jack always left her feeling a little breathless. "So, Bonnie," Jack began. "Is the nooky fabulous, or what?"

"You know it is," Bonnie said, laughing at Jack's choice of words. "I've never even *heard* of a man who can do what he does!"

Jack let out a low whistle. "Hmm," she said, tapping her chin. "I believe I need to hear some details!"

Knowing that Jack had sent him off with Lynx primarily to have him discover more about Lynx's past, Leo figured he'd better ask a few questions. If Lynx didn't want to talk, Leo couldn't very well make him, but knew that the attempt was expected of him.

"So, you are… happier now?" Leo ventured.

Lynx became instantly wary. Leo might have been an old friend, but it was hard to change deeply ingrained habits overnight. "Yes," he said cautiously.

"Being a free man is much better than being a slave, isn't it?"

Lynx thought that this went without saying, but agreed anyway.

"Being a slave wasn't always bad," Leo went on casually. "I had some good times, even then, but my life is so much better now. I have Tisana and our children to love—which is our purpose."

"Our purpose?"

"Yes," Leo replied. "Giving women joy was *always* our purpose—one which I was never privileged to fulfill until I met Tisana."

As Lynx had been required to give women joy whether he liked it or not, he hadn't seen it as being much of a privilege—though that was changing.

Noting his grim expression, Leo prompted him: "Is there anything you wish to tell me?"

"About what?"

"Anything," Leo replied with an expansive wave. "Your life since the war, the places you've been, how you came to be on this planet—I don't think you told us all of the details."

Lynx wondered when he would ever feel comfortable talking about any of it. Somehow, he didn't think he ever would. "I was first sold to a man on a planet called Paemay," he began, intending to keep his explanation to the bare minimum. "He had many female slaves. I was *their* slave for many years." Looking pointedly at Leo, he added, "Do I have to tell you anything more?"

Leo regarded him gravely. He had an idea that Lynx hadn't wasted that time polishing their fingernails or combing their hair. "Ah," Leo said with a nod. "Then you must teach me what you have learned," he said. "It would be nice to be able to give my wife something… new."

Lynx stared at Leo in disbelief. What was he saying? Was he really asking for advice on how to please a woman? In the past, Lynx had always felt like an outsider when other men discussed such things—he had never been with a woman before he became a slave, so he had nothing to contribute. This had always made him feel uncomfortable, but suddenly, he understood—it wasn't a matter of boasting or trying to prove he was better than anyone else; it was simply an exchange of useful information. Unfortunately, knowing so many things, Lynx hardly knew where to begin. "What does she like?"

Leo smiled broadly. "Everything."

Lynx paused for a moment while he tried to decide what he would know that others might not. The slave women had always been eager to try anything different, and while learning to vibrate his cock—which was *extremely* popular—had required considerable practice, there were several other positions and combinations that he felt sure any self-respecting Zetithian male should be able to accomplish.

"Standing up?"

Leo shook his head. "Done that."

"From behind?"

"Done that, too."

"Backwards?"

"Sounds peculiar," Leo said, shaking his head again.

Lynx shrugged. "You might try it anyway," he suggested, remembering that Bonnie had been particularly fond of that variation.

"What else?"

Lynx stopped to think again. "Does she enjoy very deep penetration?"

Leo grinned. "Loves it."

"Ever sit her on your cock with your legs up out of the way?"

Leo shook his head, trying to imagine just what Lynx was getting at. "Facing toward me, or away?"

"Facing away," Lynx replied. "Once you get her up there, pulse or circle your cock. Women love it."

Leo was skeptical, but after hearing Lynx's description, thought he'd better give it a shot anyway. Tisana never complained about his lack of inventiveness, but it was best to keep one's wife well pleased.

"Anything else?" Leo prompted.

Lynx knew there were other techniques, and he told Leo a few of them, but he had no way of knowing whether Leo could actually do them or not. Leo wasn't sure he could, either, but he stored the knowledge away for future reference. He might even tell Cat.

While Bonnie and Lynx were at the market, Sylor took the opportunity to explore his options and decided that the enocks were his best choice of weapons. As usual, his own hands would be clean, and he would enjoy watching the birds rip his rival to shreds. Bonnie would be horrified, of course, but with her new lover dead, she would welcome Sylor back with open arms; arms that would comfort her just as they had before. All would be forgiven. Sylor knew exactly how to handle her—always had. This time would be no different.

Chapter 20

As the *JOLLY ROGER* left orbit, Jack leaned back in the pilot's seat, biting her lip, her eyes narrowed in deep thought. Bonnie and Lynx were doing just fine, but there was something about Sylor that kept nagging at her. *The shifty-eyed snake! How a sweet woman like Bonnie ever wound up with him...* Sitting up decisively, she sent out a hail to a certain arms dealer she knew, thinking it might be best to alter course and make a little detour to one of the shadier territories in the quadrant. Lerotan Kanotay might not be anything but a shrewd businessman bent on making sales, but his line of merchandise tended to put him in contact with the criminal element on most planets he visited. He might know a little something that could help out Bonnie.

"Kanotay here," came the reply. The viewscreen projected the image of a dark-skinned, exotically handsome man with a Ralayan rune tattooed on his left temple. His black hair was long and laced up in a leather sheath that lay over the right side of his powerful chest. He was friendly enough—and could be very charming—but was definitely not a man to cross. "What's up, Jack?"

"Hey, there, Leroy! See you've let your hair grow out! Looks damn good!" Jack said, smiling. "How the hell you been?"

"Just fine, Jack," he said, eyeing her carefully. Something told him this wasn't a social call. "Don't need any more weapons, do you?" Lerotan smiled, his dark eyes alight at the prospect of a sale.

"Nope," Jack replied. "Haven't had to use them much, but so far, they work just fine. No, what I called about was this guy," she said, punching up an image of Sylor. "Ever seen him before?"

"Can't say that I have," he replied, "but I can do some checking."

"That'd be great!" she said. "Where are you?"

"Arvada," he replied. "You know, one of those nasty little planets you tend to avoid?"

"Yeah, I know it," Jack said. "Haven't been there in a while, which is probably just as well. How's Trag?"

"Just fine," he replied. "He's around here somewhere. You should drop by. You could probably do some lucrative trading here."

"Think so?" Jack chewed on her fingertip for a moment. "Might be worth it," she said reflectively. "Maybe we'll drop by. In the meantime, see if you can find out anything about this guy. Name's Sylor Halen, and he's on Terra Minor right now, but there's something fishy about him."

"And so naturally you're asking me," Lerotan said dryly. "What a low opinion you must have of the company I keep!"

Jack glared back at him with a raised eyebrow. "Come on, now, Leroy! You don't have to take it personally," she grumbled. "Not my fault you aren't dealing in legal goods."

"My weapons are all perfectly legal," he protested, but added with his flashing, piratical grin, "on some planets."

"Yeah, right," Jack snorted. "Say hello to Trag for me." Scanning the charts, she added, "We'll be there in… oh, I don't know… a week or two, maybe? That be quick enough?"

"You need a faster ship," Lerotan observed. "I could make it in five days with *my* ship."

"'I could make it in five days with *my* ship.'" Jack mimicked. "Really, Leroy! My ship is faster than your bucket of bolts, and you know it!"

Lerotan laughed. "Still won't sell it to me?"

"No way, Leroy!" she declared. "The *Jolly Roger* and I are like, you know, joined at the hip or something."

"Thought that was you and Cat," he commented with a wry smile.

"Well, yeah," she admitted. "Him, too. I'd give up the ship long before I'd give *him* up." Now that she thought about it, she would have given up *anything* to keep Cat.

"Well, you be careful out there," Lerotan advised. "It's rough territory."

"I will," Jack promised. She had only been to Arvada once and knew it was one of those worlds where a woman with a Zetithian mate needed to keep on her toes—which wasn't difficult because, thanks to Lerotan, the *Jolly Roger* was now armed to the teeth. "See you soon!"

Lerotan signed off, shaking his head. What *was* it about Terran women that made them all want to call him Leroy? He had no idea, but he had to admit, he sort of liked it…

With a few minor adjustments, Jack sent her ship hurtling off toward the planet Arvada. While she was setting the course, Tisana brought her dinner in the cockpit.

"Hey, thanks, Tisana," she said, sniffing the plate. "You always were a better cook than me."

"Must be the herbs," Tisana conceded. Jack's idea of spicing something up was to keep adding salt until even the salt monsters of Norad would consider it inedible, but Tisana's approach to seasoning was more subtle.

Jack took a bite and sighed. Yes, Tisana could definitely cook! Of course, the way she could just *look* at something and cook it was a pretty neat trick, too. Having hot food was always possible whenever Tisana was around—which put Jack in mind of Tisana's other talents. "Say, did you ever find out what Bonnie's dog wanted?"

"I completely forgot!" Tisana exclaimed. "I hope it wasn't something important! I got caught in the middle of a dispute between an ox and a badger and never got to talk to Kipper at all!"

"An ox and a badger?" Jack echoed with interest. "What the hell was that about?"

"Oh, the badger was in the right," Tisana said briskly. "The ox kept trampling his den. Couldn't blame him for biting the ox on the tail."

"What about Salan's cow?" Jack prompted her. "Did you find out what was bugging her?"

Tisana's satisfied smile was reply enough, but Jack waited for her to speak. "Didn't need to," she said.

"And why is that?"

"Let's just say that there's a time limit on the cow's behavior."

"Ha! I knew it!" Jack shook her head and lifted a forkful of Tisana's succulent baked fish to her mouth, but paused to add, "You're a dangerous woman to piss off, Tisana."

Tisana smiled. "I know."

❖ ❖ ❖

Leo, on the other hand, was never in any danger from his wife and knew *exactly* how to keep her happy. Having kissed her quite thoroughly after they retired for the night, he wasted no time in implementing Lynx's suggestion.

"You look tired, my lovely witch," Leo purred. "I think you should... sit down for a while."

"Sit down?" Tisana echoed. "But I'm already *lying* down," she pointed out. Seeing the glow in his eyes, she already had some idea as to the "chair" he might be referring to, but asked, "Just *where* do you want me to sit?"

"I have the perfect place," he replied, flipping his legs up so that his body resembled a chair with his stiff member pointing invitingly upward while his testicles lay heavily against his buttocks.

Tisana went from being merely "in the mood" to overcome with desire in the space of a heartbeat. The engorgement of her nipples and clitoris was so abrupt as to border on being painful, and her entire being was soon flooded with need for him.

"Do you enjoy the view from this perspective?"

Leo looked good from any angle, but Tisana was forced to admit that this was one of the better ones. His cock went far beyond the usual erotic fantasy, his butt was absolutely perfect, and the way his balls swayed as he moved made her breath catch in her throat.

"You are not saying anything," he chided.

Tisana swallowed with some difficulty and croaked: "I'm speechless."

Smiling, Leo pulsed his dick, causing his balls to slide up inside his scrotum and fluid to run down the shaft in gleaming rivulets that promised even greater levels of ecstasy. "Better?"

As Tisana watched her husband's coronal fluid run down over his balls, bathing them with moisture, her mind went blank. "Than what?" she gasped.

"Than anything you've seen before?"

"Well," she said, doing her best to keep breathing, "I've seen some fabulous things in my life, but this is incredibly, um, profound."

Needing no further encouragement, Leo beckoned to his wife. "Have a seat."

Tisana wasn't quite sure how to do it gracefully, but what she did soon had Leo purring louder than ever before. As she backed up to him, he was treated to the enticing view of her lovely posterior as it began its slow descent.

When his cock kissed her vaginal lips, Tisana felt the head begin to slide over her clitoris and moaned with delight. She loved it when he did that, but this new angle made it that much more… interesting.

Thanking the gods for a flexible spine, Leo raised up on his elbows, bending nearly double so he wouldn't miss anything, and sent a thought out to the glowstone on the bedside table, enhancing the light.

Tisana noted the increased level of illumination along with Leo's swift intake of air and chuckled softly. "Can you see me now?"

"Very well," Leo purred with evident appreciation. He would have given a lot to be able to see all of her—especially her face—which, so far, seemed to be the only disadvantage to this position—and thought that a strategically placed mirror would have been a nice touch. But since he didn't have one handy, he had to rely on the sounds she made—which were considerable.

"How does that feel?" he inquired after one particularly unique moan. "Good? Or would you rather I stop now?"

Her reply was almost a shout. "No!" Then she realized that he would have to stop what he was doing to get inside her. "Yes... no... I don't know..."

"It is... profound?"

Since this was one of her favorite descriptive terms, it had become something of a catchword for the couple. "Oh, yes," she breathed. *"Very* profound."

Leo pushed harder, rubbing her clit with his slick, serrated cockhead. "Is this an improvement?"

An orgasm hit Tisana so hard her head snapped backwards, sending her long, dark hair tumbling down her back.

"Yes, I believe it is," Leo murmured. He waited a moment for her to recover before trying something else. Grasping her hips, he slid her up and down the length of his hot cock. The lips that caressed him were slick with desire, and he was almost ready to push past them when he remembered how she used to be so reluctant to mate with him because she knew their time together would be short. He used to have to practically *beg...*

"Do you want more, Tisana?" he purred.

Tisana's whole body was on fire. "Mmm, yes," she panted. "Don't stop."

"Say please."

"Please."

Leo laughed wickedly. "Say it again."

"Please!"

Purring with delight, he said, "Are you certain you want more?"

"Yes!"

"How certain?"

"So certain, I'm going to scream if you don't do something quick!"

"Ah, threatening me, are you?" Leo teased. "I do not take kindly to threats."

"Leo!" Tisana said warningly. "If you don't hurry up, I'll—"

"Shoot a fireball at me?" he suggested.

The idea had merit, but Tisana didn't want any part of her beloved Leo singed. Sighing, she said, "Of course not! But would you please keep going? You're making me crazy!"

"We cannot have that, can we?" Leo lifted her slightly as he snapped his cock upwards. Hoping his aim was true, he then pulled her down hard on his stiff phallus and drilled it into her.

In the darkness of their own cabin with her beloved Cat, Jack broke off their kiss abruptly, whispering, "What the hell was that?"

Without a moment's hesitation Cat replied knowledgeably, "Tisana."

"Yes, but—" Jack listened again, quite sure that, at the very least, Tisana was being maimed. Pushing back the blanket that covered them both, she sat up, muttering, "Maybe I'd better check and see—"

"It was a cry of pleasure," Cat said, catching her by the wrist, "—possibly the result of some… suggestions from Lynx."

"Well, if you say so," Jack said dubiously. *"I've* certainly never heard her make a noise like that before."

"Perhaps not," Cat said. "But *you* have made such a sound." Chuckling softly, he added, "Many times."

"Really?" Jack said with surprise. "Must sound different when you're doing it yourself."

"Would you like to test that?" he asked innocently.

"Sure," Jack said with a shrug. "Why not?"

Cat pulled her back against his chest and eased her down on his waiting cock. Burying it to the hilt, he wrapped his arms around her, his fingers teasing her sensitive nipples as he nibbled on her ear. Jack sighed with pleasure as his cock began a slow, sinuous dance inside her. "Ah, Jacinth, my love," Cat purred. "With you in my arms, I need nothing more than the air that I breathe."

"Mmm, Kittycat," she murmured, leaning back against him as she pulled his long hair forward to cascade sensuously across her chest. She liked the way it tickled. "You say the sweetest things."

"Giving you joy is the sweetest thing I can imagine," he said. Curling his hips beneath her, he added an inward thrust and felt deep satisfaction with her long, tortured groan.

"And to think I almost left you on Orpheseus," she sighed. "Worst mistake of my life."

"I would not have let that happen," he said. "I knew you were my mate from the first moment I saw you and breathed in your scent."

"You were a lot smarter than I was," she admitted.

"I wanted to know what it would be like to make you moan," he said, using his hands on her hips to add her movement to his own. "To give you so much joy you would—" Jack's shout of rapture stopped him in mid-sentence, and with a smile she couldn't see but could hear in his voice, he added, "—do *that.*"

"Whoa!" Jack exclaimed. "I guess you're right: I do it too." Then she remembered something. "So Leo's been talking to Lynx, huh?"

"Yes," Cat purred. "Would you like to try something... different?"

"Well, sure," Jack began, "Bonnie told me some things, too..."

Cat was no slouch when it came to a challenge and was prepared for the attempt—fully intending to add his own twist to anything Lynx or Bonnie or anyone else might have come up with. "We will do whatever you wish, my lovely master," he replied.

Jack reluctantly rolled off him, but the sight of Cat's glistening cock was so enticing that she inadvertently sent out a thought which increased the illumination from a nearby glowstone. Knowing that she enjoyed looking at his cock with his balls pushed up to the base, Cat reached for the cock strap that lay on the table next to the bed and cinched it up snugly, making sure that Jack was watching as he did it.

Jack groaned as another orgasm hit her. "Just *looking* at you makes me come," she gasped desperately. "How do we ever get anything done? I could do this all day long and not get tired of it."

Cat laughed wickedly. "Yes, you would, but I would enjoy trying to *make* you tired." He got up to stand beside the bed, teasing her face with his cockhead. "Suck my balls, Jacinth. I want to feel them in your hot mouth."

Jack opened her mouth wide and sucked them in. She loved the feel of his nuts in her mouth and sucked them before flicking them with her tongue. Sliding her fingertips up his tight, wet shaft, she watched in sensuous delight as his cock quivered and pulsed, spilling more fluid down the side and onto her face. She loved the feel of his slickness on her cheeks, loved the taste of it, whether it triggered orgasms or not. It was the elixir of his love, and she couldn't get enough of it.

And he couldn't get enough of her—the sight, taste, feel, and scent of her. She lay sprawled on the bed, her fabulous, wonderful body that promised delights beyond his imagination. "Jacinth," he murmured. "You are so beautiful. Every part of you is beautiful to me."

Knowing what he liked, she let go of him and rolled over, her legs spread wide.

Cat couldn't take anymore and dove forward to taste her; she was hot and slick with desire. His hot tongue found her clitoris and teased it gently, first licking, and then sucking. Jack was treated to the view of his balls hanging down above her face, his cock swaying side to side as he licked her. "Suck me," Cat purred and thrust his cock into her mouth.

Noting that Tisana's treatment for the queasiness of pregnancy appeared to be quite effective, Jack sucked him in until his balls were resting on her nose. At one time, she'd have never dreamed she could like anything of the kind, though with Cat licking her, she probably would have enjoyed anything. But this was fabulous! She reached up and rubbed his ass, grabbing it and slapping it hard. Cat liked that, too, and purred as he licked her to a frenzy.

"Shall we do something 'different' now?" he asked innocently.

Jack was forced to let go of him long enough to reply. "No!" she shouted. "I want to suck the snard out of you."

"You may do that as well," Cat said with a slow smile. "But first, I must prove myself as good a lover as young Lynx."

"Cat," Jack said frankly, "if you were any better, I'd go completely insane from all the joy."

"Yes, but Leo has told me some of what Lynx can do."

"And you're gonna do it if it kills you, right?"

"Mating with you will not kill me, Jacinth," Cat assured her. "But *not* mating with you would be the death of me."

Not giving her a chance to reply, Cat backed up, letting his cock and balls caress her face as he went. When his face finally came into view, Jack reached up to kiss him. "I couldn't live without you, Cat—whether we were bonded together or not. You know that, don't you?"

Cat smiled. "I have never doubted it," he replied. "Come, and let me give you joy." With that, he took her in his arms as he knelt behind her and pulled her onto his lap, his cock seeking her warmth, seemingly of its own volition. That glorious feeling of penetration was one he wanted to experience again and again, and he lifted her up, pulling her off of him completely before dropping her down on his cock once more. "This was a very good suggestion," he commented. "I cannot imagine why I never tried it before."

Since Jack's comment was a shuddering, "Ohhhh!" Cat had to assume that it met with her approval as well.

Holding her firmly as he arched his back to push inside her as far as he could, Cat attempted the vibration that Lynx claimed to be capable of, and though he had been practicing, it was difficult to tell how successful he would be until he finally tried it on Jack. Unfortunately, he was only able to maintain it for a few moments before the muscles became fatigued, and he was forced to stop. Switching to a side-to-side sweep—which he could keep up until Jack simply couldn't take it anymore—he smiled to himself, knowing that this would give him something to work on—work that he would enjoy enormously.

Meanwhile, like Leo, Cat was wishing for a mirror. To see his wife's joyous expression made all the hardships of his life worthwhile, and as he buried his face in her hair, he tried to imagine her eyes—grown soft and misty with love—before his mind lost its focus, and he filled her with joy.

Landing at the spaceport, Jack and Cat headed for the nearest dive, knowing that men of Lerotan's ilk didn't frequent the trendiest spots on any planet. Still, Lerotan was a charmer, and Jack knew he'd have women draped all over him, which would make him easy to spot. Reportedly, he could do two women at once; one with his dick, and one with his long, leonine tail. Jack didn't see how a tail could possibly do as good a job as Cat's penis, but also knew that there were ignorant women everywhere.

Jack was right. Finding Lerotan wasn't difficult, as he had four women surrounding him, two of whom were Davordians who were already making eyes at

Cat. *Damned blue-eyed sluts!* Jack thought disgustedly. *They're everywhere.*

"Hey, Leroy!" Jack called out as they approached. "Good to see you!"

"So, you decided to take the risk," Lerotan said, reaching out to shake her hand and then Cat's. "Want to hear the deal?"

"Later," Jack said with a casual wave. She was shrewd enough to know that if she waited a bit, the "deal" would get even better. "Just wanted to see your handsome mug again—and Trag's, too. Where is he?" she asked, glancing around.

"Over there," Lerotan said grimly, pointing to a crowded corner that appeared to contain nothing but females—several of them Davordian.

Jack smiled. Lerotan might have been able to please two women at the same time, but Trag was Zetithian—which, in her opinion, said it all. She slid her arm around Cat's waist possessively. No Davordian was going to get their hands on *her* Zetithian! Those girls were nearly as dangerous as Nedwuts! Glancing reflexively at the doorway as a handful of newcomers entered, Jack registered the species before looking away again. Constant vigilance.

Lerotan eyed Jack speculatively. She was a tough nut to crack when it came to making deals. She could always come out ahead—though sometimes you didn't realize it until she was long gone. Still, working with Jack gave him a chance to use charm rather than intimidation to make a sale, which was a welcome change.

"I'm pleased to see you looking so well," Lerotan said graciously.

Jack grinned. "Does it show?"

Lerotan looked puzzled, but Cat supplied the answer for Jack's glowing countenance. "She is with child," he said. "Which makes her that much more beautiful."

"And you still came to Arvada?" Lerotan said wonderingly. "You should be avoiding these more… *dangerous*… worlds." *She must be more anxious to make a deal than I thought…*

"Well, yeah," Jack admitted. "We get into less trouble if we stick to planets where they actually *encourage* you to shoot Nedwuts on sight." Unlike Arvada, where such practices were merely tolerated. Jack scanned the bar with her keen eyes. *Nope, no Nedwuts here…*

"That does not stop her," Cat said. "It only takes hearing of some marvelous new thing for sale to send her to places such as *this.*" It was a little dig at Lerotan, but it was subtle, and, as always, was said with a smile, which suggested that Cat was no pretty boy toy but a force to be reckoned with in himself.

"Hey, what are you saying?" Lerotan demanded, but with a smile that took the sting out of his words. "That I only frequent the last outposts of lawlessness and disorder?"

"Not really," Cat said reasonably. "Just planets like this one."

"Aw, this place isn't so bad," said Jack, glancing around the filthy, smoke-filled room filled with its even filthier and smokier clientele. "I've been to much worse—"

"Look, boys! It's a Zetith—" The three snarling Nedwuts entering the bar didn't even have the chance to finish another sentence before they dropped in a dusty, hairy heap as Jack pulled her trusty pulse pistol and fired.

"—planets," Jack went on, holstering her weapon without comment.

"She do that often?" Lerotan asked Cat with a bemused smile.

"I believe she enjoys it," Cat replied. "Otherwise, we would not visit such worlds."

"Aw, Cat, you know you like it when I shoot the bad guys for you," protested Jack. "Makes you feel loved."

Cat smiled mysteriously. "There are much better ways of making me feel loved," he said.

"Well, yeah, but you have to be alive for that," Jack pointed out. "That last batch of Nedwuts actually got off a shot. I made myself a promise I wouldn't ever let that happen again." Jack looked over at the bartender who was eyeing the stinking pile of Nedwuts with distaste. "Hey, sorry about that!" she called out to him. "I really meant to kill them, but Tex was only set for stun. They'll probably wake up feeling pretty nasty."

"Shouldn't let them wake up at all," another man grumbled. "Allow me."

A tall, dark-haired Zetithian dressed in a long-sleeved flight suit and a heavy cloak detached himself from the bevy of women surrounding him, leveled a pulse rifle at the heap of Nedwuts and finished the job. "There," he said curtly. "Better now?"

"Hey, Trag!" Jack said, beaming at him. "Good to see you!"

Giving Trag a big hug, she then leaned back, gazing up at him appreciatively. "You handsome devil," she sighed. "I've been missing those gorgeous green eyes of

yours—and that orange streak in your hair… *way cool!"*
Trag had always believed that his lack of success with
women was because his eyes weren't blue like his brother's—a notion that Jack found completely ridiculous.

Trag grinned. "Good to see you, Jack," he said. "And
you, too, Cat," he added, gripping his old friend's hand.
"Seen Ty around?"

"You're kidding, right?" Jack scoffed. "Gotta buy
tickets about a year in advance to see *him."*

Trag's brother, Tycharian, and his rock band, *Princes
& Slaves,* were a hot act wherever they played. Jack had
only seen them once, but had come away from the performance insisting that Cat leave off his shirt and wear
a studded choker the way Tychar did. Cat had replied
that he would start dressing that way when Jack did it
herself. So far, it had only happened in private—with
some very memorable results—and Cat had gotten the
cock strap idea from the *other* collar the two brothers
had worn during their enslavement, which was an even
bigger hit. Jack had nearly fainted dead away from the
orgasm triggered from watching him wrap the choker
around the base of his cock and balls for the first time—
a sensation which Cat had also enjoyed, along with the
priceless expression on Jack's face.

"Doesn't sound too hard for you, though," Trag said
warmly. "You always had plenty of money."

Jack shrugged. "I could get tickets if I wanted, I suppose, but I'd think you'd be more interested in doing
that yourself. Don't you miss him?"

As the two brothers had both been slaves to the same
Darconian queen for twenty years, they'd probably seen
more of each other than most siblings do in a lifetime.

"Well, kinda," Trag admitted. "But we're all pretty busy, you know."

"Big fuckin' galaxy, too," Jack observed.

"Yeah," Trag agreed. "What brings you out this far?"

"Looking for information," she said lightly. "And by the way, did you hear we found another one of your friends?"

"No shit?" Trag exclaimed excitedly. "Which one?"

"Lynxsander," Cat replied. "He is... well."

"Well?" Trag scoffed. "Just, *well?* You always were one to mince words." Looking at Jack for further enlightenment, he said, "Tell me about him."

"He was a slave in a harem," Jack reported. "Fucked fifty women until they wore him out, and he was sold again—but he's doing much better now! He's living on Terra Minor with a friend of mine."

"A female friend, I take it?" Trag said with a grin.

Jack favored him with her most withering look. "Now, Trag, you know very well it's a woman! You guys attract them like flies." Glancing over at the corner where Trag had been stationed and noting the grumpy expressions on the women's faces, she added, "Which I see you've been doing yourself. Found a mate yet?"

"No," Trag replied. "Met lots of nice girls, but none I want to live with forever, so I keep looking."

"Trag was always a wanderer," Cat remarked.

"Hard to please, more like," Jack muttered under her breath. "You should take a trip to Earth, Trag," Jack suggested aloud. "Just walk down the street naked and then take your pick of the ones who follow you."

"That sounds very romantic," Trag said with a snicker.

"You didn't say you were looking for romance," Jack pointed out. "But if you think you're finding 'nice girls' in places like this… well… I guess I can't help you."

Jack glanced over at the women Trag had been sitting with and decided that they all fell into the "lover for hire" category. She wondered briefly how much it would cost to get one of them to have some of Trag's children, but then decided that she didn't want Zetithians growing up in that sort of environment. Earth would be much better, but so far, she hadn't been able to persuade Lerotan to take Trag there. Actually, Jack had an idea that, being an arms dealer, he *couldn't* go there, so she didn't press the point. Landing regulations on Earth were pretty tough.

Shifting her gaze back to Trag, she tweaked his cloak and added, " 'Course, you look like you're hiding most of your attributes under an awful lot of camouflage these days." The only skin she could see was his face and hands—and they had seemed a little chilly to her.

Trag shivered. *"You* try living on a sizzling rock like Darconia for twenty years and see how you feel when you leave!" he grumbled. "I don't know how Ty stands it! I feel like I'm freezing my nuts off all the time—no matter which planet we go to!"

"Well, I'm sure you'll adjust," Jack said kindly. "But I don't suppose you'll be walking around naked for a while—on Earth or anywhere else. Guess you'll have to get a mate based on personality alone." Trag had plenty of that, she knew.

Lerotan decided it was time to make his move. "Hey, Jack," he called out. "You know that guy you asked me to check out?"

"You mean Sylor Halen?" she said casually.

"Yeah," he said. "I think I can help you on this one."

"Good boy, Leroy!" she said with a winning smile. "I knew you would."

Lerotan smiled and motioned for her to come closer. "And now for the deal."

Jack knew he wouldn't give up the information for free. "So, Leroy," she began. "How do you feel about a sponge that makes its own soap?"

"Don't think I need that," he replied, stroking a bare Davordian thigh. "These women take great pleasure in keeping me... clean."

The Davordians looked so smug Jack wanted to slug them, but went on doggedly. "Well, then, how about some new boots? My Shoemaker in a Box could crank out a new pair in no time."

Lerotan shook his head, smiling wickedly. "Got plenty of boots."

"Well, hell, Leroy!" Jack exclaimed in exasperation. "What the devil *do* you want?"

His grin was now diabolical. "Chocolate."

Drummond got the call from Jack and immediately contacted the tracking team. "Hey, Zerk!" he said. "Need you and the boys to look up Sylor Halen again."

"Aw, c'mon, Drummond! That guy is gone!" Zerk insisted. "I don't know how, but he must have pulled his implant or something. Every time we went to pick him up, he wasn't there!"

"I've got some new info on him," Drummond said. "He's not pure Vessonian. Seems he's got a little Treslanti in his bloodline."

"Which means he can disappear," Zerk said slowly. "Damn! No wonder we could never find him! We kept checking periodically, and we went all over the place trying to locate him, but no luck. I'd about decided his implant was sending out a bad signal."

"Well, now you know the reason," Drummond said. "Where are you showing him now?"

"Hold on a minute," Zerk replied, checking the sensor array. "Hmm, looks like he's at his original address."

"Can you get there real quick?"

"Nope," Zerk replied. "We're a little tied up at the moment. Just picked up a belligerent Teonite who doesn't want to leave our charming little planet, and it might be a couple hours before we can get there."

"Well, I'll head out myself, then," Drummond said. "Bonnie needs to know about this."

"Better be careful," Zerk advised. "He could be right there in front of you, and you wouldn't see him—believe me, I know." Zerk shuddered slightly. He was as tough as any tracker, but an invisible enemy gave him the willies.

"I'll give Bonnie a call and warn her first." Drummond knew that Lynx was probably in more danger from Sylor than Bonnie was, but Drummond didn't want anything happening to him, either. Bonnie had been happier with Lynx than she'd been in a very long time, and Drummond didn't want anything to change that.

He made the call right away, but couldn't reach her because, as luck would have it, Bonnie's glitchy comlink was on the blink again.

Recognizing the scent, Lynx was instantly on the alert. Sylor was in the vicinity, but exactly where and with what intention, Lynx couldn't tell. He'd gotten several rats that evening—they liked to come out at dusk, and Lynx's keen vision had no trouble spotting them, just as he should have been able to spot Sylor. He considered hunting him down by his scent trail alone, but knew that Sylor would realize he was being hunted and leave. Lynx didn't want that; he wanted a confrontation. This cat and mouse game they were playing had him primed for a fight—and now that he had something to fight for, he was more than willing to engage.

Leaning against the feeding pen fence, he fed the rats to the enocks, letting them tear off bits of the meat while his eyes scanned the area. If Sylor moved, he would see him—but only if he happened to be looking right at him at the time. Lynx wondered just what mechanism the Vessonians used to disappear and decided that they must be capable, not of disappearing, but of projecting their surroundings to the viewer rather than their own image. This would explain why wearing clothing didn't affect the ability—Ulla had been wearing a sleeper when she did it, and Sylor must have been capable of doing the same thing.

Just then, Kipper trotted over, and Lynx remembered that the dog would know Sylor—possibly being able to see him, or somehow know where he was. He should have asked Tisana to tell the dog to point him out, but it was too late for that now. The *Jolly Roger's* crew had been gone for about two weeks, promising a return visit in a few months. Lynx had never considered just how valuable that kind of information could be, but he was thinking it now.

"He is close by," Lynx murmured to the collie. "Do you smell him?"

Kipper looked up at him questioningly. A little more time spent with Tisana and he would have been able to understand human speech better, but as it stood, Kipper only realized he was being asked a question. Not being able to talk back, he wagged his tail in reply.

Lynx noted a few eggs in the pen and decided to gather them. Giving the rest of the rats to the birds, he slid the poles in behind them and entered the larger pen.

It was only when the gate slammed shut behind him that he realized his error. Then he saw the poles to the feeding area begin to slide out all by themselves. *Ah,* thought Lynx, *he will let the birds eliminate me. His mistake…*

Sylor had been waiting for this moment for some time. Bonnie had always been nearby whenever Lynx had gone into one of the pens, but this time she was in the house and might not hear the commotion—until it was too late. Locking the gate securely, he knew very well that it was impossible for anyone—bird or man—to climb out of that pen. He'd seen to *that* modification himself, and though its purpose was to keep the birds inside, it would also make for the best, most gruesome accident he could stage. Bonnie would be horrified and in need of comfort—which Sylor would graciously provide. He might even give it some time before he approached her—let her miss having a man around the way she'd apparently missed having him. He might even wait until after the burial to return to her, though it would be difficult. Sylor hadn't been faithful to Bonnie, but that didn't mean he wasn't attracted. She was a very desirable woman—whether she cut her hair or not.

Sylor smiled, noting Lynx's expression of horror as the enocks realized that they were about to feast upon something more substantial than rats. The big male was the first to spot him, as usual—and Sylor understood the danger, having nearly been had by that one a few times himself.

Lynx had seen movement by the gate and knew that the remote control hadn't been used to close it. Sylor was there—he could smell him, he just couldn't see him. Kipper saw what was happening and barked a warning. The female enocks were milling around, not sure whether to go after Lynx or concentrate on what was left of the rats, but the male was not as indecisive. Zeroing in on his target, the bird went straight for Lynx.

Kipper barked loudly, hoping Bonnie would hear him. He wanted to go find her, but was afraid to leave. Lynx had been much kinder to him than Sylor had ever been, and Kipper knew exactly what was going on; this was a territorial battle, something a dog understood even better than a man. He knew he didn't want things to go back to the way they were. Lynx was his favorite, and he went after Sylor with a snarl.

From Lynx's perspective, the dog appeared to be attacking thin air, but he knew it had to be Sylor. The dog could obviously see the Vessonian—or smell him—and while Lynx knew he could rely on Kipper's help to track him, he first had to escape from the pen. He had to admire Sylor for his skill and cunning; setting him up to be killed by the enocks was a good plan, but he'd reckoned without an inventive Zetithian as his prey.

Lynx ignored the enocks completely and ran to the edge of the enclosure, hoping that Sylor hadn't been in the area when he'd been working on the pen. Pulling up the trapdoor on a buried box, Lynx smiled grimly. It was empty; the rope and grappling hook to be used for escape were gone. The release mechanism for the gate had also been disabled. There was only one other way out.

Lynx heard Kipper yelp as Sylor kicked him and watched the collie's renewed attack on his invisible target. If the dog kept him occupied long enough, Lynx knew he would be able to get out. The trouble was, the enocks had finished eating the rats by this time and, with nothing left to occupy them, they headed toward him with their beaks wide open, ready to rip the flesh from his bones. Lynx was under no illusions that his purring would stop them once they'd gotten a taste.

Meanwhile, Kipper was doing his best to help. He'd *tried* to tell someone what Sylor had been up to—even searching in vain for Tisana to interpret for him, but humans could be so stupid! Having seen what Sylor had done seemed strange to him at the time—and he'd wanted to tell someone then—but he understood it now.

Lynx had one last escape route, but to use it, he'd have to run toward the birds, or lure them away and then circle back to the feeding pen. They were cunning hunters, though, and they split up and fanned out in an effort to surround him. To scatter them, bold moves were required. Lynx ran right at them, doing his best to appear even more frightening than they were. Having always been quiet and soothing when he was near them had the birds unprepared for his startlingly aggressive behavior, which gave Lynx all the time he needed.

Lynx made it through the gauntlet of snapping beaks but was bleeding from several bites by the time he reached his goal. He'd carved discreet grooves in the otherwise smooth fence, which required getting a foothold in one spot and then reaching a long way for the next. The pattern was too complex for the birds to understand, but it was possible that Sylor had noticed it and sabotaged them. With the male enock hot on his heels, Lynx made it to the wall, but as he scrambled up the side and stretched his leg sideways to find the next step, he felt the beak grab at his pants leg, ripping through the tough fabric like a knife.

With no time to lose, Lynx whirled around and seized the bird by the throat, just as he had the day he rescued Bonnie. "Sorry," he said grimly, "but you must die now." Throttling the enock with one hand, Lynx punched the side of its head with the other. As he heard the neck bones snap, he pushed the body backwards to block the advance of the females. Momentarily finding the male's inert body more interesting than Lynx, the females ignored him long enough for him to climb out. From the top of the fence, he could see Kipper nearby and still on the attack, and Lynx launched himself in that direction.

His flying leap from the top of the fence took Sylor by surprise, disrupting his camouflage projection. Lynx could see him now, but was already close enough to smell and feel and knew that this was the one he truly needed to defeat—otherwise, he'd be fighting him forever.

Sylor fought back with a vengeance, using every dirty trick he could remember, even going for Lynx's eyes. Kipper managed to get a grip on Sylor's boot, but got kicked in the face. His yelp of pain set off a

fire inside Lynx and, as a lifetime of suppressed anger
was unleashed, he struck at his enemy, not to injure,
but to kill.

Sylor's head snapped back from the blow to his temple, but his kick at the dog had thrown him off balance
and he was already falling—which canceled Lynx's
advantage. Momentarily stunned, he then retaliated by
kicking Lynx in the groin. Always one of those taboos
in combat, Sylor wasn't above using it, and, at least in
this case, neither was Lynx. Recovering quickly, Lynx
whipped around, sending Sylor sprawling with a vicious
kick of his own. Then, with a snarl, Lynx advanced on
Sylor as the Vessonian scrambled to his feet. Neither
man noticed when the dog took off running.

The sensors had pinpointed his location and knowing
what he knew now, Drummond was sure Sylor was
there somewhere, but he still couldn't see him. As he
got out of his speeder, he spotted Lynx in the enock pen
and raced to his aid but stopped short as he saw Lynx's
leap from the fence and his subsequent struggle with an
invisible foe. When Sylor reappeared, Drummond knew
he should have stepped in to put an end to the fight, but
something made him let it play out.

He wished he hadn't when the Vessonian pulled
a knife.

Chapter 21

LAUNCHING HIMSELF AT HIS OPPONENT, LYNX SAW THE flash of the blade and went for the hand that held it, but missed. As the sharp point bit into his shoulder, Lynx let out a roar of fury and instinctively went for the Vessonian's throat. He heard Sylor's scream as his fangs drew blood. Snarling, Lynx shook his head—ripping through muscles, tendons, and arteries—only stopping when Sylor went limp in his grasp. Sylor's astonished eyes stared up at Lynx for a long moment before they lost their focus, and he fell back onto the grass.

Lynx pulled the knife out of his shoulder and tossed it aside, not even feeling the pain or the flow of blood that followed. His rival was dead, and as he stared down at Sylor's inert form, his whole body felt numb with the shock and the taste of another man's blood on his tongue.

Drummond stood watching, silently, until Kipper's beseeching whine finally got his attention.

"Shame about that," Drummond said gruffly as he approached. "He should have known better to get in there with those damn birds! If I was that hungry, I'd have stolen chicken eggs myself. Not as big, perhaps, but at least chickens won't kill you."

Lynx turned to face him, blood running down his chest and his yellow eyes still ablaze. "The birds did not kill him," Lynx said firmly. "I did."

Drummond scratched his head thoughtfully. "Well, now, you can believe that if you want, but that's not what *I* saw. Actually, they saved me the trouble. Seems there's more than one death warrant out on him—and Sylor Halen isn't his real name, either."

"He was a... murderer?"

"Not exactly," Drummond replied. "He's what they call a sociopath on Earth—the kind of crook who thinks only of himself and likes to manipulate people and make bad things happen. Hard to pin a murder on one of them, but we won't have to worry about trying to do that now."

"Why did he come back?" Lynx wondered aloud.

Drummond shrugged. "Don't know. Must've had some sort of plan when he left here in the first place—but it's hard to get *on* this planet legally—and even harder to leave—'specially once you've had a trace put on you. Guess whatever he had planned must have fallen through, and he decided to come back. Wish he hadn't, though," Drummond said with a rueful grimace. "Don't look forward to telling Bonnie about this."

"I am the one who will tell her," Lynx said.

"You just tell her the enocks got him, and you were trying to save him," Drummond advised. "Might be better that way."

"No," Lynx said with a defiant lift of his chin. "I will not lie to her."

"Suit yourself," Drummond said with a shrug. "But that's how the official report will read."

Lynx heard Kipper barking and looked up just as Bonnie rounded the corner of the house.

"Don't tell her," Drummond warned again. "It'll be hard enough on her as it is."

"I have to," Lynx said, wiping the blood from his chin with the back of his hand. He was already bloody from his encounter with the enocks, and Sylor's knife hadn't helped matters any.

Bonnie caught one glimpse of Lynx covered in blood and started running. Drummond tried to head her off, but she saw Sylor anyway.

Stopping short, she stared down at the body lying in the grass. "What happened?" she gasped.

Drummond looked at Lynx warningly and shook his head.

"He tried to kill me," Lynx said shortly. "So I killed him."

"That's *his* story," Drummond grumbled. "But it's not how the report will read. I was a witness, and *I* say the birds did it!"

Bonnie ignored Drummond and looked anxiously at Lynx. "Are you all right?" she asked. "You're bleeding!"

"I will heal," Lynx said. With a gesture toward Sylor, he added, "He will not."

"I kept telling you those birds were too vicious to fool with," Drummond said, "and I—"

"That's enough, Drummond," Bonnie said firmly. "I believe Lynx."

"But—"

"It doesn't matter," Bonnie said. "I know he killed Sylor in self-defense. He's incapable of murder."

"Murder? Did I say anything about murder?" Drummond demanded testily. "I just think an accidental death is easier for everyone."

"No one will believe it," Bonnie said. "Sylor knew how dangerous those birds could be, and so does everyone else around here. Nobody in their right mind would believe he would just blunder into their pen and let them rip him apart." The fact that Bonnie had done that very thing didn't occur to her at the time, though it did occur to Lynx.

"Yes, but—"

"Drummond," Bonnie said quietly. "Thank you very much for trying to help, but we will tell the truth."

"Didn't tell the truth when you filled out that birth record, did you?" Drummond countered.

Bonnie glared at him. "That was something I did to keep Sylor from having any claim on Ulla, and you know it!"

Lynx looked confused. "Ulla?"

"For your information, the name on that child's birth record is Shaulla Dackelov," Drummond told him. "And it lists you as her father—and you weren't even living on this planet when she was conceived! How's *that* for being honest and truthful?"

Lynx stared at Bonnie. "It is not possible."

"Maybe so," Bonnie admitted, "but I had Drummond put your name down when I reported Ulla's birth. I didn't want Sylor coming back and claiming her, and I figured you wouldn't care one way or the other." Sighing sadly, she added, "I never thought you'd stay this long, anyway."

"So her name is—?"

"The same as your mother's, Lynx. I think I spelled it right—not sure how it would be spelled in Zetithian, but what I came up is phonetically correct, anyway."

"You did this without telling me," Lynx said flatly. "Was I ever to be told?"

"Well, I'm telling you now, so that's a moot point, isn't it?" Sighing, she added, "Guess I should tell you the rest of it, too. When I claimed abandonment to get Sylor's name off the deed, for the price of one credit, which I withheld from your pay, you bought his share."

Lynx could hardly believe what he was hearing. "I have a daughter *and* I own this land?"

"Well, you share them both with me," Bonnie said, "but, yeah, that's about the size of it." Lynx still seemed confused, so she added, "I did it because I love you, and I didn't want Sylor coming back and trying to pick up where he left off."

"But he was the father of your child—" Lynx said, still trying to make sense of it all. "—her true father."

"Lynx," Bonnie said gently, "You *are* Ulla's true father—the only father she's ever known! You're the only one I want, and I wouldn't have let Sylor come back. Not even if I had to give up everything to keep you."

A frown furrowed his brow. "Then I should not have killed him."

"Why not?" Bonnie said with surprise. "He was trying to kill you, wasn't he?"

"Yes, but that is not why he had to die." Lynx looked into Bonnie's soft blue eyes. "I did it because of you. Because he was my rival, and I wanted to be certain that you would not be able to choose anyone but me."

"But I already have, Lynx," Bonnie said. "I love *you,* not Sylor."

"Then he did not have to die."

"Well, now, that's a matter of opinion," Drummond said briskly. He wasn't about to let Lynx go on blaming himself for killing Sylor—it wouldn't do him, or Bonnie, any good. "There are any number of people around the quadrant who want him dead. You just saved them the trouble. His name was really Ranx Prater, and he wasn't a purebred Vessonian, either; he was part Treslanti, which is why he could disappear. Vessonians can't do that. Seems Jack had some suspicions about him and did some asking around after that last visit and found someone who could identify him. He must've forged his documents to get here. That Treslanti ability doesn't show up on one of Vladen's scans, either." Drummond blew out an exasperated breath. "Damn crooks," he grumbled. "They keep getting smarter, and all I do is get older." Shaking his head, he added, "Maybe I should give it up and retire—just go back to Texas and plant avocados."

Bonnie smiled. "You can't leave!" she protested. "What would we ever do without you?"

"Probably do a lot better with someone else," he grumbled. "I must be getting senile."

"But you came here to get enough space to breathe, remember?" she reminded him. "And you can plant avocados right here. Don't leave. We need you."

"No you don't," he said gruffly. "That Zetithian boy can provide you with more protection than I can—but one thing you *do* need is a comlink that works! I tried to call you before I headed out here."

"I'll get a new one," Bonnie promised, trying to hide her smile. To Drummond, most of the people in the sector were like his children—which included Lynx. Bonnie liked that.

"See that you do," he said. "And in the meantime, you need to get to work on that boy so he doesn't bleed to death."

"Don't worry," Bonnie said, looking up at Lynx adoringly. "I'll take very good care of him."

Chapter 22

LEAVING DRUMMOND TO HANDLE THE MATTER OF Sylor's body, Bonnie took Lynx by the hand and led him back to the house. She sat him in a chair and sealed his wounds and washed away the blood, just as he had done for her on that fateful morning that seemed so long ago now.

He watched her while she worked, seeing her expression of anguish, seeing the tears in her eyes, though she avoided his own gaze. "You are not angry with me?" he asked.

"For what? Still being alive?" Bonnie shivered at the thought that Sylor's plan might have succeeded. "When I think of what I might have found if it hadn't been for— how *did* you get out of that pen?"

"I had more than one way out," he said. "I was... prepared."

"Hmph! Might have told me about it," she grumbled.

"I have never let you in the pen since I came here," Lynx said. "You did not need to know." Upon hearing his words, she realized he was right: she hadn't set foot inside either pen for any reason. He had always done it. He'd been protecting her from the very beginning.

"Would you mind telling me what else I don't need to know?"

Lynx smiled. "I will tell you everything from now on," he said. "Whether you need to know it or not."

"Well, that's a relief! Too many secrets are a bad thing! And speaking of secrets, I had no idea Sylor wasn't a pure Vessonian! Guess I'll have to check out Treslanties to know what I'm up against with Ulla."

"She will not be like him," Lynx said, understanding Bonnie's concerns immediately. "She will not use her abilities for evil as he did."

"I certainly hope not!" Bonnie said with a shudder. "I always knew he was manipulative, but this... this is... *horrifying.*"

Lynx took her hand; his grasp was warm and strong and soothed her overwrought nerves like a balm. "She will be honest and kind," Lynx said gently. "Just as her mother is."

"Are you sure about that?" Bonnie queried. "Had a vision, perhaps?" She knew it was something the other Zetithians were capable of—but she didn't know about Lynx.

"No," he said. "She will be that way because of you."

Bonnie met his gaze at last, and what she saw reassured her even more. In his shining eyes she saw nothing but the truth—however difficult it might be to accept. "Might be a little of your influence, too," she said. "I've never met a more honest man in my life."

Putting his arm around her, he pulled her close. "Nor I a kinder, more loving woman. You were kind to me even when I was not."

"I couldn't help but be kind to you, Lynx!" Bonnie protested. "You'd been a slave—I can't imagine a worse fate."

"I can," he said. "Loving someone who does not love you in return." Lynx understood just how much pain he had caused her, and he vowed never to hurt her again. He would spend the rest of his life doing anything he could to ensure her happiness. Leo had been right; it was his purpose to love her, and he would dedicate his life to it. "I am deeply sorry I could not see it in the beginning."

"See what?"

"That no matter how much hate I had stored up inside me, that I would love you and would make you my mate," he said. Gazing into her deep blue eyes, he found healing and solace there, and knew he would do so for the rest of his days. "My beautiful Bonnie," he murmured. "I love you more than you will ever know. Will you be my mate—for life?"

"I can't think of anything I'd like better," she sighed. For her part, it was already done, but hearing him say the words was a great comfort to her. "I love you, so much, Lynx. And yes, I will be your mate—forever."

Lynx felt a sense of joyous contentment wash over him. The hatred was gone. He could live again and truly be free. "I had no vision," he whispered, "but I should have known. Should have seen your face in my dreams and known that you would be the one to save me from myself."

"And I should have known when you rescued me that first day," she sighed. "You were so angry with me."

"If I was angry, it was because I knew that if you had died, any hope I ever had would have died along with you. It was very selfish of me."

Bonnie smiled. "I forgive you for that," she said, and followed it up with a loving kiss to ensure that he understood. She forgave him for everything; every tear she shed and every pain she endured. None of that mattered as long as he loved her.

The horror of Sylor's death faded slowly for Bonnie. She knew there was no longer anything to fear, but her sleep was troubled. Lynx was there to soothe her fears, as his purring soothed her soul, but she wished with all her heart that Lynx had not been placed in a situation where he was required to kill or be killed. Bonnie thought Lynx would have more difficulty as a result and was surprised that she was the one having nightmares rather than him. Lynx slept better than he had in some time; knowing that his rival was no longer plotting his death made him much more relaxed. He, too, regretted having killed, but also knew that sometimes a man must do things he does not enjoy or look back on with pride.

Late one evening, the wind began to howl and the thunder rolled as rain fell in sheets, isolating their house from the rest of the world.

"No fires?" Bonnie asked as Lynx came to bed.

"No," he replied. "The storm is moving through quickly, though."

"I'm sorry to hear that," she said. "I like the feeling of being safe inside where it's warm and dry while the storm passes around us." Looking up at him, his face illuminated by the soft light, she added, "How did you ever stand being out in the shed when it was storming like this?"

Lynx laughed. "It was better than many places I have slept." He'd told her of the tough conditions on Paemay after he left the harem; of hot, dry days and cold, sleepless nights. Of dust and dirt and the odor of sweat filling his nostrils. The pain of muscles screaming from unaccustomed use, the jostle of rough company, and the sickening smell of even rougher rations. But those things were in the past and would remain so.

"When I first came here," he said, "that shed seemed like a palace to me. I have since learned that living here with you is much better," he purred. "Here, where I can be surrounded by the scent of your love."

"Can you smell it now?"

"Always," he replied.

"Not any danger of it losing its effect—is there?" Bonnie asked hurriedly.

"None," Lynx said firmly. "But you will see that for yourself. I look forward to many years of demonstrating just how strong your effect is upon me."

Melting into his arms, Bonnie felt complete and warm and loved. And when he kissed her, the feeling grew. These were the moments she enjoyed the most: the soft, wet kisses that sent her mind to a special place—a place as special as being in his arms.

Lynx sighed and slid gently inside; flowing into her with slow, undulating moves that came as naturally to him as breathing. There was hurry, no rush to reach climax, no need to do anything spectacular; he could take his time to savor her peaceful, warm, and deliciously satisfying love. Bonnie had once said that she would have been happy just to hold him; now he knew just how true that was. He didn't need to impress her; he just needed to love her—and his need to show her how much he loved her was strong. Soft sighs escaped her,

her joy escalating with slow, potent moves designed by his love. Then heat and light and mounting passion, followed by subtle, gently rocking waves of bliss. Her soft, wet kisses on his face, her fingers tantalizingly cool on his heated skin. Her languid body surrounding him, accepting all he had to give.

Where had she come from? How had he ever found such a treasure? Out of all the women in the galaxy, she had done what no other could do. Gazing down into her deep blue eyes, her halo of golden hair framing her angelic face, he didn't know why she had saved him, he only knew that she had.

Her eyes met his, and she drank in the sight of him. "That feels so good," she whispered, her voice soft and dreamy. "You have no idea."

"But I do, my lovely Bonnie," he assured her. "I know just exactly how it feels."

"You couldn't possibly," she murmured in protest— after all, she was the one for whom the orgasms were almost continuous, and she got to look at Lynx and hold him while he loved her. "Can you read my mind and tell me what I'm feeling?"

"No," he purred. "But I know what I feel, and it feels like love. Nothing could be better than that."

"To me too," she said. "I want you to stay right where you are forever."

"If only I could," he sighed. "But I know that I cannot."

Lynx did his best to prolong the inevitable, for watching her face while he loved her was an addiction. He could never get enough of her. When his climax came, he wasn't giving it to her or taking it all for himself; it was shared joy, and he felt the euphoria for the very first time.

Lynx knew the moment it happened—the beginning of new life deep inside her. He had never had a vision before, but he knew it was a true one; the one dream he'd had all his life; the dream that never came true. Bonnie may not have had a vision, but she, too felt a change; that change which comes when two souls entwine, having no secrets from one another, no fears that the love they share will ever end. The fear and uncertainty were gone. There was no going back. They would only move forward. And with the dawn of a new day, their new lives began.

Jack received the wedding invitation with a satisfied smile. "Ha! I *knew* she could do it," she chuckled. "I had faith."

Cat smiled. "We have all been very lucky," he said. "Lynxsander perhaps even more so than the rest of us."

"How do you figure that?" demanded Jack with her hands on her hips as she tried to imagine why Cat would have thought that anyone was luckier than he. "Did you want a wife with blue eyes?"

Her chin was stuck out in that belligerent fashion that always made Cat want to sweep her off her feet and mate with her. "You are sounding like Trag," he said, doing his best to keep from taking her in his arms and kissing her so hard she would never doubt that it was she he wanted, and always would. "And no, it has nothing to do with blue eyes. It is true that you rescued me from slavery, but Lynx had already been freed when Bonnie found him. The chains on him were much more difficult to remove. It took a great deal of love to do that."

"Well, maybe you're right," she admitted. Looking questioningly at her husband, she added, "Would it have been the same for you if someone else had freed you?"

"Perhaps," Cat said, "but it was not. You, my lovely Jacinth, freed me, and bound me to you in the same moment."

"Aw, now, Cat," Jack protested. "I did no such thing!"

"But you did," he purred. "No matter where you go or what you do, I am still your slave—and it is how each of us feels about our mates."

"Natural born slave boys, huh?"

"Perhaps," he admitted. "But only when our master is a female we love."

"Ooo, and guess what?" Jack exclaimed as she remembered something else from the message.

"Bonnie is pregnant?"

"How the hell did you know?" she demanded. Then she shook her head and answered her own question before he had the opportunity to reply. "Never mind," she said. "It's what you *do,* isn't it?"

Cat shrugged. "Yes," he said, "But there is something else, as well."

"What's that?" Jack asked, her eyes dancing with glee. "Did the Nedwut homeworld finally get blown to bits?"

As hopeful as she appeared at such a grisly prospect, Cat hated not to be able to accommodate her, but also knew that his news would bring her even more delight. "It is about Kyra and Tycharian," he said. "They have had three sons."

"Really? That's fabulous!" Jack exclaimed. Looking up at her husband expectantly, she went on. "So, what are we going to have? More boys?"

Cat grinned wickedly. "I will not tell you that," he said, knowing it would drive her crazy until she knew. Cat liked his Jacinth to be a little on the crazy side. It made for much more interesting times—not that their time together was ever dull. "It will be a surprise."

Cat would tell her eventually—when he knew himself—but for now, he let her think he knew. He liked the idea of what she would do to persuade him to let her in on the secret. She could be *very* persuasive...

The wedding took place in the meeting hall at the spaceport in Nimbaza. Bonnie wore white, and Lynx thought she looked more angelic than ever. Her attendants wore emerald green, which Leo appreciated because it matched Tisana's eyes. The men were resplendent in their black formal attire with vests to match the bridesmaids dresses, and in Jack's humble opinion, all looked good enough to eat.

Drummond performed the ceremony and then announced his retirement. Vladen gave Bonnie away and then told Lynx that he had to deliver every baby in the sector from then on. Lynx said he was okay with that as long as he got paid a decent salary. Zuannis, who had made the most scrumptious wedding cake imaginable, was the matron of honor, with Cat as the best man. Jack was a bridesmaid, and it was difficult to say which of them was feeling more "desire" at seeing the other all dressed up for the event—though Cat's reaction was more obvious than Jack's.

Tisana, who made a bewitching bridesmaid, brewed up some more herbal tea for Jack and Bonnie to get them through the ceremony without throwing up. The effectiveness of the potion was tested when Gerna and Hatul showed up as guests, nearly causing Jack to lose her breakfast. Having learned a bit more about Norludian sexual practices, Bonnie was beginning to suspect that Jack had once been propositioned by one of them, which would account for her reaction. Hatul waved his suckery fingers longingly at Salan but stopped when Gerna smacked him on the butt.

Althea, who had just learned to walk, was the flower girl. Leo, along with Larry, Moe, and Curly, were the ushers, and Alrik and Aidan were ring-bearers, but could only toddle down the aisle because they were holding on to Max and Kipper. Max thought it was a lovely ceremony and did some serious howling at the end. Kipper was just glad he got to eat cake.

With her first avocados, Bonnie had made a big bowl of guacamole for the reception. Drummond ate nearly all of it and then fussed at Bonnie for not selling him her entire crop.

Salan was also a bridesmaid, but sobbed throughout the entire wedding because another Zetithian had gotten away from her. However, after dancing with Wilisan at the reception, she rebounded quickly. Lerotan and Trag sent their love, but couldn't be in attendance because arms dealers weren't allowed to land on Terra Minor—a rule that Jack had tried very hard to have changed but without any success. In fact, she'd come very close to getting herself deported—it seems that some government officials object to having someone make a request while fingering their pistol—but got off lightly, only having her permit to carry a weapon revoked.

Lynx had the opportunity to fight off yet another rival, though with less fatal results than his previous battle, when Hatul came through the receiving line.

"My dear Bonnie," Hatul said, making the most of the opportunity to hug the bride as he enfolded her in his skinny arms. "I am so pleased for you and Lynx! Words cannot express the happiness I feel on this joyous occasion."

Bonnie noted the dreamy look in Hatul's eyes as his fingertips grazed the skin exposed by the low back of her wedding gown and was about to warn him off, but Lynx reached out a hand to stop him.

"Hatul," he said gravely. "If you want to live long enough to eat some of Zuannis' cake, you should stop right now."

"So sorry," Hatul said meekly as he moved on. "Couldn't resist…"

Bonnie might have hugged him back—however reluctantly—but Jack couldn't even look at Hatul without wanting to barf. "I just can't stand those guys," she said to Cat, who merely smiled.

"Well, at least he didn't try to kiss me," Bonnie murmured to her new husband. "You know what they do with their tongues, don't you?"

"I can guess," Lynx replied, shaking Vladen's hand as he passed through the line.

"They are *so* weird," Zuannis agreed. "I'm not even sure I want him eating my cake!"

"He'll probably put fingerprints all over it," Bonnie agreed. "We'd better hurry and get a piece before it's too late."

Hatul, however, behaved impeccably during the reception, only fingering his own piece of cake, after which he and Gerna made a rather sudden departure. Seems the cake Zuannis made for the occasion tasted every bit as orgasmic as it looked.

During the reception, Jack took a moment to take Lynx aside. "So, tell me, Lynx," she said, dropping a casual arm around his shoulders. "Been thanking those lucky stars of yours?"

Jack's use of language puzzled most people, but Lynx even more so than the rest. "I do not understand."

"The ones you must have been wishing on," she said. "Those must have been some damn good stars… and you know it, don't you?" Judging from Lynx's blank expression, Jack knew she'd lost him and decided to make it easier for him. "How does it feel to be adored?"

Lynx smiled warmly. This much, he understood. "I believe you should ask Bonnie that," he said. "She understands that far better than I."

"Oh, I doubt that," said Jack, noting Bonnie's expression. If there had ever been a bride who appeared to adore her new husband more, Jack hadn't seen her yet—though if she'd happened to glance in a mirror during her own wedding, she would have seen the same thing. "I doubt that very much, indeed."

Epilogue

"PUSH AGAIN," LYNX URGED HIS WIFE. "ONCE MORE."

The head crowned, and suddenly the infant slipped from his mother and into his father's waiting hands. Lynx noted the sharply pointed ears and gazed into the blinking feline eyes of his newborn son. Then his two beautiful daughters followed their brother into the light. Out of the scores of babies he'd delivered, these were the first to be his own, and at long last, Lynx understood what it truly meant to feel joy.

**Escape to the world of
the Cat Star Chronicles,
by Cheryl Brooks**

SLAVE

WARRIOR

ROGUE

Read on for a sneak peek...

From

SLAVE

I FOUND HIM IN THE SLAVE MARKET ON ORPHESEUS Prime, and even on such a godforsaken planet as that one, their treatment of him seemed extreme. But then again, perhaps he was an extreme subject, and the fact that there was a slave market at all was evidence of a rather backward society. Slave markets were becoming extremely rare throughout the galaxy—the legal ones, anyway.

I hitched my pack higher on my shoulder and adjusted my respirator, though even with the benefit of ultrafiltration, the place still stank to high heaven. How a planet as eternally hot and dry as this one could have ever had anything on it that could possibly rot and get into the air to cause such a stench was beyond me. Most dry climates don't support a lot of decay or fermentation, but Orpheseus was different from any desert planet I'd ever had the misfortune to visit. It smelled as though at some point all of the vegetation and animal life forms had died at once and the odor of their decay had become permanently embedded in the atmosphere.

Shuddering as a wave of nausea hit me, I walked casually closer to the line of wretched creatures lined up for pre-auction inspection, but even my unobtrusive move wasn't lost on the slave owners who were bent on selling their wares.

"Come closer!" a ragged beast urged me in a rasping, unpleasant voice as he gestured with a bony arm.

I eyed him with distaste, thinking that this thing was just ugly enough to have caused the entire planet to smell bad, though I doubted he'd been there long enough to do it. On the other hand, he didn't seem to be terribly young. Okay, so older than the hills might have been a little closer to the mark. Damn, maybe he *was* responsible, after all!

"I have here just what you have been seeking!" he said. "Help to relieve you of your burden! This one is strong and loyal and will serve you well."

I glanced dubiously at the small-statured critter there before me, and its even smaller slave. "I don't think so," I replied, thinking that the weight of my pack alone would probably have crushed the poor little thing's tiny bones to powder. I know that looks can often be deceiving, but this thing looked to me like nothing more than an oversized grasshopper. Its bulbous red eyes regarded me with an unblinking and slightly unnerving stare. "Its eyes give me the creeps, anyway," I added. "I need something that looks more… humanoid."

Dismissing them with a wave, I glanced around at the others, noting that, of the group, there were only two slaves being offered that were even bipedal: one reminded me of a cross between a cow and a chimpanzee, and the other, well, the other was the one who had first caught my eye—possibly because out of all the slaves there, he was the one seeming to require the most restraint, and also because he was completely naked.

I studied him out of the corner of my eye, noting that the other prospective buyers seemed to be giving him a wide berth. His owner, an ugly Cylopean—and Cylopeans are *all* ugly, but this one would have stood out in a crowd of them—was exhorting the masses to purchase his slave.

"Come!" he shouted in heavily accented Standard Tongue, "my slave is strong and will serve you well. I part with him only out of extreme financial need, for he is as a brother to me, and it pains me greatly to lose him."

His pain wasn't as great as the slave's, obviously. I eyed the Cylopean skeptically. Surely he couldn't imagine that anyone would have suspected that his "brother" would require a genital restraint in order to drag him to the market to part him from his current master!

Rolling my eyes with disdain, I muttered, "Go ahead and admit it. You're selling him because you can't control him."

"Oh, no, my good sir!" the Cylopean exclaimed, seemingly aghast at my suggestion. "He is strong! He is willing! He is even intelligent!"

I stifled a snicker. The slave was obviously smart enough to have this one buffaloed, I thought, chuckling to myself as it occurred to me that no one around here would even know what a buffalo was, let alone the euphemism associated with the animal.

I blew out a breath hard enough to fog the eye screen on my respirator. Damn, but I was a long way from home! Earth was at least five hundred long light-years away. How the hell had I managed to end up here, searching for a lost sister whom I sometimes suspected of not wanting to be found? I'd followed her trail from planet to planet for six years now, and had always been just a few steps behind her. I was beginning to consider giving up the search, but the memory of the terror in her wild blue eyes as she was torn from my arms on Dexia Four kept me going.

And now, she had been—or so I'd been informed— taken to Statzeel, a planet where all women were slaves and upon which I didn't dare set foot, knowing that I, too, would become enslaved. The denizens of Statzeel would undoubtedly not make the same mistake that the slave trader had, for I was most definitely female, and, as such, vulnerable to the same fate that had befallen my lovely little sister. That I wasn't the delicate, winsome creature Ranata was wouldn't matter, for a female on Statzeel was a slave by definition. Free women simply did not exist there.

Which was why I needed a male slave of my own. One to pose as my owner—one that I could trust to a certain extent, though I was beginning to believe that such a creature couldn't possibly exist, and certainly not on Orpheseus Prime! I was undoubtedly wasting my time, I thought as I looked back at the slave. He was tall, dirty, and probably stank every bit as much as his owner did. I was going to have to check the filter in that damn respirator—either that or go back and beat the shit out of the scheming little scoundrel who'd taken me for ten qidnits when he sold it to me. I should have simply stolen it, but getting myself in trouble with what law there was on that nasty little planet wouldn't have done either my sister, or myself, a lick of good.

As I glanced at the man standing there before me, he raised his head ever so slightly to regard me out of the corner of one glittering, obsidian eye. Something passed between us at that moment—something almost palpable and real—making me wonder if the people of his race might have had psychic powers of some kind. That he was most definitely not human was quite evident, though at first glance he might have appeared to be, and could possibly have passed for one to the uneducated. There weren't many humans this far out for comparison, which was undoubtedly why I'd been able to get wind of Ranata's whereabouts from time to time. She seemed to have left a lasting impression wherever she was taken.

Just as this slave would do, even with the upswept eyebrows that marked him as belonging to some other alien world. His black, waving hair hung to his waist, though matted and dirty and probably crawling with vermin. I had no doubt that his owner hadn't lied when he had said that the slave was strong, for he was collared and shackled—hand, foot, and genitals. I'd been through many slave markets in my search, but I'd rarely seen any slave who was bound the way this one was, which spoke not only of strength, but also of a belligerent, and probably untrainable, nature. The muscles were all right there to see, and while they were not overly bulky—appearing, instead, to be more tough and sinewy—their level of strength was unquestionable.

This man had seen some rough work and even rougher treatment, for jagged scars laced his back and a long, straight scar sliced across his left cheekbone as though it had been made with a sword. He had a piercing in his penis, which appeared to have been done recently, for the ring through it was crusted over with dried blood. A chain ran from the metallic collar around his neck, through the ring in his cock, to another metal band that

From

WARRIOR

HE CAME TO ME IN THE DEAD OF WINTER, HIS BODY burning with fever. Even before he arrived on my doorstep, bound, beaten, and unconscious, I knew my quiet life was about to change forever. And I was ready.

As I stirred my potion, I heard the creak of saddle leather and the muffled thud of a body falling into the snow outside my isolated cottage, followed by Rafe's grunt of effort as he dragged the unconscious offworlder through the drifts. With a gust of cold air and a swirling cloud of snowflakes, he pushed my door open and burst inside without so much as a knock.

The evening had begun tranquilly enough. I had just brought in extra wood from the shed, but it was snowing so hard, I decided to go back out into the wintry darkness for more. I can conjure up fire better than any other witch I've heard of, but it helps to have some fuel. Besides, I love the cozy warmth and smell of a wood fire.

From her place by the fire, Desdemona gazed up at me with narrowed eyes, nodding her agreement. I trusted her feline intuition to alert me to danger, but Desdemona had given me no warning. Yawning, she stretched and let out a loud purr before curling up once more.

Reassured, I pushed open the heavy wooden door and peered out into the thickly falling snow. Big, fluffy flakes drifted by in the beam of light, floating gently but inexorably to the ground. It was already a handspan in depth and more was on the way. But there was something else in the air tonight—a strange feeling, heralding something altogether new and unexpected. Not a feeling of dread or fear, but something that whispered of the fulfillment of a promise. It hung there, on the edge of awareness, teasing me with its elusive aura. Just what—or who—it was, only time would tell. Time and the gods.

My woodshed was only a few paces from the door, though with the snow it seemed farther than usual. Treading softly, I sank into the snow with each step, feeling my way through the darkness. The door to the shed creaked open on its rusty hinges and I glanced up at the lantern, shooting fire into the wick, instantly illuminating the interior with a warm glow.

I had plenty of wood stored there for the winter; the people of the forest saw to that. I was too important to their well-being for them to ever let me freeze or starve, and offerings appeared almost daily on my doorstep—sometimes openly, sometimes covertly, but still they came without fail. I reminded myself frequently that one day they might not, and was, therefore, frugal with whatever I had. I knew full well that my honored status could vanish on a whim, and I wouldn't have been the first of the chosen ones to be cast out to starve. It was a tenuous existence, to be sure, but one for which I had been born and bred.

Stacking the new logs on my arm, I made my way

carefully back through the snow to my house. Although
the right to own property was denied most women on
this world, it was *my* house and had been my mother's
before me, and her mother's before her, time out of
mind—never once having a male to claim ownership.
Our children had fathers, of course, but we seldom married—at least, not in the traditional sense—and therefore traced our lineage through the female line. The one
child we were granted was of the utmost importance,
for it was she who would continue our work and our
traditions—and that child was always female. Always.

Desdemona purred her greeting as I came back inside
and dumped the logs by the fire. I had three days' worth
of wood there already, but the snow was deepening
quickly, so I thought I might as well bring in more. Pausing by the door, I listened. There was barely any wind,
and the snow fell silently until, just on the fringes of my
hearing, I was at last able to hear what I'd been waiting
for: hooves in the snow, and heavily laden, by the sound
of them. A rider was coming, but that was not all.

I could hear the effort the horse was making as he
strained to climb. He was coming from the east, and I
could place him now. It was Sinjar; I sent a greeting of
thought out to him and heard him nicker in reply. We
knew each other well, for his master, Rafe, had been my
lover once. Too arrogant now to trouble with the likes of
me, he'd been charming enough in his youth. I'd known
that Rafe wasn't the one—had always known, even from
the beginning—but loneliness sometimes drives one to
seek out solace in places where happiness can never be
found. It had been over for many years; Rafe had a wife
and sons now and had never once strayed back to my

bed. That it was for the best, I was well aware, because he had become too powerful and had too much to lose by consorting with a witch.

Sinjar's thoughts reached into my mind. *"I'm tired and hungry,"* he said. *"They are heavy."*

"They?" I asked.

"The master and another," he replied. *"Sick and hurt. A slave, I think. He is... strange. An offworlder."*

"I'll have food and water waiting for you, Sinjar," I promised.

"Good. It's not far now. I'll be glad to see you again, Tisana."

"And I, you."

Returning to the shed, I gathered up buckets and feed and carried them back to the house, filling one of them with water from the pump by my door. Rafe might want food and drink as much as his horse did, but he would have to ask for it when he arrived.

Rafe and I had not parted company on the best of terms, though he did use my talents when it served his purpose. He must need my help very badly to come out on a night like this—and for a slave, no less. An offworlder, which didn't bode well, for my skills and medicines were sometimes useless with other species. My knowledge had grown with time, but there were still those whose physiology was too different to respond to my treatments. Many of the basic principles were the same, but they were usually strangers, and often didn't trust me completely, which was half the battle. This one might already be beyond my aid, for I could sense something ominous about him, a life-force on the wane. Rafe may have been too late.

I set Sinjar's food and water down and went inside, leaving the door unlatched, and gathered what herbs I thought I might need. Water was already hot in the kettle hanging from a hook over the fire, and I mixed the pungent potion in an earthenware bowl on a heavy wooden table that was probably as old as the cottage itself. Powdered comfrey root mixed with sage and rosemary tea would help to heal his battered body, but an infusion of thyme, lavender, rosemary, and vervain would help restore the will to live, which I could tell even from a distance was the chief problem afflicting my newest client. I doubted that many slaves would prefer death to slavery, but some might. Rafe was a stern man and could be an exacting master. On the other hand, Rafe would presumably have paid good money for him, and see him as an investment to be protected. He wouldn't be coming at such a time if it didn't matter to him.

Putting my fingertips to my temples, I wished for perhaps the millionth time that I could read the thoughts of humans as well as those of animals. My grandmother had had that gift. My mother had had both, though to a lesser degree, but I could read only the beasts of the forest and farm. It was a useful skill, for very few others could ask their horse which foot was hurting them, or if the girth was pulled too tight. I always knew where to find the juiciest berries and the lushest patches of wild rosemary, because the rabbits knew, and their minds were much occupied with these matters. Animals had a feel for weather, too, and were a much more reliable source of information than your typical village sage.

Still, with sick or injured humans, you can ask what the trouble is—if they're conscious enough to reply—

From

ROGUE

"I WILL NOT KEEP YOU MUCH LONGER." SHE PAUSED, calling out to a servant in the next room before taking another delicate sip of her wine and continuing, "But before you go, you must see my cats."

"Your cats?"

Nodding, she said, "I'd like your opinion of them."

That sounded odd. What did it matter what I thought of her pets? The little toad creature was told to fetch the cats, so I had a little time to think. Okay, if this was a desert planet with intelligent life forms that looked for all the world like dinosaurs, what kind of cats would they have here? Saber-toothed tigers?

On that thought, the door opened again, and the two cats entered—but they weren't cats, at least, not in the ordinary sense. They were tall male humanoids— undoubtedly more of Scalia's "exotic slaves"—and they certainly were exotic! Separately, each one would have been stunning, but together, they took my breath away—would have taken *anyone's* breath away, even Nindala's. For myself, I was just glad I happened to be sitting down when I saw them for the first time. Staring back at them in awe, I had barely managed to take another breath when one of them turned his startlingly blue eyes on me and, no doubt noting my open-mouthed expression, lowered his eyelids ever so slightly and sent a roguish smile in my direction.

And I had an orgasm.

Scalia probably thought I'd choked on my wine, but that wasn't it at all! I felt a fire begin to burn deep inside me when I first laid eyes on him, and his smile sent me over the edge. I'd never felt anything quite like it before in my life—nor had I ever seen anything to compare with him.

"They are my most prized possessions," Scalia said. "Very beautiful, are they not?"

I'm not entirely sure what I said in reply, but it was affirmative, though undoubtedly inarticulate.

Scalia smiled. "I hoped you would like them."

I took another sip of my wine—actually, it was more of a gulp than a sip—and asked, "W—where did you find them?"

"The slave traders in this region know of my penchant for interesting specimens and brought them to me," she replied. "You would not believe what I had to pay for them! The trader said that there had been a bounty placed on them, which, of course, meant that I was required to pay about twenty times that amount in order to get them—and also to keep him quiet as to their whereabouts! Apparently, someone holds a grudge against their kind and set out to exterminate them entirely—which would have been most unfortunate, as I am certain you will agree."

I think I nodded, but sitting there trying to imagine a whole planet full of these guys nearly made my uterus go into another spasm. I decided that a group of jealous men must have gotten an army together and plotted against them, for certainly no female in the known universe would have gone along with such a scheme. I mean, Scalia was a lizard, and even *she* liked them!

"But they are safe here," she added firmly. "They are kept under lock and key at night, and no one beyond the palace walls knows they exist. And, unlike my other slaves, even my daughter has never seen them."

The fact that they were both entirely nude except for jeweled collars around their necks and genitals might have been one reason Zealon had never been permitted to see them. She was much too young for such things, though I didn't think that anyone under the age of—oh, I don't know, a hundred, perhaps?—could look at them and not be affected.

"These two are brothers," Scalia went on, as though she were truly talking about a pair of pet cats who happened to be littermates. "I would dearly love to breed more of them, but they are a mammalian species and will not cross with our kind. Nor are they... aroused... by our females."

Which, of course, made me wonder whether or not they liked humans. I, for one, certainly liked *them*, especially the one who'd smiled at me. The other one didn't seem terribly pleased to see me—not quite scowling, but certainly not smiling.

As they had positioned themselves on either side of Scalia's chair, across the table from me, I had an excellent view of them both. They didn't seem particularly shy, either, not minding a bit that I couldn't take my eyes off them. The blue-eyed one was fair-skinned with the most spectacular hair—jet black with a thick streak of white running through it near his temple—hanging to his waist in perfect spirals. The other also had black hair which curled to his waist, but with a similarly placed orange stripe, green eyes, and more tawny skin. They both possessed upswept eyebrows and pointed ears, as well as vertical pupils that seemed to glow slightly. The green-eyed one yawned just then, revealing a mouthful of sharp white teeth with canines that looked downright dangerous. All in all, they put me in mind of Earth's tigers—the one Bengal, and the other Siberian—but they had body hair more like that of human males, not the fur you would expect to find on a cat. Neither of them had beards, but I wasn't close enough to determine whether or not this was natural. Both were tall, broad-chested, and lean, with smooth, rippling muscles and perfectly proportioned limbs. It was no wonder Scalia had paid a fortune for them!

All of this possibly wouldn't have mattered if they hadn't had one other notable attribute: they were both hung like horses. A crass description, perhaps, but it was accurate, nonetheless. Unfortunately, they were not, as Scalia had mentioned before, aroused. The mere thought of what they might look like if they *were* aroused made my mouth go dry, and I attempted to take another sip from an empty glass.

"My guest needs more wine," Scalia said, crooking a finger toward the Siberian tiger.

Nodding, he collected a flask from the sideboard and came around the table. When he leaned over to pour the wine, his cock was just below my eye level, but as my eyes were slightly downcast, I had an excellent view of it. Among other things, I noted that the jewels on his genital cuff were every bit as blue as his eyes. Scalia, it seemed, was not the slightest bit color-blind and had paid attention to detail when decorating her slaves.

"Thank you," I said hoarsely.

"You are very welcome," he replied. "It is my pleasure to serve you."

His deep voice was like melted butter and, even though polite, his choice of words had me envisioning all manner of pleasurable things—none of them having *anything* to do with food or drink. I couldn't help but look up at him, and, when our eyes met, he smiled again and blinked slowly. Then I watched, fascinated, as his nostrils flared with a deep inhalation—and his smile intensified, as did the hot blue of his eyes.

"Oh, excellent!" Scalia said in hushed tones.

Yes, he is! Excellent, perfect, amazing, unbelievable—and just about any other superlative you'd care to use. Still gazing up at him, I felt as though I were about to melt into a puddle and slide off my chair. Honestly, if I'd ever felt a more overwhelming sense of desire for any other man in the galaxy, this one would have made me forget it.

I felt something wet drop onto my hand. Glancing down to see if I was, indeed, melting, I saw what Scalia had undoubtedly been referring to, for the tiger's penis was now fully erect. As thick and long as a well-endowed human's would have been, it also had a wide, scalloped corona at the base of the head that was obviously there for one reason only: to give the greatest possible pleasure to any woman fortunate enough to be penetrated by it. Looking closer, I noted that the clear fluid that had fallen on my hand appeared to be coming, not from the opening at the apex, but from the starlike points of the corona.

I tried to swallow and couldn't. I looked up at him again with what must have been an expression of raw hunger mingled with guilt written clearly upon my face. In return, what I saw on his face was the most open invitation to partake of anything I'd ever seen. His mesmerizing eyes beckoned, his full lips promised sensuous delights beyond my wildest imaginings, and his provocative smile assured me of his knowledge of every possible way to drive a woman wild. He was offering himself to me—completely—without saying a word.

Unfortunately, just as I was about to take a taste of him, I suddenly remembered where I was. We were not alone, and he was a slave who belonged to the lizard queen sitting across the table from me. Reaching awkwardly for my wineglass, my sleeve slid across the head of his cock, soaking it with his fluid and drawing a barely audible groan from him.

Trying desperately to ignore his reaction, I looked away from him and saw that Scalia was watching us intently, but she had her hand on the Bengal tiger's thigh, stroking him, though without any erotic response on his part whatsoever. I would have thought that such a pornographic vision right across the table from him would have been enough to stimulate him, but apparently, it wasn't.

Then I remembered the blue-eyed tiger inhaling as though he was taking a whiff of me. It was something to do with scent, then—though it was surprising that I was clearheaded enough to figure that out at the time. What was also surprising was the fact that my "scent" hadn't reached the other man, because if the way I was feeling was any indication, it had to have been pretty heavy on the sex pheromones.

Breaking the silence, the Queen's voice was now brisk and businesslike. "You will require a personal attendant during your stay with us," Scalia said. "I believe he will suit you very nicely."

"Who, him?" I gasped. As I sat staring at his cock, I decided that if anyone could "suit me," it would have been him, but he was far more… *man*… than I'd ever so much as touched in my life! He could turn me to mush in a heartbeat—and, of course, in that state, I'd never play piano again… "Oh, but I don't really need—" I protested, before she cut me off with an imperious wave of her hand.

"Yes, you do," she said firmly. "You are new to this world, Kyra. He will be able to help you… adjust."

Adjust. What an interesting choice of words! He probably could have helped me adjust to just about anything— even daily torture—if only he were to hold my hand for the duration. And speaking of hands, I wondered if I'd be able to keep mine off of him when we were alone together. Having been within a hairbreadth of licking his cock just moments before—and in full view of two other people, I might add—I thought I'd probably have some difficulty with that. I also wondered if he'd go running to Scalia to complain if I did something of that nature—or what he would do if I didn't.

To be honest, I doubted that I needed a servant of any kind, though due to the scarcity of water and fabrics, it was a given that there wouldn't be any easy way to wash my clothes. I wondered if my bed would have sheets on it, or if I'd be sleeping on a bed of stones or sand. Hopefully, Zealon had done some homework in that area as well.

My tiger was still standing next to me, flanking my chair just as his counterpart did for Scalia—quite slave-like behavior, despite his persistent erection—and it occurred to me that he might like to have some say in the matter.

"What about you?" I asked, looking up at him curiously. "Do you think I need a personal attendant?"

"Absolutely," he replied, his luscious lips curling in a smile. "There are a great many things I can do for you."

I'll just bet you can, I thought grimly. "But do you *want* to?" I said aloud. For some reason, I felt it was important that his service to me be voluntary. Not that he wouldn't have done whatever he was told to do by his owner; after all, he *was* a slave, though a very valuable one. What would happen if he refused? I doubted that Scalia would punish him—doubted that she ever had, for neither of them had a mark on him, nor did they have the cowed expressions of people who were habitually abused or bullied. In fact, they appeared to have been well cared for, if not cosseted, by their owner—truly more like cherished pets than slaves.

"I can think of nothing I would like more," he assured me.

"Because you have been told to." I said this not as a question, but as a statement.

He seemed uncertain about how to reply to that, glancing at Scalia out of the corner of his eye as if for direction, but she gave him none that I could see.

"Because you smell of desire," he said finally. "Being

near you pleases me… and I have no doubt that I can please *you*."

"An honest answer," Scalia asserted. "You may believe what he tells you. They are both very truthful."

I nodded. "Yes, I can believe that much," I said. This man undoubtedly could please the most stone-cold woman imaginable, but I secretly wondered if it was my desire which pleased him, or if any woman's desire would do.

Sighing deeply, I relented, knowing that while I might regret my decision in the end, if I refused, I'd regret it even more.

"It is settled, then," Scalia said to my tiger. "You may escort Kyra to her rooms." Turning to me, she added, "Your quarters have been adapted to suit human needs. I believe you will find them to your liking."

"I'm sure I will," I replied, "but, if you don't mind my asking, how are you going to keep him a secret if he's with me? The Princess, or someone else, may see him."

"We will take that risk," Scalia said with conviction. "I believe it to be worthwhile."

And her word was law. After all, she *was* the queen.

About the Author

Cheryl Brooks has been a critical care nurse since 1977, graduating from the Kentucky Baptist Hospital School of Nursing in 1976, and earning a BSN from Indiana University in 1986. Cheryl is an avid reader of romance novels and has been a fan of science fiction ever since watching that first episode of *Star Trek*. Always in need of a creative outlet, she has written numerous novels, with *The Cat Star Chronicles: Outcast* being her fourth published work. She lives on a farm near Bloomfield, Indiana, with her husband, two sons, four horses, and five cats. You can visit her website at: http://cherylbrooksonline.com, or email her at: cheryl.brooks52@yahoo.com.

IN OVER HER HEAD

by Judi Fennell

"Holy mackerel! *In Over Her Head* is a
fantastically fun romantic catch!"

—Michelle Rowen, author of *Bitten & Smitten*

∘ ∘ ∘ ∘ ∘ ∘ **HE LIVES UNDER THE SEA** ∘ ∘ ∘ ∘ ∘ ∘

Reel Tritone is the rebellious royal second son of the ruler
of a vast undersea kingdom. A Merman, born with legs
instead of a tail, he's always been fascinated by humans,
especially one young woman he once saw swimming near
his family's reef…

∘ ∘ ∘ ∘ ∘ **SHE'S TERRIFIED OF THE OCEAN** ∘ ∘ ∘ ∘ ∘

Ever since the day she swam out too far and heard voices
in the water, marina owner Erica Peck won't go swimming
for anything—until she's forced into the water by a shady
ex-boyfriend searching for stolen diamonds, and is nearly
eaten by a shark…luckily Reel is nearby to save her, and
discovers she's the woman he's been searching for…

978-1-4022-2001-2 • $6.99 U.S. / $7.99 CAN

Heart
of the
Wolf

BY TERRY SPEAR

A *Publisher's Weekly* Best Book of the Year

"A fast-paced, sexy read with lots of twists and turns!" —Nicole North, author of *Devil in a Kilt*

THEIR FORBIDDEN LOVE MAY GET THEM BOTH KILLED

"Red werewolf Bella flees her adoptive pack of gray werewolves when the alpha male Volan tries forcibly to claim her as his mate. Her real love, beta male Devlyn, is willing to fight Volan to the death to claim her. That problem pales, however, as a pack of red werewolves takes to killing human females in a crazed quest to claim Bella for their own. Bella and Devlyn must defeat the rogue wolves before Devlyn's final confrontation with Volan. The vulpine couple's chemistry crackles off the page, but the real strength of the book lies in Spear's depiction of pack power dynamics...her wolf world feels at once palpable and even plausible."

—*Publisher's Weekly*

978-1-4022-1157-7 • $6.99 U.S. / $8.99 CAN

call of the highland moon

BY KENDRA LEIGH CASTLE

A Highlands werewolf fleeing his destiny, and the warm-hearted woman who takes him in…

Not ready for the responsibilities of an alpha wolf, Gideon MacInnes leaves Scotland and seeks the quiet hills of upstate New York. When he is attacked by rogue wolves and collapses on Carly Silver's doorstep, she thinks she's rescuing a wounded animal. But she awakens to find that the beast has turned into a devastatingly handsome, naked man.

With a supernatural enemy stalking them, their only hope is to get back to Scotland, where Carly has to risk becoming a werewolf herself, or give up the one man she's ever truly loved.

"*Call of the Highland Moon* thrills with seductive romance and breathtaking suspense." —Alyssa Day, *USA Today* bestselling author of *Atlantis Awakening*

978-1-4022-1158-4 • $6.99 U.S. / $8.99 CAN

Wicked by Any Other Name

BY LINDA WISDOM

"Do not miss this wickedly entertaining treat."

—Annette Blair,
Sex and the Psychic Witch

STASI ROMANOV USES A LITTLE WITCH MAGIC IN HER LINGERIE shop, running a brisk side business in love charms. A disgruntled customer threatening to sue over a failed spell brings wizard attorney Trevor Barnes to town—and witches and wizards make a volatile combination. The sparks fly, almost everyone's getting singed, and the whole town seems on the verge of a witch hunt.

Can the feisty witch and the gorgeous wizard overcome their objections and settle out of court—and in the bedroom?

978-1-4022-1773-9 • $6.99 U.S. / $7.99 CAN

SLAVE

BY CHERYL BROOKS

"I found him in the slave market on Orpheseus Prime, and even on such a god-forsaken planet as that one, their treatment of him seemed extreme."

Cat may be the last of a species whose sexual talents were the envy of the galaxy. Even filthy, chained, and beaten, his feline gene gives him a special aura.

Jacinth is on a rescue mission… and she needs a man she can trust with her life.

PRAISE FOR CHERYL BROOKS' *SLAVE*:

"A sexy adventure with a hero you can't resist!"

—Candace Havens, author of *Charmed & Deadly*

"Fascinating world customs, a bit of mystery, and the relationship between the hero and heroine make this a very sensual romance."

—*Romantic Times*

978-1-4022-1192-8 • $6.99 U.S. / $8.99 CAN